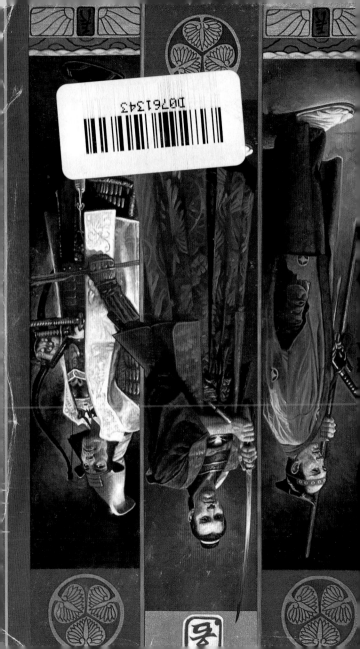

**Across a Land of Great Beauty,
in an Age of Heroism,
a Lone Swordsman
Challenges Japan's Greatest Fighters . . .**

Yoshioka Seijūrō: Son of a famous swordsman, he was the Young Master of the Yoshioka school. Challenged by Musashi, he could not escape—nor heed—his own fear . . .

Sasaki Kojirō: A raw-boned young samurai who traveled with a monkey, an enormous sword and an air of arrogance. Like Musashi, his reputation was beginning to spread. Like Musashi, he feared no one in the world . . .

Otsū: Young and beautiful, she gave up her old, sheltered life to search for Musashi. Now she was on a journey of her own—in a world where a woman alone was easy prey . . .

Shishido Baiken: The famed maker of a deadly new weapon. When Musashi went to visit him, he met a ghost from his past—and a host bent on murder . . .

Osugi: Mother of Musashi's best friend, the furious old woman wanted vengeance for her son's disgrace. She would not rest until she saw the spilled blood of Musashi and Otsū . . .

Books in the Musashi Saga by Eiji Yoshikawa

Book I: The Way of the Samurai
Book II: The Art of War

Published by POCKET BOOKS

Book III: The Way of the Sword
Book IV: The Bushido Code
Book V: The Way of Life and Death

Coming Soon from POCKET BOOKS

MUSASHI

BOOK II:
THE ART OF WAR

EIJI YOSHIKAWA

Translated from the Japanese by Charles S. Terry
Foreword by Edwin O. Reischauer

POCKET BOOKS

New York   London   Toronto   Sydney   Tokyo

Map design by Ray Lundgren Graphics, Ltd.
Map research by Jim Moser

POCKET BOOKS, a division of Simon & Schuster Inc.
1230 Avenue of the Americas, New York, NY 10020

Copyright © 1971 by Fumiko Yoshikawa
English translation copyright © 1981 by Kodansha International Ltd.
Cover art copyright © 1989 Osyczka Limited
Inside cover art copyright © 1989 Sanjulian

Published by arrangement with Kodansha International
Library of Congress Catalog Card Number: 80-8791

ISBN: 0-671-67720-9

First Pocket Books printing March 1989

10 9 8 7 6 5 4 3 2 1

POCKET and colophon are trademarks of
Simon & Schuster Inc.

Printed in the U.S.A.

CONTENTS

Contents

PLOT SUMMARY
Book I: *The Way of the Samurai*

Wounded in the great battle of Sekigahara, Takezō (later Musashi) and Matahachi were taken in by a beautiful girl, Akemi, and her lascivious mother, Okō. After a violent confrontation with local bandits, in which he slayed the leader, Takezō left his friend with the two women and traveled back to his home province of Mimasaka. There, he was accused of having murdered Matahachi. A wild and undisciplined youth, Takezō was hunted by his own townspeople, and reacted with bitter rage—until the Buddhist town monk, Takuan Sōhō, was able to capture him without a single blow. Takuan tied Takezō up in the branches of a tall tree, but Matahachi's beloved, Otsū, took pity on him and freed him. Begging him to run away with her, she forsook Matahachi forever, but the eccentric Takuan had an even greater power over Takezō—and led him to Himeji Castle. There, by the light of a single lamp in a windowless room, Takezō began to study Suntzu's *The Art of War*, the Books of Zen and the history of Japan. Weeks stretched into months, and gradually Takezō was transformed. When the day came for him to leave, he took the name Miyamoto Musashi, and set off for Kyoto—and his first tests as a man of the sword.

CHARACTERS AND LOCALES

AKEMI, the daughter of Okō

ARAKIDA HOUSE, a temple

SHISHIDO BAIKEN, a blacksmith and sword maker

YOSHIOKA DENSHICHIRŌ, brother of Yoshioka Seijūrō

FUSHIMI CASTLE, a residence of Ieyasu, south of Kyoto

HIDEYORI, ruler of Osaka Castle and rival of Ieyasu

TOKUGAWA IEYASU, the Shōgun, ruler of Japan

JŌTARŌ, a young follower of Musashi

MATSUO KANAME, uncle of Musashi

YOSHIOKA KEMPŌ, father of Yoshioka Seijūrō

SHŌDA KIZAEMON, an official and samurai of the House of Yagyū

SASAKI KOJIRŌ, a young samurai whose identity Matahachi assumes

KOYAGYŪ CASTLE, home of the Yagyū family

KYOTO, city in southwestern Japan, rival to Osaka

DEBUCHI MAGOBEI, an official and samurai of the House of Yagyū

HON'IDEN MATAHACHI, childhood friend of Musashi

MIMASAKA, home province of Musashi

LORD KARASUMARU MITSUHIRO, a Kyoto nobleman

MIYAMOTO MUSASHI, a swordsman of growing fame

SHIMMEN OGIN, the sister of Musashi

OKŌ, a lascivious woman

Characters and Locales

OSAKA, city in southwestern Japan, rival to Kyoto

HON'IDEN OSUGI, the mother of Matahachi and bitter enemy of Musashi

OTSŪ, a young woman in love with Musashi

UEDA RYŌHEI, a swordsman of the House of Yoshioka

YOSHIOKA SEIJŪRŌ, Young Master of the Yoshioka school

SEKIGAHARA, battle in which Ieyasu defeated the combined armies of the western daimyō for control of Japan

YAGYŪ SEKISHŪSAI, aging master of the Yagyū style of swordsmanship

SHIMMEN TAKEZŌ, former name of Musashi

TAKUAN SŌHŌ, an eccentric monk

AOKI TANZAEMON, a beggar priest

TSUJIKAZE TEMMA, bandit slain by Musashi

GION TŌJI, samurai of the Yoshioka school and suitor of Okō

HOUSE OF YAGYŪ, a powerful family known for their style of swordsmanship

AKAKABE YASOMA, a drifter

FOREWORD[1]
by Edwin O. Reischauer[2]

Musashi might well be called the *Gone with the Wind* of Japan. Written by Eiji Yoshikawa (1892–1962), one of Japan's most prolific and best-loved popular writers, it is a long historical novel, which first appeared in serialized form between 1935 and 1939 in the *Asahi Shimbun,* Japan's largest and most prestigious newspaper. It has been published in book form no less than fourteen times, most recently in four volumes of the 53-volume complete works of Yoshikawa issued by Kodansha. It has been produced as a film some seven times, has been repeatedly presented on the stage, and has often been made into television mini-series on at least three nationwide networks.

Miyamoto Musashi was an actual historical person, but through Yoshikawa's novel he and the other main characters of the book have become part of Japan's living folklore. They are so familiar to the public that people will frequently be compared to them as personalities everyone knows. This gives the novel an added interest to the foreign reader. It not only provides a romanticized slice of Japanese history, but

---

[1]This Foreword has been taken in its entirety from the original single-volume American hardcover edition of *Musashi: An Epic Novel of the Samurai Era.*

[2]Edwin O. Reischauer was born in Japan in 1910. He has been a professor at Harvard University since 1946, and is now Professor Emeritus. He left the university temporarily to be the United States Ambassador to Japan from 1961 to 1966, and is one of the best-known authorities on the country. Among his numerous works are *Japan: The Story of a Nation* and *The Japanese.*

gives a view of how the Japanese see their past and themselves. But basically the novel will be enjoyed as a dashing tale of swashbuckling adventure and a subdued story of love, Japanese style.

Comparisons with James Clavell's *Shōgun* seem inevitable, because for most Americans today *Shōgun*, as a book and a television mini-series, vies with samurai movies as their chief source of knowledge about Japan's past. The two novels concern the same period of history. *Shōgun*, which takes place in the year 1600, ends with Lord Toranaga, who is the historical Tokugawa Ieyasu, soon to be the Shōgun, or military dictator of Japan, setting off for the fateful battle of Sekigahara. Yoshikawa's story begins with the youthful Takezō, later to be renamed Miyomoto Musashi, lying wounded among the corpses of the defeated army on that battlefield.

With the exception of Blackthorne, the historical Will Adams, *Shōgun* deals largely with the great lords and ladies of Japan, who appear in thin disguise under names Clavell has devised for them. *Musashi*, while mentioning many great historical figures under their true names, tells about a broader range of Japanese and particularly about the rather extensive group who lived on the ill-defined borderline between the hereditary military aristocracy and the commoners—the peasants, tradesmen and artisans. Clavell freely distorts historical fact to fit his tale and inserts a Western-type love story that not only flagrantly flouts history but is quite unimaginable in the Japan of that time. Yoshikawa remains true to history or at least to historical tradition, and his love story, which runs as a background theme in minor scale throughout the book, is very authentically Japanese.

Yoshikawa, of course, has enriched his account with much imaginative detail. There are enough strange coincidences and deeds of derring-do to delight the heart of any lover of adventure stories. But he sticks faithfully to such facts of history as are known. Not only Musashi himself but many of the other people who figure prominently in the story are real historical individuals. For example, Takuan, who serves as a guiding light and mentor to the youthful Musashi, was a famous Zen monk, calligrapher, painter, poet and tea-master of the time, who became the youngest abbot of the Daitokuji in Kyoto in 1609 and later founded a major monastery in Edo, but is best remembered today for having left his name to a popular Japanese pickle.

The historical Miyamoto Musashi, who may have been born in 1584 and died in 1645, was like his father a master swordsman and became known for his use of two swords. He was an ardent cultivator of self-discipline as the key to martial skills and the author of a famous work on swordsmanship, the *Gorin no sho*. He probably took part as a youth in the battle of Sekigahara, and his clashes with the Yoshioka school of swordsmanship in Kyoto, the warrior monks of the Hōzōin in Nara and the famed swordsman Sasaki Kojirō, all of which figure prominently in this book, actually did take place. Yoshikawa's account of him ends in 1612, when he was still a young man of about 28, but subsequently he may have fought on the losing side at the siege of Osaka castle in 1614 and participated in 1637–38 in the annihilation of the Christian peasantry of Shimabara in the western island of Kyushu, an event which marked the extirpation of that religion from Japan for the next two centuries and helped seal Japan off from the rest of the world.

Ironically, Musashi in 1640 became a retainer of the Hosokawa lords of Kumamoto, who, when they had been the lords of Kumamoto, had been the patrons of his chief rival, Sasaki Kojirō. The Hosokawas bring us back to *Shōgun*, because it was the older Hosokawa, Tadaoki, who figures quite unjustifiably as one of the main villains of that novel, and it was Tadaoki's exemplary Christian wife, Gracia, who is pictured without a shred of plausibility as Blackthorne's great love, Mariko.

The time of Musashi's life was a period of great transition in Japan. After a century of incessant warfare among petty diamyō, or feudal lords, three successive leaders had finally reunified the country through conquest. Oda Nobunaga had started the process but, before completing it, had been killed by a treacherous vassal in 1582. His ablest general, Hideyoshi, risen from the rank of common foot soldier, completed the unification of the nation but died in 1598 before he could consolidate control in behalf of his infant heir. Hideyoshi's strongest vassal, Tokugawa Ieyasu, a great daimyō who ruled much of eastern Japan from his castle at Edo, the modern Tokyo, then won supremacy by defeating a coalition of western daimyō at Sekigahara in 1600. Three years later he took the traditional title of Shō-gun, signifying his military dictatorship over the whole land, theoretically in behalf of the ancient but impotent imperial line in Kyoto. Ieyasu in 1605 transferred the position of Shōgun to his son, Hidetada, but remained in actual control himself until he had destroyed the supporters of Hideyoshi's heir in sieges of Osaka castle in 1614 and 1615.

The first three Tokugawa rulers established such firm control over Japan that their rule was to last more than two and a half centuries, until it finally collapsed in 1868 in the tumultuous aftermath of the reopening of Japan to contact with the West a decade and a half earlier. The Tokugawa ruled through semi-autonomous hereditary daimyō, who numbered around 265 at the end of the period, and the daimyō in turn controlled their fiefs through their hereditary samurai retainers. The transition from constant warfare to a closely regulated peace brought the drawing of sharp class lines between the samurai, who had the privilege of wearing two swords and bearing family names, and the commoners, who though including well-to-do merchants and land owners, were in theory denied all arms and the honor of using family names.

During the years of which Yoshikawa writes, however, these class divisions were not yet sharply defined. All local-ities had their residue of peasant fighting men, and the country was overrun by rōnin, or masterless samurai, who were largely the remnants of the armies of the daimyō who had lost their domains as the result of the battle of Sekiga-hara or in earlier wars. It took a generation or two before society was fully sorted out into the strict class divisions of the Tokugawa system, and in the meantime there was consid-erable social ferment and mobility.

Another great transition in early seventeenth century Japan was in the nature of leadership. With peace restored and major warfare at an end, the dominant warrior class found that military prowess was less essential to successful rule than administrative talents. The samurai class started a slow transformation from being warriors of the gun and sword to being bureaucrats of the writing brush and paper. Disciplined self-control and education in a society at peace was becoming more important than skill in warfare. The Western reader may be surprised to see how widespread literacy already was at the beginning of the seventeenth century and at the constant references the Japanese made to Chinese history and literature, much as Northern Europeans of the same time continually referred to the traditions of ancient Greece and Rome.

A third major transition in the Japan of Musashi's time was in weaponry. In the second half of the sixteenth century matchlock muskets, recently introduced by the Portuguese, had become the decisive weapons of the battlefield, but in a land at peace the samurai could turn their backs on distasteful firearms and resume their traditional love affair with the sword. Schools of swordsmanship flourished. However, as the chance to use swords in actual combat diminished, martial skills were gradually becoming martial arts, and these increasingly came to emphasize the importance of inner self-control and the character-building qualities of swordsmanship rather than its untested military efficacy. A whole mystique of the sword grew up, which was more akin to philosophy than to warfare.

Yoshikawa's account of Musashi's early life illustrates all these changes going on in Japan. He was himself a typical rōnin from a mountain village and became a settled samurai retainer only late in life. He was the founder of a school of swordsmanship. Most important, he gradually transformed himself from an instinctive fighter into a man who fanatically pursued the goals of Zen-like self-discipline, complete inner mastery over oneself, and a sense of oneness with surrounding nature. Although in his early years lethal contests, reminiscent of the tournaments of medieval Europe, were still possible, Yoshikawa portrays Musashi as consciously turning his martial skills from service in warfare to a means of character building for a time of peace. Martial skills, spiritual self-discipline and aesthetic sensitivity became merged into a single indistinguishable whole. This picture of

Musashi may not be far from the historical truth. Musashi is known to have been a skilled painter and an accomplished sculptor as well as a swordsman.

The Japan of the early seventeenth century which Musashi typified has lived on strongly in the Japanese consciousness. The long and relatively static rule of the Tokugawa preserved much of its forms and spirit, though in somewhat ossified form, until the middle of the nineteenth century, not much more than a century ago. Yoshikawa himself was a son of a former samurai who failed like most members of his class to make a successful economic transition to the new age. Though the samurai themselves largely sank into obscurity in the new Japan, most of the new leaders were drawn from this feudal class, and its ethos was popularized through the new compulsory educational system to become the spiritual background and ethics of the whole Japanese nation. Novels like *Musashi* and the films and plays derived from them aided in the process.

The time of Musashi is as close and real to the modern Japanese as is the Civil War to Americans. Thus the comparison to *Gone with the Wind* is by no means far-fetched. The age of the samurai is still very much alive in Japanese minds. Contrary to the picture of the modern Japanese as merely group oriented "economic animals," many Japanese prefer to see themselves as fiercely individualistic, high-principled, self-disciplined and aesthetically sensitive modern-day Musashis. Both pictures have some validity, illustrating the complexity of the Japanese soul behind the seemingly bland and uniform exterior.

Musashi is very different from the highly psychological and often neurotic novels that have been the mainstay of translations of modern Japanese literature into English. But it is nevertheless fully in the mainstream of traditional Japanese fiction and popular Japanese thought. Its episodic presentation is not merely the result of its original appearance as a newspaper serial but is a favorite technique dating back to the beginnings of Japanese storytelling. Its romanticized view of the noble swordsman is a stereotype of the feudal past enshrined in hundreds of other stories and samurai movies. Its emphasis on the cultivation of self-control and inner personal strength through austere Zen-like self-discipline is a major feature of Japanese personality today. So also is the pervading love of nature and sense of closeness to it. *Musashi* is not just a great adventure story. Beyond that, it gives both a glimpse into Japanese history and a view into the idealized self-image of the contemporary Japanese.

January 1981

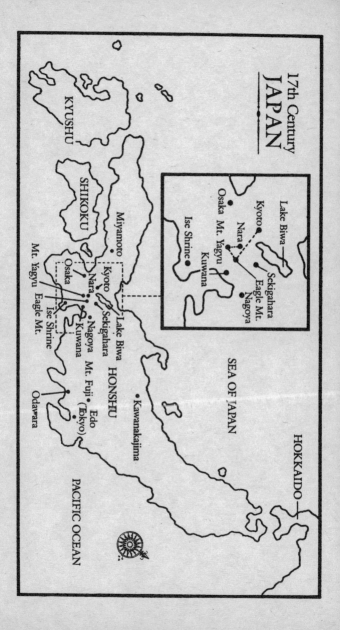

1

The Koyagyū Fief

Yagyū Valley lies at the foot of Mount Kasagi, northeast of
Nara. In the early seventeenth century, it was the site of a
prosperous little community, too large to be described as a
mere village, yet not populous or bustling enough to be
called a town. It might naturally have been called Kasagi
Village, but instead its inhabitants referred to their home as
the Kambe Demesne, a name inherited from the bygone age
of the great privately owned manorial estates.

In the middle of the community stood the Main House,
a castle that served as both a symbol of governmental
stability and the cultural center of the region. Stone ramparts, reminiscent of ancient fortresses, surrounded the
Main House. The people of the area, as well as their lord's
ancestors, had been comfortably settled there since the tenth
century, and the present ruler was a country squire in the
best tradition, who spread culture among his subjects and
was at all times prepared to protect his territory with his
life. At the same time, however, he carefully avoided any
serious involvement in the wars and feuds of his fellow lords
in other districts. In short, it was a peaceful fief, governed
in an enlightened manner.

Here one saw no traces of the depravity or degeneracy
associated with footloose samurai; it was quite unlike Nara,
where ancient temples celebrated in history and folklore
were being left to go to seed. Disruptive elements simply
were not permitted to enter into the life of this community.

The setting itself militated against ugliness. The mountains in the Kasagi Range were no less strikingly beautiful at eventide than at sunrise, and the water was pure and clean—ideal water, it was said, for making tea. The plum blossoms of Tsukigase were nearby, and nightingales sang from the season of the melting snow to that of the thunderstorms, their tones as crystal clear as the waters of the mountain streams.

A poet once wrote that "in the place where a hero is born, the mountains and rivers are fresh and clear." If no hero had been born in Yagyū Valley, the poet's words would have been empty; but this was indeed a birthplace of heroes. No better proof could be offered than the lords of Yagyū themselves. In this great house even the retainers were men of nobility. Many had come from the rice fields, distinguished themselves in battle, and gone on to become loyal and competent aides.

Yagyū Muneyoshi Sekishūsai, now that he'd retired, had taken up residence in a small mountain house some distance behind the Main House. He no longer showed any interest in local government, and had no idea who was in direct control at the moment. He had a number of capable sons and grandsons, as well as trustworthy retainers to assist and guide them, and he was safe in assuming that the people were being as well governed as they had been when he was in charge.

When Musashi arrived in this district, about ten days had passed since the battle on Hannya Plain. On the way he had visited some temples, Kasagidera and Jōruriji, where he'd seen relics of the Kemmu era. He put up at the local inn with the intention of relaxing for a time, physically and spiritually.

Dressed informally, he went out one day for a walk with Jōtarō. "It's amazing," said Musashi, his eyes roving over the crops in the fields and the farmers going about their work. "Amazing," he repeated several times.

Finally Jōtarō asked, "What's amazing?" For him, the most amazing thing was the way Musashi was talking to himself.

"Since leaving Mimasaka, I've been in Settsu, Kawachi

2

and Izumi provinces, Kyoto and Nara, and I've never seen a place like this."

"Well, so what? What's so different about it?"

"For one thing, there are lots of trees in the mountains here."

Jōtarō laughed. "Trees? There are trees everywhere. Well, aren't there?"

"Yes, but here it's different. All the trees in Yagyū are old. That means there haven't been any wars here, no enemy troops burning or cutting down the forests. It also means there haven't been any famines, at least for a long, long time."

"That's all?"

"No. The fields are green too, and the new barley has been well trampled to strengthen the roots and make it grow well. Listen! Can't you hear the sound of spinning wheels? It seems to be coming from every house. And haven't you noticed that when travelers in fine clothing pass by, the farmers don't look at them enviously?"

"Anything else?"

"As you can see, there are many young girls working the fields. This means that the district is well off, that life is normal here. The children are growing up healthy, the old people are treated with due respect, and the young men and women aren't running off to live uncertain lives in other places. It's a safe bet that the lord of the district is wealthy, and that the swords and guns in his armory are kept polished and in the best condition."

"I don't see anything so interesting in all that," complained Jōtarō.

"Hmm, I don't imagine you would."

"Anyway, you didn't come here to admire the scenery. Aren't you going to fight the samurai in the House of Yagyū?"

"Fighting isn't all there is to the Art of War. The men who think that way, and are satisfied to have food to eat and a place to sleep, are mere vagabonds. A serious student is much more concerned with training his mind and disciplining his spirit than with developing martial skills. He has to learn about all sorts of things—geography, irrigation, the people's

3

feelings, their manners and customs, their relationship with the lord of their territory. He wants to know what goes on inside the castle, not just what goes on outside it. He wants, essentially, to go everywhere he can and learn everything he can.''

Musashi realized this lecture probably meant little to Jōtarō, but he felt it necessary to be honest with the child and not give him halfway answers. He showed no impatience at the boy's many questions, and as they walked along, he continued to give thoughtful and serious replies.

After they had seen what there was to see of the exterior of Koyagyū Castle, as the Main House was properly known, and taken a good look all around the valley, they started back to the inn.

There was only one inn, but it was a large one. The road was a section of the Iga highroad, and many people making pilgrimages to the Jōruriji or Kasagidera stayed the night here. In the evening, ten or twelve packhorses were always to be found tied to the trees near the entrance or under the front eaves.

The maid who followed them to their room asked, ''Have you been out for a walk?'' In her mountain-climbing trousers, she might have been mistaken for a boy, were it not for her girl's red obi. Without waiting for an answer, she said, ''You can take your bath now, if you like.''

Musashi started for the bathroom, while Jōtarō, sensing that here was a new friend of his own age, asked, ''What's your name?''

''I don't know,'' answered the girl.

''You must be crazy if you don't know your own name.''

''It's Kocha.''

''That's a funny name.'' Jōtarō laughed.

''What's funny about it?'' demanded Kocha, striking him with her fist.

''She hit me!'' yelled Jōtarō.

From the folded clothing on the floor of the anteroom, Musashi knew there were other people in the bath. He took off his own clothes and opened the door into the steamy bathroom. There were three men, talking jovially, but catch-

4

ing sight of his brawny body, they stopped as though a foreign element had been introduced into their midst.

Musashi slipped into the communal bath with a contented sigh, his six-foot frame causing the hot water to overflow. For some reason, this startled the three men, and one of them looked straight at Musashi, who had leaned his head against the edge of the pool and closed his eyes.

Gradually they took up their conversation where they had left off. They were washing themselves outside the pool; the skin on their backs was white and their muscles pliant. They were apparently city people, for their manner of speech was polished and urbane.

"What was his name—the samurai from the House of Yagyū?"

"I think he said it was Shōda Kizaemon."

"If Lord Yagyū sends a retainer to convey a refusal to a match, he can't be as good as he's said to be."

"According to Shōda, Sekishūsai's retired and never fights anyone anymore. Do you suppose that's the truth, or was he just making it up?"

"Oh, I don't think it's true. It's much more likely that when he heard the second son of the House of Yoshioka was challenging him, he decided to play it safe."

"Well, he was tactful at least, sending fruit and saying he hoped we'd enjoy our stopover."

Yoshioka? Musashi lifted his head and opened his eyes. Having overheard someone mention Denshichirō's trip to Ise while he was at the Yoshioka School, Musashi assumed that the three men were on their way back to Kyoto. One of them must be Denshichirō. Which one?

"I don't have much luck with baths," thought Musashi ruefully. "First Osugi tricked me into taking a bath, and now, again with no clothes on, I run into one of the Yoshiokas. He's bound to have heard of what happened at the school. If he knew my name was Miyamoto, he'd be out that door and back with his sword in no time."

But the three paid him no attention. To judge from their talk, as soon as they had arrived they had sent a letter to the House of Yagyū. Apparently Sekishūsai had had some connection with Yoshioka Kempō back in the days when Kempō

5

was tutor to the shōguns. No doubt because of this, Sekishū-sai could not let Kempō's son go away without acknowledging his letter and had therefore sent Shōda to pay a courtesy call at the inn.

In response to this, the best these city youths could say was that Sekishūsai was "tactful," that he had decided to "play it safe," and that he couldn't be "as good as he's said to be." They seemed exceedingly satisfied with themselves, but Musashi thought them ridiculous. In contrast to what he had seen of Koyagyū Castle and the enviable state of the area's inhabitants, they appeared to have nothing better to offer than clever conversation.

It reminded him of a saying about the frog at the bottom of a well, unable to see what was going on in the outside world. Sometimes, he was thinking, it works the other way around. These pampered young sons of Kyoto were in a position to see what was happening at the center of things and to know what was going on everywhere, but it would not have occurred to them that while they were watching the great open sea, somewhere else, at the bottom of a deep well, a frog was steadily growing larger and stronger. Here in Koyagyū, well away from the country's political and economic center, sturdy samurai had for decades been leading a healthy rural life, preserving the ancient virtues, correcting their weak points and growing in stature.

With the passage of time, Koyagyū had produced Yagyū Muneyoshi, a great master of the martial arts, and his son Lord Munenori of Tajima, whose prowess had been recognized by Ieyasu himself. And there were also Muneyoshi's older sons, Gorōzaemon and Toshikatsu, famous throughout the land for their bravery, and his grandson Hyōgo Toshitoshi, whose prodigious feats had earned him a highly paid position under the renowned general Katō Kiyomasa of Higo. In fame and prestige, the House of Yagyū did not rank with the House of Yoshioka, but in terms of ability, the difference was a thing of the past. Denshichirō and his companions were blind to their own arrogance. Musashi, nevertheless, felt a little sorry for them.

He went over to a corner where water was piped into the room. Undoing his headband, he seized a handful of clay

6

and began scrubbing his scalp. For the first time in many weeks, he treated himself to the luxury of a good shampoo.

In the meantime, the men from Kyoto were finishing their bath.

"Ah, that felt good."

"Indeed it did. Now why don't we have some girls in to pour our sake for us?"

"Splendid idea! Splendid!"

The three finished drying themselves and left. After a thorough wash and another soak in the hot water, Musashi too dried off, tied up his hair, and went back to his room. There he found the boyish-looking Kocha in tears.

"What happened to you?"

"It's that boy of yours, sir. Look where he hit me!"

"That's a lie!" Jōtarō cried angrily from the opposite corner.

Musashi was about to scold him, but Jōtarō protested. "The dope said you were weak!"

"That's not true. I didn't."

"You did too!"

"Sir, I didn't say you or anybody else was weak. This brat started bragging about how you were the greatest swordsman in the country, because you'd killed dozens of rōnin at Hannya Plain, and I said there wasn't anybody in Japan better with the sword than the lord of this district, and then he started slapping me on the cheeks."

Musashi laughed. "I see. He shouldn't have done that, and I'll give him a good scolding. I hope you'll forgive us, Jō!" he said sternly.

"Yes, sir," said the boy, still sulking.

"Go take a bath!"

"I don't like to take baths."

"Neither do I," Musashi lied. "But you, you're so sweaty you stink."

"I'll go swimming in the river tomorrow morning."

The boy was becoming more and more stubborn as he grew more accustomed to Musashi, but Musashi did not really mind. In fact, he rather liked this side of Jōtarō. In the end, the boy did not go to the bath.

Before long Kocha brought the dinner trays. They ate

in silence, Jōtarō and the maid glaring at each other, while she served the meal.

Musashi was preoccupied with his private objective of meeting Sekishūsai. Considering his own lowly status, perhaps this was asking too much, but maybe, just maybe, it was possible.

"If I'm going to match arms with anybody," thought Musashi, "it should be with somebody strong. It's worth risking my life to see whether I can overcome the great Yagyū name. There's no use in following the Way of the Sword if I haven't the courage to try."

Musashi was aware that most people would laugh outright at him for entertaining the idea. Yagyū, though not one of the more prominent daimyō, was the master of a castle, his son was at the shōgun's court, and the whole family was steeped in the traditions of the warrior class. In the new age now dawning, they were riding the crest of the times.

"This will be the true test," thought Musashi, who, even as he ate his rice, was preparing himself for the encounter.

2

The Peony

The old man's dignity had grown with the years, until now he resembled nothing so much as a majestic crane, while at the same time retaining the appearance and manner of the well-bred samurai. His teeth were sound, his eyes wonderfully sharp. "I'll live to be a hundred," he frequently assured everyone.

Sekishūsai firmly believed this himself. "The House of Yagyū has always been long-lived," he liked to point out. "The ones who died in their twenties and thirties were killed in battle; all the others lived well beyond sixty." Among the countless wars he himself had taken part in were several major ones, including the revolt of the Miyoshi and the battles marking the rise and fall of the Matsunaga and Oda families.

Even if Sekishūsai had not been born in such a family, his way of life, and especially his attitude after he reached old age, gave reason to believe he would live to reach a hundred. At the age of forty-seven, he had decided for personal reasons to give up warfare. Nothing since had altered this resolution. He had turned a deaf ear to the entreaties of the shōgun Ashikaga Yoshiaki, as well as to repeated requests from Nobunaga and Hideyoshi to join forces with them. Though he lived almost in the shadow of Kyoto and Osaka, he refused to become embroiled in the frequent battles of those centers of power and intrigue. He preferred to remain in Yagyū, like a bear in a cave, and tend his fifteen-thousand-bushel estate in such a way that it could be handed on to his descendants in good condition. Sekishūsai once remarked, "I've done well to hold on to this estate. In this uncertain age, when leaders rise today and fall tomorrow, it's almost incredible that this one small castle has managed to survive intact."

This was no exaggeration. If he had supported Yoshiaki, he would have fallen victim to Nobunaga, and if he had supported Nobunaga, he might well have run afoul of Hideyoshi. Had he accepted Hideyoshi's patronage, he would have been dispossessed by Ieyasu after the Battle of Sekigahara.

His perspicacity, which people admired, was one factor, but to survive in such turbulent times, Sekishūsai had to have an inner fortitude lacking in the ordinary samurai of his time; they were all too apt to side with a man one day and shamelessly desert him the next, to look after their own interests—with no thought to propriety or integrity—or even to slaughter their own kinsmen should they interfere with personal ambitions.

"I am unable to do things like that," Sekishūsai said simply. And he was telling the truth. However, he had not renounced the Art of War itself. In the alcove of his living room hung a poem he had written himself. It said:

> I have no clever method
> For doing well in life.
> I rely only
> On the Art of War.
> It is my final refuge.

When he was invited by Ieyasu to visit Kyoto, Sekishūsai found it impossible not to accept and emerged from decades of serene seclusion to make his first visit to the shōgun's court. With him he took his fifth son, Munenori, who was twenty-four, and his grandson Hyōgo, then only sixteen. Ieyasu not only confirmed the venerable old warrior in his landholdings but asked him to become tutor in the martial arts to the House of Tokugawa. Sekishūsai, declining the honor on grounds of age, requested that Munenori be appointed in his stead, and this met with Ieyasu's approval.

The legacy Munenori carried with him to Edo encompassed more than a superb ability in martial arts, for his father had also passed on to him a knowledge of the higher plane of the Art of War that enables a leader to govern wisely.

In Sekishūsai's view, the Art of War was certainly a means of governing the people, but it was also a means of controlling the self. This he had learned from Lord Kōizumi, who, he was fond of saying, was the protective deity of the Yagyū household. The certificate Lord Kōizumi had given him to attest to his mastery of the Shinkage Style of swordsmanship was always kept on a shelf in Sekishūsai's room, along with a four-volume manual of military techniques presented him by his lordship. On anniversaries of Lord Kōizumi's death, Sekishūsai never neglected to place an offering of food before these treasured possessions.

In addition to descriptions of the hidden-sword techniques of the Shinkage Style, the manual contained illustrative pictures, all by the hand of Lord Kōizumi himself. Even in his retirement, Sekishūsai took pleasure in rolling the scrolls out and looking through them. He was constantly surprised to rediscover how skillfully his teacher had wielded the brush. The pictures showed people fighting and fencing in every conceivable position and stance. When Sekishūsai looked at them, he felt that the swordsmen were about to descend from heaven to join him in his little mountain house.

Lord Kōizumi had first come to Koyagyū Castle when Sekishūsai was thirty-seven or thirty-eight and still brimming with military ambition. His lordship, together with two nephews, Hikida Bungorō and Suzuki Ihaku, was going around the country seeking experts in the martial arts, and one day he arrived at the Hōzōin. This was in the days when In'ei often called at Koyagyū Castle, and In'ei told Sekishūsai about the visitor. That was the beginning of their relationship.

Sekishūsai and Kōizumi held matches for three days in a row. In the first bout, Kōizumi announced where he would attack, then proceeded to take the match doing exactly as he had said.

The same thing happened the second day, and Sekishūsai, his pride injured, concentrated on figuring out a new approach for the third day.

Upon seeing his new stance, Kōizumi merely said, "That won't do. If you are going to do that, I will do this." Without further ado, he attacked and defeated Sekishūsai for the third time. From that day on, Sekishūsai gave up the egotistic approach to swordsmanship; as he later recalled, it was on that occasion that he first had a glimpse of the true Art of War.

At Sekishūsai's strong urging, Lord Kōizumi remained at Koyagyū for six months, during which time Sekishūsai studied with the single-minded devotion of a neophyte. When they finally parted, Lord Kōizumi said, "My way of swordsmanship is still imperfect. You are young, and you should try to carry it to perfection." He then gave Sekishūsai a Zen riddle: "What is sword fighting without a sword?"

For a number of years, Sekishūsai pondered this, considering it from every angle and finally arriving at an answer that satisfied him. When Lord Kōizumi came to visit again, Sekishūsai greeted him with clear, untroubled eyes and suggested that they have a match. His lordship scrutinized him for a moment, then said, "No, it would be useless. You have discovered the truth!"

He then presented Sekishūsai with the certificate and the four-volume manual, and in this fashion the Yagyū Style was born. This in turn gave birth to Sekishūsai's peaceful way of life in his old age.

That Sekishūsai lived in a mountain house was due to his no longer liking the imposing castle with all its elaborate trappings. Despite his almost Taoist love of seclusion, he was happy to have the company of the girl Shōda Kizaemon had brought to play the flute for him, for she was thoughtful, polite and never a nuisance. Not only did her playing please him immensely, but she added a welcome touch of youth and femininity to the household. Occasionally she would talk of leaving, but he would always tell her to stay a little longer.

The Peony

* * *

Putting the finishing touches on the single peony he was arranging in an Iga vase, Sekishūsai asked Otsū, "What do you think? Is my flower arrangement alive?"

Standing just behind him, she said, "You must have studied flower arranging very hard."

"Not at all. I'm not a Kyoto nobleman, and I've never studied either flower arranging or the tea ceremony under a teacher."

"Well, it looks as though you had."

"I use the same method with flowers that I use with the sword."

Otsū looked surprised. "Can you really arrange flowers the way you use the sword?"

"Yes. You see, it's all a matter of spirit. I have no use for rules—twisting the flowers with your fingertips or choking them at the neck. The point is to have the proper spirit—to be able to make them seem alive, just as they were when they were picked. Look at that! My flower isn't dead."

Otsū felt that this austere old man had taught her many things she needed to know, and since it had all begun with a chance meeting on the highroad, she felt she had been very lucky. "I'll teach you the tea ceremony," he would say. Or: "Do you compose Japanese poems? If you do, teach me something about the courtly style. The Man'yōshū is all well and good, but living here in this secluded place, I'd rather hear simple poems about nature."

In return, she did little things for him that no one else thought of. He was delighted, for example, when she made him a little cloth cap like the tea masters wore. He kept it on his head much of the time now, treasuring it as though there were nothing finer anywhere. Her flute playing, too, pleased him immensely, and on moonlit nights, the hauntingly beautiful sound of her flute often reached as far as the castle itself.

While Sekishūsai and Otsū were discussing the flower arrangement, Kizaemon came quietly to the entrance of the mountain house and called to Otsū. She came out and invited him in, but he hesitated.

13

"Would you let his lordship know I've just come back from my errand?" he asked.

Otsū laughed. "That's backwards, isn't it?"

"Why?"

"You're the chief retainer here. I'm only an outsider, called in to play the flute. You're much closer to him than I. Shouldn't you go to him directly, rather than through me?"

"I suppose you're right, but here in his lordship's little house, you're special. Anyway, please give him the message." Kizaemon, too, was pleased by the way things had turned out. He had found in Otsū a person whom his master liked very much.

Otsū returned almost immediately to say that Sekishūsai wanted Kizaemon to come in. Kizaemon found the old man in the tea room, wearing the cloth cap Otsū had made.

"Are you back already?" asked Sekishūsai.

"Yes. I called on them and gave them the letter and the fruit, just as you instructed."

"Have they gone?"

"No. No sooner had I arrived back here than a messenger came from the inn with a letter. It said that since they'd come to Yagyū, they didn't want to leave without seeing the dōjō. If possible, they'd like to come tomorrow. They also said they'd like to meet you and pay their respects."

"Impudent boors! Why must they be such a nuisance?" Sekishūsai looked extremely annoyed. "Did you explain that Munenori is in Edo, Hyōgo in Kumamoto, and that there's no one else around?"

"I did."

"I despise people like that. Even after I send a message to tell them I can't see them, they try to push their way in."

"I don't know what—"

"It would appear that Yoshioka's sons are as shiftless as they're said to be."

"The one at the Wataya is Denshichirō. He didn't impress me."

"I'd be surprised if he did. His father was a man of considerable character. When I went to Kyoto with Lord Kōizumi, we saw him two or three times and drank some sake together. It appears that the house has gone downhill

14

since then. The young man seems to think that being Kempō's son gives him the right not to be refused entry here, and so he's pressing his challenge. But from our viewpoint, it makes no sense to accept the challenge and then send him away beaten."

"This Denshichirō seems to have a good deal of self-confidence. If he wants so badly to come, perhaps I myself should take him on."

"No, don't even consider it. These sons of famous people usually have a high opinion of themselves; moreover, they're prone to try and twist things to their own advantage. If you were to beat him, you can depend on it that he'd try to destroy our reputation in Kyoto. As far as I'm concerned, it makes no difference, but I don't want to burden Munenori or Hyōgo with something like that."

"What shall we do, then?"

"The best thing would be to appease him in some way, make him feel he's being treated the way a son from a great house should be treated. Maybe it was a mistake to send a man to see him." Shifting his gaze to Otsū, he continued: "I think a woman would be better. Otsū is probably just the right person."

"All right," she said. "Do you want me to go now?"

"No, there's no hurry. Tomorrow morning will do."

Sekishūsai quickly wrote a simple letter, of the sort a tea master might compose, and handed it to Otsū, with a peony like the one he had put in the vase. "Give these to him, and tell him that you've come in my stead because I have a cold. Let's see what his answer is."

The next morning, Otsū draped a long veil over her head. Although veils were already out of style in Kyoto, even among the higher classes, the upper- and middle-class women in the provinces still prized them.

At the stable, which was in the outer grounds of the castle, she asked to borrow a horse.

The keeper of the stables, who was busy cleaning up, asked, "Oh, are you going somewhere?"

"Yes, I have to go to the Wataya on an errand for his lordship."

"Shall I go with you?"

"There's no need for that."

"Will you be all right?"

"Of course. I like horses. The ones I used to ride in Mimasaka were wild, or nearly so."

As she rode off, the reddish-brown veil floated in the wind behind her. She rode well, holding the letter and the slightly weary peony in one hand and deftly handling the horse with the other. Farmers and workers in the field waved to her, for in the short time she had been here, she had already become fairly well known among the local people, whose relations with Sekishūsai were much friendlier than were usual between lord and peasants. The farmers here all knew that a beautiful young woman had come to play the flute for their lord, and their admiration and respect for him were extended to Otsū.

Arriving at the Wataya, she dismounted and tied her horse to a tree in the garden.

"Welcome!" called Kocha, coming out to greet her. "Are you staying for the night?"

"No, I've just come from Koyagyū Castle with a message for Yoshioka Denshichirō. He's still here, isn't he?"

"Would you wait a moment, please?"

In the brief time Kocha was gone, Otsū created a mild stir among the travelers who were noisily putting on their leggings and sandals and strapping their luggage to their backs.

"Who's that?" asked one.

"Who do you suppose she's come to see?"

Otsū's beauty, a graceful elegance seldom encountered in the country, kept the departing guests whispering and ogling until she followed Kocha out of sight.

Denshichirō and his companions, having drunk until late the night before, had only just arisen. When told that a messenger had come from the castle, they assumed it would be the man who had come the day before. The sight of Otsū with her white peony came as a distinct surprise.

"Oh, please forgive the room! It's a mess."

With abjectly apologetic faces, they straightened their kimonos and sat properly and a little stiffly on their knees.

"Please, come in, come in."

"I've been sent by the lord of Koyagyū Castle," Otsū said simply, placing the letter and the peony before Denshichirō. "Would you be so kind as to read the letter now?"

"Ah, yes . . . this is the letter? Yes, I'll read it."

He opened the scroll, which was no more than a foot long. Written in thin ink, suggestive of the light flavor of tea, it said: "Forgive me for sending my greetings in a letter, rather than meeting you in person, but unfortunately I have a slight cold. I think a pure white peony will give you more pleasure than the runny nose of an old man. I send the flower by the hand of a flower, with the hope that you will accept my apology. My ancient body rests outside the everyday world. I hesitate to show my face. Please smile with pity on an old man."

Denshichirō sniffed with contempt and rolled up the letter. "Is that all?" he asked.

"No, he also said that although he'd like to have a cup of tea with you, he hesitates to invite you to his house, because there is no one there but warriors ignorant of the niceties of tea. Since Munenori is away in Edo, he feels that the serving of the tea would be so crude as to bring laughter to the lips of people from the imperial capital. He asked me to beg your pardon, and tell you that he hopes to see you on some future occasion."

"Ha, ha!" exclaimed Denshichirō, putting on a suspicious face. "If I understand you correctly, Sekishūsai is under the impression we were looking forward to observing the niceties of the tea ceremony. To tell the truth, being from samurai families, we don't know anything about tea. Our intention was to inquire personally after Sekishūsai's health and persuade him to give us a lesson in swordsmanship."

"He understands that perfectly, of course. But he's spending his old age in retirement and has acquired the habit of expressing many of his thoughts in terms of tea."

In obvious disgust, Denshichirō replied, "Well, he hasn't left us any choice but to give up. Please tell him that if we come again, we'd like to see him." He handed the peony back to Otsū.

"Don't you like it? He thought it might cheer you up on

the road. He said you might hang it in the corner of your palanquin, or if you're on horseback, attach it to your saddle."

"He meant it to be a souvenir?" Denshichirō lowered his eyes as though insulted, then with a sour face said, "This is ridiculous! You can tell him we have peonies of our own in Kyoto!"

If that was the way he felt, Otsū decided, there was no point in pressing the gift on him. Promising to deliver his message, she took her leave as delicately as she would have removed the bandage from an open sore. In ill temper, her hosts barely acknowledged her departure.

Once in the hallway, Otsū laughed softly to herself, glanced at the shiny black floor leading to the room where Musashi was staying, and turned in the other direction.

Kocha came out of Musashi's room and ran to catch up with her.

"Are you leaving already?" she asked.

"Yes, I've finished what I came to do."

"My, that was fast, wasn't it?" Looking down at Otsū's hand, she asked, "Is that a peony? I didn't know they bloomed white."

"Yes. It's from the castle garden. You can have it, if you like."

"Oh, please," said Kocha, stretching out her hands.

After bidding Otsū good-bye, Kocha went to the servants' quarters and showed everyone the flower. Since no one was inclined to admire it, she went disappointedly back to Musashi's room.

Musashi, sitting by the window with his chin in his hands, was gazing in the direction of the castle and thinking hard about his objective: how could he manage, first, to meet Sekishūsai and, second, to overcome him with his sword?

"Do you like flowers?" Kocha asked as she entered.

"Flowers?"

She showed him the peony.

"Hmm. It's nice."

"Do you like it?"

"Yes."

"It's supposed to be a peony, a white peony."

18

"Is it? Why don't you put it in that vase over there."

"I don't know how to arrange flowers. You do it."

"No, you do it. It's better to do it without thinking how it's going to look."

"Well, I'll go and get some water," she said, taking the vase out with her.

Musashi's eye happened to light on the cut end of the peony stem. His head tilted in surprise, though he couldn't pinpoint what it was that attracted his attention.

Casual interest had become intent scrutiny by the time Kocha came back. She put the vase in the alcove and tried sticking the peony in it, but with poor results.

"The stem's too long," said Musashi. "Bring it here; I'll cut it. Then when you stand it up, it'll look natural."

Kocha brought the flower over and held it up to him. Before she knew what had happened, she had dropped the flower and burst into tears. Small wonder, for in that split second Musashi had whipped out his short sword, uttered a vigorous cry, slashed through the stem between her hands, and resheathed his sword. To Kocha, the glint of steel and the sound of the sword snapping back into its scabbard seemed simultaneous.

Making no attempt to comfort the terrified girl, Musashi picked up the piece of stem he had cut off and began comparing one end of it with the other. He seemed completely absorbed. Finally, taking notice of her distraught state, he apologized and patted her on the head.

Once he had coaxed her out of her tears, he asked, "Do you know who cut this flower?"

"No. It was given to me."

"By whom?"

"A person from the castle."

"One of the samurai?"

"No, it was a young woman."

"Mm. Then you think the flower came from the castle?"

"Yes, she said it did."

"I'm sorry I scared you. If I buy you some cakes later, will you forgive me? In any case, the flower should be just right now. Try putting it in the vase."

"Will this do?"

19

"Yes, that's fine."

Kocha had taken an instant liking to Musashi, but the flash of his sword had chilled her to the marrow. She left the room, unwilling to return until her duties made it absolutely unavoidable.

Musashi was far more fascinated by the eight-inch piece of stem than by the flower in the alcove. He was sure the first cut had not been made with either scissors or a knife. Since peony stems are lithe and supple, the cut could only have been made with a sword, and only a very determined stroke would have made so clean a slice. Whoever had done it was no ordinary person. Although he himself had just tried to duplicate the cut with his own sword, upon comparing both ends he was immediately aware that his own cut was by far the inferior one. It was like the difference between a Buddhist statue carved by an expert and one made by a craftsman of average skill.

He asked himself what it could mean. "If a samurai working the castle garden can make a cut like this, then the standards of the House of Yagyū must be even higher than I thought."

His confidence suddenly deserted him. "I'm nowhere near ready yet."

Gradually, however, he recovered from this feeling. "In any event, the Yagyū people are worthy opponents. If I should lose, I can fall at their feet and accept defeat with good grace. I've already decided I'm willing to face anything, even death." Sitting and mustering up his courage, he felt himself grow warmer.

But how was he to go about it? Even if a student arrived at his doorstep with a proper introduction, it seemed unlikely Sekishūsai would agree to a match. The innkeeper had said as much. And with Munenori and Hyōgo both away, there was no one to challenge but Sekishūsai himself.

He again tried to devise a way of gaining admittance to the castle. His eyes returned to the flower in the alcove, and the image of someone the flower unconsciously reminded him of began to take form. Seeing Otsū's face in his mind's eye quieted his spirit and soothed his nerves.

Otsū herself was well on her way back to Koyagyū

20

Castle when suddenly she heard a raucous shout behind her. She turned to see a child emerging from a clump of trees at the base of a cliff. He was clearly coming after her, and since children of the area were much too timid to accost a young woman such as herself, she brought her horse to a halt out of sheer curiosity.

Jōtarō was stark naked. His hair was wet, and his clothes were rolled up in a ball under his arm. Unabashed by his nudity, he said, "You're the lady with the flute. Are you still staying here?" Having eyed the horse with distaste, he looked directly at Otsū.

"It's you!" she exclaimed, before averting her eyes in embarrassment. "The little boy who was crying on the Yamato highroad."

"Crying? I wasn't crying!"

"Never mind. How long have you been here?"

"Just came the other day."

"By yourself?"

"No; with my teacher."

"Oh, that's right. You did say you were studying swordsmanship, didn't you? What are you doing with your clothes off?"

"You don't think I'd jump in the river with my clothes on, do you?"

"River? But the water must be freezing. People around here would laugh at the idea of going swimming this time of year."

"I wasn't swimming; I was taking a bath. My teacher said I smelled sweaty, so I went to the river."

Otsū chuckled. "Where are you staying?"

"At the Wataya."

"Why, I've just come from there."

"Too bad you didn't come to see us. How about coming back with me now?"

"I can't now. I have an errand to do."

"Well, bye!" he said, turning to go.

"Jōtarō, come see me at the castle sometime."

"Could I really?"

The words were barely out before Otsū began to regret

them, but she said, "Yes, but make sure you don't come dressed the way you are now."

"If that's the way you feel about it, I don't want to go. I don't like places where they make a fuss about things."

Otsū felt relieved and still had a smile on her face when she rode back through the castle gate. After returning her horse to the stable, she went to report to Sekishūsai.

He laughed and said, "So they were angry! Fine! Let them be angry. There's nothing they can do about it." After a moment, he seemed to remember something else. "Did you throw the peony away?" he asked.

She explained that she had given it to the maid at the inn, and he nodded his approval. "Did the Yoshioka boy take the peony in his hand and look at it?" he asked.

"Yes. When he read the letter."

"And?"

"He just handed it back to me."

"He didn't look at the stem?"

"Not that I noticed."

"He didn't examine it, or say anything about it?"

"No."

"It's just as well that I refused to meet him. He's not worth meeting. The House of Yoshioka might just as well have ended with Kempō.

The Yagyū dōjō could quite appropriately be described as grand. Situated in the outer grounds of the castle, it had been rebuilt around the time when Sekishūsai was forty, and the sturdy timber used in its construction gave it an air of indestructibility. The gloss of the wood, acquired over the years, seemed to echo the rigors of the men who had undergone training here, and the building was ample enough to have served as samurai barracks during times of war.

"Lightly! Not with your sword point! With your gut, your gut!" Shōda Kizaemon, seated on a slightly elevated platform and clad in underrobe and *hakama*, was roaring angry instructions at two aspiring swordsmen. "Do it again! You don't have it right at all!"

The target of Kizaemon's scolding was a pair of Yagyū samurai, who though dazed and bathed in sweat fought doggedly on. Stances were taken, weapons readied, and the two came together again like fire against fire.

"A-o-o-oh!"

"Y-a-a-ah!"

At Yagyū, beginners were not allowed to use wooden swords. Instead they used a staff devised specifically for the Shinkage Style. A long, thin leather bag filled with strips of bamboo, it was, in effect, a leather stick, with no handle or sword guard. Though less dangerous than a wooden sword, it could still remove an ear or turn a nose into a pomegranate. There were no restrictions regarding what part of the body a combatant could attack. Knocking down an opponent by striking him horizontally in the legs was permitted, and there was no rule against hitting a man once he was down.

"Keep it up! Keep at it! Same as last time!" Kizaemon drove the students on.

The custom here was not to let a man quit until he was ready to drop. Beginners were driven especially hard, never praised and treated to no small amount of verbal abuse. Because of this, the average samurai knew that entering into the service of the House of Yagyū was not something to be taken lightly. Newcomers rarely lasted long, and the men now serving under Yagyū were the result of very careful sifting. Even the common foot soldiers and stablemen had made some progress in the study of swordsmanship.

Shōda Kizaemon was, needless to say, an accomplished swordsman, having mastered the Shinkage Style at an early age and, under the tutelage of Sekishūsai himself, gone on to learn the secrets of the Yagyū Style. To this he had added some personal techniques of his own, and he spoke proudly now of the "True Shōda Style."

The Yagyū horse trainer, Kimura Sukekurō, was also an adept, as was Murata Yozō, who, though employed as keeper of the storehouse, was said to have been a good match for Hyōgo. Debuchi Magobei, another relatively minor official, had studied swordsmanship from childhood and wielded a powerful weapon indeed. The Lord of Echizen had tried to persuade Debuchi to come into his service, and the Tokugawas of Kii had tried to lure Murata away, but both of them had chosen to stay in Yagyū, though the material benefits were fewer.

The House of Yagyū, now enjoying a peak in its fortunes, was turning out a seemingly unending stream of great swordsmen. By the same token, the Yagyū samurai were not recognized as swordsmen until they had proved their ability by surviving the merciless regimen.

"You there!" called Kizaemon to a guard passing by outside. He had been surprised by the sight of Jōtarō following along after the soldier.

"Hello!" shouted Jōtarō in his friendly manner.

"What are you doing inside the castle?" asked Kizaemon sternly.

"The man at the gate brought me in," answered Jōtarō, truthfully enough.

"He did, did he?" To the guard, he said, "Why did you bring this boy here?"

"He said he wanted to see you."

"Do you mean to say you brought this child here on his word alone? . . . Boy!"

"Yes, sir."

"This is no playground. Get along with you."

"But I didn't come to play. I brought a letter from my teacher."

"From your teacher? Didn't you say he was one of those wandering students?"

"Look at the letter, please."

"I don't need to."

"What's the matter? Can't you read?"

Kizaemon snorted.

"Well, if you can read, read it."

"You're a tricky brat. The reason I said I don't need to read it is that I already know what it says."

"Even so, wouldn't it be more polite to read it?"

"Student warriors swarm here like mosquitoes and maggots. If I took time to be polite to all of them, I wouldn't be able to do anything else. I feel sorry for you, however, so I'll tell you what the letter says. All right?

"It says that the writer would like to be allowed to see our magnificent dōjō, that he would like to bask, even for a minute, in the shadow of the greatest master in the land, and that for the sake of all those successors who will follow the Way of the Sword, he would be grateful to have a lesson bestowed upon him. I imagine that's about the long and short of it.''

Jōtarō's eyes rounded. "Is that what the letter says?"

"Yes, so I don't need to read it, do I? Let it not be said, however, that the House of Yagyū coldheartedly turns away those who call upon it." He paused and continued, as though having rehearsed the speech: "Ask the guard there to explain everything to you. When student warriors come to this house, they enter through the main gate and proceed to the middle gate, to the right of which is a building called the Shin'indō. It is identified by a hanging wooden plaque. If they apply to the caretaker there, they are free to rest for a time, and there are facilities for them to stop over for a night or two. When they leave, they are given a small amount of money to help them along the way. Now, the thing for you to do is to take this letter to the caretaker at the Shin'indō— understand?''

"No!" said Jōtarō. He shook his head and raised his right shoulder slightly. "Listen, sir!"

"Well?"

"You shouldn't judge people by their appearance. I'm not the son of a beggar!"

"I do have to admit you have a certain knack with words.''

"Why don't you just take a look at the letter? It may say something completely different from what you think. What would you do then? Would you let me cut off your head?''

"Hold on a minute!" Kizaemon laughed, and his face, with its red mouth behind his spiky beard, looked like the inside of a broken chestnut burr. "No, you can't cut my head off.''

"Well, then, look at the letter."

"Come in here."

"Why?" Jōtarō had a sinking feeling he'd gone too far.

"I admire your determination not to let your master's message go undelivered. I'll read it."

"And why shouldn't you? You're the highest-ranking official in the House of Yagyū, aren't you?"

"You wield your tongue superbly. Let's hope you can do the same with your sword when you grow up." He broke the seal of the letter and silently read Musashi's message. As he read, his face became serious. When he was finished, he asked, "Did you bring anything along with this letter?"

"Oh, I forgot! I was to give you this too." Jōtarō quickly pulled the peony stem from his kimono.

Silently, Kizaemon examined both ends of the stem, looking somewhat puzzled. He could not completely understand the meaning of Musashi's letter.

It explained how the inn's maid had brought him a flower, which she said had come from the castle, and that upon examining the stem, he had discovered that the cut had been made by "no ordinary person." The message continued: "After putting the flower in a vase, I sensed some special spirit about it, and I feel that I simply have to find out who made the cut. The question may seem trivial, but if you would not mind telling me which member of your household did it, I would appreciate your sending a reply by the boy who delivers my letter."

That was all—no mention of the writer's being a student, no request for a bout.

"What an odd thing to write," thought Kizaemon. He looked at the peony stem again, again examining both ends closely, but without being able to discern whether one end differed from the other.

"Murata!" he called. "Come look at this. Can you see any difference between the cuts at the ends of this stem? Does one cut, perhaps, seem to be keener?"

Murata Yozō looked at the stem this way and that, but had to confess that he saw no difference between the two cuts.

"Let's show it to Kimura."

They went to the office at the back of the building and put the problem to their colleague, who was as mystified as they were. Debuchi, who happened to be in the office at the time, said, "This is one of the flowers the old lord himself cut the day before yesterday. Shōda, weren't you with him at the time?''

"No, I saw him arranging a flower, but I didn't see him cut it."

"Well, this is one of the two he cut. He put one in the vase in his room and had Otsū take the other one to Yoshioka Denshichirō with a letter."

"Yes, I remember that," said Kizaemon, as he started to read Musashi's letter again. Suddenly, he looked up with startled eyes. "This is signed 'Shimmen Musashi,' " he said. "Do you suppose this Musashi is the Miyamoto Musashi who helped the Hōzōin priests kill all that riffraff at Hannya Plain? It must be!"

Debuchi and Murata passed the letter back and forth, rereading it. "The handwriting has character," said Debuchi.

"Yes," mumbled Murata. "He seems to be an unusual person."

"If what the letter says is true," Kizaemon said, "and he really could tell that this stem had been cut by an expert, then he must know something we don't. The old master cut it himself, and apparently that's plain to someone whose eyes really see."

Debuchi said, "Mm. I'd like to meet him. . . . We could check on this and also get him to tell us what happened at Hannya Plain." But rather than commit himself on his own, he asked Kimura's opinion. Kimura pointed out that since they weren't receiving any *shugyōsha*, they couldn't have him as a guest at the practice hall, but there was no reason why they couldn't invite him for a meal and some sake at the Shin'indō. The irises were already in bloom there, he noted, and the wild azaleas were about to blossom. They could have a little party and talk about swordsmanship and things like that. Musashi would in all likelihood be glad to come, and the old lord certainly wouldn't object if he heard about it.

Kizaemon slapped his knee and said, "That's a splendid suggestion."

"It'll be a party for us too," Murata added. "Let's send him an answer right away."

As he sat down to write the reply, Kizaemon said, "The boy's outside. Have him come in."

A few minutes earlier, Jōtarō had been yawning and grumbling, "How can they be so slow," when a big black dog caught his scent and came over to sniff at him. Thinking he had found a new friend, Jōtarō spoke to the dog and pulled him forward by the ears.

"Let's wrestle," he suggested, then hugged the dog and threw him over. The dog went along with this, so Jōtarō caught him in his hands and threw him two or three more times.

Then, holding the dog's jaws together, he said, "Now, bark!"

This made the dog angry. Breaking away, he caught the skirt of Jōtarō's kimono with his teeth and tugged tenaciously.

Now it was Jōtarō's turn to get mad. "Who do you think I am? You can't do that!" he shouted.

He drew his wooden sword and held it menacingly over his head. The dog, taking him seriously, started barking loudly to attract the attention of the guards. With a curse, Jōtarō brought his sword down on the dog's head. It sounded as though he had hit a rock. The dog hurled himself against the boy's back, and catching hold of his obi, brought him to the ground. Before he could get to his feet, the dog was at him again, while Jōtarō frantically tried to protect his face with his hands.

He tried to escape, but the dog was right on his heels, the echoes of his barking reverberating through the mountains. Blood began to ooze between the fingers covering his face, and soon his own anguished howls drowned out those of the dog.

3

Jōtarō's Revenge

On his return to the inn, Jōtarō sat down before Musashi and with a smug look reported that he had carried out his mission. Several scratches criss-crossed the boy's face, and his nose looked like a ripe strawberry. No doubt he was in some pain, but since he offered no explanation, Musashi asked no questions.

"Here's their reply," said Jōtarō, handing Musashi the letter from Shōda Kizaemon and adding a few words about his meeting with the samurai, but saying nothing about the dog. As he spoke, his wounds started to bleed again.

"Will that be all?" he asked.

"Yes, that's all. Thanks."

As Musashi opened Kizaemon's letter, Jōtarō put his hands to his face and hurriedly left the room. Kocha caught up with him and examined his scratches with worried eyes.

"How did that happen?" she asked.

"A dog jumped on me."

"Whose dog was it?"

"One of the dogs at the castle."

"Oh, was it that big black Kishū hound? He's vicious. I'm sure, strong as you are, you wouldn't be able to handle him. Why, he's bitten prowlers to death!"

Although they were not on the best of terms, Kocha led him to the stream out back and made him wash his face. Then she went and fetched some ointment, which she applied to his face. For once, Jōtarō behaved like a gentleman.

When she had finished her ministrations, he bowed and thanked her over and over again.

"Stop bobbing your head up and down. You're a man, after all, and it looks ridiculous."

"But I appreciate what you've done."

"Even if we do fight a lot, I still like you," she confessed.

"I like you too."

"Really?"

The parts of Jōtarō's face that showed between the patches of ointment turned crimson, and Kocha's cheeks burst into subdued flame. There was no one around. The sun shone through the pink peach blossoms.

"Your master will probably be going away soon, won't he?" she asked with a trace of disappointment.

"We'll be here for a while yet," he replied reassuringly.

"I wish you could stay for a year or two."

The two went into the shed where the fodder for the horses was kept and lay down on their backs in the hay. Their hands touched, sending a warm tingle through Jōtarō. Quite without warning, he pulled Kocha's hand toward him and bit her finger.

"Ouch!"

"Did that hurt? I'm sorry."

"It's all right. Do it again."

"You don't mind?"

"No, no, go on and bite! Bite harder!"

He did just that, tugging at her fingers like a puppy. Hay was falling over their heads, and soon they were hugging each other, just for the sake of hugging, when Kocha's father came looking for her. Appalled at what he saw, his face took on the stern expression of a Confucian sage.

"You idiots, what are you up to? Both of you, still only children!" He dragged them out by the scruff of the neck and gave Kocha a couple of smart whacks on the behind.

The rest of that day, Musashi said very little to anyone. He sat with his arms folded and thought.

Once, in the middle of the night, Jōtarō woke up and, raising his head a little, stole a look at his master. Musashi

30

was lying in bed with his eyes wide open, staring at the ceiling with intense concentration.

The next day, too, Musashi kept to himself. Jōtarō was frightened; his master might have heard about his playing with Kocha in the shed. Nothing was said, however. Late in the afternoon, Musashi sent the boy to ask for their bill and was making preparations to depart when the clerk brought it. Asked if he would need dinner, he said no.

Kocha, standing idly in a corner, asked, "Won't you be coming back to sleep here tonight?"

"No. Thank you, Kocha, for taking such good care of us. I'm sure we've been a lot of trouble for you. Good-bye."

"Take good care of yourself," said Kocha. She was holding her hands over her face, hiding her tears.

At the gate, the manager of the inn and the other maids lined up to see them off. Their setting off just before sunset seemed very odd.

After walking a bit, Musashi looked around for Jōtarō. Not seeing him, he turned back toward the inn, where the boy was under the storehouse, saying farewell to Kocha. When they saw Musashi approaching, they drew hastily away from each other.

"Good-bye," said Kocha.

"Bye," called Jōtarō, as he ran to Musashi's side. Though fearful of Musashi's eyes, the boy could not resist stealing backward glances until the inn was out of sight.

Lights began to appear in the valley. Musashi, saying nothing and not once looking back, strode on ahead. Jōtarō followed along glumly.

After a time, Musashi asked, "Aren't we there yet?"

"Where?"

"At the main gate of Koyagyū Castle."

"Are we going to the castle?"

"Yes."

"Will we stay there tonight?"

"I have no idea. That depends on how things turn out."

"There it is. That's the gate."

Musashi stopped and stood before the gate, feet together. Above the moss-grown ramparts, the huge trees made a soughing sound. A single light streamed from a square window.

Musashi called out, and a guard appeared. Giving him the letter from Shōda Kizaemon, he said, "My name is Musashi, and I've come on Shōda's invitation. Would you please tell him that I'm here?"

The guard had been expecting him. "They're waiting for you," he said, motioning for Musashi to follow him.

In addition to its other functions, the Shin'indō was the place where the young people in the castle studied Confucianism. It also served as the fief's library. The rooms along the passageway to the rear of the building were all lined with bookshelves, and though the fame of the House of Yagyū stemmed from its military prowess, Musashi could see it also placed great emphasis on scholarship. Everything about the castle seemed to be steeped in history.

And everything seemed to be well run, to judge from the neatness of the road from the gate to the Shin'indō, the courteous demeanor of the guard, and the austere, peaceful lighting visible in the vicinity of the keep.

Sometimes, upon entering a house for the first time, a visitor has the feeling he's already familiar with the place and its inhabitants. Musashi had that impression now, as he sat down on the wooden floor of the large room to which the guard brought him. After offering him a hard round cushion of woven straw, which he accepted with thanks, the guard left him alone. On the way, Jōtarō had been dropped off at the attendants' waiting room.

The guard returned a few minutes later and told Musashi that his host would arrive soon.

Musashi slid the round cushion over to a corner and leaned back against a post. From the light of the low lamp shining into the garden, he saw trellises of blossoming wisteria vines, both white and lavender. The sweetish scent of wisteria was in the air. He was startled by the croak of a frog, the first he had heard that year.

Water gurgled somewhere in the garden; the stream apparently ran under the building, for after he was settled, he noticed the sound of flowing water beneath him. Indeed, before long it seemed to him that the sound of water was coming from the walls, the ceiling, even the lamp. He felt cool and relaxed. Yet simmering deep inside him there was an unsuppressible sense of disquiet. It was his insatiable fighting spirit, coursing through his veins even in this quiet atmosphere. From his cushion by the post, he looked questioningly at his surroundings.

"Who is Yagyū?" he thought defiantly. "He's a swordsman, and I'm a swordsman. In this respect we are equal. But tonight I will advance a step farther and put Yagyū behind me."

"Sorry to have kept you waiting."

Shōda Kizaemon entered the room with Kimura, Debuchi and Murata.

"Welcome to Koyagyū," Kizaemon said warmly.

After the other three men had introduced themselves, servants brought in trays of sake and snacks. The sake was a thick, rather syrupy, local brew, served in large old-style sake bowls with high stems.

"Here in the country," said Kizaemon, "we aren't able to offer you much, but please feel at home."

The others too, with great cordiality, invited him to make himself comfortable, not to stand on ceremony.

With a little urging, Musashi accepted some sake, though he was not particularly fond of it. It was not so much that he disliked it as that he was still too young to appreciate its subtlety. The sake this evening was palatable enough but had little immediate effect on him.

"Looks as though you know how to drink," said Kimura Sukekurō, offering to refill his cup. "By the way, I hear the peony you asked about the other day was cut by the lord of this castle himself."

Musashi slapped his knee. "I thought so!" he exclaimed. "It was splendid!"

Kimura moved closer. "What I'd like to know is just how you could tell that the cut in that soft, thin stem had been made by a master swordsman. We, all of us, were deeply impressed by your ability to discern that."

Uncertain as to where the conversation was leading, Musashi said, to gain time, "You were? Really?"

"Yes, no mistake about it!" said Kizaemon, Debuchi and Murata almost simultaneously.

"We ourselves couldn't see anything special about it," said Kizaemon. "We arrived at the conclusion that it must take a genius to recognize another genius. We think it would be of great help in our future studies if you'd explain it to us."

Musashi, taking another sip of sake, said, "Oh, it wasn't anything in particular—just a lucky guess."

"Come now, don't be modest."

"I'm not being modest. It was a feeling I got—from the look of the cut."

"Just what sort of feeling was it?"

As they would with any stranger, these four senior disciples of the House of Yagyū were trying to analyze Musashi as a human being and at the same time test him. They had already taken note of his physique, admiring his carriage and the expression in his eyes. But the way he held his sake cup and his chopsticks betrayed his country up-bringing and made them inclined to be patronizing. After only three or four cups of sake, Musashi's face turned copper red. Embarrassed, he touched his hand to his forehead and cheeks two or three times. The boyishness of the gesture made them laugh.

"This feeling of yours," repeated Kizaemon. "Can't you tell us more about it? You know, this building, the Shin'indō, was built expressly for Lord Kōizumi of Ise to stay in during his visits. It's an important building in the history of swordsmanship. It's a fitting place for us to hear a lecture from you tonight."

Realizing that protesting their flattery was not going to get him off the hook, Musashi decided to take the plunge.

"When you sense something you sense it," he said. "There's really no way to explain it. If you want me to demonstrate what I mean, you'll have to unsheath your sword and face me in a match. There's no other way."

The smoke from the lamp rose as black as squid ink in the still night air. The croaking frog was heard again.

Kizaemon and Debuchi, the two eldest, looked at each other and laughed. Though he had spoken quietly, the statement about testing him had undeniably been a challenge, and they recognized it as such.

Letting it pass without comment, they talked about swords, then about Zen, events in other provinces, the Battle of Sekigahara. Kizaemon, Debuchi and Kimura had all taken part in the bloody conflict, and to Musashi who had been on the opposing side, their stories had the ring of bitter truth. The hosts appeared to be enjoying the conversation immensely, and Musashi found it fascinating just to listen.

He was nonetheless conscious of the swift passage of time, knowing in his heart that if he did not meet Sekishūsai tonight, he would never meet him.

Kizaemon announced it was time for the barley mixed with rice, the customary last course, to be served, and the sake was removed.

"How can I see him?" thought Musashi. It became increasingly clear that he might be forced to employ some underhanded scheme. Should he goad one of his hosts into losing his temper? Difficult, when he was not angry himself, so he purposefully disagreed several times with what was being said and spoke in a rude and brash manner. Shōda and Debuchi chose to laugh at this. None of these four was about to be provoked into doing anything rash.

Desperation set in. Musashi could not bear the idea of leaving without accomplishing his objective. For his crown, he wanted a brilliant star of victory, and for the record, he wanted it known that Musashi had been here, had gone, had left his mark on the House of Yagyū. With his own sword, he wanted to bring Sekishūsai, this great patriarch of the martial arts, this "ancient dragon" as he was called, to his knees.

Had they seen through him completely? He was considering this possibility when matters took an unexpected turn.

"Did you hear that?" asked Kimura.

Murata went out on the veranda, then, reentering the room, said, "Tarō's barking—not his usual bark, though. I think something must be wrong."

Tarō was the dog Jōtarō had had a run-in with. There was no denying that the barking, which seemed to come from the second encirclement of the castle, was frightening.

It sounded too loud and terrible to be coming from a single dog.

Debuchi said, "I think I'd better have a look. Forgive me, Musashi, for spoiling the party, but it may be important. Please go on without me."

Shortly after he left, Murata and Kimura excused themselves, politely begging Musashi's forgiveness.

The barking grew more urgent; the dog was apparently trying to give warning of some danger. When one of the castle's dogs acted this way, it was almost a sure sign something untoward was going on. The peace the country was enjoying was not so secure that a daimyō could afford to relax his vigilance against neighboring fiefs. There were still unscrupulous warriors who might stoop to anything to satisfy their own ambition, and spies roamed the land searching out complacent and vulnerable targets.

Kizaemon seemed extremely upset. He kept staring at the ominous light of the little lamp, as if counting the echoes of the unearthly noise.

Eventually there was one long, mournful wail. Kizaemon grunted and looked at Musashi.

"He's dead," said Musashi.

"Yes, he's been killed." No longer able to contain himself, Kizaemon stood up. "I can't understand it."

He started to leave, but Musashi stopped him, saying, "Wait. Is Jōtarō, the boy who came with me, still in the waiting room?"

They directed their inquiry to a young samurai in front of the Shin'indō, who after searching reported the boy was nowhere to be found.

A look of concern came over Musashi's face. Turning to Kizaemon, he said, "I think I know what happened. Would you mind my going with you?"

"Not at all."

About three hundred yards from the dōjō, a crowd had gathered, and several torches had been lit. Besides Murata, Debuchi and Kimura, there were a number of foot soldiers and guards, forming a black circle, all talking and shouting at once.

From the outer rim of the circle, Musashi peered into

the open space in the middle. His heart sank. There, just as he had feared, was Jōtarō, covered with blood and looking like the devil's own child—wooden sword in hand, his teeth tightly clenched, his shoulders rising and falling with his heavy breathing.

By his side lay Tarō, teeth bared, legs outstretched. The dog's sightless eyes reflected the light of the torches; blood trickled from his mouth.

"It's his lordship's dog," someone said mournfully.

A samurai went toward Jōtarō and shouted, "You little bastard! What have you done? Are you the one who killed this dog?" The man brought his hand down in a furious slap, which Jōtarō just managed to dodge.

Squaring his shoulders, he shouted defiantly, "Yes, I did it!"

"You admit it?"

"I had a reason!"

"Ha!"

"I was taking revenge."

"What?" There was general astonishment at Jōtarō's answer; the whole crowd was angry. Tarō was the favorite pet of Lord Munenori of Tajima. Not only that; he was the pedigreed offspring of Raiko, a bitch belonging to and much loved by Lord Yorinori of Kishū. Lord Yorinori had personally given the pup to Munenori, who had himself reared it. The slaying of the animal would consequently be investigated thoroughly, and the fate of the two samurai who had been paid to take good care of the dog was now in jeopardy.

The man now facing Jōtarō was one of these two.

"Shut up!" he shouted, aiming his fist at Jōtarō's head. This time Jōtarō did not duck in time. The blow landed in the vicinity of his ear.

Jōtarō raised his hand to feel his wound. "What are you doing?" he screamed.

"You killed the master's dog. You don't mind if I beat you to death the same way, do you? Because that's exactly what I'm going to do."

"All I did was get even with him. Why punish me for that? A grown man should know that's not right!"

In Jōtarō's view, he had only protected his honor, and

risked his life in doing so, for a visible wound was a great disgrace to a samurai. To defend his pride, there was no alternative to killing the dog; indeed, in all likelihood he had expected to be praised for his valiant conduct. He stood his ground, determined not to flinch.

"Shut your impudent mouth!" screamed the keeper. "I don't care if you are only a child. You're old enough to know the difference between a dog and a human being. The very idea—taking revenge on a dumb animal!"

He grabbed Jōtarō's collar, looked to the crowd for approval, and declared it his duty to punish the dog's murderer. The crowd silently nodded in agreement. The four men who had so recently been entertaining Musashi looked distressed but said nothing.

"Bark, boy! Bark like a dog!" the keeper shouted. He swung Jōtarō around and around by his collar and with a black look in his eye threw him to the ground. Seizing an oak staff, he raised it above his head, ready to strike.

"You killed the dog, you little hoodlum. Now it's your turn! Stand up so I can kill you! Bark! Bite me!"

Teeth tightly clenched, Jōtarō propped himself up on one arm and struggled to his feet, wooden sword in hand. His features had not lost their spritelike quality, but the expression on his face was anything but childlike, and the howl that issued from his throat was eerily savage.

When an adult gets angry, he often regrets it later, but when a child's wrath is aroused, not even the mother who brought him into the world can placate him.

"Kill me!" he screamed. "Go on, kill me!"

"Die, then!" raged the keeper. He struck.

The blow would have killed the boy if it had connected, but it didn't. A sharp crack reverberated in the ears of the bystanders, and Jōtarō's wooden sword went flying through the air. Without thinking about it, he had parried the keeper's blow.

Weaponless, he closed his eyes and charged blindly at the enemy's midriff, latching on to the man's obi with his teeth. Holding on for dear life, he tore with his nails at the keeper's groin, while the keeper made futile swings with his staff.

Musashi had remained silent, arms folded and face expressionless, but then another oak staff appeared. A second man had dashed into the ring and was on the verge of attacking Jōtarō from behind. Musashi moved into action. His arms came down and in no time he forced his way through the solid wall of men into the arena.

"Coward!" he shouted at the second man.

An oak stick and two legs described an arc in the air, coming to rest in a clump about four yards away.

Musashi shouted, "And now for you, you little devil!" Gripping Jōtarō's obi with both hands, he lifted the boy above his head and held him there. Turning to the keeper, who was taking a fresh grip on his staff, he said, "I've been watching this from the start, and I think you're going about it the wrong way. This boy is my servant, and if you're going to question him, you ought to question me too."

In fiery tones, the keeper answered, "All right, we'll do that. We'll question the two of you!"

"Good! We'll take you on together. Now, here's the boy!"

He threw Jōtarō straight at the man. The crowd let out an appalled gasp and fell back. Was the man mad? Who ever heard of using one human being as a weapon against another human?

The keeper stared in disbelief as Jōtarō sailed through the air and rammed into his chest. The man fell straight back, as though a prop holding him up had suddenly been removed. It was difficult to tell whether he had struck his head against a rock, or whether his ribs had been broken. Hitting the ground with a howl, he began vomiting blood. Jōtarō bounced off the man's chest, did a somersault in the air, and rolled like a ball to a point twenty or thirty feet away.

"Did you see that?" a man shouted.

"Who is this crazy rōnin?"

The fracas no longer involved only the dog's keeper; the other samurai began abusing Musashi. Most of them were unaware that Musashi was an invited guest, and several suggested killing him then and there.

"Now," said Musashi, "everybody listen!"

They watched him closely as he took Jōtarō's wooden sword in his hand and faced them, a terrifying scowl on his face.

"The child's crime is his master's crime. We are both prepared to pay for it. But first let me tell you this: we have no intention of letting ourselves be killed like dogs. We are prepared to take you on."

Instead of acknowledging the crime and taking his punishment, he was challenging them! If at this point Musashi had apologized for Jōtarō and spoken in his defense, if he had made even the slightest effort to soothe the ruffled feelings of the Yagyū samurai, the whole incident might have passed by quietly. But Musashi's attitude precluded this. He seemed set on creating a still greater disturbance.

Shōda, Kimura, Debuchi and Murata all frowned, wondering anew what sort of freak they had invited to the castle. Deploring his lack of sense, they gradually edged around the crowd while keeping a watchful eye on him.

The crowd had been seething to begin with, and Musashi's challenge exacerbated their anger.

"Listen to him! He's an outlaw!"

"He's a spy! Tie him up!"

"No, cut him up!"

"Don't let him get away!"

For a moment it looked as though Musashi and Jōtarō, who was again by his side, would be swallowed up by a sea of swords, but then an authoritative voice cried, "Wait!"

It was Kizaemon, who together with Debuchi and Murata was trying to hold the crowd in check.

"This man seems to have planned all this," said Kizaemon. "If you let him entice you and you're wounded or killed, we shall have to answer to his lordship for it. The dog was important, but not as important as a human life. The four of us will assume all responsibility. Rest assured no harm will befall you because of anything we do. Now calm down and go home."

With some reluctance, the others dispersed, leaving the four men who had entertained Musashi in the Shin'indō. It was no longer a case of guest and hosts, but one of an outlaw facing his judges.

"Musashi," said Kizaemon, "I'm sorry to tell you your plot has failed. I suppose someone put you up to spying on Koyagyū Castle or just stirring up trouble, but I'm afraid it didn't work."

As they pressed in on Musashi, he was keenly aware that there was not one among them who was not an expert with the sword. He stood quite still, his hand on Jōtarō's shoulder. Surrounded, he couldn't have escaped even if he'd had wings.

"Musashi!" called Debuchi, working his sword a little way out of its scabbard. "You've failed. The proper thing for you to do is commit suicide. You may be a scoundrel, but you showed a great deal of bravery coming into this castle with only that child at your side. We had a friendly evening together; now we'll wait while you prepare yourself for harakiri. When you're ready, you can prove that you're a real samurai!"

That would have been the ideal solution; they had not consulted with Sekishūsai, and if Musashi died now, the whole affair could be buried along with his body.

Musashi had other ideas. "You think I should kill myself? That's absurd! I have no intention of dying, not for a long time." His shoulders shook with laughter.

"All right," said Debuchi. The tone was quiet, but the meaning was crystal clear. "We've tried to treat you decently, but you've done nothing but take advantage of us—"

Kimura broke in, saying, "There's no need for further talk!"

He went behind Musashi and pushed him. "Walk!" he commanded.

"Walk where?"

"To the cells."

Musashi nodded and started walking, but in the direction of his own choice, straight toward the castle keep.

"Where do you think you're going?" cried Kimura, jumping in front of Musashi and stretching his arms out to block him. "This isn't the way to the cells. They're in back of you. Turn around and get going!"

"No!" cried Musashi. He looked down at Jōtarō, who

41

was still clinging to his side, and told him to go sit under a pine tree in the garden in front of the keep. The ground around the pine trees was covered with carefully raked white sand.

Jōtarō darted from under Musashi's sleeve and hid behind the tree, wondering all the while what Musashi intended to do next. The memory of his teacher's bravery at Hannya Plain came back to him, and his body swelled with excitement.

Kizaemon and Debuchi took positions on either side of Musashi and tried to pull him back by the arms. Musashi didn't budge.

"Let's go!"

"I'm not going."

"You intend to resist?"

"I do!"

Kimura lost patience and started to draw his sword, but his seniors, Kizaemon and Debuchi, ordered him to hold off.

"What's the matter with you? Where do you think you're going?"

"I intend to see Yagyū Sekishūsai."

"You *what?*"

Never had it crossed their minds that this insane youth could have even thought of anything so preposterous.

"And what would you do if you met him?" asked Kizaemon.

"I'm a young man, I'm studying the martial arts, and it is one of my goals in life to receive a lesson from the master of the Yagyū Style."

"If that's what you wanted, why didn't you just ask?"

"Isn't it true that Sekishūsai never sees anyone and never gives lessons to student warriors?"

"Yes."

"Then what else can I do but challenge him? I realize, of course, that even if I do, he'll probably refuse to come out of retirement, so I'm challenging this whole castle to a battle instead."

"A battle?" chorused the four.

His arms still held by Kizaemon and Debuchi, Musashi

looked up at the sky. There was a flapping sound, as an eagle flew toward them from the blackness enveloping Mount Kasagi. Like a giant shroud, its silhouette hid the stars from view before it glided noisily down to the roof of the rice storehouse.

To the four retainers, the word "battle" sounded so melodramatic as to be laughable, but to Musashi it barely sufficed to express his concept of what was to come. He was not talking about a fencing match to be decided by technical skill only. He meant total war, where the combatants concentrate every ounce of their spirit and ability—and their fates are decided. A battle between two armies might be different in form, but in essence it was the same. It was simple: a battle between one man and one castle. His willpower was manifest in the firmness with which his heels were now implanted in the ground. It was this iron determination that made the word "battle" come naturally to his lips.

The four men scrutinized his face, wondering again if he had an iota of sanity left.

Kimura took up the challenge. Kicking his straw sandals into the air and tucking up his *hakama*, he said, "Fine! Nothing I like better than a battle! I can't offer you rolling drums or clanging gongs, but I can offer you a fight. Shōda, Debuchi push him over here." Kimura had been the first to suggest that they should punish Musashi, but he had held himself back, trying to be patient. Now he had had his fill.

"Go ahead!" he urged. "Leave him to me!"

At exactly the same time, Kizaemon and Debuchi shoved Musashi forward. He stumbled four or five paces toward Kimura. Kimura stepped back a pace, lifted his elbow above his face, and sucking in his breath, swiftly brought his sword down toward Musashi's stumbling form. There was a curious gritty sound as the sword flashed through the air.

At the same time a shout was heard—not from Musashi but from Jōtarō, who had jumped out from his position behind the pine tree. The handful of sand he had thrown was the source of the strange noise.

Realizing that Kimura would be gauging the distance so

as to strike effectively, Musashi had deliberately added speed to his stumbling steps and at the time of the strike was much closer to Kimura than the latter had anticipated. His sword touched nothing but air, and sand.

Both men quickly jumped back, separating themselves by three or four paces. There they stood, staring menacingly at one another in the tension-filled stillness.

"This is going to be something to watch," said Kizaemon softly.

Debuchi and Murata, though not within the sphere of battle, both took up new positions and assumed defensive stances. From what they had seen so far, they had no illusions about Musashi's competence as a fighter. His evasion and recovery had already convinced them he was a match for Kimura.

Kimura's sword was positioned slightly lower than his chest. He stood motionless. Musashi, equally still, had his hand on the hilt of his sword, right shoulder forward and elbow high. His eyes were two white, polished stones in his shadowy face.

For a time, it was a battle of nerves, but before either man moved, the darkness around Kimura seemed to waver, to change indefinably. Soon it was obvious that he was breathing faster and with greater agitation than Musashi.

A low grunt, barely audible, issues from Debuchi. He knew now that what had started as a comparatively trivial matter was about to turn into a catastrophe. Kizaemon and Murata, he felt sure, understood this as well as he. It was not going to be easy to put an end to this.

The outcome of the fight between Musashi and Kimura was as good as decided, unless extraordinary steps were taken. Reluctant as the three other men were to do anything that suggested cowardice, they found themselves forced to act to prevent disaster. The best solution would be to rid themselves of this strange, unbalanced intruder as expeditiously as possible, without themselves suffering needless wounds. No exchange of words was needed. They communicated perfectly with their eyes.

Acting in unison, the three moved in on Musashi. At the same instant, Musashi's sword, with the twang of a bowstring, pierced the air, and a thunderous shout filled the empty space. The battle cry came not from his mouth alone but from his whole body, the sudden peal of a temple bell resounding in all directions. From his opponents, arrayed to both sides of him, to front and back, came a hissing gurgle.

Musashi felt vibrantly alive. His blood seemed about to burst from every pore. But his head was as cool as ice. Was this the flaming lotus of which the Buddhist spoke? The ultimate heat made one with the ultimate cold, the synthesis of flame and water?

No more sand sailed through the air. Jōtarō had disappeared. Gusts of wind whistled down from the peak of Mount Kasagi; tightly held swords glinted luminescently.

One against four, yet Musashi felt himself at no great disadvantage. He was conscious of a swelling in his veins. At times like this, the idea of dying is said to assert itself in the mind, but Musashi had no thought of death. At the same time, he felt no certainty of his ability to win.

The wind seemed to blow through his head, cooling his brain, clearing his vision, though his body was growing sticky, and beads of oily sweat glistened on his forehead.

There was a faint rustle. Like a beetle's antennae, Musashi's sword told him that the man on his left had moved his foot an inch or two. He made the necessary adjustment in the position of his weapon, and the enemy, also perceptive, made no further move to attack. The five formed a seemingly static tableau.

Musashi was aware that the longer this continued, the less advantageous it was for him. He would have liked somehow to have his opponents not around him but stretched out in a straight line—to take them on one by one—but he was not dealing with amateurs. The fact was that until one of them shifted of his own accord, Musashi could make no move. All he could do was wait and hope that eventually one would make a momentary misstep and give him an opening.

His adversaries took little comfort from their superiority in numbers. They knew that at the slightest sign of a relaxed attitude on the part of any one of them, Musashi would strike. Here, they understood, was the type of man that one did not ordinarily encounter in this world.

Even Kizaemon could make no move. "What a strange man!" he thought to himself.

Swords, men, earth, sky—everything seemed to have frozen solid. But then into this stillness came a totally unexpected sound, the sound of a flute, wafted by the wind.

As the melody stole into Musashi's ears, he forgot himself, forgot the enemy, forgot about life and death. Deep in the recesses of his mind, he knew this sound, for it was the one that had enticed him out of hiding on Mount Takateru—the sound that had delivered him into the hands of Takuan. It was Otsū's flute, and it was Otsū playing it.

He went limp inside. Externally, the change was barely perceptible, but that was enough. With a battle cry rising from his loins, Kimura lunged forward, his sword arm seeming to stretch out six or seven feet.

Musashi's muscles tensed, and the blood seemed to rush through him toward a state of hemorrhage. He was sure he had been cut. His left sleeve was rent from shoulder to wrist, and the sudden exposure of his arm made him think the flesh had been cut open.

For once, his self-possession left him and he screamed out the name of the god of war. He leaped, turned suddenly, and saw Kimura stumble toward the place where he himself had been standing.

"Musashi!" shouted Debuchi Magobei.

"You talk better than you fight!" taunted Murata, as he and Kizaemon scrambled to head Musashi off.

But Musashi gave the earth a powerful kick and sprang high enough to brush against the lower branches of the pine trees. Then he leaped again and again, and off he flew into the darkness, never looking back.

"Coward!"

"Musashi!"

"Fight like a man!"

When Musashi reached the edge of the moat around the inner castle, there was a cracking of twigs, and then silence. The only sound was the sweet melody of the flute in the distance.

4

The Nightingales

There was no way of knowing how much stagnant rainwater might be at the bottom of the thirty-foot moat. After diving into the hedge near the top and rapidly sliding halfway down, Musashi stopped and threw a rock. Hearing no splash, he leapt to the bottom, where he lay down on his back in the grass, not making a sound.

After a time his ribs stopped heaving and his pulse returned to normal. As the sweat cooled, he began to breathe regularly again.

"Otsū couldn't be here at Koyagyū!" he told himself. "My ears must be playing tricks on me. . . . Still, it's not impossible. It could have been her."

As he debated with himself, he envisioned Otsū's eyes among the stars above him, and soon he was carried away by memories: Otsū at the pass on the Mimasaka-Harima border, where she had said she could not live without him, there was no other man in the world for her. Then at Hanada Bridge in Himeji, when she had told him how she had waited for him for nearly a thousand days and would have waited ten years, or twenty—until she was old and gray. Her begging him to take her with him, her assertion that she could bear any hardship.

His headlong flight at Himeji had been a betrayal. How she must have hated him after that! How she must have bit her lips and cursed the unpredictability of men.

"Forgive me!" The words he had carved on the railing

47

of the bridge slipped from his lips. Tears seeped from the corners of his eyes.

He was startled by a cry from the top of the moat. It sounded like, "He's not here." Three or four pine torches flickered among the trees, then disappeared. They hadn't spotted him.

He was annoyed to find himself weeping. "What do I need with a woman?" he said scornfully, wiping his eyes with his hands. He jumped to his feet and looked up at the black outline of Koyagyū Castle.

"They called me a coward, said I couldn't fight like a man! Well, I haven't surrendered yet, not by a long shot. I didn't run away. I just made a tactical retreat."

Almost an hour had passed. He began walking slowly along the bottom of the moat. "No point in fighting those four anyway. That wasn't my aim to begin with. When I find Sekishūsai himself, then the real battle will start."

He stopped and began gathering fallen branches, which he broke into short sticks over his knee. Shoving them one by one into cracks in the stone wall, he used them for footholds and climbed out of the moat.

He could no longer hear the flute. For a second he had the vague feeling Jōtarō was calling, but when he stopped and listened closely, he could hear nothing. He wasn't really worried about the boy. He could take care of himself; he was probably miles away by now. The absence of torches indicated the search had been called off, at least for the night.

The thought of finding and defeating Sekishūsai was once again his controlling passion, the immediate shape taken by his overpowering desire for recognition and honor.

He had heard from the innkeeper that Sekishūsai's retreat was in neither of the castle encirclements but in a secluded spot in the outer grounds. He walked through the woods and valleys, at times suspecting he had strayed outside the castle grounds. Then a bit of moat, a stone wall or a rice granary would reassure him he was still inside.

All night he searched, compelled by a diabolic urge. He intended, once he had found the mountain house, to burst in with his challenge on his lips. But as the hours wore on, he

would have welcomed the sight of even a ghost appearing in
Sekishūsai's form.

It was getting on toward daybreak when he found himself at the back gate of the castle. Beyond it rose a precipice
and above that Mount Kasagi. On the verge of screaming
with frustration, he retraced his steps southward. Finally, at
the bottom of a slope inclined toward the southeast quarter
of the castle, well-shaped trees and well-trimmed grass told
him he'd found her hideaway. His conjecture was soon
confirmed by a gate, with a thatched roof, in the style
favored by the great tea master Sen no Rikyū. Inside he
could make out a bamboo grove shrouded in morning mist.

Peeking through a crack in the gate, he saw that the
path meandered through the grove and up the hill, as in Zen
Buddhist mountain retreats. For a moment he was tempted
to leap over the fence, but he checked himself; something
about the surroundings held him back. Was it the loving care
that had been lavished on the area, or the sight of white
petals on the ground? Whatever it was, the sensitivity of the
occupant came through, and Musashi's agitation subsided.
He suddenly thought of his appearance. He must look like a
tramp, with his disheveled hair and his kimono in disarray.

"No need to rush," he said to himself, conscious now
of his exhaustion. He had to pull himself together before
presenting himself to the master inside.

"Sooner or later," he thought, "someone's bound to
come to the gate. That'll be time enough. If he still refuses
to see me as a wandering student, then I'll use a different
approach." He sat down under the eaves of the gate, leaned
his back against the post and dropped off to sleep.

The stars were fading and white daisies swaying in the
breeze when a large drop of dew fell coldly on his neck and
woke him up. Daylight had come, and as he stirred from his
nap, his head was cleansed by the morning breeze and the
singing of the nightingales. No vestige of weariness remained: he felt reborn.

Rubbing his eyes and looking up, he saw the bright red
sun climbing over the mountains. He jumped up. The sun's
heat had already rekindled his ardor, and the strength stored

up in his limbs demanded action. Stretching, he said softly, "Today's the day."

He was hungry, and for some reason this made him think about Jōtarō. Perhaps he had treated the boy too roughly the night before, but it had been a calculated move, a part of the lad's training. Musashi again assured himself that Jōtarō, wherever he was, wasn't in any real danger.

He listened to the sound of the brook, which ran down the mountainside, detoured inside the fence, circled the bamboo grove and then emerged from under the fence on its journey toward the lower castle grounds. Musashi washed his face and drank his fill, in lieu of breakfast. The water was good, so good that Musashi imagined it might well be the main reason Sekishūsai had chosen this location for his retirement from the world. Still, knowing nothing of the art of the tea ceremony, he had no inkling that water of such purity was in fact the answer to a tea master's prayer.

He rinsed his hand towel in the stream, and having wiped the back of his neck thoroughly, cleaned the grime from his nails. He then tidied his hair with the stiletto attached to his sword. Since Sekishūsai was not only the master of the Yagyū Style but one of the greatest men in the land, Musashi intended to look his best; he himself was nothing but a nameless warrior, as different from Sekishūsai as the tiniest star is from the moon.

Patting his hair and straightening his collar, he felt inwardly composed. His mind was clear; he was resolved to knock at the gate like any legitimate caller.

The house was quite a way up the hill, and it wasn't likely an ordinary knock would be heard. Looking around for a clapper of some kind, he saw a pair of plaques, one on either side of the gate. They were beautifully inscribed, and the carved writing had been filled in with a bluish clay which gave off a bronzelike patina. On the right were the words:

> Be not suspicious, ye scribes,
> Of one who likes his castle closed.

And on the left:

> No swordsman will you find here,
> Only the young nightingales in the fields.

The Nightingales

The poem was addressed to the "scribes," referring to the officials of the castle, but its meaning was deeper. The old man had not shut his gate merely to wandering students but to all the affairs of this world, to its honors as well as its tribulations. He had put behind him worldly desire, both his own and that of others.

"I'm still young," thought Musashi. "Too young! This man is completely beyond my reach."

The desire to knock on the gate evaporated. Indeed, the idea of barging in on the ancient recluse now seemed barbarian, and he felt totally ashamed of himself.

Only flowers and birds, the wind and the moon, should enter this gate. Sekishūsai was no longer the greatest swordsman in the land, no longer the lord of a fief, but a man who had returned to nature, renouncing the vanity of human life. To upset his household would be a sacrilege. And what honor, what distinction, could possibly be derived from defeating a man to whom honor and distinction had become meaningless?

"It's a good thing I read this," Musashi said to himself. "If I hadn't, I'd have made a perfect fool of myself!"

With the sun now fairly high in the sky, the nightingales' singing had subsided. From a distance up the hill came the sound of rapid footsteps. Apparently frightened by the clatter, a flock of little birds arced up into the sky. Musashi peeped through the gate to see who was coming.

It was Otsū.

So it had been her flute he had heard! Should he wait and meet her? Go away? "I want to talk with her," he thought. "I must!"

Indecision seized him. His heart palpitated and his self-confidence fled.

Otsū ran down the path to a point a few feet from where he stood. Then she stopped and turned back, uttering a little cry of surprise.

"I thought he was right behind me," she murmured, looking all around. Then she ran back up the hill, calling, "Jōtarō! Where are you?"

Hearing her voice, Musashi flushed with embarrassment and began to sweat. His lack of confidence disgusted him.

51

He couldn't move from his hiding place in the shadow of the trees.

After a short interval, Otsū called again, and this time there was an answer. "I'm here. Where are you?" shouted Jōtarō from the upper part of the grove.

"Over here!" she replied. "I told you not to wander off like that."

Jōtarō came running toward her. "Oh, is this where you are?" he exclaimed.

"Didn't I tell you to follow me?"

"Well, I did, but then I saw a pheasant, so I chased it."

"Of all things, chasing after a pheasant! Did you forget you have to go look for somebody important this morning?"

"Oh, I'm not worried about him. He's not the kind to get hurt."

"Well, that's not the way it was last night when you came running to my room. You were ready to burst into tears."

"I was not! It just happened so fast, I didn't know what to do."

"I didn't either, especially after you told me your teacher's name."

"But how do you know Musashi?"

"We come from the same village."

"Is that all?"

"Of course that's all."

"That's funny. I don't see why you should start crying just because somebody from the same village turned up here."

"Was I crying that much?"

"How can you remember everything I did, when you can't remember what you did yourself? Anyway, I guess I was pretty scared. If it'd just been a matter of four ordinary men against my teacher, I wouldn't have worried, but they say all of them are experts. When I heard the flute I remembered you were here in the castle, so I thought maybe if I could apologize to his lordship—"

"If you heard me playing, Musashi must have heard it too. He may even have known it was me." Her voice softened. "I was thinking of him as I played.

"I don't see what difference that makes. Anyway, I could tell from the sound of the flute where you were."

"And that was quite a performance—storming into the house and screaming about a 'battle' going on somewhere. His lordship was pretty shocked."

"But he's a nice man. When I told him I'd killed Tarō, he didn't get mad like all the others."

Suddenly realizing she was wasting time, Otsū hurried toward the gate. "We can talk later," she said. "Right now there are more important things to do. We've got to find Musashi. Sekishūsai even broke his own rule by saying he'd like to meet the man who'd done what you said."

Otsū looked as cheerful as a flower. In the bright sun of early summer, her cheeks shone like ripening fruit. She sniffed at the young leaves and felt their freshness fill her lungs.

Musashi, hidden in the trees, watched her intently, marveling at how healthy she looked. The Otsū he saw now was very different from the girl who had sat dejectedly on the porch of the Shippōji, looking out at the world with vacant eyes. The difference was that then Otsū had had no one to love. Or at least, such love as she had felt had been vague and difficult to pin down. She had been a sentimental child, self-conscious about being an orphan, and somewhat resentful of the fact.

Coming to know Musashi, having him to look up to, had given birth to the love that now dwelt inside her and gave meaning to her life. During the long year she'd spent wandering around in search of him, body and mind had developed the courage to face anything fate might fling at her.

Quickly perceiving her new vitality and how beautiful it made her, Musashi yearned to take her somewhere where they could be alone and tell her everything—how he longed for her, how he needed her physically. He wanted to reveal that hidden in his heart of steel was a weakness; he wanted to retract the words he had carved on Hanada Bridge. If no one were to know, he could show her how tender he could be. He would tell her he felt the same love for her that she felt for him. He could hug her, rub his cheek against hers, cry the tears he wanted to cry. He was strong enough now to admit to himself that these feelings were real.

Things Otsū had said to him in the past came back to him and he saw how cruel and ugly it was for him to reject the simple, straightforward love she had offered.

He was miserable, yet there was something in him that couldn't surrender to these feelings, something that told him it was wrong. He was two different men, one longing to call out to Otsū, the other telling him he was a fool. He couldn't be sure which was his real self. Staring from behind the tree, lost in indecision, he seemed to see two paths ahead, one of light and another of darkness.

Otsū, unaware of his presence, walked a few paces out from the gate. Looking back, she saw Jōtarō stooping to pick something up.

"Jōtarō, what on earth are you doing? Hurry up!"

"Wait!" he cried excitedly. "Look at this!"

"It's nothing but a dirty old rag! What do you want that for?"

"It belongs to Musashi."

"To Musashi?" she exclaimed, running back to him.

"Yes, it's his," replied Jōtarō as he held the hand towel up by the corners for her to see. "I remember it. It came from the widow's house where we stayed in Nara. See, here: there's a maple leaf design dyed on it and a character reading 'Lin.' That's the name of the owner of the dumpling restaurant there."

"Do you think Musashi was right here?" Otsū cried, looking frantically around.

Jōtarō drew himself up almost to the girl's height and at the top of his voice yelled, *"Sensei!"*

In the grove there was a rustling sound. With a gasp, Otsū spun around and darted toward the trees, the boy chasing after her.

"Where are you going?" he called.

"Musashi just ran away!"

"Which way?"

"That way."

"I don't see him."

"Over there in the trees!"

She had caught a glimpse of Musashi's figure, but the momentary joy she experienced was immediately replaced by apprehension, for he was rapidly increasing the distance between them. She ran after him with all the strength her legs possessed. Jōtarō ran along with her, not really believing she'd seen Musashi.

"You're wrong!" he shouted. "It must be somebody else. Why would Musashi run away?"

"Just look!"

"Where?"

"There!" She took a deep breath, and straining her voice to the utmost, screamed, "Mu—sa—shi!" But no more had the frantic cry come from her lips than she stumbled and fell. As Jōtarō helped her up, she cried, "Why don't you call him too? Call him! Call him!"

Instead of doing as she said, he froze in shock and stared at her face. He had seen that face before, with its bloodshot eyes, its needlelike eyebrows, its waxen nose and jaw. It was the face of the mask! The madwoman's mask the widow in Nara had given him. Otsū's face lacked the curiously curved mouth, but otherwise the likeness was the same. He quickly withdrew his hands and recoiled in fright.

Otsū continued her scolding. "We can't give up! He'll never come back if we let him get away now! Call him! Get him to come back!"

Something inside Jōtarō resisted, but the look on Otsū's face told him it was useless to try to reason with her. They started running again, and he, too, began to shout for all he was worth.

Beyond the woods was a low hill, along the bottom of which ran the back road from Tsukigase to Iga. "It is Musashi!" cried Jōtarō. Having reached the road, the boy could see his master clearly, but Musashi was too far ahead of them to hear their shouts.

Otsū and Jōtarō ran as far as their legs would carry them, shouting themselves hoarse. Their screams echoed through the fields. At the edge of the valley they lost sight of Musashi, who ran straight into the heavily wooded foothills. They stopped and stood there, forlorn as deserted children. White clouds stretched out emptily above them, while the murmuring of a stream accented their loneliness.

"He's crazy! He's out of his mind! How could he leave me like this?" Jōtarō cried, stamping the ground.

Otsū leaned against a large chestnut tree and let the tears gush forth. Even her great love for Musashi—a love for which she would have sacrificed anything—was incapable of holding him. She was puzzled, bereft and angry. She knew what his purpose in life was, and why he was avoiding her. She had known since that day at Hanada Bridge. Still, she could not comprehend why he considered her a barrier between him and his goal. Why should his determination be weakened by her presence?

Or was that just an excuse? Was the real reason that he didn't like her enough? It would make more sense perhaps. And yet . . . and yet . . . Otsū had come to understand Musashi when she had seen him tied up in the tree at the Shippōji. She could not believe him to be the sort who would lie to a woman. If he didn't care about her, he would say so, but in fact he had told her at Hanada Bridge that he did like her very much. She recalled his words with sadness.

Being an orphan, she was prevented by a certain coldness from trusting many people, but once she trusted someone, she trusted him completely. At this moment, she felt there was no one but Musashi worth living for or relying on. Matahachi's betrayal had taught her, the hard way, how careful a girl must be in judging men. But Musashi was not Matahachi. She had not only decided that she would live for him, whatever happened, but had already made up her mind never to regret doing so.

But why couldn't he have said just one word? It was more than she could bear. The leaves of the chestnut tree were shaking, as though the tree itself understood and sympathized.

The angrier she became, the more she was possessed by her love for him. Whether it was fate or not, she couldn't say, but her grief-torn spirit told her there was no real life for her apart from Musashi.

Jōtarō glanced down the road and muttered, "Here comes a priest." Otsū paid no attention to him.

The Nightingales

With the approach of noon, the sky above had turned a deep, transparent blue. The monk descending the slope in the distance had the look of having stepped down from the clouds, of having no connection whatever with this earth. As he neared the chestnut tree, he looked toward it and saw Otsū.

"What's all this?" he exclaimed, and at the sound of his voice, Otsū looked up.

Her swollen eyes wide with astonishment, she cried, "Takuan!" In her present condition, she saw Takuan Sōhō as a savior. She wondered if she was dreaming.

Although the sight of Takuan was a shock to Otsū, the discovery of Otsū was for Takuan no more than confirmation of something he had suspected. As it happened, his arrival was neither accident nor miracle.

Takuan had been on friendly terms with the Yagyū family for a long time, his acquaintance with them going back to the days when, as a young monk at the Sangen'in in the Daitokuji, his duties had included cleaning the kitchen and making bean paste.

In those days, the Sangen'in, then known as the "North Sector" of the Daitokuji, had been famous as a gathering place for "unusual" samurai, which is to say, samurai who were given to thinking philosophically about the meaning of life and death; men who felt the need to study affairs of the spirit, as well as the technical skills of the martial arts. Samurai flocked there in greater numbers than did Zen monks, and one result of this was that the temple became known as a breeding ground for revolt.

Among the samurai who came frequently were Suzuki Ihaku, the brother of Lord Kōizumi of Ise; Yagyū Gorōzaemon, the heir of the House of Yagyū; and Gorōzaemon's brother Munenori. Munenori had quickly taken a liking to Takuan, and the two had remained friends ever since. In the course of a number of visits to Koyagyū Castle, Takuan had met Sekishūsai and had acquired great respect for the older man. Sekishūsai had also taken a liking to the young monk, who struck him as having a great deal of promise.

Recently Takuan had stopped for a time at the Nansōji in Izumi Province and from there had sent a letter to inquire

57

after the health of Sekishūsai and Munenori. He had received a long reply from Sekishūsai, saying in part:

> I have been very fortunate lately. Munenori has taken a post with the Tokugawas, in Edo, and my grandson, who left the service of Lord Katō of Higo and went out to study on his own, is making progress. I myself have in my service a beautiful young girl who not only plays the flute well but talks with me, and together we have tea, arrange flowers and compose poems. She is the delight of my old age, a flower blooming in what might otherwise be a cold, withered old hut. Since she says that she comes from Mimasaka, which is near your birthplace, and was brought up in a temple called the Shippōji, I imagine that you and she have much in common. It is unusually pleasant to drink one's evening sake to the accompaniment of a flute well played, and since you are so close to here, I hope you will come and enjoy this treat with me.

It would have been difficult for Takuan to refuse the invitation under any circumstances, but the certainty that the girl described in the letter was Otsū made him all the more eager to accept.

As the three of them walked toward Sekishūsai's house, Takuan asked Otsū many questions, which she answered without reservation. She told him what she'd been doing since last seeing him in Himeji, what had happened that morning, and how she felt about Musashi.

Nodding patiently, he heard out her tearful story. When she was finished, he said, "I guess women are able to choose ways of life that would not be possible for men. You want me, I take it, to advise you on the path that you should follow in the future."

"Oh, no."

"Well . . ."

"I've already decided what I'm going to do."

Takuan scrutinized her closely. She had stopped walking and was looking at the ground. She seemed to be in the depths of despair, yet there was a certain strength in the tone of her voice that forced Takuan to a reappraisal.

"If I'd had any doubts, if I'd thought I'd give up," she said, "I'd never have left the Shippōji. I'm still determined to meet Musashi. The only question in my mind is whether this will cause him trouble, whether my continuing to live will bring him unhappiness. If it does, I'll have to do something about it!"

"Just what does that mean?"

"I can't tell you."

"Be careful, Otsū!"

"Of what?"

"Under this bright, cheerful sun, the god of death is tugging at you."

"I . . . I don't know what you mean."

"I don't suppose you would, but that's because the god of death is lending you strength. You'd be a fool to die, Otsū, particularly over nothing more than a one-sided love affair." Takuan laughed.

Otsū was getting angry again. She might as well have been talking to thin air, she thought, for Takuan had never been in love. It was impossible for anyone who'd never been in love to understand how she felt. For her to try to explain her feelings to him was like him trying to explain Zen Buddhism to an imbecile. But just as there was truth in Zen, whether an imbecile could understand it or not, there were people who would die for love, whether Takuan could understand it or not. To a woman at least, love was a far more serious matter than the troublesome riddles of a Zen priest. When one was swayed by a love that meant life or death, what difference did it make what the clapping of one hand sounded like? Biting her lips, Otsū vowed to say no more.

Takuan became serious. "You should have been born a man, Otsū. A man with the kind of willpower you have would certainly accomplish something for the good of the country."

"Does that mean it's wrong for a woman like me to exist? Because it might bring harm to Musashi?"

"Don't twist what I said. I wasn't talking about that.

But no matter how much you love Musashi, he still runs away, doesn't he? And I daresay you never will catch him!''

"I'm not doing this because I enjoy it. I can't help it. I love him!''

"I don't see you for a while, and the next thing I know, you're carrying on like all the other women!''

"But can't you see? Oh, never mind, let's not talk about it anymore. A brilliant priest like you would never understand a woman's feelings!''

"I don't know how to answer that. It's true, though; women do puzzle me.''

Otsū turned away from him and said, "Let's go, Jō-tarō!''

As Takuan stood watching, the two of them started down a side road. With a sad flicker of his eyebrows, the monk came to the conclusion that there was nothing more for him to do. He called after her, "Aren't you going to say good-bye to Sekishūsai before setting out on your own?''

"I'll say good-bye to him in my heart. He knows I never meant to stay at his house this long anyway.''

"Won't you reconsider?''

"Reconsider what?''

"Well, it was nice living in the mountains of Mimasaka, but it's nice here too. It's peaceful and quiet, and life is simple. Instead of seeing you go out in the ordinary world, with all its misery and hardships, I'd like to see you live your life out in peace, among these mountains and streams, like those nightingales we hear singing.''

"Ha, ha! Thanks so much, Takuan!''

Takuan sighed, realizing he was helpless before this strong-willed young woman, so determined to go blindly on her chosen way. "You may laugh, Otsū, but the path you are embarking on is one of darkness.''

"Darkness?''

"You were brought up in a temple. You should know that the path of darkness and desire leads only to frustration and misery—frustration and misery beyond salvation.''

"There's never been a path of light for me, not since I was born.''

60

"But there is, there is!" Putting his last drop of energy into this plea, Takuan came up to the girl and took her hand. He wanted desperately for her to trust him.

"I'll talk to Sekishūsai about it," he offered. "About how you can live and be happy. You can find yourself a good husband here in Koyagyū, have children, and do the things that women do. You'd make this a better village. That would make you happier too."

"I understand you're trying to be helpful, but—"

"Do it! I beg you!"

Pulling her by the hand, he looked at Jōtarō and said, "You come too, boy!"

Jōtarō shook his head decisively. "Not me. I'm going to follow my master."

"Well, do as you like, but at least go back to the castle and say good-bye to Sekishūsai."

"Oh, I forgot!" gasped Jōtarō. "I left my mask there. I'll go get it." He streaked off, untroubled by paths of darkness and paths of light.

Otsū, however, stood still at the crossroads. Takuan relaxed, becoming again the old friend she had known before. He warned her of the dangers lurking in the life she was trying to lead and tried to convince her there were other ways to find happiness. Otsū remained unmoved.

Presently Jōtarō came running back with the mask over his face. Takuan froze when he saw it, instinctively feeling that this was the future face of Otsū, the one he would see after she had suffered on her long journey along the path of darkness.

"I'll go now," said Otsū, stepping away from him.

Jōtarō, clinging to her sleeve, said, "Yes, let's go! Now!"

Takuan lifted his eyes to the white clouds, lamenting his failure. "There's nothing more I can do," he said. "The Buddha himself despaired of saving women."

"Good-bye, Takuan," said Otsū. "I'm bowing here to Sekishūsai, but would you also tell him thank you and good-bye for me?"

"Ah, even I'm beginning to think priests are crazy.

61

Everywhere they go they meet no one but people rushing toward hell." Takuan raised his hands, let them drop and said very solemnly, "Otsū, if you begin to drown in the Six Evil Ways or the Three Crossings, call out my name. Think of me, and call my name! Until then, all I can say is, travel on as far as you can and try to be careful!"

5

Sasaki Kojirō

Just south of Kyoto, the Yodo River wound around a hill called Momoyama (the site of Fushimi Castle), then flowed on through the Yamashiro Plain toward the ramparts of Osaka Castle, some twenty miles farther to the southwest. Partly owing to this direct water link, each political ripple in the Kyoto area produced immediate repercussions in Osaka, while in Fushimi it seemed that every word spoken by an Osaka samurai, let alone an Osaka general, was reported as a portent of the future.

Around Momoyama, a great upheaval was in progress, for Tokugawa Ieyasu had decided to transform the way of life that had flourished under Hideyoshi. Osaka Castle, occupied by Hideyori and his mother, Yodogimi, still clung desperately to the vestiges of its faded authority, as the setting sun holds fast to its vanishing beauty, but real power resided at Fushimi, where Ieyasu had chosen to live during his extended trips to the Kansai region. The clash between old and new was visible everywhere. It could be discerned in the boats plying the river, in the deportment of the people on the highways, in popular songs, and in the faces of the displaced samurai searching for work.

The castle at Fushimi was under repair, and the rocks disgorged from the boats onto the riverbank formed a virtual mountain. Most of them were huge boulders, at least six feet square and three or four feet high. They fairly sizzled under a boiling sun. Though it was autumn by the calendar, the sweltering heat was reminiscent of the dog days immediately following the early summer rainy season.

Willow trees near the bridge shimmered with a whitish glint, and a large cicada zigzagged crazily from the river into a small house near the bank. The roofs of the village, deprived of the gentle colors their lanterns swathed them in at twilight, were a dry, dusty gray. In the heat of high noon, two laborers, mercifully freed for half an hour from their backbreaking work, lay sprawled on the broad surface of a boulder, chatting about what was on everybody's lips.

"You think there'll be another war?"

"I don't see why not. There doesn't seem to be anybody strong enough to keep things under control."

"I guess you're right. The Osaka generals seem to be signing up all the rōnin they can find."

"They would, I suppose. Maybe I shouldn't say this too loud, but I heard the Tokugawas are buying guns and ammunition from foreign ships."

"If they are, why is Ieyasu letting his granddaughter Senhime marry Hideyori?"

"How should I know? Whatever he's doing, you can bet he has his reasons. Ordinary people like us can't be expected to know what Ieyasu has in mind."

Flies buzzed about the two. A swarm covered two nearby oxen. Still hitched to empty timber carts, the beasts lazed in the sun, stolid, impassive and drooling at the mouth.

The real reason the castle was undergoing repairs was not known to the lowly laborer, who assumed that Ieyasu was to stay there. Actually, it was one phase of a huge building program, an important part of the Tokugawa scheme of government. Construction work on a large scale was also being carried out in Edo, Nagoya, Suruga, Hikone, Ōtsu and a dozen other castle towns. The purpose was to a large extent political, for one on Ieyasu's methods of maintaining control over the daimyō was to order them to undertake various engineering projects. Since none was powerful enough to refuse, this kept the friendly lords too busy to grow soft, while simultaneously forcing the daimyō who'd opposed Ieyasu at Sekigahara to part with large portions of their incomes. Still another aim of the government was to win the support of the common people, who profited both directly and indirectly from extensive public works.

At Fushimi alone, nearly a thousand laborers were engaged in extending the stone battlements, with the incidental result that the town around the castle experienced a sudden influx of peddlers, prostitutes and horseflies—all symbols of prosperity. The masses were delighted with the good times Ieyasu had brought, and merchants relished the thought that on top of all this there was a good chance of war—bringing even greater profits. Goods were moving briskly, and even now the bulk of them were military supplies. After fingering their collective abacus, the larger entrepreneurs had concluded that this was where the big money was.

City folk were fast forgetting the balmy days of Hideyoshi's regime and instead speculating on what might be gained in the days ahead. It made little difference to them who was in power; so long as they could satisfy their own petty wants, they saw no reason to complain. Nor did Ieyasu disappoint them in this respect, for he contrived to scatter money as he might pass out candy to children. Not his own money, to be sure, but that of his potential enemies.

In agriculture, too, he was instituting a new system of control. No longer were local magnates allowed to govern as they pleased or to conscript farmers at will for outside labor. From now on, the peasants were to be permitted to farm their lands—but to do very little else. They were to be kept ignorant of politics and taught to rely on the powers that be.

The virtuous ruler, to Ieyasu's way of thinking, was one who did not let the tillers of the soil starve but at the same time ensured that they did not rise above their station; this was the policy by which he intended to perpetuate Tokugawa rule. Neither the townspeople nor the farmers nor the daimyō realized that they were being carefully fitted into a feudal system that would eventually bind them hand and foot. No one was thinking of what things might be like in another hundred years. No one, that is, except Ieyasu.

Nor were the laborers at Fushimi Castle thinking of tomorrow. They had modest hopes of getting through the day, the quicker the better. Though they talked of war and when it might break out, grand plans to maintain peace and increase prosperity had nothing to do with them. Whatever happened they could not be much worse off than they were.

"Watermelon! Anybody want a watermelon?" called a farmer's daughter, who came around at this time every day. Almost as soon as she appeared, she managed to make a sale to some men matching coins in the shadow of a large rock. Jauntily, she went on from group to group, calling, "Won't you buy my melons?"

"You crazy? You think we've got money for watermelons?"

"Over here! I'll be glad to eat one—if it's free."

Disappointed because her initial luck had been deceptive, the girl approached a young worker sitting between two boulders, his back propped against one, his feet against the other, and his arms around his knees. "Watermelon?" she asked, not very hopefully.

He was thin, his eyes sunken, and his skin ruddily sunburned. A shroud of fatigue dimmed his obvious youth; still, his closer friends would have recognized him as Hon'iden Matahachi. Wearily he counted some grimy coins into the palm of his hand and gave them to the girl.

When he leaned back against the rock again, his head dropped morosely. The slight effort had exhausted him. Gagging, he leaned to one side and began to spit up on the grass. He lacked the little strength it would have taken to retrieve the watermelon, which had tumbled from his knees. He stared dully at it, his black eyes revealing no trace of strength or hope.

"The swine," he mumbled weakly. He meant the people he would like to strike back at: Okō, with her whitened face; Takezō, with his wooden sword. His first mistake had been to go to Sekigahara; his second to succumb to the lascivious widow. He had come to believe that but for these two events, he would be at home in Miyamoto now, the head of the Hon'iden family, a husband with a beautiful wife, and the envy of the village.

"I suppose Otsū must hate me now . . . though I wonder what she's doing." In his present circumstances, thinking occasionally of his former fiancée was his only comfort.

When Okō's true nature had finally sunk in, he had begun to long for Otsū again. He had thought of her more and more since the day he'd had the good sense to break loose from the Yomogi Teahouse.

On the night of his departure, he had discovered that the Miyamoto Musashi who was acquiring a reputation as a swordsman in the capital was his old friend Takezō. This severe shock was followed almost immediately by strong waves of jealousy.

With Otsū in mind, he had stopped drinking and attempted to slough off his laziness and his bad habits. But at first he was unable to find any suitable work. He cursed himself for having been out of the swim of things for five years, while an older woman supported him. For a time it appeared as though it was too late to change.

"*Not* too late," he'd assured himself. "I'm only twenty-two. I can do whatever I want, if I try!" While anyone might experience this sentiment, in Matahachi's case it meant shutting his eyes, leaping over an abyss of five years, and hiring himself out as a day laborer at Fushimi.

Here he had worked hard, slaving steadily day after day while the sun beat down on him from summer into fall. He was rather proud of himself for sticking to it.

"I'll show them all!" he was thinking now, despite his queasiness. "No reason I can't make a name for myself. I can do anything Takezō can do! I can do even more, and I will. Then I'll have my revenge, despite Okō. Ten years is all I need."

Ten years? He stopped to calculate how old Otsū would be by then. Thirty-one! Would she stay single, wait for him all that time? Not likely. Matahachi had no inkling of recent developments in Mimasaka, no way of knowing that his was but a pipe dream, but ten years—never! It would have to be no more than five or six. Within that time he would have to make a success of himself; that was all there was to it. Then he could go back to the village, apologize to Otsū and persuade her to marry him. "That's the only way!" he exclaimed. "Five years, six at most." He stared at the watermelon and a glimmer of light returned to his eyes.

Just then one of his fellow workers rose up beyond the

rock in front of him, and resting his elbows on the boulder's broad top, called, "Hey, Matahachi. What're you mumbling to yourself about? Say, your face is green. Watermelon rotten?"

Matahachi, though he forced a wan smile, was seized by another wave of dizziness. Saliva streamed from his mouth as he shook his head. "It's nothing, nothing at all," he managed to gasp. "Guess I got a little too much sun. Let me take it easy here for an hour or so."

The burly stone haulers gibed at his lack of strength, albeit good-naturedly. One of them asked, "Why'd you buy a watermelon when you can't eat it?"

"I bought it for you fellows," answered Matahachi. "I thought it'd make up for not being able to do my share of the work."

"Now, that was smart. Hey, men! Watermelon! Have some, on Matahachi."

Splitting the melon on the corner of a rock, they fell to it like ants, snatching greedily at the sweet, dripping hunks of red pulp. It was all gone when moments later a man jumped up on a rock and yelled, "Back to work, all of you!"

The samurai in charge emerged from a hut, whip in hand, and the stench of sweat spread over the earth. Presently the melody of a rock haulers' chantey rose from the site, as a gigantic boulder was shifted with large levers onto rollers and dragged along with ropes as thick as a man's arm. It advanced ponderously, like a moving mountain.

With the boom in castle construction, these rhythmical songs proliferated. Though the words were rarely written down, no less a personage than Lord Hachisuka of Awa, who was in charge of building Nagoya Castle, quoted several verses in a letter. His lordship, who would hardly have had occasion to so much as touch construction materials, had apparently learned them at a party. Simple compositions, like the following, they'd become something of a fad in society as well as among work crews.

> From Awataguchi we've pulled them—
> Dragged rock after rock after rock.
> For our noble Lord Tōgorō.

Ei, sa, ei, sa . . .
Pull—ho! Drag—ho! Pull—ho! Drag—ho!
His lordship speaks,
Our arms and legs tremble.
We're loyal to him—to the death.

The letter writer commented, "Everybody, young and old alike, sings this, for it is part of the floating world we live in."

While the laborers at Fushimi were not aware of these social reverberations, their songs did reflect the spirit of the times. The tunes popular when the Ashikaga shogunate was in decline had been on the whole decadent and had been sung mostly in private, but during the prosperous years of Hideyoshi's regime, happy, cheerful songs were often heard in public. Later, with the stern hand of Ieyasu making itself felt, the melodies lost some of their rollicking spirit. As Tokugawa rule became stronger, spontaneous singing tended to give way to music composed by musicians in the shōgun's employ.

Matahachi rested his head on his hands. It burned with fever, and the heave-ho singing buzzed indistinctly in his ears, like a swarm of bees. All alone now, he lapsed into depression.

"What's the use," he groaned. "Five years. Suppose I do work hard—what'll it get me? For a whole day's work, I make only enough to eat that day. If I take a day off, I don't eat."

Sensing someone standing near him, he looked up and saw a tall young man. His head was covered with a deep, coarsely woven basked hat, and at his side hung a bundle of the sort carried by *shugyōsha*. An emblem in the form of a half-open steel-ribbed fan adorned the front of his hat. He was gazing thoughtfully at the construction work and sizing up the terrain.

After a time he seated himself next to a flat, broad rock, which was just the right height to serve as a writing table. He blew away the sand on top, along with a line of ants marching across it, then with his elbows propped on the rock and his head on his hands, resumed his intense survey of the surroundings. Though the sun's glare hit him full in the face, he remained motionless, seemingly impervious to the discomforting heat. He did not notice Matahachi, who was still too miserable to care whether anyone was around or not. The other man meant nothing to him. He sat with his back to the newcomer and spasmodically retched.

By and by the samurai became aware of his gagging. "You there," he said. "What's the matter?"

"It's the heat," answered Matahachi.

"You're in pretty bad shape, aren't you?"

"I'm a little better than I was, but I still feel dizzy."

"I'll give you some medicine," said the samurai, opening his black-lacquered pillbox and shaking some black pills into the palm of his hand. He walked over and put the medicine in Matahachi's mouth.

"You'll be all right in no time," he said.

"Thanks."

"Do you plan to rest here for a while longer?"

"Yes."

"Then do me a favor. Let me know if anybody comes— throw a pebble or something."

He went back to his own rock, sat down, and took a brush from his writing kit and a notebook from his kimono. He opened the pad on the rock and began to draw. Under the brim of his hat, his eyes moved back and forth from the castle to its immediate surroundings, taking in the main tower, the fortifications, the mountains in the background, the river and the smaller streams.

Just before the Battle of Sekigahara, this castle had been attacked by units of the Western Army, and two compounds, as well as part of the moat, had suffered considerable damage. Now the bastion was not only being restored but also being strengthened, so that it would outclass Hideyori's stronghold at Osaka.

Quickly but in great detail, the student warrior sketched a bird's-eye view of the entire castle and on a second page began making a diagram of the approaches from the rear.

"Uh-oh!" exclaimed Matahachi softly. From out of nowhere the inspector of works appeared and was standing behind the sketcher. Clad in half-armor, with straw sandals on his feet, he stood there silently, as if waiting to be noticed. Matahachi felt a pang of guilt for not having seen him in time to give warning. It was too late now.

Presently the student warrior lifted his hand to brush a fly off his sweaty collar and in doing so caught sight of the intruder. As he looked up with startled eyes, the inspector stared back angrily for a moment before stretching out a hand toward the drawing. The student warrior grabbed his wrist and jumped up.

"What do you think you're doing?" he shouted.

The inspector seized the notebook and held it high in the air. "I'd like to have a look at this," he barked.

"You have no right."

"Just doing my job!"

"Butting into other people's business—is that your job?"

"Why? Shouldn't I look at it?"

"An oaf like you wouldn't understand it."

"I think I'd better keep it."

"Oh, no you don't!" cried the student warrior, making a grab for the notebook. Both pulled at it, ripping it in half.

"Watch yourself!" shouted the inspector. "You'd better have a good explanation, or I'll turn you in."

"On whose authority? You an officer?"

"That's right."

"What's your group? Who's your commander?"

"None of your business. But you might as well know that I'm under orders to investigate anyone around here who looks suspicious. Who gave you permission to make sketches?"

"I'm making a study of castles and geographic features for future reference. What's wrong with that?"

"The place is swarming with enemy spies. They all have excuses like that. It doesn't matter who you are. You'll have to answer some questions. Come with me!"

"Are you accusing me of being a criminal?"

"Just hold your tongue and come along."

"Rotten officials! Too used to making people cringe every time you open your big mouths!"

"Shut up—let's go!"

"Try and make me!" The student warrior was adamant.

Angry veins popping up in his forehead, the inspector dropped his half of the notebook, ground it under foot, and pulled out his truncheon. The student warrior jumped back a pace to improve his position.

"If you're not going to come along willingly, I'll have to tie you up and drag you," said the inspector.

Before the words were out, his adversary went into action. Uttering a great howl, he seized the inspector by the neck with one hand, grabbed the lower edge of his armor with the other, then hurled him at a large rock.

"Worthless lout!" he screamed, but not in time to be heard by the inspector, whose head split open on the rock like a watermelon. With a cry of horror, Matahachi covered his face with his hands to protect it from the globs of red pasty matter flying his way, while the student warrior quickly reverted to an attitude of complete calm.

Matahachi was appalled. Could the man be accustomed to murdering in this brutal fashion? Or was his sangfroid merely the letdown that follows an explosion of rage? Matahachi, shocked to the core, began to sweat profusely. From all he could tell, the other man could hardly have reached the age of thirty. His bony, sunburned face was blemished by pockmarks, and he appeared to have no chin, though this may have been due to a curiously shrunken scar from a deep sword wound.

The student warrior was in no hurry to flee. He gathered up the torn fragments of his notebook. Then he began looking quietly about for his hat, which had flown off when he made his mighty throw. After finding it, he placed it with care upon his head, once again concealing his eerie face from view. At a brisk pace he took his leave, gathering speed until he seemed to be flying on the wind.

The whole incident had happened so fast that neither the hundreds of laborers in the vicinity nor their overseers had noticed it. The workmen continued to toil like drones, as the supervisors, armed with whips and truncheons, bellowed orders at their sweating back.

But one particular pair of eyes had seen it all. Standing atop a high scaffold commanding a view of the whole area was the general overseer of carpenters and log cutters. Seeing that the student warrior was escaping, he roared out a command, setting into motion a group of foot soldiers who had been drinking tea below the scaffold.

"What happened?"

"Another fight?"

Others heard the call to arms and soon stirred up a cloud of yellow dust near the wooden gate of the stockade, which divided the construction site from the village. Angry shouts rose from the gathering swarm of people.

"It's a spy! A spy from Osaka!"

"They'll never learn."

"Kill him! Kill him!"

Rock haulers, earth carriers and others, screaming as though the "spy" were their personal enemy, bore down on the chinless samurai. He darted behind an oxcart shambling through the gate and tried to slip out, but a sentinel caught sight of him and tripped him with a nail-studded staff.

From the overseer's scaffold came the cry: "Don't let him escape!"

With no hesitation, the crowd fell upon the miscreant, who counterattacked like a trapped beast. Wresting the staff from the sentinel, he turned on him and with the point of the weapon knocked him down headfirst. After downing four or five more men in similar fashion, he drew his huge sword and took an offensive stance. His captors fell back in terror, but as he prepared to cut his way out of the circle, a barrage of stones descended on him from all directions.

The mob vented its wrath in earnest, its mood all the more murderous because of a deep-seated distaste for all *shugyōsha*. Like most commoners, these laborers considered the wandering samurai useless, nonproductive and arrogant.

"Stop acting like stupid churls!" cried the beleaguered samurai, appealing for reason and restraint. Though he fought back, he seemed more concerned with chiding his attackers than with avoiding the rocks they hurled. More than a few innocent bystanders were injured in the melee.

Then, in a trice, it was all over. The shouting ceased, and the laborers began moving back to their work stations.

In five minutes, the great construction site was exactly as it had been before, as though nothing had happened. The sparks flying from the various cutting instruments, the whinnying of horses half addled by the sun, the mind-numbing heat—all returned to normal.

Two guards stood over the collapsed form, which had been trussed up with a thick hemp rope. "He's ninety percent dead," said one, "so we may as well leave him here till the magistrate comes." He looked around and spotted Matahachi. "Hey, you there! Stand watch over this man. If he dies, it doesn't make any difference."

Matahachi heard the words, but his head could not quite take in either their import or the meaning of the event he had just witnessed. It all seemed like a nightmare, visible to his eyes, audible to his ears, but not comprehensible to his brain.

"Life's so flimsy," he thought. "A few minutes ago he was absorbed in his sketching. Now he's dying. He wasn't very old."

He felt sorry for the chinless samurai, whose head, lying sideways on the ground, was black with dirt and gore, his face still contorted with anger. The rope anchored him to a large rock. Matahachi wondered idly why the officials had taken such precautions when the man was too near death to make a sound. Or maybe already dead. One of his legs lay grotesquely exposed through a long rip in his *hakama,* the white shinbone protruding from the crimson flesh. Blood was sprouting from his scalp, and wasps had begun to hover around his matted hair. Ants nearly covered his hands and feet.

"Poor wretch," thought Matahachi. "If he was studying seriously, he must have had some great ambition in life. Wonder where he's from . . . if his parents are still alive." Matahachi was seized by a peculiar doubt: was he really bemoaning the man's fate, or was he bothered by the vagueness of his own future? "For a man with ambition," he reflected, "there ought to be a cleverer way to get ahead."

This was an age that fanned the hopes of the young, urged them to cherish a dream, prodded them to improve their status in life. An age, indeed, in which even someone like Matahachi might have visions of rising from nothing to become the master of a castle. A modestly talented warrior could get by traveling from temple to temple and living on the charity of the priests. If he was lucky, he might be taken in by one of the provincial gentry, and if he was still more fortunate, might receive a stipend from a daimyō.

Still, of all the young men who set out with high hopes, only one in a thousand actually ended up finding a position with an acceptable income. The rest had to be content with what satisfaction they could derive from the knowledge that theirs was a difficult and dangerous calling.

As Matahachi contemplated the samurai lying before him, the whole idea began to seem utterly stupid. Where could the path Musashi was following possibly lead? Matahachi's desire to equal or surpass his boyhood friend hadn't abated, but the sight of the bloodied warrior made the Way of the Sword seem vain and foolish.

Horror-stricken, he realized that the warrior was moving, and his train of thought stopped short. The man's hand reached out like a turtle's flipper and clawed at the ground. Feebly he lifted his torso, raised his head and pulled the rope taut.

Matahachi could hardly believe his eyes. As the man inched along the ground, he dragged behind him the four-hundred-pound rock securing his rope. One foot, two feet— it was a display of superhuman strength. No muscle man on any rock-hauling crew could have done it, though many boasted of the strength of ten or twenty men. The samurai lying on the threshold of death was possessed by some demonic force, which enabled him to far surpass the power of an ordinary mortal.

A gurgle came from the dying man's throat. He was trying desperately to speak, but his tongue had turned black and dry, making it impossible for him to form the words. Breath came in cracked, hollow hisses; eyes popping from their sockets stared imploringly at Matahachi.

"Pl—lul—poo—loo—ees . . ."

Matahachi gradually understood he was saying "please." Then a different sound, all but inarticulate, Matahachi made out to be "beg you." But it was the man's eyes that really spoke. Therein were the last of his tears and the certainty of death. His head fell back; his breathing ceased. As more ants started coming out of the grass to explore the dust-whitened hair, a few even entering a blood-caked nostril, Matahachi could see the skin under his kimono collar take on a blackish-blue cast.

What had the man wanted him to do? Matahachi felt haunted by the thought that he had incurred an obligation. The samurai had come upon him when he was sick and had had the kindness to give him medicine. Why had fate blinded Matahachi when he should have been warning the man of the inspector's approach? Was this destined to have occurred?

Matahachi tentatively touched the cloth-wrapped bundle on the dead man's obi. The contents would surely reveal who the man was and where he was from. Matahachi suspected that his dying wish had been to have some memento delivered to his family. He detached the bundle, as well as the pillbox, and stuffed them quickly inside his own kimono.

He debated whether to cut off a lock of hair for the man's mother, but while staring into the fearsome face, he heard footsteps approaching. Peeking from behind a rock, he saw samurai coming for the corpse. If he were caught with the dead man's possessions, he'd be in serious trouble. He crouched down low and made his way from shadow to shadow behind the rocks, sneaking away like a field rat.

Two hours later he arrived at the sweetshop where he was staying. The shopkeeper's wife was by the side of the house, rinsing herself off from a washbasin. Hearing him moving about inside, she showed a portion of her white flesh from behind the side door and called, "Is that you, Matahachi?"

Answering with a loud grunt, he dashed into his own room and grabbed a kimono and his sword from a cabinet; he then knotted a rolled towel around his head and prepared to slip into his sandals again.

"Isn't it dark in there?" called the woman.

"No, I can see well enough."

"I'll bring you a lamp."

"No need to. I'm going out."

"Aren't you going to wash?"

"No. Later."

He rushed out into the field and swiftly moved away from the shabby house. A few minutes later he looked back to see a group of samurai, no doubt from the castle, come from beyond the miscanthus in the field. They entered the sweetshop from both front and rear.

"That was a close call," he thought. "Of course, I didn't really steal anything. I just took it in custody. I had to. He begged me to."

To his way of thinking, as long as he admitted that the articles were not his, he had committed no crime. At the same time, he realized he could never again show his face at the construction site.

The miscanthus came up to his shoulders, and a veil of evening mist floated above it. No one could see him from a distance; it would be easy to get away. But which way to go was a difficult choice, all the more so since he strongly felt that good luck lay in one direction and bad luck in another.

Osaka? Kyoto? Nagoya? Edo? He had no friends in any of those places; he might as well roll dice to decide where to go. With dice, as with Matahachi, all was chance. When the wind blew, it would waft him along with it.

It seemed to him that the farther he walked, the deeper he went into the miscanthus. Insects buzzed about him, and the descending mist dampened his clothes. The soaked hems curled around his legs. Seeds caught at his sleeves. His shins itched. The memory of his noonday nausea was gone now and he was painfully hungry. Once he felt himself out of the reach of his pursuers, it became agony to walk.

An overwhelming urge to find a place to lie down and rest carried him the length of the field, beyond which he spotted the roof of a house. Drawing nearer, he saw that the fence and gate were both askew, apparently damaged by a recent storm. The roof needed fixing too. Yet at one time the house must have belonged to a wealthy family, for there was a certain faded elegance about it. He imagined a beautiful court lady seated in a richly curtained carriage approaching the house at a stately pace.

Going through the forlorn-looking gate, he found that

both the main house and a smaller detached house were nearly buried in weeds. The scene reminded him of a passage by the poet Saigyō that he had been made to learn as a child:

> I heard that a person I knew lived in Fushimi and went to pay him a call, but the garden was so overgrown! I couldn't even see the path. As the insects sang, I composed this poem.

> > Pressing through the weeds,
> > I hide my tearful feelings
> > In the folds of my sleeve.
> > In the dew-laden garden
> > Even lowly insects weep.

Matahachi's heart was chilled as he crouched near the house, whispering the words so long forgotten.

Just as he was about to conclude the house was empty, a red light appeared from deep inside. Presently he heard the pining strains of a *shakuhachi,* the bamboo flute mendicant priests played when begging on the streets. Looking inside, he discovered the player was indeed a member of that class. He was seated beside the hearth. The fire he had just lit grew brighter, and his shadow loomed larger on the wall. He was playing a mournful tune, a solitary lament on the loneliness and melancholy of autumn, intended for no ears but his own. The man played simply, without flourish, giving Matahachi the impression he took little pride in his playing.

When the melody came to an end, the priest sighed deeply and launched into a lament.

"They say when a man is forty, he is free from delusion. But look at me! Forty-seven when I destroyed my family's good name. Forty-seven! And still I was deluded; contrived to lose everything—income, position, reputation. Not only that; I left my only son to fend for himself in this wretched world. . . . For what? An infatuation?

"It's mortifying—never again could I face my dead wife, nor the boy, wherever he is. Ha! When they say you're wise after forty, they must be talking about great men, not dolts like me. Instead of thinking myself wise because of my years, I should have been more careful than ever. It's madness not to, where women are concerned.''

Standing his *shakuhachi* on end in front of him and propping both hands on the mouthpiece, he went on. ''When that business with Otsū came up, nobody would forgive me any longer. It's too late, too late.''

Matahachi had crept into the next room. He listened but was repelled by what he saw. The priest's cheeks were sunken, his shoulders had a pointed, stray-dog air, and his hair was sheenless. Matahachi crouched in silence; in the flickering firelight the man's form summoned up visions of demons of the night.

''Oh, what am I to do?'' moaned the priest, lifting his sunken eyes to the ceiling. His kimono was plain and dingy, but he also wore a black cassock, indicating he was a follower of the Chinese Zen master P'u-hua. The reed matting on which he sat, and which he rolled up and carried with him wherever he went, was probably his only household possession—his bed, his curtain, and in bad weather, his roof.

''Talking won't bring back what I've lost,'' he said. ''Why wasn't I more careful! I thought I understood life. I understood nothing, let my status go to my head! I behaved shamelessly toward a woman. No wonder the gods deserted me. What could be more humiliating?''

The priest lowered his head as though apologizing to someone, then lowered it still farther. ''I don't care about myself. The life I have now is good enough for me. It's only right I should do penance and have to survive without outside help.

''But what have I done to Jōtarō? He'll suffer more for my misconduct than I. If I were still in Lord Ikeda's service, he'd now be the only son of a samurai with an income of five thousand bushels, but because of my stupidity, he's nothing. What's worse, one day, when he's grown, he'll learn the truth.''

For a time he sat with his hands covering his face, then suddenly stood up. ''I must stop this—feeling sorry for myself again. The moon's out; I'll go walk in the field—rid myself of these old grievances and ghosts.''

The priest picked up his *shakuhachi* and shuffled list-lessly out of the house. Matahachi thought he saw a hint of a stringy mustache under the emaciated nose. ''What a strange person!'' he thought. ''He's not really old, but he's so unsteady on his feet.'' Suspecting the man might be a little insane, he felt a tinge of pity for him.

Fanned by the evening breeze, the flames from the broken kindling were beginning to scorch the floor. Entering the empty room, Matahachi found a pitcher of water and poured some on the fire, reflecting as he did so on the priest's carelessness.

It wouldn't matter much if this old deserted house burned to the ground, but what if instead it were an ancient temple of the Asuka or Kamakura period? Matahachi felt a rare spasm of indignation. ''It's because of people like him that the ancient temples in Nara and on Mount Kōya are destroyed so often,'' he thought. ''These crazy vagabond priests have no property, no family of their own. They don't give a thought to how dangerous fire is. They'll light one in the main hall of an old monastery, right next to the murals, just to warm their own carcasses, which are of no use to anyone.

''Now, there's something interesting,'' he mumbled, turning his eyes toward the alcove. It wasn't the graceful design of the room nor the remains of a valuable vase that had attracted his attention, but a blackened metal pot, beside which stood a sake jar with a chipped mouth. In the pot was some rice gruel, and when he shook the jar, it made a cheerful gurgling sound. He smiled broadly, grateful for his good fortune and oblivious, as any hungry man might be, to the property rights of others.

He promptly drained off the sake in a couple of long swallows, emptied the rice pot and congratulated himself on the fullness of his belly.

Nodding sleepily beside the hearth, he became con-scious of the rainlike buzz of insects coming from the dark field outside—not only from the field but from the walls, the ceiling and the rotting tatami mats.

Just before drifting off to sleep, he remembered the bundle he had taken from the dying warrior. He roused himself and untied it. The cloth was a soiled piece of crepe dyed with a dark red sappanwood dye. It contained a washed and bleached undergarment, together with the usual articles travelers carry. Unfolding the garment, he found an object the size and shape of a letter scroll, wrapped with great care in oil paper. There was also a purse, which fell with a loud clink from a fold in the fabric. Made of purple-dyed leather, it contained enough gold and silver to make Matahachi's hand shake with fear. "This is someone else's money, not mine," he reminded himself.

Undoing the oil paper around the longer object revealed a scroll, wound on a Chinese-quince roller, with a gold brocade end cloth. He immediately sensed that it contained some important secret and with great curiosity put the scroll down in front of him and slowly unrolled it. It said:

CERTIFICATE

On sacred oath I swear that I have transmitted to Sasaki Kojirō the following seven secret methods of the Chūjō Style of swordsmanship:

Overt—Lightning style, wheel style, rounded style, floating-boat style
Secret—The Diamond, The Edification, The Infinite

Issued in the village of Jōkyōji in the Usaka Demesne of Echizen Province on the —————— day of the —————— month.

Kanemaki Jisai, Disciple of Toda Seigen

On a piece of paper that seemed to have been attached later, there followed a poem:

The moon shining on
The waters not present
In an undug well
Yields forth a man
With neither shadow nor form.

Matahachi realized he was holding a diploma given to a
disciple who had learned all his master had to teach, but the
name Kanemaki Jisai meant nothing to him. He would have
recognized the name of Itō Yagorō, who under the name
Ittōsai had created a famous and highly admired style of
swordsmanship. He did not know that Jisai was Itō's
teacher. Nor did he know that Jisai was a samurai of splendid
character, who had mastered the true style of Toda Seigen
and had retired to a remote village to pass his old age in
obscurity, thereafter transmitting Seigen's method to only a
few select students.

Matahachi's eyes went back to the first name. "This
Sasaki Kojirō must have been the samurai who was killed at
Fushimi today," he thought. "He must have been quite a
swordsman to be awarded a certificate in the Chūjō Style,
whatever that is. Shame he had to die! But now I'm sure of
it. It's just as I suspected. He must've wanted me to deliver
this to somebody, probably someone in his birthplace."

Matahachi said a short prayer to the Buddha for Sasaki
Kojirō, then vowed to himself that somehow he would carry
out his new mission.

To ward off the chill, he rebuilt the fire, then lay down
by the hearth and presently fell asleep.

From somewhere in the distance came the sound of the
old priest's *shakuhachi*. The mournful tune, seemingly
searching for something, calling out to someone, went on
and on, a poignant wave hovering over the rushes of the
field.

6

Reunion in Osaka

The field lay under a gray mist, and the chill in the early air hinted that autumn was beginning in earnest. Squirrels were up and about, and in the doorless kitchen of the deserted house, fresh fox tracks crossed the earthen floor.

The beggar priest, having stumbled back before sunrise, had succumbed to fatigue on the pantry floor, still clutching his *shakuhachi*. His dirty kimono and cassock were wet with dew and spotty with grass stains picked up while he wandered like a lost soul through the night. As he opened his eyes and sat up, his nose crinkled, his nostrils and his eyes opened wide, and he shook with a mighty sneeze. He made no effort to wipe off the snot trickling from his nose into his wispy mustache.

He sat there for a few minutes before recalling that he still had some sake left from the night before. Grumbling to himself, he made his way down a long hallway to the hearth room at the back of the house. By daylight, there were more rooms than there had seemed to be at night, but he found his way without difficulty. To his astonishment, the sake jar was not where he had left it.

Instead there was a stranger by the hearth, with his head on his arm and saliva seeping from his mouth, sound asleep. The whereabouts of the sake was all too clear.

The sake, of course, was not all that was missing. A quick check revealed that not a drop of the rice gruel intended for breakfast remained. The priest turned scarlet

83

with rage; he could get by without the sake, but rice was a matter of life and death. With a fierce yelp, he kicked the sleeper with all his might, but Matahachi grunted sleepily, took his arm from underneath him, and lazily raised his head.

"You . . . you . . . !" sputtered the priest, giving him another kick.

"What are you doing?" cried Matahachi. The veins popped out on his sleepy face as he jumped to his feet. "You can't kick me like that!"

"Kicking's not good enough for you! Who told you you could come in her and steal my rice and sake?"

"Oh, were they yours?"

"Of course they were!"

"Sorry."

"You're sorry? What good does that do me?"

"I apologize."

"You'll have to do more than that!"

"What do you expect me to do?"

"Give them back!"

"Heh! They're already inside me; they kept me alive for a night. Can't get them back now!"

"I have to live too, don't I? The most I ever get for going around and playing music at people's gates is a few grains of rice or a couple of drops of sake. You imbecile! Do you expect me to stand silently by and let you steal my food? I want it back—give it back!" His tone as he made his irrational demand was imperious, and his voice sounded to Matahachi like that of a hungry devil straight from hell.

"Don't be so stingy," said Matahachi disparagingly. "What's there to get so upset about—a little rice and less than half a jar of third-rate sake."

"You ass, maybe you turn your nose up at leftover rice, but for me it's a day's food—a day's life!" The priest grunted and grabbed Matahachi's wrist. "I won't let you get away with this!"

"Don't be a fool!" countered Matahachi. Wresting his arm free and seizing the old man by his thin hair, he tried to throw him down with a quick yank. To his surprise, the starved-cat body didn't budge. The priest got a firm grip on Matahachi's neck and clung to it.

"You bastard!" barked Matahachi, reassessing his opponent's fighting power.

He was too late. The priest, planting his feet solidly on the floor, sent Matahachi stumbling backward with a single push. It was a skillful move, utilizing Matahachi's own strength, and Matahachi did not stop until he banged against the plastered wall on the far side of the adjacent room. The posts and lathing being rotten, a good part of the wall collapsed, showering him with dirt. Spitting out a mouthful, he jumped up, drew his sword and lunged at the old man.

The latter prepared to parry the attack with his *shakuhachi*, but he was already gasping for air.

"Now see what you've got yourself into!" yelled Matahachi as he swung. He missed but went on swinging relentlessly, giving the priest no chance to catch his breath. The old man's face took on a ghostly look. He jumped back time and again, but there was no spring in his step; he appeared to be on the verge of collapse. Each time he dodged, he let out a plaintive cry, like a whimper of a dying man. Still, his constant shifting made it impossible for Matahachi to connect with his sword.

Eventually Matahachi was undone by his own carelessness. When the priest jumped into the garden, Matahachi followed blindly, but the moment his foot hit the rotted floor of the veranda, the boards cracked and gave way. He landed on his backside, one leg dangling through a hole.

The priest leaped to the attack. Grabbing the front of Matahachi's kimono, he started beating him on the head, the temples, the body—anywhere his *shakuhachi* happened to fall—grunting loudly with each whack. With his leg caught, Matahachi was helpless. His head seemed ready to swell to the size of a barrel, but luck was with him, for at this point pieces of gold and silver began dropping from his kimono. Each new blow was followed by the happy tinkling of coins falling on the floor.

"What's this?" gasped the priest, letting go of his victim. Matahachi hastily freed his leg and jumped clear, but the old man had already vented his anger. His aching fist and labored breathing didn't stop him from staring in wonder at the money.

Matahachi, hands on his throbbing head, shouted, "See, you old fool? There was no reason to get excited over a little bit of rice and sake. I've got money to throw away! Take it if you want it! But in return you're going to get back the beating you gave me. Stick out your silly head, and I'll pay you with interest for your rice and booze!"

Instead of responding to this abuse, the priest put his face to the floor and began weeping. Matahachi's wrath abated somewhat, but he said venomously, "Look at you! The minute you see money, you fall apart."

"How shameful of me!" wailed the priest. "Why am I such a fool?" Like the strength with which he had so lately fought, his self-reproach was more violent than that of an ordinary man. "What an ass I am!" he continued. "Haven't I come to my senses yet? Not even at my age? Not even after being cast out of society and sinking as low as a man can sink?"

He turned toward the black column beside him and started beating his head against it, all the time moaning to himself. "Why do I play this *shakuhachi?* Isn't it to expel through its five openings my delusions, my stupidity, my lust, my selfishness, my evil passions? How could I possibly have allowed myself to get into a life-and-death struggle over a bit of food and drink? And with a man young enough to be my son?"

Matahachi had never seen anyone like this. The old man would weep for a moment, then ram his head against the column again. He seemed intent on beating his forehead until it split in two. More numerous by far were his inflictions on himself than the blows he had dealt Matahachi. Presently, blood began to flow from his brow.

Matahachi felt obliged to prevent him from torturing himself further. "Look now," he said. "Stop that. You don't know what you're doing!"

"Leave me alone," pleaded the priest.

"But what's wrong with you?"

"Nothing's wrong."

"There must be something. Are you sick?"

"No."

"Then what is it?"

"I'm disgusted with myself. I'd like to beat this evil body of mine to death and feed it to the crows, but I don't want to die a stupid fool. I'd like to be as strong and upright as the next person before I discard this flesh. Losing my self-control makes me furious. I guess you could call it sickness after all."

Feeling sorry for him, Matahachi picked up the fallen money and tried to press some of it into his hand. "It was partly my fault," he said apologetically. "I'll give you this, and then maybe you'll forgive me."

"I don't want it!" cried the priest, quickly withdrawing his hand. "I don't need money. I tell you, I don't need it!" Though he had previously exploded in anger over a bit of rice gruel, he now looked at the money with loathing. Shaking his head vigorously, he backed away, still on his knees.

"You're an odd one," said Matahachi.

"Not really."

"Well, you certainly act strange."

"Don't let it worry you."

"You sound like you come from the western provinces. Your accent, I mean."

"I guess I would. I was born in Himeji."

"Is that so? I'm from that area too—Mimasaka."

"Mimasaka?" repeated the priest, fixing his eye on Matahachi. "Just where in Mimasaka?"

"The village of Yoshino. Miyamoto, to be exact."

The old man seemed to relax. Sitting down on the porch, he spoke quietly. "Miyamoto? That's a name that brings back memories. I was once on guard duty at the stockade in Hinagura. I know that area fairly well."

"Does that mean you used to be a samurai in the Himeji fief?"

"Yes. I suppose I don't look it now, but I used to be something of a warrior. My name is Aoki Tan—"

He broke off, then just as abruptly went on: "That's not true. I just made it up. Forget I said anything at all." He stood up, saying, "I'm going into town, play my *shakuhachi* and get some rice." With that, he turned and walked rapidly toward the field of miscanthus.

After he was gone, Matahachi started wondering whether it had been right of him to offer the old priest money from the dead samurai's pouch. Soon he'd solved his dilemma by telling himself there couldn't be any harm in just borrowing some, provided it wasn't a lot. "If I deliver these things to the dead man's home, the way he wanted me to," he thought, "I'll have to have money for expenses, and what choice do I have but to take it out of the cash I have here?" This easy rationalization was so comforting that from that day on he began using the money little by little.

There remained the question of the certificate made out to Sasaki Kojirō. The man appeared to have been a rōnin, but mightn't he instead have been in the service of some daimyō? Matahachi had found no clue to where the man was from, hence had no idea where to take the certificate. His only hope, he decided, would be to locate the master swordsman Kanemaki Jisai, who no doubt knew all there was to know about Sasaki.

As Matahachi made his way from Fushimi toward Osaka, he asked at every teahouse, eating house and inn whether anyone knew of Jisai. All the replies were negative; even the added information that Jisai was an accredited disciple of Toda Seigen elicited no response.

Finally, a samurai with whom Matahachi struck up an acquaintance on the road displayed a glimmer of recognition. "I've heard of Jisai, but if he's still alive, he must be very old. Somebody said he went east and became a recluse in a village in Kōzuke, or somewhere. If you want to find out more about him, you should go to Osaka Castle and talk to a man named Tomita Mondonoshō." Mondonoshō, it seemed, was one of Hideyori's teachers in the martial arts, and Matahachi's informant was fairly sure he belonged to the same family as Seigen.

Though disappointed at the vagueness of his first real lead, Matahachi resolved to follow it up. Upon his arrival in Osaka, he took a room at a cheap inn on one of the busier streets and as soon as he was settled in asked the innkeeper whether he knew of a man named Tomita Mondonoshō at Osaka Castle.

"Yes, I've heard the name," replied the innkeeper. "I believe he's the grandson of Toda Seigen. He's not Lord Hideyori's personal instructor, but he does teach swordsmanship to some of the samurai in the castle. Or at least he used to. I think he might have gone back to Echizen some years ago. Yes, that's what he did.

"You could go to Echizen and look for him, but there's no guarantee he's still there. Instead of taking such a long trip on a hunch, wouldn't it be easier to look up Itō Ittōsai? I'm pretty sure he studied the Chūjō Style under Jisai before developing his own style."

The innkeeper's suggestion seemed sensible, but when Matahachi began looking for Ittōsai, he found himself in another blind alley. As far as he could learn, the man had until recently been living in a small hut in Shirakawa, just east of Kyoto, but he was no longer there and hadn't been seen in Kyoto or Osaka for some time.

Before long, Matahachi's resolution flagged and he was ready to drop the whole business. The bustle and excitement of the city rekindled his ambition and stirred his youthful soul. In a wide-open town like this, why should he spend his time looking for a dead man's family? There was plenty of things to do here; people were looking for young men like him. At Fushimi Castle, the authorities had been singlemindedly implementing the policies of the Tokugawa government. Here, however, the generals running Osaka Castle were searching out rōnin to build up an army. Not publicly, of course, but openly enough so that it was common knowledge. It was a fact that rōnin were more welcome and could live better here than in any other castle town in the country.

Heady rumors circulated among the townspeople. It was said, for instance, that Hideyori was quietly providing funds for such fugitive daimyō as Gotō Matabei, Sanada Yukimura, Akashi Kamon and even the dangerous Chōsokabe Morichika, who now lived in a rented house in a narrow street on the outskirts of town.

Chōsokabe had, despite his youth, shaved his head like a Buddhist priest and changed his name to Ichimusai—"The

Man of a Single Dream.'' It was a declaration that the affairs of this floating world no longer concerned him, and ostensibly he passed his time in elegant frivolities. It was widely known, however, that he had in his service seven or eight hundred rōnin, all of them firm in their confidence that when the proper time came, he would rise up and vindicate his late benefactor Hideyoshi. It was rumored that his living expenses, including the pay for his rōnin, all came from Hideyori's private purse.

For two months Matahachi wandered about Osaka, increasingly confident that this was the place for him. Here was where he would catch the straw that would lead to success. For the first time in years he felt as brave and dauntless as when he'd gone off to war. He was healthy and alive again, unperturbed by the gradual depletion of the dead samurai's money, for he believed luck was finally turning his way. Every day was a joy, a delight. He was sure he was about to stumble over a rock and come up covered with money. Good fortune was on the verge of finding him.

New clothes! That was what he needed. And so he bought himself a complete new outfit, carefully choosing material that would be suitable in the cold of approaching winter. Then, having decided living in an inn was too expensive, he rented a small room belonging to a saddle-maker in the vicinity of the Junkei Moat and began taking his meals out. He went to see what he wanted to see, came home when he felt like it, and stayed out all night from time to time, as the spirit moved him. While basking in this happy-go-lucky existence, he remained on the lookout for a friend, a connection who would lead him to a good-paying position in the service of a great daimyō.

It required a certain amount of self-restraint for Matahachi to live within his means, but he felt he was behaving himself better than ever before. He was repeatedly buoyed up by stories of how this or that samurai had not long ago been hauling dirt away from a construction site but was now to be seen riding pompously through town with twenty retainers and a spare horse.

At other times he felt a trace of dejection. "The world's a stone wall," he would think. "And they've put the rocks so close together there's not a chink where anybody can get in." But his frustration always eddied away. "What am I talking about? It just looks that way when you still haven't seen your chance. It's always difficult to break in, but once I find an opening . . ."

When he asked the saddle-maker whether he knew of a position, the latter replied optimistically, "You're young and strong. If you apply at the castle, they're sure to find a place for you."

But finding the right work was not as easy as that. The last month of the year found Matahachi still unemployed, his money diminished by half.

Under the wintry sun of the busiest month of the year, the hordes of people milling about the streets looked surprisingly unrushed. In the center of town there were empty lots, where in early morning the grass was white with frost. As the day progressed, the streets became muddy, and the feeling of winter was driven away by the sound of merchants hawking their goods with clanging gongs and booming drums. Seven or eight stalls, surrounded by shabby straw matting to keep outsiders from looking in, beckoned with paper flags and lances decorated with feathers to advertise shows being presented inside. Barkers competed stridently to lure idle passersby into their flimsy theaters.

The smell of cheap soy sauce permeated the air. In the shops, hairy-legged men, skewers of food stuffed in their mouths, whinnied like horses, and at twilight long-sleeved women with whitened faces simpered like ewes, walking together in flocks and munching on parched-bean tidbits.

One evening a fight broke out among the customers of a man who had set up a sake shop by placing some stools on the side of the street. Before anyone could tell who had won, the combatants turned tail and ran off down the street, leaving a trail of dripping blood behind them.

"Thank you, sir," said the sake vendor to Matahachi, whose glaring presence had caused the fighting townsmen to flee. "If you hadn't been here, they would have broken all my dishes." The man bowed several times, then served Matahachi another jar of sake, which he said he trusted was warmed to just the right temperature. He also presented some snacks as a token of his appreciation.

Matahachi was pleased with himself. The brawl had erupted between two workmen, and when he had scowled at them, threatening to kill them both if they did any damage to the stall, they had fled.

"Lots of people around, aren't there?" he remarked amiably.

"It's the end of the year. They stay awhile and move on, but others keep coming."

"Nice that the weather's holding up."

Matahachi's face was red from drink. As he lifted his cup, he remembered having sworn off before he went to work at Fushimi, and vaguely wondered how he had started again. "Well, what of it?" he thought. "If a man can't have a drink now and then . . ."

"Bring me another, old boy," he said aloud.

The man sitting quietly on the stool next to Matahachi's was also a rōnin. His long and short swords were impressive; townsmen would be inclined to steer clear of him, even though he wore no cloak over his kimono, which was quite dirty around the neck.

"Hey, bring me another one too, and make it quick!" he shouted. Propping his right leg on his left knee, he scrutinized Matahachi from the feet up. When his eyes came to the face, he smiled and said, "Hello."

"Hello," said Matahachi. "Have a sip of mine while yours is being heated."

"Thanks," said the man, holding out his cup. "It's humiliating to be a drinker, isn't it? I saw you sitting here with your sake, and then this nice aroma floated through the air and pulled me over here—by the sleeve, sort of." He drained his cup in one gulp.

Matahachi liked his style. He seemed friendly, and there was something dashing about him. He could drink too; he put down five jars in the next few minutes, while Matahachi was taking his time over one. Yet he was still sober.

"How much do you usually drink?" asked Matahachi.

"Oh, I don't know," replied the man offhandedly. "Ten or twelve jars, when I feel like it."

They fell to talking about the political situation, and after a time the rōnin straightened up his shoulders and said, "Who's Ieyasu anyway? What kind of nonsense is it for him to ignore Hideyori's claims and go around calling himself the 'Great Overlord'? Without Honda Masazumi and some of his other old supporters, what have you got? Cold-bloodedness, foxiness and a little political ability—I mean, all he has is a certain flair for politics that you usually don't find in military men.

"Personally, I wish Ishida Mitsunari had won at Seki-gahara, but he was too high-minded to organize the daimyō. And his status wasn't high enough." Having delivered himself of this appraisal, he suddenly asked, "If Osaka were to clash with Edo again, which side would you be on?"

Not without hesitation, Matahachi replied, "Osaka."

"Good!" The man stood up with his sake jar in his hand. "You're one of us. Let's drink to that! What fief do you— Oh, I guess I shouldn't ask that until I tell you who I am. My name is Akakabe Yasoma. I'm from Gamō. Perhaps you've heard of Ban Dan'emon? I'm a good friend of his. We'll be together again one of these days. I'm also a friend of Susukida Hayato Kanesuke, the distinguished general at Osaka Castle. We traveled together when he was still a rōnin. I've also met Ōno Shurinosuke three or four times, but he's too gloomy for me, even if he does have more political influence than Kanesuke."

He stepped back, paused for a moment, seemingly having second thoughts about talking too much, then asked, "Who are you?"

Matahachi, though he did not believe everything the man had said, felt somehow that he had been put temporarily in the shade.

"Do you know of Toda Seigen?" he asked. "The man who originated the Tomita Style."

"I've heard the name."

"Well, my teacher was the great and selfless hermit Kanemaki Jisai, who received the true Tomita Style from Seigen and then developed the Chūjō Style."

"Then you must be a real swordsman."

"That's right," replied Matahachi. He was beginning to enjoy the game.

"You know," said Yasoma, "I've been thinking that's what you must be. Your body looks disciplined, and there's an air of capability about you. What were you called when you were training under Jisai? I mean, if I'm not being too bold in asking."

"My name is Sasaki Kojirō," said Matahachi with a straight face. "Itō Yagorō, the creator of the Ittō Style, is a senior disciple from the same school."

"Is that a fact?" said Yasoma with astonishment.

For a jittery moment, Matahachi thought of retracting everything, but it was too late. Yasoma had already knelt on the ground and was making a deep bow. There was no turning back.

"Forgive me," he said several times. "I've often heard Sasaki Kojirō was a splendid swordsman, and I must apologize for not having spoken more politely. I had no way of knowing who you were."

Matahachi was vastly relieved. If Yasoma had happened to be a friend or acquaintance of Kojirō, he would have had to fight for his life.

"You needn't bow like that," said Matahachi magnanimously. "If you insist on standing on formalities, we won't be able to talk as friends."

"But you must have been annoyed by my spouting off so."

"Why? I have no particular status or position. I'm only a young man who doesn't know much about the ways of the world."

"Yes, but you're a great swordsman. I've heard your name many times. Now that I think about it, I can see you must be Sasaki Kojirō." He stared intently at Matahachi. "What's more, I don't think it's right that you should have no official position."

Matahachi replied innocently, "Well, I've devoted myself so single-mindedly to my sword that I haven't had time to make many friends."

"I see. Does that mean you aren't interested in finding a good position?"

"No; I've always thought that one day I'd have to find a lord to serve. I just haven't reached that point yet."

"Well, it should be simple enough. You have your reputation with the sword to back you up, and that makes all the difference in the world. Of course, if you remain silent, then no matter how much talent you have, nobody's likely to search you out. Look at me. I didn't even know who you were until you told me. I was completely taken by surprise."

Yasoma paused, then said, "If you'd like me to help you, I'd be glad to. To tell the truth, I've asked my friend Susukida Kanesuke to see whether he can find a position for me too. I'd like to be taken on at Osaka Castle, even though there might not be much pay in it. I'm sure Kanesuke would be happy to recommend a person like you to the powers that be. If you'd like, I'll be glad to speak to him."

As Yasoma waxed enthusiastic about the prospects, Matahachi could not avoid the feeling that he had stumbled straight into something it wouldn't be easy to get out of. Eager as he was to find work, he feared he'd made a mistake passing himself off as Sasaki Kojirō. On the other hand, if he had said he was Hon'iden Matahachi, a country samurai from Mimasaka, Yasoma would never have offered his help. Indeed, he probably would have looked down his nose at him. There was no getting around it: the name Sasaki Kojirō had certainly made a strong impression.

But then—was there actually anything to worry about? The real Kojirō was dead, and Matahachi was the only person who knew that, for he had the certificate, the dead man's only identification. Without it, there was no way for the authorities to know who the rōnin was; it was extremely unlikely they would have gone to the trouble of conducting an investigation. After all, who was the man but a "spy" who had been stoned to death. Gradually, as Matahachi convinced himself that his secret would never be discovered, a bold scheme took definite shape in his mind: he would become Sasaki Kojirō. As of this moment.

"Bring the bill," he called, taking some coins from his money pouch.

As Matahachi rose to leave, Yasoma, thrown into confusion, blurted, "What about my proposal?"

"Oh," replied Matahachi, "I'd be very grateful if you'd speak to your friend on my behalf, but we can't discuss this sort of thing here. Let's go somewhere quiet where we can have some privacy."

"Why, of course," said Yasoma, obviously relieved. He appeared to think it only natural that Matahachi paid his bill too.

Soon they were in a district some distance from the main streets. Matahachi had intended to take his newfound friend to an elegant drinking establishment, but Yasoma pointed out that going to such a place would be a waste of money. He suggested someplace cheaper and more interesting, and while singing the praises of the red-light district, led Matahachi to what was euphemistically called the Town of Priestesses. Here, it was said, with only slight exaggeration, there were a thousand houses of pleasure, and a trade so thriving that a hundred barrels of lamp oil were consumed in a single night. Matahachi was a little reluctant at first but soon found himself attracted by the gaiety of the atmosphere.

Nearby was an offshoot of the castle moat, into which tidewater flowed from the bay. If one looked very closely, one could discern fish lice and river crabs crawling about under the projecting windows and red lanterns. Matahachi did look closely and ended up slightly unsettled, for they reminded him of deadly scorpions.

The district was peopled to a large extent by women with thickly powdered faces. Among them a pretty face was to be seen now and then, but there were many others who seemed to be more than forty, women stalking the streets with sad eyes, heads wrapped in cloth to fend off the cold, teeth blackened, but trying wanly to stir the hearts of the men who gathered here.

"There sure are lots of them," said Matahachi with a sigh.

"I told you so," replied Yasoma, who was at pains to make excuses for the women. "And they're better than the next teahouse waitress or singing girl you might take up with. People tend to be put off by the idea of selling sex, but if you spend a winter's night with one of them and talk with her about her family and so on, you're likely to find she's just like any other woman. And not really to blame for having become a whore.

"Some were once concubines of the shōgun, and there are lots whose fathers were once retainers of some daimyō who have since lost power. It was the same centuries ago when the Taira fell to the Minamoto. You'll find, my friend, that in the gutters of this floating world, much of the trash consists of fallen flowers."

They went into a house, and Matahachi left everything to Yasoma, who seemed to be quite experienced. He knew how to order the sake, how to deal with the girls; he was flawless. Matahachi found the experience quite entertaining.

They spent the night, and even at noon on the next day, Yasoma showed no sign of tiring. Matahachi felt recompensed to some extent for all those times he had been pushed off into a back room at the Yomogi, but he was beginning to run down.

Finally, admitting he'd had enough, he said, "I don't want any more to drink. Let's go."

Yasoma did not budge. "Stay with me until evening," he said.

"What happens then?"

"I have an appointment to see Susukida Kanesuke. It's too early to go to his house now, and anyway I won't be able to discuss your situation until I have a better idea of what you want."

"I guess I shouldn't ask for too large an allowance at first."

"There's no point in selling yourself cheap. A samurai of your caliber should be able to command any figure he names. If you say you'll settle for any old position, you'll be demeaning yourself. Why don't I tell him you want an allowance of twenty-five hundred bushels? A samurai with self-confidence is always better paid and treated. You shouldn't give the impression you'd be satisfied with just anything."

As evening approached, the streets in this area, lying as

they did in the immense shadow of Osaka Castle, darkened early. Having left the brothel, Matahachi and Yasoma made their way through the town to one of the more exclusive samurai residential areas. They stood with their backs to the moat, the cold wind driving away the effects of the sake they'd been pouring into themselves all day.

"That's Susukida's house there," said Yasoma.

"The one with the bracketed roof over the gate?"

"No, the corner house next to it."

"Hmm. Big, isn't it?"

"Kanesuke's made a name for himself. Until he was thirty or so, nobody had ever heard of him, but now . . ."

Matahachi pretended to pay no attention to what Yasoma was saying. Not that he did not believe it; on the contrary, he had come to trust Yasoma so thoroughly that he no longer questioned what the man said. He felt, however, that he should remain nonchalant. As he gazed at the mansions of the daimyō, which ringed the great castle, his still youthful ambition told him, "I'll live in a place like that too—one of these days."

"Now," said Yasoma, "I'll see Kanesuke and talk him into hiring you. But before that, what about the money?"

"Oh, sure," said Matahachi, aware that a bribe was in order. Taking the money pouch from his breast, he realized that it had shrunk to about a third of its original bulk. Pouring it all out in his hand, he said, "This is all I have. Is it enough?"

"Oh, sure, quite enough."

"You'll want to wrap it up in something, won't you?"

"No, no. Kanesuke's not the only man around here who takes a fee for finding somebody a position. They all do it, and very openly. There's nothing to be embarrassed about."

Matahachi kept back a little of the cash, but after handing over the rest began to feel uneasy. When Yasoma walked away, he followed for a few steps. "Do the best you can," he implored.

"Don't worry. If it looks as though he's going to be difficult, all I have to do is keep the money and return it to you. He's not the only influential man in Osaka. I could just as easily ask help from Ōno or Gotō. I've got lots of contacts.''

"When will I get an answer?"

"Let's see. You could wait for me, but you wouldn't want to stand here in this wind, would you? Anyway, people might suspect you were up to no good. Let's meet again tomorrow."

"Where?"

"Come to that vacant lot where they're holding side-shows."

"All right."

"The surest way would be for you to wait at that sake vendor's where we first met."

After they settled on the time, Yasoma waved his hand and walked grandly through the gate to the mansion, swinging his shoulders and showing not the slightest hesitation. Matahachi, duly impressed, felt Yasoma must indeed have known Kanesuke since his less prosperous days. Confidence swept over him, and that night he dreamed pleasant dreams of his future.

At the appointed time, Matahachi was walking through the melting frost on the open lot. As on the previous day, the wind was cold, and there were a lot of people about. He waited until sundown but saw no sign of Akakabe Yasoma.

The day after that, Matahachi went again. "Something must have detained him," he thought charitably, as he sat staring at the faces of the passing crowd. "He'll show up today." But again the sun set without Yasoma's appearing.

On the third day, Matahachi said to the sake vendor, somewhat timidly, "I'm here again."

"Are you waiting for someone?"

"Yes, I'm supposed to meet a man named Akakabe Yasoma. I met him here the other day." Matahachi went on to explain the situation in detail.

"That scoundrel?" gasped the sake vendor. "Do you mean he told you he'd find you a good position and then stole your money?"

"He didn't steal it. I gave him some money to give to a man named Susukida Kanesuke. I'm waiting here to find out what happened."

"You poor man! You can wait a hundred years, but I daresay you won't see him again."

"Wh-what? Why do you say that?"

"Why, he's a notorious crook! This area's full of parasites like him. If they see anybody who looks a little innocent, they pounce on him. I thought of warning you, but I didn't want to interfere. I thought you'd know from the way he looked and acted what sort of character he was. Now you've gone and lost your money. Too bad!"

The man was all sympathy. He tried to assure Matahachi that it was no disgrace to be taken in by the thieves operating here. But it wasn't embarrassment that troubled Matahachi; it was finding his money gone, and with it his high hopes, that made his blood boil. He stared helplessly at the crowd moving about them.

"I doubt it'll do any good," said the sake vendor, "but you might try asking over there at the magician's stall. The local vermin often gather behind there to gamble. If Yasoma came by some money, he may be trying to build it into something bigger."

"Thanks," said Matahachi, jumping up excitedly. "Which is the magician's stall?"

The enclosure to which the man pointed was surrounded by a fence of pointed bamboo stakes. Out in front, barkers were drumming up trade, and flags suspended near the wooden gate announced the names of several famous sleight-of-hand artists. From within the curtains and strips of straw matting lining the fence came the sound of strange music, mingled with the loud, rapid patter of the performers and the applause of the audience.

Going around to the rear, Matahachi found another gate. When he glanced in, a lookout asked, "You here to gamble?"

He nodded and the man let him in. He found himself in a space surrounded by tenting but open to the sky. About twenty men, all unsavory types, sat in a circle playing a game. All eyes turned toward Matahachi and one man silently made room for him to sit down.

"Is Akakabe Yasoma here?" Matahachi asked.

"Yasoma?" repeated one gambler in a puzzled tone. "Come to think of it, he hasn't been around lately. Why?"

"Do you think he'll come later?"

"How should I know? Sit down and play."

"I didn't come to play."

"What're you doing here if you don't want to play?"

"I'm looking for Yasoma. Sorry to bother you."

"Well, why don't you go look somewhere else!"

"I said I'm sorry," said Matahachi, exiting hastily.

"Hold on there!" commanded one of the gamblers, getting up and following him. "You can't get away with just saying you're sorry. Even if you don't play, you'll pay for your seat!"

"I don't have any money."

"No money! I see. Just waiting for a chance to swipe some cash, huh? Damned thief, that's what you are."

"I'm no thief! You can't call me that!" Matahachi pushed the hilt of his sword forward, but this merely amused the gambler.

"Idiot!" he barked. "If threats from the likes of you scared me, I wouldn't be able to stay alive in Osaka for one day. Use your sword, if you dare!"

"I warn you, I mean it!"

"Oh, you do, do you?"

"Do you know who I am?"

"Why should I?"

"I'm Sasaki Kojirō, successor of Toda Seigen of Jōkyōji Village in Echizen. He created the Tomita Style," Matahachi declared proudly, thinking this pronouncement alone would put the man to flight. It didn't. The gambler spat and turned back into the enclosure.

"Hey, come on, all of you! This guy's just called himself some fancy name; seems to want to pull his sword on us. Let's have a look at his swordsmanship. It ought to be fun."

Matahachi, seeing that the man was off guard, suddenly drew his sword and sliced across his backside.

The man jumped straight up in the air. "You son of a bitch!" he screamed.

Matahachi dived into the crowd. By sneaking from one cluster of people to the next, he managed to stay hidden, but every face he saw looked like one of the gamblers. Deciding he couldn't hide that way forever, he looked around for more substantial shelter.

Directly in front of him, draped on a bamboo fence, was a curtain with a large tiger painted on it. There was also a banner on the gate bearing a design of a forked spear and a snake-eye crest, and a barker standing on an empty box, shouting hoarsely, "See the tiger! Come in and see the tiger! Take a trip of a thousand miles! This enormous tiger, my friends, was captured personally by the great general Katō Kiyomasa in Korea. Don't miss the tiger!" His spiel was frenetic and rhythmical.

Matahachi threw down a coin and darted through the entrance. Feeling relatively safe, he looked around for the beast. At the far end of the tent a large tiger skin lay stretched out like laundry drying on a wooden panel. The spectators were staring at it with great curiosity, seemingly unperturbed by the fact that the creature was neither whole nor alive.

"So that's what a tiger looks like," said one man.

"Big, isn't it?" marveled another.

Matahachi stood a little to one side of the tiger skin, until suddenly he spotted an old man and woman, and his ears perked up in disbelief as he listened to their voices.

"Uncle Gon," said the woman, "that tiger there is dead, isn't it?"

The old samurai, stretching his hand over the bamboo railing and feeling the skin, replied gravely, "Of course it's dead. This is only the hide."

"But that man outside was talking as though it was alive."

"Well, maybe that's what they mean by a fast talker," he said with a little laugh.

Osugi didn't take it so lightly. Pursing her lips, she protested, "Don't be silly! If it's not real, the sign outside should say so. If all I was going to see was a tiger's skin, I'd just as soon see a picture. Let's go and get our money back."

"Don't make a fuss, Granny. People will laugh at you."

"That's all right. I'm not too proud. If you don't want

to go, I'll go myself." As she started pushing her way back through the spectators, Matahachi ducked, but too late. Uncle Gon had already seen him.

"Hey, there, Matahachi! Is that you?" he shouted.

Osugi, whose eyes were none too good, stammered, "Wh-what's that you said, Uncle Gon?"

"Didn't you see? Matahachi was standing there, just behind you."

"Impossible!"

"He was there, but he ran away."

"Where? Which way?"

The two scampered out the wooden gate into the crowd, already veiled in the hues of evening. Matahachi kept bumping into people but disentangled himself and ran on.

"Wait, son, wait!" cried Osugi.

Matahachi glanced behind him and saw his mother chasing him like a madwoman. Uncle Gon, too, was waving his hands frantically.

"Matahachi!" he cried. "Why are you running away? What's wrong with you? Matahachi! Matahachi!"

Seeing she was not going to be able to catch him, Osugi stuck her wrinkled neck forward and, at the top of her lungs, screamed, "Stop, thief! Robber! Catch him!"

Immediately a throng of bystanders took up the chase, and those in the forefront soon fell upon Matahachi with bamboo poles.

"Keep him there!"

"The scoundrel!"

"Give him a good beating!"

The mob had Matahachi cornered, and some even spat on him. Arriving with Uncle Gon, Osugi quickly took in the scene and turned furiously on Matahachi's attackers. Pushing them away, she seized the hilt of her short sword and bared her teeth.

"What are you doing?" she cried. "Why are you attacking this man?"

"He's a thief!"

"He is not! He's my son."

"Your son?"

"Yes, he's my son, the son of a samurai, and you have

no business beating him. You're nothing but common towns-people. If you touch him again I'll . . . I'll take you all on!"

"Are you joking? Who shouted 'thief' a minute ago?"

"That was me, all right, I don't deny it. I'm a devoted mother, and I thought if I cried 'thief,' my son would stop running. But who asked you stupid oafs to hit him? It's outrageous!"

Startled by her volte-face, yet admiring her mettle, the crowd slowly dispersed. Osugi seized her wayward son by the collar and dragged him to the grounds of a nearby shrine.

After standing and looking on from the shrine gate for a few minutes, Uncle Gon came forward and said, "Granny, you don't have to treat Matahachi like that. He's not a child." He tried to pull her hand away from Matahachi's collar, but the old woman elbowed him roughly out of the way.

"You stay out of this! He's my son, and I'll punish him as I see fit, with no help from you. Just keep quiet and mind your own business! . . . Matahachi, you ungrateful . . . I'll show you!"

It is said that the older people grow, the simpler and more direct they become, and watching Osugi, one could not help but agree. At a time when other mothers might have been weeping for joy, Osugi was seething with rage.

She forced Matahachi to the ground and beat his head against it.

"The very idea! Running away from your own mother! You weren't born from the fork of a tree, you lout—you're my son!" She began spanking him as though he were still a child. "I didn't think you could possibly be alive, and here you are loafing around Osaka! It's shameful! You brazen, good-for-nothing . . . Why didn't you come home and pay the proper respects to your ancestors? Why didn't you so much as show your face just once to your old mother? Didn't you know all your relatives were worried sick about you?"

"Please, Mama," begged Matahachi, crying like a baby. "Forgive me. Please forgive me! I'm sorry. I know what I did was wrong. It was because I knew I'd failed you that I couldn't go home. I didn't really mean to run away from you. I was so surprised to see you, I started running without thinking. I was so ashamed of the way I'd been living, I couldn't face you and Uncle Gon." He covered his face with his hands.

Osugi's nose crinkled, and she, too, started to bawl, but almost immediately she stopped herself. Too proud to show weakness, she renewed her attack, saying sarcastically, "If you're so ashamed of yourself and feel you've disgraced your ancestors, then you really must have been up to no good all this time."

Uncle Gon, unable to restrain himself, pleaded, "That's enough. If you keep on like that, it'll surely twist his nature."

"I told you to keep your advice to yourself. You're a man; you shouldn't be so soft. As his mother, I have to be just as stern as his father would be if he were still alive. I'll do the punishing, and I'm not finished yet! . . . Matahachi! Sit up straight! Look me in the face."

She sat down formally on the ground and pointed to the place where he was to sit.

"Yes, Mama," he said obediently, lifting his dirt-stained shoulders and getting into a kneeling position. He was afraid of his mother. She could on occasion be an indulgent parent, but her readiness to raise the subject of his duty to his ancestors made him uncomfortable.

"I absolutely forbid you to hide anything from me," said Osugi. "Now, what exactly have you been doing since you ran off to Sekigahara? Start explaining, and don't stop till I've heard all I want to hear."

"Don't worry, I won't hold anything back," he began, having lost the desire to fight. True to his word, he blurted out the whole story in detail: about escaping from Sekigahara, hiding at Ibuki, becoming involved with Okō, living off her—though hating it—for several years. And how he now sincerely regretted what he'd done. It was a relief, like throwing up bile from his stomach, and he felt much better after he'd confessed.

"Hmm . . ." mumbled Uncle Gon from time to time.

Osugi clicked her tongue, saying, "I'm shocked at your conduct. And what are you doing now? You seem to be able to dress well. Have you found a position that pays adequately?"

"Yes," said Matahachi. The answer slipped out without forethought, and he hastened to correct himself. "I mean, no, I don't have a position."

"Then where do you get money to live on?"

"My sword—I teach swordsmanship." There was the ring of truth in the way he said this, and it had the desired effect.

"Is that so?" said Osugi with obvious interest. For the first time, a glimmer of good humor appeared in her face. "Swordsmanship, is it? Well, it doesn't really surprise me that a son of mine would find time to polish his swordsmanship—even leading the kind of life you were. Hear that, Uncle Gon? He is my son, after all."

Uncle Gon nodded enthusiastically, grateful to see the old woman's spirits rise. "We might have known," he said. "That shows he does have the blood of his Hon'iden ancestors in his veins. So what if he went astray for a time? It's clear he's got the right spirit!"

"Matahachi," said Osugi.

"Yes, Mama."

"Here in this area, who did you study swordsmanship under?"

"Kanemaki Jisai."

"Oh? Why, he's famous." Osugi had a happy expression on her face. Matahachi, eager to please her even more, brought out the certificate and unrolled it, taking care to cover Sasaki's name with his thumb.

"Look at this," he said.

"Let me see," said Osugi. She reached for the scroll, but Matahachi kept a firm grip on it.

"See, Mama, you don't have to worry about me."

She nodded. "Yes, indeed, this is fine. Uncle Gon, look at this. Isn't it splendid? I always thought, even when Matahachi was a baby, that he was smarter and more capable than Takezō and the other boys." She was so overjoyed she began spitting as she spoke.

At just this moment, Matahachi's hand slipped, and the name on the scroll became visible.

106

"Wait a minute," said Osugi. "Why does it say 'Sasaki Kojirō'?"

"Oh, that? Why, uh, that's my nom de guerre."

"Nom de guerre? Why do you need that? Isn't Hon'iden Matahachi good enough for you?"

"Yes, fine!" replied Matahachi, thinking fast. "But when I thought it over, I decided not to use my own name. With my shameful past, I was afraid of disgracing our ancestors."

"I see. That was good thinking, I suppose. Well, I don't imagine you know anything about what's gone on in the village, so I'll tell you. Now pay attention; it's important."

Osugi launched into a spirited account of the incident that had occurred in Miyamoto, choosing her words in a way calculated to spur Matahachi to action. She explained how the Hon'iden family had been insulted, how she and Uncle Gon had been searching for years for Otsū and Takezō. Although she tried not to get emotional, she did get carried away with her story; her eyes moistened and her voice thickened.

Matahachi, listening with bowed head, was struck by the vividness of her narrative. At times like this, he found it easy to be a good and obedient son, but whereas his mother's main concern was family honor and the samurai spirit, he was most deeply moved by something else: if what she was saying was true, Otsū didn't love him anymore. This was the first time he had actually heard this. "Is that really true?" he asked.

Osugi, seeing his face change color, drew the mistaken conclusion that her lecture on honor and spirit was taking effect. "If you think I'm lying," she said, "ask Uncle Gon. That trollop abandoned you and ran off with Takezō. To put it another way, you could say Takezō, knowing you wouldn't be back for some time, lured Otsū into going away with him. Isn't that right, Uncle Gon?"

"Yes. When Takezō was tied up in the tree, he got Otsū to help him escape, and the two made off together. Everybody said there must have been something going on between them."

This brought out the worst in Matahachi and inspired a new revulsion against his boyhood friend.

Sensing this, his mother fanned the spark. "Do you see now, Matahachi! Do you understand why Uncle Gon and I left the village? We're going to have our revenge on those two. Unless I kill them, I can't ever show my face in the village again or stand before the memorial tablets of our ancestors."

"I understand."

"And do you see that unless we avenge ourselves, you can't return to Miyamoto either?"

"I won't go back. I'll never go back."

"That's not the point. You've got to kill those two. They're our mortal enemies."

"Yeah, I guess so."

"You don't sound very enthusiastic. What's the matter? Don't you think you're strong enough to kill Takezō?"

"Of course I am," he protested.

Uncle Gon spoke up. "Don't worry, Matahachi. I'll stick by you."

"And your old mother will too," added Osugi. "Let's take their heads back to the village as souvenirs for the people. Isn't that a good idea, son? If we do, then you can go ahead and find yourself a wife and settle down. You'll vindicate yourself as a samurai and earn a fine reputation as well. There's no better name in the whole Yoshino area than Hon'iden, and you will have proved that to everyone beyond a doubt. Can you do it, Matahachi? Will you do it?"

"Yes, Mama."

"That's a good son. Uncle Gon, don't just stand there, congratulate the boy. He's sworn to take revenge on Takezō and Otsū." Seemingly satisfied at last, she started to rise from the ground with visible difficulty. "Oh, that hurts!" she cried.

"What's the matter?" asked Uncle Gon.

"The ground is freezing. My stomach and hips ache."

"That's not so good. Are you coming down with piles again?"

Matahachi, in a show of filial devotion, said, "Climb on my back, Mama."

"Oh, you want to carry me? Isn't that nice!" Grasping his shoulders, she shed tears of joy. "How many years has it been? Look, Uncle Gon, Matahachi's going to carry me on his back."

As her tears fell on his neck, Matahachi himself felt strangely pleased. "Uncle Gon, where are you staying?" he asked.

"We still have to find an inn, but any will do. Let's go look for one."

"All right." Matahachi bounced his mother lightly on his back as he walked. "Say, Mama, you're light! Very light! Much lighter than a rock!"

7

The Handsome Young Man

Gradually obscured by the wintry noonday mist, the sunlit island of Awaji faded into the distance. The flapping of the great sail in the wind drowned out the sound of the waves. The boat, which plied several times each month between Osaka and Awa Province in Shikoku, was crossing the Inland Sea on its way to Osaka. Although its cargo consisted mostly of paper and indigo dye, a distinctive odor betrayed it was carrying contraband, in the form of tobacco, which the Tokugawa government had forbidden the people to smoke, sniff or chew. There were also passengers on board, mostly merchants, either returning to the city or visiting it for the year-end trading.

"How's it going? Making lots of money, I bet."

"Not at all! Everybody says things are booming in Sakai, but you couldn't prove it by me."

"I hear there's a shortage of workmen there. Heard they need gunsmiths."

Conversation in another group went along similar lines.

"I supply battle equipment myself—flagstaffs, armor, that sort of thing. I'm certainly not making as much as I used to, though."

"Is that so?"

"Yes, I guess the samurai are learning how to add."

"Ha, ha!"

"It used to be that when the freebooters brought in their loot, you could redye or repaint things and sell them

111

right back to the armies. Then after the next battle, the stuff would come back and you could fix it up and sell it again.''

One man was gazing out over the ocean and extolling the riches of the countries beyond it. ''You can't make money at home anymore. If you want real profits, you have to do what Naya 'Luzon' Sukezaemon or Chaya Sukejirō did. Go into foreign trade. It's risky, but if you're lucky, it can really pay off.''

''Well,'' said another man, ''even if things aren't so good for us these days, from the samurai's viewpoint we're doing very well. Most of them don't even know what good food tastes like. We talk about the luxuries the daimyō enjoy, but sooner or later they have to put on their leather and steel and go out and get killed. I feel sorry for them; they're so busy thinking about their honor and the warrior's code they can't ever sit back and enjoy life.''

''Isn't that the truth? We complain about bad times and all, but the only thing to be today is a merchant.''

''You're right. At least we can do what we want.''

''All we really have to do is make a show of bowing down before the samurai, and a little money makes up for a lot of that.''

''If you're going to live in this world, might as well have a good time.''

''That's the way I see it. Sometimes I feel like asking the samurai what they're getting out of life.''

The woolen carpet this group had spread for themselves to sit on was imported—evidence that they were better off than other elements of the population. After Hideyoshi's death, the luxuries of the Momoyama period had passed largely into the hands of merchants, rather than samurai, and these days the richer townspeople were the ones with elegant sake-serving sets and beautiful, expensive travel equipment. Even a small businessman was normally better off than a samurai with an allowance of five thousand bushels of rice per year, which was considered a princely income by most samurai.

''Never much to do on these trips, is there?''

''No. Why don't we have a little card game to pass the time.''

"Why not?"

A curtain was hung, mistresses and underlings brought sake, and the man began playing *umsummo*, a game recently introduced by Portuguese traders, for unbelievable stakes. The gold on the table could have saved whole villages from famine, but the players tossed it about like gravel.

Among the passengers were several people the rich merchants might well have questioned as to what they were getting out of life—a wandering priest, some rōnin, a Confucian scholar, a few professional warriors. Most of them, after witnessing the beginning of the ostentatious card game, sat down beside their baggage and stared disapprovingly at the sea.

One young man was holding something round and furry in his lap, telling it from time to time to "Sit still!"

"What a nice little monkey you have. Is it trained?" asked another passenger.

"Yes."

"You've had him for some time, then?"

"No, I found him not long ago in the mountains between Tosa and Awa."

"Oh, you caught him yourself?"

"Yes, but the older monkeys almost scratched me to pieces before I got away."

As he talked, the young man concentrated intently on picking fleas off the animal. Even without the monkey, he would have attracted attention, for both his kimono and the short red cloak he wore over it were decidedly fancy. His front hair wasn't shaved, and his topknot was tied with an unusual purple band. His clothing suggested he was still a boy, but these days it wasn't as easy as it used to be to tell a person's age from his apparel. With the rise of Hideyoshi, clothing in general had become more colorful. It was not unknown for men of twenty-five or so to continue to dress like boys of fifteen or sixteen and leave their forelocks uncut.

His skin glowed with youth, his lips were a healthy red, and his eyes were bright. On the other hand, he was solidly built, and there was a certain adult severity about his thick eyebrows and the upward curve at the corners of his eyes.

"Why do you keep squirming?" he said impatiently,

rapping the monkey sharply on the head. The innocence with which he was picking off the fleas added to the impression of youthfulness.

His social status was also difficult to ascertain. Since he was traveling, he wore the same straw sandals and leather socks everyone else wore. So there was no clue there, and he seemed perfectly at home among the wandering priest, the puppeteer, the ragged samurai and the unwashed peasants on board. He could easily be taken for a rōnin, yet there was something that hinted at a higher status, namely the weapon slung slantwise across his back on a leather strap. It was a long, straight battle sword, large and splendidly made. Nearly everyone who spoke to the youth remarked on its fineness.

Gion Tōji, standing some distance away, was impressed by the weapon. Yawning and thinking that not even in Kyoto were swords of such high quality often seen, he grew curious as to its owner's background.

Tōji was bored. His trip, which had lasted fourteen days, had been vexing, tiring and fruitless, and he longed to be once again among people he knew. "I wonder if the runner arrived in time," he mused. "If he did, she'll certainly be at the dock in Osaka to meet me." He tried, by conjuring up Okō's face, to alleviate his boredom.

The reason behind his trip was the shaky financial condition of the House of Yoshioka, brought on by Seijūrō's having lived beyond his means. The family was no longer wealthy. The house on Shijō Avenue was mortgaged and in danger of being seized by merchant creditors. Aggravating the situation were countless other year-end obligations; selling every single family possession would not produce enough funds to meet the bills that had already piled up. Faced with this, Seijūrō's only comment had been, "How did this happen?"

Tōji, feeling responsible for having encouraged the Young Master's extravagance, had said that the matter should be left up to him. He promised that he would settle things somehow.

After racking his brains, he'd come up with the idea of building a new and bigger school on the vacant lot next to the Nishinotōin, where a much larger number of students could be accommodated. According to his reasoning, this was no time to be exclusive. With all sorts of people around wanting to learn the martial arts and the daimyō crying for trained warriors, it would be in the interests of everyone to have a bigger school and turn out a great number of trained swordsmen. The more he thought about it, the more he deluded himself into thinking it was the school's sacred duty to teach Kempō's style to as many men as possible.

Seijūrō wrote a circular to that effect, and thus armed, Tōji set out to solicit contributions from former students in western Honshu, Kyushu and Shikoku. There were many men in various feudal domains who had studied under Kempō, and most of those still alive were now samurai of enviable status. As it turned out, however, for all the earnestness of Tōji's pleas, not many were ready to make substantial donations or subscribe on such short notice. With discouraging frequency, the answer had been, "I'll write you about it later," "We'll see about it the next time I'm in Kyoto," or something equally evasive. The contributions Tōji was returning with amounted to but a fraction of what he'd anticipated.

The endangered household was not, strictly speaking, Tōji's own, and the face that came to mind now was not Seijūrō's but Okō's. But even hers could divert him only superficially, and soon he became fidgety again. He envied the young man picking the fleas off his monkey. He had something to do to kill time. Tōji walked over and tried to strike up a conversation.

"Hello, there, young fellow. Going to Osaka?"

Without actually raising his head, the young man lifted his eyes a bit and said, "Yes."

"Does your family live there?"

"No."

"Then you must be from Awa."

"No, not there either." This was said with a certain finality.

Tōji lapsed into silence for a time before he made another try. "That's quite a sword you have there," he said.

Seemingly happy to have the weapon praised, the young

man rearranged himself to face Tōji and replied genially, "Yes, it's been in my family a long time. It's a battle sword, but I plan to get a good swordsmith in Osaka to remount it, so I can draw it from my side."

"It's too long for that, isn't it?"

"Oh, I don't know. It's only three feet."

"That's pretty long."

Smiling, the youth replied confidently, "Anybody should be able to handle a sword that long."

"Oh, it could be used if it was three feet long, or even four feet," said Tōji reproachfully. "But only an expert could handle it with ease. I see a lot of fellows swaggering around with huge swords these days. They look impressive, but when the going gets rough, they turn and run. What style did you study?" In matters pertaining to swordsmanship, Tōji could not conceal a feeling of superiority over this mere boy.

The young man flashed a questioning look at Tōji's smug face and replied, "The Tomita Style."

"The Tomita Style is for use with a shorter sword than that," said Tōji authoritatively.

"The fact that I learned the Tomita Style doesn't mean I have to use a shorter sword. I don't like to be imitative. My teacher used a shorter sword, so I decided to use a long one. That got me thrown out of the school."

"You young people do seem to take pride in being rebellious. What happened then?"

"I left Jōkyōji Village in Echizen and went to Kanemaki Jisai. He'd also discarded the Tomita Style, then developed the Chūjō Style. He sympathized with me, took me in as a disciple, and after I'd studied under him four years, he said I was ready to go out on my own."

"These country teachers are all quick to pass out certificates."

"Oh, not Jisai. He wasn't like that. In fact, the only other person he had ever given his certificate to was Itō Yagorō Ittōsai. After I made up my mind to be the second man to get formally certified, I worked at it very hard. Before I was through, though, I was suddenly called home because my mother was dying."

The Handsome Young Man

"Where's your home?"

"Iwakuni in Suō Province. After I went home, I practiced every day in the neighborhood of Kintai Bridge, cutting down swallows on the wing and slicing willow branches. That way I developed some techniques of my own. Before my mother died, she gave me this sword and told me to take good care of it, because it was made by Nagamitsu."

"Nagamitsu? You don't say!"

"It doesn't bear his signature on the tang, but it's always been thought to be his work. Where I come from, it's a well-known sword; people call it the Drying Pole." Though reticent earlier, on subjects he liked he would talk at great length, even volunteer information. Once started, he rattled on, paying little attention to his listener's reaction. From this, as well as from his account of his earlier experiences, it appeared that he was of stronger character than might have been inferred from his taste in clothes.

At one point, the youth stopped talking for a moment. His eyes grew cloudy and pensive. "While I was in Suō," he murmured, "Jisai took sick. When I heard about it from Kusanagi Tenki, I actually broke down and cried. Tenki was at the school long before I was and was still there when the master was on his sickbed. Tenki was his nephew, but Jisai didn't even consider giving him a certificate. Instead he told him he'd like to give me a certificate, along with his book of secret methods. He not only wanted me to have them but had hoped to see me and give them to me personally." The young man's eyes moistened with the recollection.

Tōji had not the slightest whit of empathy with this handsome, emotional youth, but talking to him was better than being alone and bored. "I see," he said, feigning great interest. "And he died while you were away?"

"I wish I could have gone to him as soon as I heard of his illness, but he was in Kōzuke, hundreds of miles from Suō. And then my mother finally died about the same time, so it was impossible for me to be with him at the end."

Clouds hid the sun, giving the whole sky a grayish cast. The ship began to roll, and foam blew in over the gunwales.

The young man continued his sentimental tale, the gist of which was that he had closed up the family residence in

Suō and, in an exchange of letters, had arranged to meet his friend Tenki on the spring equinox. It was unlikely that Jisai, who had no close kin, had left much property, but he had entrusted Tenki with some money for the young man, along with the certificate and the book of secrets. Until they met on the appointed day at Mount Hōraiji in Mikawa Province, halfway between Kōzuke and Awa, Tenki was supposedly traveling around studying. The young man himself planned to spend the time in Kyoto, studying and doing some sightseeing.

Having finished his story, he turned to Tōji and asked, "Are you from Osaka?"

"No, I'm from Kyoto."

For a while, they were both silent, distracted by the noise of the waves and the sail.

"Then you plan to try to make your way in the world through the martial arts?" said Tōji. While the remark was innocent enough in itself, the look on Tōji's face revealed condescension bordering on contempt. He had long since had his fill of conceited young swordsmen who went around bragging about their certificates and their books of secrets. It was his considered opinion that there could not possibly be all that many expert swordsmen just wandering around. Had not he himself been in the Yoshioka School for nearly twenty years, and was he not still only a disciple, although a highly privileged one?

The young man shifted his position and looked intently at the gray water. "Kyoto?" he muttered, then turned again to Tōji and said, "I'm told there's a man there named Yoshioka Seijūrō, the eldest son of Yoshioka Kempō. Is he still active?"

Tōji was in the mood to do some teasing.

"Yes," he replied simply. "The Yoshioka School seems to be flourishing. Have you visited the place?"

"No, but when I get to Kyoto, I'd like to have a match with this Seijūrō and see how good he is."

Tōji coughed to suppress a laugh. He was fast growing to detest the young man's brash self-confidence. Of course, he had no way of knowing Tōji's position in the school, but if he were to find out, he would no doubt regret what he had just said. With a twisted face and a contemptuous tone, Tōji asked, "And I suppose you think you'd come away unscathed?"

"Why not?" the truth snapped back. Now he was the one who wanted to laugh, and laugh he did. "Yoshioka has a big house and a lot of prestige, so I imagine Kempō must have been a great swordsman. But they say neither of his sons amounts to much."

"How can you be so sure before you've actually met them?"

"Well, that's what the samurai in the other provinces say. I don't believe everything I hear, but almost everybody seems to think the House of Yoshioka will come to an end with Seijūrō and Denshichirō."

Tōji longed to tell the youth to hold his tongue. He even thought for a moment of making his identity known, but to bring the matter to a head at this point would make him appear the loser. With as much restraint as he could manage, he replied, "The provinces seem to be full of know-it-alls these days, so I wouldn't be surprised if the House of Yoshioka is being underrated. But tell me more about yourself. Didn't you say a while ago you'd figured out a way to kill swallows on the wing?"

"Yes, I said that."

"And you did it with that great long sword?"

"That's right."

"Well, if you can do that, it should be easy for you to cut down one of the sea gulls swooping down over the ship."

The youth did not answer immediately. It had suddenly dawned on him that Tōji was up to no good. Staring at Tōji's grim lips, he said, "I could do it, but I think it would be silly."

"Well," said Tōji magniloquently, "if you're so good that you can disparage the House of Yoshioka without having been there . . ."

"Oh, have I annoyed you?"

"No; not at all," said Tōji. "But no one from Kyoto likes to hear the Yoshioka School talked down."

"Ha! I wasn't telling you what I thought; I was repeating what I'd heard."

"Young man!" said Tōji sternly.

"What?"

"Do you know what is meant by 'half-baked samurai'? For the sake of your future, I warn you! You'll never get anywhere underestimating other people. You brag about cutting down swallows and talk about your certificate in the Chūjō Style, but you'd better remember that not everybody is stupid. And you'd better start taking a good look at whoever you're talking to before you start boasting."

"You think it's only bragging?"

"Yes, I do." Thrusting out his chest, Tōji came closer. "Nobody really minds listening to a young man boast of his accomplishments, but you shouldn't carry it too far."

When the young man said nothing, Tōji continued. "From the beginning I've been listening to you carry on about yourself, and I haven't complained. But the fact of the matter is that I am Gion Tōji, the chief disciple of Yoshioka Seijūrō, and if you make one more disparaging remark about the House of Yoshioka, I'll have it out of your hide!"

By this time they had attracted the attention of the other passengers. Tōji, having revealed his name and exalted status, swaggered off toward the stern of the ship, growling ominously about the insolence of young people these days. The youth followed him in silence, while the passengers gaped from a safe distance.

Tōji was not at all happy about the situation. Okō would be waiting for him when the ship docked, and if he got into a fight now, there was bound to be trouble with the officials later. Looking as unconcerned as possible, he propped his elbows on the rail and gazed intently at the blue-black eddies forming under the rudder.

The youth tapped him on the back lightly. "Sir," he said, in a quiet voice that showed neither anger nor resentment.

Tōji did not answer.

"Sir," the young man repeated.

Unable to keep up his show of nonchalance, Tōji asked, "What do you want?"

"You called me a braggart in front of a lot of strangers, and I have my honor to uphold. I feel constrained to do what you challenged me to do a few minutes ago. I want you to be a witness."

"What did I challenge you to do?"

"You can't have forgotten already. You laughed when I told you I'd cut down swallows on the wing and dared me to try cutting down a sea gull."

"Hmm, I did suggest that, didn't I?"

"If I cut one down, will it convince you I'm not just talking?"

"Well . . . yes, it will."

"All right, I'll do it."

"Fine, splendid!" Tōji laughed sarcastically. "But don't forget, if you undertake this just for pride's sake and fail, you'll *really* be laughed at."

"I'll take that chance."

"I've no intention of stopping you."

"And you will stand by as a witness?"

"Why, I'd be only too glad to!"

The young man took a position on a lead plate in the center of the afterdeck and moved his hand toward his sword. As he did so, he called out Tōji's name. Tōji, staring curiously, asked what he wanted, and the youth, speaking with great seriousness, said, "Please have some sea gulls fly down in front of me. I'm ready to cut down any number of them."

Tōji suddenly recognized the similarity between what was going on and the plot of a certain humorous tale attributed to the priest Ikkyū; the young man had succeeded in making an ass of him. Angrily he shouted, "What sort of nonsense is this? Anyone who could make sea gulls fly in front of him would be able to cut them down."

"The sea stretches out for thousands of miles, and my sword is only three feet long. If the birds won't come near, I can't cut them down."

Advancing a couple of paces, Tōji gloated, "You're just trying to work yourself out of a bad spot. If you can't kill a sea gull on the wing, say you can't, and apologize."

"If I intended to do that, I wouldn't be standing here waiting. If the birds won't come near, then I'll cut something else for you."

"Such as . . . ?"

"Just come another five steps closer. I'll show you."

Tōji came nearer, growling, "What are you up to now?"

"I just want you to let me make use of your head—the head with which you dared me to prove I wasn't just boasting. When you consider the matter, it would be more logical to cut that off than to kill innocent sea gulls."

"Have you lost your mind?" shouted Tōji. His head ducked reflexively, for just at that instant, the young man whipped his sword from its scabbard and used it. The action was so fast that the three-foot sword seemed no larger than a needle.

"Wh-wh-what?" cried Tōji, as he staggered backward and put his hands to his collar. His head was still there, fortunately, and as far as he could tell, he was unharmed.

"Do you understand now?" asked the youth, turning his back and walking off between the piles of baggage.

Tōji was already crimson with embarrassment, when looking down at a sunlit patch of the deck, he saw a peculiar-looking object, something like a little brush. A horrible thought came into his mind, and he put his hand to the top of his head. His topknot was gone! His precious topknot—the pride and joy of any samurai! Horror on his face, he rubbed the top of his head and found that the band tying his hair at the back was undone. The locks it had held together had fanned out over his scalp.

"That bastard!" Unmitigated rage swept through his heart. He knew now, only too well, that the youth had been neither lying nor voicing an empty boast. Young he was, but he was a spectacular swordsman. Tōji was amazed that anyone so young could be so good, but the respect he felt in his mind was one thing, and the choler in his heart something else again.

When he rasied his head and looked toward the bow, he saw that the youth had returned to his previous seat and was searching around on the deck for something. He was obviously off guard, and Tōji sensed that the opportunity for revenge had presented itself. Spitting on the hilt of his sword, he grasped it tightly and sneaked up behind his tormenter. He was not sure his aim was good enough to take off the man's topknot without taking off his head too, but he did not care. Body swollen and red, breathing heavily, he steeled himself to strike.

Just then, a commotion arose among the card-playing merchants.

"What's going on here? There aren't enough cards!"

"Where'd they go?"

"Look over there!"

"I've already looked."

As they were shouting and shaking out their carpet, one of them happened to glance skyward.

"Up there! That monkey has them!"

The other passengers, welcoming still another diversion, all looked up at the simian in question, which was perched at the very top of the thirty-foot mast.

"Ha, ha!" laughed one. "Quite a monkey—stole the cards, he did."

"He's chewing them up."

"No, he's making like he's dealing them."

A single card came floating down. One of the merchants swept it up and said, "He must still have three or four more."

"Somebody get up there and get the cards! We can't play without them."

"Nobody's going to climb up there."

"Why not the captain?"

"I guess he could if he wanted to."

"Let's offer him a little money. Then he'll do it."

The captain heard the proposal, agreed, and took the money, but apparently felt that as the master of the ship, he must first fix responsibility for the incident. Standing on a pile of cargo, he addressed the passengers. "Just who does that monkey belong to? Will the owner please come forward?"

Not a soul answered, but a number of people who knew the monkey belonged to the handsome young man eyed him expectantly. The captain also knew, and his anger rose when the youth did not reply. Raising his voice still higher, he said, "Isn't the owner here? . . . If nobody owns the monkey, I'll take care of him, but I don't want any complaints afterward.''

The monkey's owner was leaning against some luggage, apparently deep in thought. A few passengers began to whisper disapprovingly; the captain looked daggers at the youth. The cardplayers grumbled malevolently, and others began to ask whether the young man was deaf and dumb or just insolent. The youth, however, merely shifted his position a little to the side and acted as though nothing had happened.

The captain spoke again. "It appears that monkeys thrive on sea as well as on land. As you can see, one has wandered in on us. Since it is ownerless, I suppose we can do whatever we wish with it. Passengers, be my witness! As captain, I have appealed to the owner to make himself known, but he hasn't done so. If he later complains that he could not hear me, I ask you to stand by me!''

"We're your witnesses!'' cried the merchants, who by this time were verging on apoplexy.

The captain disappeared down the ladder into the hold. When he reemerged, he was holding a musket with the slow-burning fuse already lit. There was no question in anybody's mind but that he was ready to use it. Faces turned from the captain to the monkey's owner.

The monkey was enjoying himself immensely. High in the air, he was playing with the cards and doing everything he could to annoy the people on deck. Suddenly he bared his teeth, chattered, and ran to the yardarm, but once there he did not seem to know what to do.

The captain raised the musket and took aim. But as one of the merchants pulled at his sleeve and urged him to fire, the owner called out, "Stop, Captain!''

It was now the captain's turn to pretend not to hear. He squeezed the trigger, the passengers bent down with their hands over their ears, and the musket fired with a huge bang. But the shot went high and wide. At the last instant, the young man had pushed the barrel of the gun out of line.

Screaming with rage, the captain caught hold of the young man's chest. He seemed for a time almost to be suspended there, for though he was strongly built, he was short by the side of the handsome youth.

"What's the matter with you?" shouted the young man. "You were about to shoot down an innocent monkey with that toy of yours, weren't you?"

"I was."

"That's not a very nice thing to do, is it?"

"I gave fair warning!"

"And just how did you do that?"

"Don't you have eyes and ears?"

"Shut up! I'm a passenger on this ship. What's more, I'm a samurai. Do you expect me to answer when a mere ship's captain stands up before his customers and bellows as though he were their lord and master?"

"Don't be impertinent! I repeated my warning three times. You must have heard me. Even if you didn't like the way I said it, you could have shown some consideration for the people who were inconvenienced by your monkey."

"What people? Oh, you mean that bunch of tradesmen who've been gambling behind their curtain?"

"Don't talk so big! They paid three times as much fare as the others."

"That doesn't make them anything but what they are— low-class, irresponsible merchants, throwing around their gold where everybody can see it, drinking their sake, and acting as though they owned the ship. I've been watching them, and I don't like them at all. What if the monkey did run away with their cards? I didn't tell him to. He was just imitating what they themselves were doing. I see no need for me to apologize!"

The young man looked fixedly at the rich merchants and directed a loud, sardonic laugh their way.

8

The Seashell of Forgetfulness

It was evening when the ship entered the harbor at Kizu-gawa, where it was met by the all-pervading odor of fish. Reddish lights twinkled onshore, and the waves hummed steadily in the background. Little by little, the distance between the raised voices coming from the ship and those issuing from the shore closed up. With a white splash, the anchor was dropped; ropes were cast and the gangplank was moved into place.

A flurry of excited cries filled the air.

"Is the son of the priest at the Sumiyoshi Shrine aboard?"

"Is there a runner around?"

"Master! Here we are, over here!"

Like a wave, paper lanterns bearing the names of various inns rolled across the dock toward the ship, as the touts vied with each other for business.

"Anyone for the Kashiwaya Inn?"

The young man with the monkey on his shoulder pushed his way through the crowd.

"Come to our place, sir—no charge for the monkey."

"We're right in front of Sumiyoshi Shrine. It's a great place for pilgrims. You can have a beautiful room with a beautiful view!"

No one had come to meet the youth. He walked straight away from the dock, paying no attention to the touts or anyone else.

"Who does he think he is?" growled one passenger. "Just because he knows a little swordsmanship!"

"If I weren't just a townsman, he wouldn't have gotten away without a fight."

"Oh, calm down! Let the warriors think they're better than anybody else. As long as they're strutting around like kings, they're happy. The thing for us townsmen to do is to let them have the flowers while we take the fruit. Why get excited over today's little incident?"

While talking on in this fashion, the merchants saw to it that their mountains of baggage were properly gathered together, then disembarked, to be met by swarms of people and lanterns and vehicles. There was not one among them who was not immediately surrounded by several solicitous women.

The last person off the ship was Gion Tōji, on whose face there was an expression of extreme discomfort. Never in all his life had he spent a more unpleasant day. His head was decently covered with a kerchief to conceal the mortifying loss of his topknot, but the cloth did nothing to hide his downcast eyebrows and sullen lips.

"Tōji! Here I am!" called Okō. Though her head was also covered with a kerchief, her face had been exposed to the cold wind while she was waiting, and her wrinkles showed through the white powder that was meant to hide them.

"Okō! So you came after all."

"Isn't that what you expected? You sent me a letter telling me to meet you here, didn't you?"

"Yes, but I thought it might not have reached you in time."

"Is something the matter? You look upset."

"Oh, it's nothing. Just a little seasick. Come on, let's go to Sumiyoshi and find a nice inn."

"Come this way. I have a palanquin waiting."

"Thanks. Did you reserve a room for us?"

"Yes. Everybody's waiting at the inn."

A look of consternation crossed Tōji's face. "*Everybody?* What are you talking about? I thought just the two of us were going to spend a couple of pleasant days here at some quiet place. If there are a lot of people around, I'm not going.''

Refusing the palanquin, he strode angrily on ahead. When Okō tried to explain, he cut her off and called her an idiot. All the rage that had built up inside him on the ship exploded.

"I'll stay somewhere by myself!" he bellowed. "Send the palanquin away! How could you be such a fool? You don't understand me at all." He snatched his sleeve away from her and hurried on.

They were in the fish market by the waterfront; all the shops were closed, and the scales strewn about the street glittered like tiny silver seashells. Since there was virtually no one around to see them, Okō hugged Tōji and attempted to soothe him.

"Let go of me!" he shouted.

"If you go off by yourself, the others will think something's wrong."

"Let them think what they want!"

"Oh, don't talk like that!" she pleaded. Her cool cheek pressed against his. The sweetish odor of her powder and her hair penetrated his being, and gradually his anger and frustration ebbed.

"Please," begged Okō.

"It's just that I'm so disappointed," he said.

"I know, but we'll have other chances to be together."

"But these two or three days with you—I was really looking forward to them."

"I understand that."

"If you understood, why did you drag a lot of other people along? It's because you don't feel about me the way I feel about you!"

"Now you're starting on that again," said Okō reproachfully, staring ahead and looking as if the tears were about to flow. But instead of weeping, she made another attempt to get him to listen to her explanation. When the runner had arrived with Tōji's letter, she had, of course, made plans to come to Osaka alone, but as luck would have it, that very night Seijūrō had come to the Yomogi with six or seven of his students, and Akemi had let it slip out that

Tōji was arriving. In no time at all, the men had decided that they should all accompany Okō to Osaka and that Akemi should come along with them. In the end, the party that checked into the inn in Sumiyoshi numbered ten.

While Tōji had to admit that under the circumstances there was not much Okō could have done, his gloomy mood did not improve. This had clearly not been his day, and he was sure there was worse to come. For one thing, the first question he expected to hear would concern how he had made out on his canvassing campaign, and he hated to have to give them the bad news. What he dreaded far more was the prospect of having to take the kerchief off his head. How could he ever explain the missing topknot? Ultimately he realized there was no way out and resigned himself to his fate.

"Oh, all right," he said, "I'll go with you. Have the palanquin brought here."

"Oh, I'm so happy!" cooed Okō, as she turned back toward the dock.

At the inn, Seijūrō and the others had taken a bath, wrapped themselves up snugly in the cotton-padded kimonos provided by the inn, and settled down to wait for Tōji and Okō's return. When, after a time, they failed to reappear, someone said, "Those two will be here sooner or later. There's no reason to sit here doing nothing."

The natural consequence of this statement was the ordering of sake. At first they drank merely to pass the time, but soon legs began to stretch out comfortably, and the sake cups to pass back and forth more rapidly. It was not long before everybody had more or less forgotten about Tōji and Okō.

"Don't they have any singing girls in Sumiyoshi?"

"Say, that's a good idea! Why don't we call in three or four nice girls?"

Seijūrō looked hesitant until someone suggested that he and Akemi retire to another room, where it would be quieter. The none-too-subtle move to get rid of him brought a wistful smile to his face, but he was nevertheless happy to leave. It would be far more pleasant to be alone with Akemi in a room with a warm *kotatsu* than to be drinking with this crew of ruffians.

As soon as he was out of the room, the party began in earnest, and before long several singing girls of the class known locally as the "pride of Tosamagawa" appeared in the garden outside the room. Their flutes and shamisen were old, of poor quality and battered from use.

"Why are you making so much noise?" one of the women asked saucily. "Did you come here to drink or to have a brawl?"

The man who had appointed himself ringleader called back, "Don't ask foolish questions. Nobody pays money to fight! We called you in so we could drink and have some fun."

"Well," said the girl tactfully, "I'm glad to hear that, but I do wish you'd be a little quieter."

"If that's the way you want it, fine! Let's sing some songs."

In deference to the feminine presence, several hairy shins were retracted under kimono skirts, and a few horizontal bodies became vertical. The music started, spirits rose, and the party gained momentum. It was in full swing when a young maid came in and announced that the man who had come in on the ship from Shikoku had arrived with his companion.

"What'd she say? Somebody coming?"

"Yeah, she said somebody named Tōji's coming."

"Great! Wonderful! Good old Tōji's coming . . . Who's Tōji?"

Tōji's entrance with Okō did not interrupt the proceedings in the least; in fact, they were ignored. Having been led to believe the gathering was all for his sake, Tōji was disgusted.

He called back the maid who had shown them in and asked to be taken to Seijūrō's room. But as they went into the hall, the ringleader, reeking of sake, staggered over and threw his arms around Tōji's neck.

"Hey, Tōji!" he slurred. "Just get back? You must have been having a good time with Okō somewhere while we sat here waiting. Now, that's not the thing to do!"

Tōji tried unsuccessfully to shake him off. The man dragged him struggling into the room. In the process, he stepped on a tray or two, kicked over several sake jars, then fell to the floor, bringing Tōji down with him.

"My kerchief!" gasped Tōji. His hand sped to his head, too late. On his way down, the ringleader had snatched at the kerchief and now had it in his hand. With a collective gasp, all eyes looked straight at the spot where Tōji's topknot should have been.

"What happened to your head?"

"Ha, ha, ha! That's some hairdo!"

"Where did you get it?"

Tōji's face flushed blood red. Grabbing the kerchief and replacing it, he sputtered, "Oh, it's nothing. I had a boil."

To a man, they doubled up with laughter.

"He brought a boil back with him as a souvenir!"

"Cover the vile spot!"

"Don't talk about it. Show us!"

It was obvious from the feeble jokes that nobody believed Tōji, but the party went on, and no one had much to say about the topknot.

The next morning it was a different matter altogether. Ten o'clock found the same group assembled on the beach behind the inn, sober now and engaged in a very serious conference. They sat in a circle, some with shoulders squared, some with arms crossed, but all looking grim.

"Any way you look at it, it's bad."

"The question is, is it true?"

"I heard it with my own ears. Are you calling me a liar?"

"We can't let it pass without doing anything. The honor of the Yoshioka School is at stake. We have to act!"

"Of course, but what do we do?"

"Well, it's still not too late. We'll find the man with the monkey and cut off *his* topknot. We'll show him that it's not just Gion Tōji's pride that's involved. It's a matter that concerns the dignity of the whole Yoshioka School! Any objections?" The drunken ringleader of the night before was now a gallant lieutenant, spurring his men on to battle.

Upon awakening, the men had ordered the bath heated,

so as to wash away their hangovers, and while they were in the bath, a merchant had come in. Not knowing who they were, he told them about what had happened on the ship the day before. He furnished them with a humorous account of the cutting off of the topknot and concluded his tale by saying that "the samurai who had lost his hair claimed to be a leading disciple of the House of Yoshioka in Kyoto. All I can say is that if he really is, the House of Yoshioka must be in worse shape than anyone imagines."

Sobering up fast, the Yoshioka disciples had gone looking for their wayward senior to question him about the incident. They soon discovered he had risen early, spoken a few words with Seijūrō, and departed with Okō for Kyoto right after breakfast. This confirmed the essential accuracy of the story, but rather than pursue the cowardly Tōji, they decided it would make better sense to find the unknown youth with the monkey and vindicate the Yoshioka name.

Having agreed upon a plan at their seaside council of war, they now stood up, brushed the sand off their kimonos and moved into action.

A short distance away, Akemi, bare-legged, had been playing at the edge of the water, picking up seashells one by one, then discarding them almost immediately. Even though it was winter, the sun was shining warmly, and the smell of the sea rose from the froth of the breakers, which stretched out like chains of white roses as far as the eye could see.

Akemi, wide-eyed with curiosity, watched the Yoshioka men as they all ran off in different directions, the tips of their scabbards in the air. When the last of them passed her, she called out to him, "Where are you all going?"

"Oh, it's you!" he said. "Why don't you come search with me? Everybody's been assigned a territory to cover."

"What are you looking for?"

"A young samurai with a long forelock. He's carrying a monkey."

"What did he do?"

"Something that will disgrace the Young Master's name unless we act fast."

He told her what had happened, but failed to raise even a spark of interest.

"You people are always looking for a fight!" she said disapprovingly.

"It's not that we like to fight, but if we let him get away with this, it'll bring shame on the school, the greatest center of the martial arts in the country."

"Oh, what if it does?"

"Are you crazy?"

"You men spend all your time running after the silliest things."

"Huh?" He squinted at her suspiciously. "And what have you been doing out here all this time?"

"Me?" She dropped her eyes to the beautiful sand around her feet and said, "I'm looking for seashells."

"Why look for them? There are millions of them all over the place. It just goes to show you—women waste their time in crazier ways than men."

"I'm looking for a very particular type of shell. It's called the seashell of forgetfulness."

"Oh? And is there really such a shell?"

"Yes, but they say you can only find it here on the shore at Sumiyoshi."

"Well, I'll bet there's no such thing!"

"There is too! If you don't believe it, come with me. I'll show you."

She pulled the reluctant youth over to a row of pine trees and pointed to a stone on which an ancient poem was carved.

> Had I but the time
> I'd find it on the Sumiyoshi shore.
> They say it comes there—
> The shell that brings
> Oblivion to love.

Proudly, Akemi said, "See? What more proof do you need?"

"Aw, that's only a myth, one of those useless lies they tell in poetry."

"But in Sumiyoshi they also have flowers that make you forget, and water too."

"Well, suppose it does exist. What magic will it work for you?"

"It's simple. If you put one in your obi or sleeve, you can forget everything."

The samurai laughed. "You mean you want to be more absentminded than you already are?"

"Yes. I'd like to forget everything. Some things I can't forget, so I'm unhappy in the daytime and lie awake nights. That's why I'm looking for it. Why don't you stay and help me look?"

"This is no time for child's play!" the samurai said scornfully, then suddenly remembering his duty, flew off at full speed.

When she was sad, Akemi often thought her problems would be solved if she could only forget the past and enjoy the present. Right now she was hugging herself and wavering between holding on to the few memories she cherished and wanting to cast them out to sea. If there really were such a thing as a seashell of forgetfulness, she decided, she wouldn't carry it herself, but instead sneak it into Seijūrō's sleeve. She sighed, imagining how lovely life would be if he would just forget all about her.

The very thought of him turned her heart cold. She was tempted to believe he existed for the sole purpose of ruining her youth. When he importuned her with his wheedling protestations of love, she comforted herself by thinking of Musashi. But if Musashi's presence in her heart was at times her salvation, it was also a frequent source of misery, for it made her want to run away to escape into a world of dreams. Yet she hesitated to give herself up entirely to fantasy, knowing it was likely that Musashi had forgotten her completely.

"Oh, if there was some way I could erase his face from my mind!" she thought.

The blue water of the Inland Sea looked suddenly tempting. Staring at it, she grew frightened. How easy it would be to run straight in and disappear.

Her mother had no idea Akemi entertained such desperate thoughts, let alone Seijūrō. All the people around her considered her a very happy creature, a little flippant perhaps, but nonetheless a bud still so far from blossoming that she couldn't possibly accept the love of a man.

To Akemi, her mother and the men who came to the teahouse were something outside her own self. In their presence, she laughed and joked, tinkled her bell and pouted as the occasion seemed to demand, but when she was alone, her sighs were care-filled and sullen.

Her thoughts were interrupted by a servant from the inn. Spotting her by the stone inscription, he ran up and said, "Young lady, where've you been? The Young Master's been calling for you, and he's getting very worried."

Back at the inn, Akemi found Seijūrō all alone, warming his hands under the red quilt covering the *kotatsu*. The room was silent. In the garden a breeze rustled through the withered pines.

"Have you been out in this cold?" he asked.

"What do you mean? I don't think it's cold. It's very sunny on the beach."

"What have you been doing?"

"Looking for seashells."

"You act like a child."

"I *am* a child."

"How old do you think you'll be on your next birthday?"

"It doesn't make any difference. I'm still a child. What's wrong with that?"

"There's a great deal wrong with it. You ought to think about your mother's plans for you."

"My mother? She's not thinking about me. She's convinced she's still young herself."

"Sit down here."

"I don't want to. I'd get too hot. I'm still young, remember?"

"Akemi!" He seized her wrist and pulled her toward him. "There's no one else here today. Your mother had the delicacy to return to Kyoto."

Akemi looked at Seijūrō's burning eyes; her body stiffened. She tried unconsciously to back away, but he held her wrist tightly.

"Why are you trying to run away?" he asked accusingly.

"I'm not trying to run away."

"There's no one here now. It's a perfect opportunity, isn't it, Akemi?"

"For what?"

"Don't be so obstinate! We've been seeing each other for nearly a year. You know how I feel about you. Okō gave her permission long ago. She says you won't give in to me because I don't go about it the right way. So today, let's—"

"Stop! Let go of my arm! Let go, I tell you!" Akemi suddenly bent over and lowered her head in embarrassment.

"You won't have me, whatever happens?"

"Stop! Let go!"

Though her arm had turned red under his grasp, he still refused to release her, and the girl was hardly strong enough to resist the military techniques of the Kyōhachi Style.

Seijūrō was different today from his usual self. He often sought comfort and consolation in sake, but today he had drunk nothing. "Why do you treat me this way, Akemi? Are you trying to humiliate me?"

"I don't want to talk about it! If you don't let me go, I'll scream!"

"Scream away! Nobody'll hear you. The main house is too far away, and anyway, I told them we were not to be disturbed."

"I want to leave."

"I won't let you."

"My body doesn't belong to you!"

"Is that the way you feel? You'd better ask your mother about that! I've certainly paid her enough for it."

"Well, my mother may have sold me, but I haven't sold myself! Certainly not to a man I despise more than death itself!"

"What's that?" shouted Seijūrō, throwing the red quilt over her head.

Akemi screamed for all she was worth.

"Scream, you bitch! Scream all you want! Nobody's coming."

On the shoji the pale sunlight mingled with the restless

shadow of the pines as though nothing had happened. Outside, all was quiet, save for the distant lapping of the waves and the chatter of the birds.

Deep silence followed Akemi's muffled wails. After a time, Seijūrō, his face deathly pale, appeared in the outer corridor, holding his right hand over his scratched and bleeding left hand.

Shortly afterward, the door opened again with a bang, and Akemi emerged. With a cry of surprise, Seijūrō, his hand now wrapped in a towel, moved as though to stop her, but not in time. The half-crazed girl fled with lightning speed.

Seijūrō's face creased worriedly, but he did not pursue her as she crossed the garden and went into another part of the inn. After a moment, a thin, crooked smile appeared on his lips. It was a smile of deep satisfaction.

9

A Hero's Passing

"Uncle Gon!"

"What?"

"Are you tired?"

"Yes, a little."

"I thought so. I'm about walked out myself. But this shrine has splendid buildings, doesn't it? Say, isn't that the orange tree they call the secret tree of Wakamiya Hachiman?"

"Seems to be."

"It's supposed to be the first item in the eighty shiploads of tribute presented by the King of Silla to Empress Jingū when she conquered Korea."

"Look over there in the Stable of the Sacred Horses! Isn't that a fine animal? It'd certainly come in first at the annual horse race in Kamo."

"You mean the white one?"

"Yes. Hmm, what does that signboard say?"

"It says if you boil the beans used in the horse fodder and drink the juice, it'll keep you from crying or gritting your teeth at night. Do you want some?"

Uncle Gon laughed. "Don't be silly!" Turning around, he asked, "What happened to Matahachi?"

"He seems to have wandered off."

"Oh, there he is, resting by the stage for the sacred dances."

The old lady lifted her hand and called to her son. "If

we go over that way, we can see the original Great Torii, but let's go to the High Lantern first.''

Matahachi followed along lazily. Ever since his mother had collared him in Osaka, he'd been with them—walking, walking, walking. His patience was beginning to wear thin. Five or ten days of sightseeing might be all well and good, but he dreaded the thought of accompanying them to take their revenge. He had tried to persuade them that traveling together was a poor way to go about it, that it would be better for him to go and look for Musashi on his own. His mother wouldn't hear of it.

"It'll be New Year's soon," she pointed out. "And I want you to spend it with me. We haven't been together to celebrate the New Year holiday for a long time, and this may be our last chance."

Though Matahachi knew he couldn't refuse her, he had made up his mind to leave them a couple of days after the first of the year. Osugi and Uncle Gon, possibly fearing they hadn't long to live, had become so wrapped up in religion they stopped at every shrine or temple possible, leaving offerings and making long supplications to the gods and Buddhas. They had spent nearly all of the present day at Sumiyoshi Shrine.

Matahachi, bored stiff, was dragging his feet and pouting.

"Can't you walk faster?" Osugi asked in a testy voice.

Matahachi's pace did not change. Fully as annoyed with his mother as she was with him, he grumbled, "You hurry me along and make me wait! Hurry and wait, hurry and wait!"

"What am I to do with a son like you? When people come to a sacred place, it's only proper to stop and pray to the gods. I've never seen you bow before either a god or a Buddha, and mark my words, you'll live to regret it. Besides, if you prayed with us, you wouldn't have to wait so long."

"What a nuisance!" growled Matahachi.

"Who's a nuisance?" cried Osugi indignantly.

For the first two or three days everything had been as sweet as honey between them, but once Matahachi had got used to his mother again, he began to take exception to everything she did and said and to make fun of her every chance he got. When night came and they returned to the inn, she would make him sit down in front of her and give him a sermon, which served to put him in worse humor than before.

"What a pair!" Uncle Gon lamented to himself, trying to figure out a way to soothe the old woman's pique and restore a measure of calmness to his nephew's scowling face. Sensing yet another sermon in the making, he moved to head it off. "Oh," he called cheerily. "I thought I smelled something good! They're selling broiled clams at that tea-house over by the beach. Let's stop in and have some."

Neither mother nor son displayed much enthusiasm, but Uncle Gon managed to steer them to the seaside shop, which was sheltered with thin reed blinds. While the other two got comfortable on a bench outside, he went in and came back with some sake.

Offering a cup to Osugi, he said amiably, "This will cheer Matahachi up a little. Maybe you're being a little hard on him."

Osugi looked away and snapped, "I don't want anything to drink."

Uncle Gon, caught in his own web, offered the cup to Matahachi, who, though still grumpy, proceeded to empty three jars as fast as he could, knowing full well this would make his mother livid. When he asked Uncle Gon for a fourth, Osugi had had all she could take.

"You've had enough!" she scolded. "This isn't a picnic, and we didn't come here to get drunk! And you watch yourself too, Uncle Gon! You're older than Matahachi, and should know better."

Uncle Gon, as mortified as if only he had been drinking, tried to hide his face by rubbing his hands over it. "Yes, you're quite right," he said meekly. He got up and ambled off a few paces.

Then it began in earnest, for Matahachi had struck at the roots of Osugi's violent though brittle sense of maternal love and anxiety, and it was out of the question for her to wait until they returned to the inn. She lashed out furiously at him, not caring whether other people were listening.

Matahachi stared at her with a look of sullen disobedience until she finished.

"All right," he said. "I take it you've made up your mind that I'm an ungrateful lout with no self-respect. Right?"

"Yes! What have you done up till now that shows any pride or self-respect?"

"Well, I'm not as worthless as you seem to think, but then you wouldn't have any way of knowing that."

"Oh, I wouldn't, would I? Well, nobody knows a child better than his parents, and I think the day you were born was a bad day for the House of Hon'iden!"

"You just wait and see! I'm still young. One day when you're dead and buried, you'll be sorry you said that."

"Ha! I wish that were so, but I doubt that would happen in a hundred years. It's so sad, when you think of it."

"Well, if it makes you so terribly sad to have a son like me, there's not much use in my hanging around any longer. I'm leaving!" Steaming with rage, he stood up and walked away in long, determined strides.

Taken by surprise, the old woman tried in a pitifully trembling voice to call him back. Matahachi paid no heed. Uncle Gon, who could have run and tried to stop him, stood looking intently toward the sea, his mind apparently occupied with other thoughts.

Osugi got up, then sat back down again. "Don't try to stop him," she said needlessly to Uncle Gon. "It's no use."

Uncle Gon turned toward her, but instead of answering, said, "That girl out there is acting very funny. Wait here a minute!" Almost before the words were out, he had chucked his hat under the eaves of the shop and headed like an arrow toward the water.

"Idiot!" cried Osugi. "Where are you going? Matahachi's—"

She chased after him, but about twenty yards from the shop, snagged her foot in a clump of seaweed and fell flat on her face. Mumbling angrily, she picked herself up, her face and shoulders covered with sand. When she caught sight of Uncle Gon again, her eyes opened like mirrors.

"You old fool! Where are you going? Have you lost your mind?" she screamed.

So excited that she looked as if she might be mad herself, she ran as fast as she could, following Uncle Gon's footsteps. But she was too late. Uncle Gon was already in up to his knees and pushing out farther.

Enveloped in the white spray, he seemed almost in a trance. Still farther out was a young girl, feverishly making her way toward deep water. When he had first spotted her, she had been standing in the shadow of the pines, looking blankly at the sea; then suddenly she sped across the sand and into the water, her black hair streaming out behind her. The water was now halfway up to her waist, and she was rapidly approaching the point where the bottom fell off sharply.

As he neared her, Uncle Gon called out frantically, but she pressed on. Suddenly, with an odd sound, her body disappeared, leaving a swirl on the surface.

"Crazy child!" cried Uncle Gon. "Are you determined to kill yourself?" Then he himself sank below the surface with a glug.

Osugi was running back and forth along the edge of the water. When she saw the two go down, her screaming turned to strident calls for help.

Waving her hands, running, stumbling, she ordered the people on the beach to the rescue as though they were the cause of the accident. "Save them, you idiots! Hurry, or they'll drown."

Minutes later, some fishermen brought the bodies in and laid them on the sand.

"A love suicide?" asked one.

"Are you joking?" said another, laughing.

Uncle Gon had caught hold of the girl's obi and was still holding it, but neither he nor she was breathing. The girl presented a strange appearance, for though her hair was matted and messy, her powder and lipstick had not washed away, and she looked as if she were alive. Even with her teeth still biting her lower lip, her purple mouth bore the suggestion of a laugh.

"I've seen her before somewhere," somebody said.

"Isn't she the girl who was looking for shells on the beach a while ago?"

"Yes, that's right! She was staying at the inn over there."

From the direction of the inn, four or five men were already approaching, among them Seijūrō, who breathlessly pushed his way through the crowd.

"Akemi!" he cried. His face went pale, but he stood perfectly still.

"Is she a friend of yours?" asked one of the fishermen.

"Y-y-yes."

"You'd better try and get the water out of her fast!"

"Can we save her?"

"Not if you just stand there gaping!"

The fishermen loosened Uncle Gon's grip, laid the bodies side by side, and began slapping them on the back and pressing them in the abdomen. Akemi regained her breathing fairly rapidly, and Seijūrō, eager to escape the stares of the bystanders, had the men from the inn carry her back.

"Uncle Gon! Uncle Gon!" Osugi had her mouth to the old man's ear and was calling to him through her tears. Akemi had come back to life because she was young, but Uncle Gon . . . Not only was he old, but he had had a fair amount of sake in him when he went to the rescue. His breath was stilled forever; no amount of urging on Osugi's part would open his eyes again.

The fishermen, giving up, said, "The old man's gone."

Osugi stopped crying long enough to turn on them as though they were enemies rather than people trying to help. "What do you mean? Why should he die when that young girl was saved?" Her attitude suggested she was ready to attack them physically. She pushed the men aside and said firmly, "I'll bring him back to life myself! I'll show you."

She set to work on Uncle Gon, putting to use every method she could think of. Her determination brought tears to the eyes of the onlookers, a few of whom stayed to help her. Far from being appreciative, however, she ordered them around like hired help—complained that they were not pressing the right way, told them that what they were doing would not work, ordered them to build a fire, sent them off for medicine. Everything she did, she did in the surliest fashion imaginable.

To the men on the shore, she was neither a relative nor a friend but just a stranger, and eventually even the most sympathetic became angry.

"Who is this old hag anyway?" growled one.

"Humph! Can't tell the difference between somebody who's unconscious and somebody who's dead. If she can bring him back, let her do it."

Before long, Osugi found herself alone with the body. In the gathering darkness, mist rose from the sea, and all that remained of the day was a strip of orange clouds near the horizon. Building a fire and sitting down beside it, she held Uncle Gon's body close to her.

"Uncle Gon. Oh, Uncle Gon!" she wailed.

The waves darkened. She tried and tried to bring warmth back to his body. The look on her face said that she expected him at any minute to open his mouth and speak to her. She chewed up pills from the medicine box in his obi and transferred them to his mouth. She held him close and rocked him.

"Open your eyes, Uncle Gon!" she pleaded. "Say something! You can't go away and leave me alone. We still haven't killed Musashi or punished that hussy Otsū."

Inside the inn, Akemi lay in a fretful sleep. When Seijūrō attempted to adjust her feverish head on the pillow, she mumbled deliriously. For a time, he sat by her side in utter stillness, his face paler than hers. As he observed the agony he himself had heaped on her, he suffered too.

It was he himself who by animal force had preyed on her and satisfied his own lust. Now he sat gravely and stiffly beside her, worrying about her pulse and her breathing, praying that the life that had for a time left her would be safely restored. In one short day, he had been both a beast and a man of compassion. But to Seijūrō, given as he was to extremes, his conduct didn't seem inconsistent.

His eyes were sad, the set of his mouth humble. He stared at her and murmured, "Try to be calm, Akemi. It's not just me; most other men are the same way. . . . You'll soon come to understand, though you must have been shocked by the violence of my love." Whether this speech was actually directed toward the girl or was intended to quiet his own spirit would have been difficult to judge, but he kept voicing the same sentiment over and over.

The gloom in the room was like ink. The paper-covered shoji muffled the sound of the wind and waves.

Akemi stirred and her white arms slipped out from under the covers. When Seijūrō tried to replace the quilt, she mumbled, "Wh-what's the date?"

"What?"

"How . . . how many days . . . till New Year's?"

"It's only seven days now. You'll be well by then, and we'll be back in Kyoto." He lowered his face toward hers, but she pushed it away with the palm of her hand.

"Stop! Go away! I don't like you."

He drew back, but the half-crazed words poured from her lips.

"Fool! Beast!"

Seijūrō remained silent.

"You're a beast. I don't . . . I don't want to look at you."

"Forgive me, Akemi, please!"

"Go away! Don't talk to me." Her hand waved nervously in the dark. Seijūrō swallowed sadly but continued to stare at her.

"What . . . what's the date?"

This time he did not answer.

"Isn't it New Year's yet? . . . Between New Year's and the seventh . . . Every day . . . He said he'd be on the bridge. . . . The message from Musashi . . . every day . . . Gojō Avenue bridge . . . It's so long till New Year's. . . . I must go back to Kyoto. . . . If I go to the bridge, he'll be there."

"Musashi?" said Seijūrō in wonderment.

The delirious girl was silent.

"This Musashi . . . Miyamoto Musashi?"

Seijūrō peered into her face, but Akemi said no more. Her blue eyelids were closed; she was fast asleep.

Dried pine needles tapped against the shoji. A horse

whinnied. A light appeared beyond the partition, and a maid's voice said, "The Young Master is in here."

Seijūrō hastily went into the adjoining room, carefully shutting the door behind him. "Who is it?" he asked. "I'm in here."

"Ueda Ryōhei," came the answer. Clad in full travel garb and covered with dust, Ryōhei came in and sat down.

While they exchanged greetings, Seijūrō wondered what could have brought him here. Since Ryōhei, like Tōji, was one of the senior students and was needed at home, Seijūrō would never have brought him on a spur-of-the-moment excursion.

"Why have you come? Has something happened in my absence?" asked Seijūrō.

"Yes, and I must ask you to return immediately."

"What is it?"

As Ryōhei put both hands into his kimono and felt around, Akemi's voice came from the next room. "I don't like you! . . . Beast! . . . Go away!" The clearly spoken words were filled with fear; anyone would have thought she was awake and in real danger.

Startled, Ryōhei asked, "Who's that?"

"Oh, that? Akemi took sick after she got here. She's feverish. Every once in a while she gets a little delirious."

"That's Akemi?"

"Yes, but never mind. I want to hear why you came."

From the stomach wrapper under his kimono, Ryōhei finally extracted a letter and presented it to Seijūrō. "It's this," he said without further explanation, then moved the lamp the maid had left over to Seijūrō's side.

"Hmm. It's from Miyamoto Musashi."

"Yes!" said Ryōhei with force.

"Have you opened it?"

"Yes. I talked it over with the others, and we decided it might be important, so we opened and read it."

Instead of seeing for himself what was in the letter, Seijūrō asked, somewhat hesitantly, "What does it say?" Though nobody had dared mention the subject to him, Musashi had remained in the back of Seijūrō's mind. Even so, he had nearly convinced himself he'd never run into the man again. The sudden arrival of the letter right after Akemi had spoken Musashi's name sent chills up and down his spine.

Ryōhei bit his lip angrily. "It's finally come. When he went away talking so big last spring, I was sure he'd never set foot in Kyoto again, but—can you imagine the conceit? Go on, look at it! It's a challenge, and he has the gall to address it to the entire House of Yoshioka, signing it with only his own name. He thinks he can take us all on himself!"

Musashi hadn't written any return address, nor was there any clue to his whereabouts in the letter. But he had not forgotten the promise he had written to Seijūrō and his disciples, and with this second letter the die was cast. He was declaring war on the House of Yoshioka; the battle would have to be fought, and it would be a fight to the finish—one in which samurai struggle to the death to preserve their honor and vindicate their skill with the sword. Musashi was laying his life on the line and challenging the Yoshioka School to do the same. When the time came, words and clever technical ploys would count for little.

That Seijūrō still did not grasp this fact was the greatest source of danger to him. He did not see that the day of reckoning was at hand, that this was no time to be idling away his days on empty pleasures.

When the letter had arrived in Kyoto, some of the stauncher disciples, disgusted with the Young Master's undisciplined way of life, had grumbled angrily over his absence at so crucial a moment. Riled by the insult from this lone rōnin, they lamented that Kempō was no longer alive. After much discussion, they had agreed to inform Seijūrō of the situation and make sure he returned to Kyoto immediately. Yet now that the letter had been delivered, Seijūrō merely put it on his knees and made no move to open it.

With obvious irritation, Ryōhei asked, "Don't you think you ought to read it?"

"What? Oh, this?" said Seijūrō vacantly. He unrolled the letter and read it. His fingers began to tremble beyond his control, an unsteadiness caused not by the strong language and tone of Musashi's challenge but by his own feeling of weakness and vulnerability. Akemi's harsh words of rejection had already destroyed his composure and upset his pride as a samurai. He had never before felt so powerless.

Musashi's message was simple and straightforward:

> Have you been in good health since I last wrote? In accordance with my previous promise, I am writing to ask where, on what day and at what hour we will meet. I have no particular preference and am willing to hold our promised match at the time and place designated by you. I request that you post a sign by the bridge at Gojō Avenue giving me your reply sometime before the seventh day of the New Year.
>
> I trust that you have been polishing your swordsmanship as usual. I myself feel that I have improved to a certain small extent. Shimmen Miyamoto Musashi.

Seijūrō stuffed the letter into his kimono and stood up. "I'll return to Kyoto now," he said.

This was said less out of resolution than because his emotions were so tangled he couldn't bear to remain where he was a moment longer. He had to get away and put the whole dreadful day behind him as soon as possible.

With much commotion, the innkeeper was called and requested to take care of Akemi, a task he accepted only with reluctance, despite the money Seijūrō pressed on him.

"I'll use your horse," he said summarily to Ryōhei. Like a fleeing bandit, he jumped into the saddle and rode rapidly away through the dark rows of trees, leaving Ryōhei to follow along at a dead run.

10

The Drying Pole

"A guy with a monkey? Yes, he came by a while ago."

"Did you notice which way he went?"

"That way, toward Nōjin Bridge. Didn't cross it, though—looked like he went into the swordsmith's shop down there."

After conferring briefly, the Yoshioka students stormed off, leaving their informant gaping in wonder at what the fuss was all about.

Although it was just past closing time for the shops along the East Moat, the sword shop was still open. One of the men went in, consulted with the apprentice and emerged shouting, "Temma! He's headed toward Temma!" And away they raced.

The apprentice had said that just as he was about to hang the shutters for the night, a samurai with a long forelock had thrown a monkey down near the front door, seated himself on a stool and asked to see the master. Told he was out, the samurai had said that he wanted to have his sword sharpened, but that it was much too valuable to entrust to anyone but the master himself. He had also insisted on seeing samples of the swordsmith's work.

The apprentice had politely shown him some blades, but the samurai, after looking them over, showed nothing but disgust. "It seems all you handle here are ordinary weapons," he said dryly. "I don't think I'd better give you mine. It's much too good, the work of a Bizen master. It's called the Drying Pole. See? It's perfect." He had then held it up with obvious pride.

The apprentice, amused by the young man's boasting, mumbled that the only remarkable features of the sword seemed to be its length and its straightness. The samurai, apparently offended, abruptly stood up and asked directions to the Temma-Kyoto ferry landing.

"I'll have my sword taken care of in Kyoto," he snapped. "All the Osaka swordsmiths I've visited seem to deal only in junk for ordinary foot soldiers. Sorry to have bothered you." With a cold look in his eye, he had departed.

The apprentice's story infuriated them all the more, as fresh evidence of what they already considered to be the young man's excessive conceit. It was clear to them that cutting off Gion Tōji's topknot had made the braggart cockier than ever.

"That's our man for sure!"

"We've got him now. He's as good as caught."

The men continued their pursuit, not once stopping to rest, even when the sun began to set. Nearing the dock at Temma, someone exclaimed, "We've missed it," referring to the last boat of the day.

"That's impossible."

"What makes you think we've missed it?" another asked.

"Can't you see? Down there," said the first man, pointing to the wharf. "The teashops are piling up their stools. The boat must've already pulled out."

For a moment they all stood stock-still, the wind gone from their sails. Then, on making inquiries, they found that the samurai had indeed boarded the last boat. They also learned it had just left and wouldn't be docking at the next stop, Toyosaki, for some time. The boats going upstream toward Kyoto were slow; they would have plenty of time to catch it at Toyosaki without even hurrying.

Knowing this, they took their time over tea, rice cakes and some cheap sweets before setting off at a brisk pace up the road along the riverbank. Ahead the river looked like a silver snake winding away into the distance. The Nakatsu and Temma rivers joined to form the Yodo, and near this fork a light flickered midstream.

"It's the ship!" one man shouted.

The seven became animated and soon forgot the piercing cold. In the bare fields by the road, dry rushes covered with frost glittered like slender steel swords. The wind seemed laden with ice.

As the distance between themselves and the floating light narrowed, they were able to see the boat quite clearly. Soon one of the man, without thinking, shouted, "Hey, there. Slow down!"

"Why?" came a response from on board.

Annoyed at having attention drawn to themselves, his companions chided the loudmouth. The boat was stopping at the next landing anyway; it was sheer stupidity to give advance warning. Now that they had, however, everyone agreed that the best thing to do would be to make their demand for the passenger then and there.

"There's only one of him, and if we don't challenge him outright, he may get suspicious, jump overboard and escape."

Keeping pace with the boat, they again called out to those on board. An authoritative voice, undoubtedly the captain's, demanded to know what they wanted.

"Bring the boat to the bank!"

"What! Are you crazy?" came the reply, accompanied by raucous laughter.

"Land here!"

"Not on your life."

"Then we'll be waiting for you at the next landing. We have some business with a young man you've got on board. Wears a forelock and has a monkey. Tell him if he has any sense of honor, he'll show himself. And if you let him get away, we'll drag every one of you ashore."

"Captain, don't answer them!" pleaded a passenger.

"Whatever they say, just ignore it," counseled another. "Let's go on to Moriguchi. There are guards there."

Most of the passengers were huddled in fear and talking in subdued tones. The one who had spoken so jauntily to the samurai on shore a few minutes earlier now stood mute.

For him as well as the others, safety lay in keeping some distance between the boat and the riverbank.

The seven men, sleeves hitched up and hands on their swords, stayed with the boat. Once they stopped and listened, apparently expecting an answer to their challenge, but heard none.

"Are you deaf?" one of them shouted. "We told you to tell that young braggart to come to the rail!"

"Do you mean me?" bellowed a voice from the boat.

"He's there, all right, and brazen as ever!"

While the men pointed their fingers and squinted toward the boat, the murmuring of the passengers grew frenzied. To them it looked as though the men on the shore might at any moment leap onto the deck.

The young man with the long sword stood firmly poised on the gunwale, his teeth shining like white pearls in the reflected moonlight. "There's no one else on board with a monkey, so I suppose it's me you're looking for. Who are you, freebooters down on your luck? A troupe of hungry actors?"

"You still don't know who you're talking to, do you, Monkey Man? Watch your tongue when you address men from the House of Yoshioka!"

As the shouting match intensified, the boat neared the dike at Kema, which had both mooring posts and a shed. The seven ran forward to seal off the landing, but no sooner reached it than the boat stopped midriver and began turning around in circles.

The Yoshioka men grew livid.

"What do you think you're doing?"

"You can't stay out there forever!"

"Come in or we'll come out after you."

The threats continued unabated till the prow of the boat began to move toward the bank. A voice roared through the cold air: "Shut up, you fools! We're coming in! Better get ready to defend yourselves."

Despite the other passengers' pleas, the young man had seized the boatman's pole and was bringing the ferry in. The seven samurai immediately assembled around where the prow would touch shore and watched the figure poling the boat grow larger as he neared them. But then suddenly the boat's speed picked up, and he was upon them before they knew it. As the hull scraped bottom, they fell back, and a dark, round object came sailing across the reeds and locked itself around one man's neck. Before realizing it was only the monkey, they had all instinctively drawn their swords and sliced through the empty air around them. To disguise their embarrassment, they shouted impatient orders at one another.

Hoping to stay out of the fray, the passengers huddled in a corner of the boat. The mayhem among the seven on the bank was encouraging, if somewhat puzzling, but no one yet dared to speak. Then, in an instant, all heads turned with a gasp as the boat's self-appointed pilot rammed his pole into the riverbed and vaulted, more lightly than the monkey, over the rushes to shore.

This caused even greater confusion, and without pausing to regroup, the Yoshioka men scampered toward their enemy in single file. This couldn't have put him in a better position to defend himself.

The first man had already advanced too far to turn back when he realized the stupidity of his move. At that moment every martial skill he'd ever learned deserted him. It was all he could do to bare his teeth and wave his sword erratically in front of him.

The handsome young man, aware of his psychological advantage, seemed to grow in stature. His right hand was behind him, on his sword hilt, and his elbow protruded above his shoulder.

"So you're from the Yoshioka School, are you? That's good. I feel as if I know you already. One of your men was kind enough to allow me to remove his topknot. Apparently that wasn't enough for you. Have you all come for a haircut? If you have, I'm sure I can oblige you. I'm having this blade sharpened soon anyway, so I don't mind putting it to good use."

As the declaration ended, the Drying Pole split first the air and then the cringing body of the nearest swordsman.

Seeing their comrade slain so easily paralyzed their brains; one by one they backed into one another in retreat, like so many colliding balls. Taking advantage of their obvious disorganization, the attacker swung his sword sideways at the next man, delivering a blow so solid it sent him tumbling with a shriek into the rushes.

The young man glared at the remaining five, who had in the meantime arranged themselves around him like flower petals. Reassuring each other that their present tactic was foolproof, they regained their confidence to the point of taunting the young man again. But this time their words had a tremulous, hollow ring.

Finally, with a loud battle cry, one of the man sprang forward and swung. He was sure he had made a cut. In fact, his sword point fell short of its target by two full feet and finished its arc by clanging loudly against a rock. The man fell forward, leaving himself wide open.

Rather than slay such easy prey, the young man leaped sideways and swung at the next man over. While the death scream still rang through the air, the other three took to their heels.

The young man, looking murderous, stood holding his sword with both hands. "Cowards!" he shouted. "Come back and fight! Is this the Yoshioka Style you boast of? To challenge a person and then run away? No wonder the House of Yoshioka's become a laughingstock."

To any self-respecting samurai, such insults were worse than being spat on, but the young man's former pursuers were too busy running to care.

Just then, from the vicinity of the dike, the sound of a horse's bells rang out. The river and the frost in the fields reflected enough light for the young man to make out a form on horseback and another running along behind. Though frosty breath steamed from their nostrils, they seemed oblivious of the cold as they sped along. The three fleeing samurai nearly collided with the horse as his rider brutally reined him up short.

Recognizing the three, Seijūrō scowled furiously. "What are you doing here?" he barked. "Where are you running to?"

"It's . . . it's the Young Master!" one of them stammered.

The Drying Pole

Ueda Ryōhei, appearing from behind the horse, lit into them. "What's the meaning of this? You're supposed to be escorting the Young Master, you pack of fools! I suppose you were too busy getting yourselves into another drunken brawl."

The three, rattled but righteously indignant, spilled out the story of how, far from being in a drunken fight, they had been defending the honor of the Yoshioka School and its master and how they had come to grief at the hands of a young but demonic samurai.

"Look!" cried one of them. "He's coming this way."

Terrified eyes watched the approaching enemy.

"Quiet down!" Ryōhei ordered in a disgusted voice. "You talk too much. Fine ones you are to protect the honor of the school. We'll never be able to live down that perform-ance. Stand aside! I'll take care of him myself." He took a challenging stance and waited.

The young man rushed toward them. "Stand and fight!" he was shouting. "Is running away the Yoshioka version of the Art of War? I personally don't want to kill you, but my Drying Pole's still thirsty. The least you can do, cowards that you are, is leave your heads behind." He was running along the dike with enormous, confident strides and seemed likely to leap right over the head of Ryōhei, who spat on his hands and regripped his sword with resolution.

At the moment the young man flew by, Ryōhei uttered a piercing cry, raised his sword over the young man's gold-colored coat, brought it down fiercely, and missed.

Halting instantly, the young man turned around, crying, "What's this? A new one?"

As Ryōhei stumbled forward with the momentum of his swing, the young man swiped viciously at him. In all his life, Ryōhei had never seen such a powerful stroke, and although he managed to dodge it just in time, he plunged headfirst into the paddy field below. Luckily for him, the dike was fairly low and the field frozen over, but he lost his weapon as well as his confidence when he fell.

When he clambered back up, the young man was mov-ing with the strength and speed of an enraged tiger, scatter-

ing the three disciples with a flash of his sword and making
for Seijūrō.

Seijūrō hadn't yet felt any fear. He had thought it would
be all over before he himself became involved. But now
danger was rushing directly at him, in the form of a rapacious
sword.

Moved by a sudden inspiration, Seijūrō cried, "Ganryū!
Wait!" He disengaged one foot from its stirrup, put it on the
saddle, and stood straight up. As the horse sprang forward
over the young man's head, Seijūrō flew backward through
the air and landed on his feet about three paces away.

"What a feat!" cried the young man in genuine admiration as he moved in on Seijūrō. "Even if you are my enemy,
that was really magnificent! You must be Seijūrō himself. On
guard!"

The blade of the long sword became the embodiment of
the young man's fighting spirit. It loomed ever closer to
Seijūrō, but Seijūrō, for all his failings, was Kempō's son,
and he was able to face the danger calmly.

Addressing the young man confidently, he said, "You're
Sasaki Kojirō from Iwakuni. I can tell. It is true, as you
surmise, that I am Yoshioka Seijūrō. However, I have no
desire to fight you. If it's really necessary, we can have it
out some other time. Right now I'd just like to find out how
all this came about. Put your sword away."

When Seijūrō had called him Ganryū, the young man
had apparently not heard; now, being addressed as Sasaki
Kojirō startled him. "How did you know who I am?" he
asked.

Seijūrō slapped his thigh. "I knew it! I was only guess-
ing, but I was right!" Then he came forward and said, "It's
a pleasure to meet you. I've heard a good deal about you."

"Who from?" asked Kojirō.

"From your senior, Itō Yagorō."

"Oh, are you a friend of his?"

"Yes. Until last fall, he had a hermitage on Kagura Hill
in Shirakawa, and I often visited him there. He came to my
house a number of times too."

Kojirō smiled. "Well, then, this is not exactly like
meeting for the first time, is it?"

"No. Ittōsai mentioned you rather often. He said there was a man from Iwakuni named Sasaki who had learned the style of Toda Seigen and then studied under Kanemaki Jisai. He told me this Sasaki was the youngest man in Jisai's school but would one day be the only swordsman who could challenge Ittōsai."

"I still don't see how you knew so quickly."

"Well, you're young and you fit the description. Seeing you wield that long sword reminded me that you're also called Ganryū—'The Willow on the Riverbank.' I had a feeling it must be you, and I was right."

"That's amazing. It really is."

As Kojirō chuckled with delight, his eyes dropped to his bloody sword, which reminded him that there had been a fight and made him wonder how they would straighten everything out. As it happened, however, he and Seijūrō hit it off so well that an understanding was soon reached, and after a few minutes they were walking along the dike shoulder to shoulder, like old friends. Behind them were Ryōhei and the three dejected disciples. The little group headed toward Kyoto.

Kojirō was saying, "From the beginning, I couldn't see what the fight was all about. I had nothing against them."

Seijūrō's thoughts were on Gion Tōji's recent conduct. "I'm disgusted with Tōji," he said. "When I get back, I'll call him to account. Please don't think I have any grudge against you. I'm simply mortified to find that the men in my school aren't better disciplined."

"Well, you can see what sort of man I am," Kojirō replied. "I talk too big and I'm always ready to fight anybody. Your disciples weren't the only ones to blame. In fact, I think you should give them some credit for trying to defend your school's good name. It's unfortunate they're not much as fighters, but at least they tried. I feel a little sorry for them."

"I'm the one to blame," Seijūrō said simply. The expression on his face was one of genuine pain.

"Let's just forget the whole thing."

"Nothing would please me more."

The sight of the two making up came as a relief to the

others. Who would have thought this handsome, overgrown boy was the great Sasaki Kojirō, whose praises Ittōsai had sung? ("The prodigy of Iwakuni" were his actual words.) No wonder Tōji, in his ignorance, had been tempted to do some teasing. And no wonder he had ended up looking ridiculous.

It made Ryōhei and the other three shiver to think how close they had come to being mowed down by the Drying Pole. Now that their eyes had been opened, the sight of Kojirō's broad shoulders and sturdy back made them wonder how they could have been so stupid as to underestimate him in the first place.

After a time, they came again to the landing. The corpses were already frozen, and the three were assigned to bury them, while Ryōhei went to find the horse. Kojirō went about whistling for his monkey, which suddenly appeared out of nowhere and jumped on his master's shoulder.

Seijūrō not only urged Kojirō to come along to the school on Shijō Avenue and stay awhile but even proffered his horse. Kojirō refused.

"That wouldn't be right," he said, with unaccustomed deference. "I'm just a young rōnin, and you're the master of a great school, the son of a distinguished man, the leader of hundreds of followers." Taking hold of the bridle, he continued, "Please, you ride. I'll just hold on to this. It's easier to walk that way. If it's really all right for me to go with you, I'd like to accept your offer and stay with you in Kyoto for a time."

Seijūrō, with equal cordiality, said, "Well, then, I'll ride for now, and when your feet get tired, we can change places."

Seijūrō, faced with the certain prospect of having to fight Miyamoto Musashi at the beginning of the New Year, was reflecting that it was not a bad idea to have a swordsman like Sasaki Kojirō around.

11

Eagle Mountain

In the 1550s and 1560s, the most famous master swordsmen in eastern Japan were Tsukahara Bokuden and Lord Kōizumi of Ise, whose rivals in central Honshu were Yoshioka Kempō of Kyoto and Yagyū Muneyoshi of Yamato. In addition there was Lord Kitabatake Tomonori of Kuwana, a master of the martial arts and an outstanding governor. Long after his death, the people of Kuwana spoke of him with affection, since to them he symbolized the essence of good government and prosperity.

When Kitabatake studied under Bokuden, the latter passed on to him his Supreme Swordsmanship: his most secret of secret methods. Bokuden's son, Tsukahara Hikoshirō, inherited his father's name and estate but had not been bequeathed his secret treasure. It was for this reason that Bokuden's style spread not in the east, where Hikoshirō was active, but in the Kuwana region, where Kitabatake ruled.

Legend has it that after Bokuden's death, Hikoshirō came to Kuwana and tried to trick Kitabatake into revealing the secret method to him. "My father," he allegedly claimed, "long ago taught it to me, and I'm told he did the same with you. But lately I've been wondering whether what we were taught was, in fact, the same thing. Since the ultimate secrets of the Way are our mutual concern, I think we should compare what we've learned, don't you?"

Though Kitabatake immediately realized Bokuden's

heir was up to no good, he quickly agreed to a demonstration, but what Hikoshirō then became privy to was only the outward form of the Supreme Swordsmanship, not its innermost secret. As a result, Kitabatake remained the sole master of the true Bokuden Style and to learn it students had to go to Kuwana. In the east, Hikoshirō passed on as genuine the spurious hollow shell of his father's skill: its form without its heart.

Or such, in any case, was the story told to any traveler who happened to set foot in the Kuwana region. It was not a bad story, as such stories go, and being based on fact, it was both more plausible and less inconsequential than most of the myriad local folk tales people told to reaffirm the uniqueness of their beloved towns and provinces.

Musashi, descending Tarusaka Mountain on his way from the castle town of Kuwana, heard it from his groom. He nodded and said politely, "Really? How interesting." It was the middle of the last month of the year, and though the Ise climate is relatively warm, the wind blowing up into the pass from Nako inlet was cold and biting.

He wore only a thin kimono, a cotton undergarment and a sleeveless cloak, clothing too light by any standard, and distinctly dirty as well. His face was not so much bronzed as blackened from exposure to the sun. Atop his weather-beaten head, his worn and frayed basket hat looked absurdly superfluous. Had he discarded it along the road, no one would have bothered to pick it up. His hair, which could not have been washed for many days, was tied in back, but still managed to resemble a bird's nest. And whatever he had been doing for the past six months had left his skin looking like well-tanned leather. His eyes shone pearly white in their coal-dark setting.

The groom had been worrying ever since he took on this unkempt rider. He doubted he would ever receive his pay and was certain he would see no return fare from their destination deep in the mountains.

"Sir," he said, somewhat timidly.

"Mm?"

"We'll reach Yokkaichi a little before noon and Kameyama by evening, but it'll be the middle of the night before we get to the village of Ujii.''

"Mm.''

"Is that all right?''

"Mm.'' Musashi was more interested in the view of the inlet than in talking, and the groom, try though he did, could elicit no more response than a nod and a noncommittal "Mm.''

He tried again. "Ujii's nothing but a little hamlet about eight miles into the mountains from the ridge of Mount Suzuka. How do you happen to be going to a place like that?''

"I'm going to see someone.''

"There's nobody there but a few farmers and woodcutters.''

"In Kuwana I heard there's a man there who's very good with the chain-ball-sickle.''

"I guess that would be Shishido.''

"That's the man. His name is Shishido something or other.''

"Shishido Baiken.''

"Yes.''

"He's a blacksmith, makes scythes. I remember hearing how good he is with that weapon. Are you studying the martial arts?''

"Mm.''

"Well, in that case, instead of going to see Baiken, I'd suggest you go to Matsuzaka. Some of the best swordsmen in Ise Province are there.''

"Who, for instance?''

"Well, there's Mikogami Tenzen, for one.''

Musashi nodded. "Yes, I've heard of him.'' He said no more, leaving the impression that he was quite familiar with Mikogami's exploits.

When they reached the little town of Yokkaichi, he limped painfully to a stall, ordered a box lunch and sat down to eat. One of his feet was bandaged around the instep, because of a festering wound on the sole, which explained why he had chosen to rent a horse rather than walk. Despite his usual habit of taking good care of his body, a few days earlier in the crowded port town of Narumi, he had stepped on a board with a nail in it. His red and swollen foot looked like a pickled persimmon, and since the day before, he had had a fever.

To his way of thinking, he had had a battle with a nail, and the nail had won. As a student of the martial arts, he was humiliated at having let himself be taken unawares. "Is there no way to resist an enemy of this sort?" he asked himself several times. "The nail was pointed upward and plainly visible. I stepped on it because I was half asleep— no, blind, because my spirit is not yet active throughout my whole body. What's more, I let the nail penetrate deep, proof my reflexes are slow. If I'd been in perfect control, I would have noticed the nail as soon as the bottom of my sandal touched it."

His trouble, he concluded, was immaturity. His body and his sword were still not one; though his arms grew stronger every day, his spirit and the rest of his body were not in tune. It felt to him, in his self-critical frame of mind, like a crippling deformity.

Still, he did not feel he'd entirely wasted the past six months. After fleeing from Yagyū, he had gone first to Iga, then up the Ōmi highroad, then through the provinces of Mino and Owari. At every town, in every mountain ravine, he had sought to master the true Way of the Sword. At times he felt he had brushed up against it, but its secret remained elusive, something not to be found lurking in either town or ravine.

He couldn't remember how many warriors he had clashed with; there had been dozens of them, all well-trained, superior swordsmen. It was not hard to find able swordsmen. What was hard to find was a real man. While the world was full of people, all too full, finding a genuine human being was not easy. In his travels, Musashi had come to believe this very deeply, to the point of pain, and it discouraged him. But then his mind always turned to Takuan, for there, without doubt, was an authentic, unique individual.

"I guess I'm lucky," thought Musashi. "At least I've

had the good fortune to know one genuine man. I must make sure the experience of having known him bears fruit."

Whenever Musashi thought of Takuan, a certain physical pain spread from his wrists throughout his body. It was a strange feeling, a physiological memory of the time when he had been bound fast to the cryptomeria branch. "Just wait!" vowed Musashi. "One of these days, I'll tie Takuan up in that tree, and I'll sit on the ground and preach the true way of life to him!" It was not that he resented Takuan or had any desire for revenge. He simply wanted to show that the state of being one could attain through the Way of the Sword was higher than any one could reach by practicing Zen. It made Musashi smile to think he might someday turn the tables on the eccentric monk.

It could happen, of course, that things would not go exactly as planned, but supposing he did make great progress, and supposing he was eventually in a position to tie Takuan up in the tree and lecture him; what would Takuan be able to say then? Surely he would cry out for joy and proclaim, "It's magnificent! I'm happy now."

But no, Takuan would never be that direct. Being Takuan, he would laugh and say, "Stupid! You're improving, but you're still stupid!"

The actual words wouldn't really matter. The point was that Musashi felt, in a curious way, that hitting Takuan over the head with his personal superiority was something he owed to the monk, a kind of debt. The fantasy was innocent enough; Musashi had set out upon a Way of his own and was discovering day by day how infinitely long and difficult the path to true humanity is. When the practical side of his nature reminded him of how much farther along that path Takuan was than he, the fantasy vanished.

It unsettled him even more to consider how immature and inept he was compared to Sekishūsai. Thinking of the old Yagyū master both maddened and saddened him, making him keenly aware of his own incompetence to speak of the Way, the Art of War or anything else with any confidence.

At times like this, the world, which he had once thought so full of stupid people, seemed frighteningly large. But then life, Musashi would tell himself, is not a matter of logic. The sword is not logic. What was important was not talk or speculation but action. There may be other people much greater than he right now, but he, too, could be great!

When self-doubt threatened to overwhelm him, it was Musashi's habit to make straight for the mountains, in whose seclusion he could live to himself. His style of life there was evident from his appearance on returning to civilization—his cheeks hollow as a deer's, his body covered with scratches and bruises, his hair dry and stiff from long hours under a cold waterfall. He would be so dirty from sleeping on the ground that the whiteness of his teeth seemed unearthly, but these were mere superficialities. Inside he would be burning with a confidence verging on arrogance and bursting with eagerness to take on a worthy adversary. And it was this search for a test of mettle that always brought him down from the mountains.

He was on the road now because he wondered whether the chain-ball-sickle expert of Kuwana might do. In the ten days left before his appointment in Kyoto, he had time to go and find out whether Shishido Baiken was that rare entity a real man, or just another of the multitude of rice-eating worms who inhabit the earth.

It was late at night before he reached his destination deep in the mountains. After thanking the groom, he told him he was free to leave, but the groom said that since it was so late he would prefer to accompany Musashi to the house he was looking for and spend the night under the eaves. The next morning he could go down from Suzuka Pass and, if he was lucky, pick up a return fare on the way. Anyhow, it was too cold and dark to try making his way back before sunup.

Musashi sympathized with him. They were in a valley enclosed on three sides, and any way the groom went, he'd have to climb the mountains knee-deep in snow. "In that case," said Musashi, "come with me."

"To Shishido Baiken's house?"

"Yes."

"Thank you sir. Let's see if we can find it."

Since Baiken ran a smithy, any of the local farmers would have been able to direct them to his place, but at this hour of the night, the whole village was in bed. The only sign of life was the steady thud of a mallet beating on a fulling block. Walking through the frigid air toward the sound, they eventually spied a light.

It turned out to be the blacksmith's house. In front was a pile of old metal and the underside of the eaves was smoke-stained. At Musashi's command, the groom pushed open the door and went in. There was a fire in the forge, and a woman with her back to the flames was pounding cloth.

"Good evening, ma'am! Oh! You've got a fire. That's wonderful!" The groom made straight for the forge.

The woman jumped at the sudden intrusion and dropped her work. "Who in the world are you?" she asked.

"Just a moment, I'll explain," he said, warming his hands. "I've brought a man from a long way off who wants to meet your husband. We just got here. I'm a groom from Kuwana."

"Well, of all . . ." The woman looked sourly in Musashi's direction. The frown on her face made it evident that she had seen more than enough *shugyōsha* and had learned how to handle them. With a touch of arrogance, she said to him, as though to a child, "Shut the door! The baby will catch cold with all that freezing air blowing in."

Musashi bowed and complied. Then, taking a seat on a tree stump beside the forge, he surveyed his surroundings, from the blackened foundry area to the three-room living space. On a board nailed to one section of the wall hung about ten chain-ball-sickle weapons. He assumed that was what they were, since if the truth be told, he'd never laid eyes on the device. As a matter of fact, another reason for his having made the journey here was that he thought a student like himself should become acquainted with every type of weapon. His eyes sparkled with curiosity.

The woman, who was about thirty and rather pretty, put down her mallet and went back into the living area. Musashi thought perhaps she would bring some tea, but instead she went to a mat where a small child was sleeping, picked him up and began to suckle him.

To Musashi she said, "I suppose you're another one of those young samurai who come here to get bloodied up by my husband. If you are, you're in luck. He's off on a trip, so you don't have to worry about getting killed." She laughed merrily.

Musashi did not laugh with her; he was thoroughly annoyed. He had not come to this out-of-the-way village to be made fun of by a woman, all of whom, he mused, tended to overestimate their husbands' status absurdly. This wife was worse than most; she seemed to think her spouse the greatest man on earth.

Not wanting to give offense, Musashi said, "I'm disappointed to learn that your husband's away. Where did he go?"

"To the Arakida house."

"Where's that?"

"Ha, ha! You've come to Ise, and you don't even know the Arakida family?"

The baby at her breast began to fret, and the woman, forgetting about her guests, started to sing a lullaby in the local dialect.

> Go to sleep, go to sleep.
> Sleeping babies are sweet.
> Babies who wake and cry are naughty,
> And they make their mothers cry too.

Thinking he might at least learn something by taking a look at the blacksmith's weapons, Musashi asked, "Are those the weapons your husband wields so well?"

The woman grunted, and when he asked to examine them, she nodded and grunted again.

He took one down from its hook. "So this is what they're like," he said, half to himself. "I've heard people are using them a good deal these days." The weapon in his hand consisted of a metal bar about a foot and a half long (easily carried in one's obi), with a ring at one end to which a long chain was attached. At the other end of the chain was a heavy metal ball, quite substantial enough to crack a person's skull. In a deep groove on one side of the bar, Musashi could see the back of a blade. As he pulled at it with his fingernails, it snapped out sideways, like the blade of a sickle. With this, it would be a simple matter to cut off an opponent's head.

"I suppose you hold it like this," said Musashi, taking the sickle in his left hand and the chain in his right. Imagining an enemy in front of him, he assumed a stance and considered what movements would be necessary.

The woman, who had turned her eyes from the baby's bed to watch, chided him. "Not that way! That's terrible!" Stuffing her breast back in her kimono, she came over to where he was standing. "If you do that, anyone with a sword can cut you down with no trouble at all. Hold it this way."

She snatched the weapon from his hands and showed him how to stand. It made him queasy to see a woman take a battle stance with such a brutal-looking weapon. He stared with open mouth. While nursing the baby, she had appeared distinctly bovine, but now, ready for combat, she looked handsome, dignified, and, yes, beautiful. As Musashi watched, he saw that on the blade, which was blackish blue like the back of a mackerel, there was an inscription reading "Style of Shishido Yaegaki."

She kept the stance only momentarily. "Well, anyway, it's something like that," she said, folding the blade back into the handle and hanging the weapons on its hook.

Musashi would have liked to see her handle the device again, but she obviously had no intention of doing so. After clearing up the fulling block, she clattered about near the sink, evidently washing pots or preparing to cook something.

"If this woman can take a stance as imposing as that," thought Musashi, "her husband must really be something to see." By this time he was nearly sick with the desire to meet Baiken and quietly asked the groom about the Arakidas. The groom, leaning against the wall and baking in the warmth of the fire, mumbled that they were the family charged with guarding Ise Shrine.

If this was true, Musashi thought, they would not be difficult to locate. He resolved to do just that, then curled up on a mat by the fire and went to sleep.

In the early morning, the blacksmith's apprentice got up and opened the outside door to the smithy. Musashi got up too and asked the groom to take him to Yamada, the town nearest Ise Shrine. The groom, satisfied because he'd been paid the day before, agreed at once.

By evening they had reached the long, tree-lined road that led to the shrine. The teashops looked particularly desolate, even for winter. There were few travelers, and the road itself was in poor condition. A number of trees blown down by autumn storms were still lying where they had fallen.

From the inn in Yamada, Musashi sent a servant to inquire at the Arakida house whether Shishido Baiken was staying there. A reply came saying that there must be some mistake; no one of that name was there. In his disappointment, Musashi turned his attention to his injured foot, which had swollen up considerably overnight.

He was exasperated, for only a few days remained before he was due in Kyoto. In the letter of challenge he had sent to the Yoshioka School from Nagoya, he had given them the choice of any day during the first week of the New Year. He couldn't very well beg off now because of a sore foot. And besides, he had promised to meet Matahachi at the Gojō Avenue bridge.

He spent the whole of the next day applying a remedy he had once heard about. Taking the dregs left after making bean curd, he put them in a cloth sack, squeezed the warm water out, and soaked his foot in it. Nothing happened, and to make matters worse, the smell of the bean curd was nauseating. As he fretted over his foot, he bemoaned his stupidity in making this detour to Ise. He should have gone to Kyoto straightaway.

That night, with his foot wrapped up under the quilt, his fever shot higher and the pain became unendurable. The next morning, he desperately tried more prescriptions, including smearing on some oily medicine given him by the innkeeper, who swore his family had used it for generations. Still the swelling did not go down. The foot began to look to Musashi like a large, bloated wad of bean curd and felt as heavy as a block of wood.

The experience set him to thinking. He had never in his life been bedridden for three days. Aside from having a carbuncle on his head as a child, he couldn't remember ever having been ill.

"Sickness is the worst kind of enemy," he reflected. "Yet I'm powerless in its grip." Until now he had assumed his adversaries would be coming at him from without, and the fact of being immobilized by a foe within was both novel and thought-provoking.

"How many more days are there in the year?" he wondered. "I can't just stay here doing nothing!" As he lay there chafing, his ribs seemed to press in on his heart, and his chest felt constricted. He kicked the quilt off his swollen foot. "If I can't even beat this, how can I hope to overcome the whole House of Yoshioka?"

Thinking he would pin down and stifle the demon inside him, he forced himself to sit on his haunches in formal style. It was painful, excruciatingly so. He nearly fainted. He faced the window but closed his eyes, and quite some time passed before the violent redness in his face began to subside and his head to cool a bit. He wondered if the demon was yielding to his unflinching tenacity.

Opening his eyes, he saw before him the forest around Ise Shrine. Beyond the trees he could see Mount Mae, and a little to the east Mount Asama. Rising above the mountains between these two was a soaring peak that looked down its nose at its neighbors and stared insolently at Musashi.

"It's an eagle," he thought, not knowing its name actually was Eagle Mountain. The peak's arrogant appearance offended him; its haughty pose taunted him until his fighting spirit was once again stirred. He could not help thinking of Yagyū Sekishūsai, the old swordsman who resembled this proud peak, and as time passed, it began to seem the peak *was* Sekishūsai, looking down at him from above the clouds and laughing at his weakness and insignificance.

Staring at the mountain, he became for a time oblivious of his foot, but presently the pain reasserted its claim on his consciousness. Had he rammed his leg into the fire of the blacksmith's forge, it couldn't have hurt any more, he thought bitterly. Involuntarily he drew the big round thing out from under him and glared at it, unable to accept the fact that it was really a part of him.

In a loud voice he summoned the maid. When she did not appear promptly, he beat on the tatami with his fist. "Where is everybody?" he shouted. "I'm leaving! Bring the bill! Fix me some food—some fried rice—and get me three pairs of heavy straw sandals!"

Soon he was out on the street, limping through the old marketplace where the famous warrior Taira no Tadakiyo, the hero of the "Story of the Hōgen War," was supposed to have been born. But now little about it suggested a birthplace of heroes; it was more like an open-air brothel, lined with tea stalls and teeming with women. More temptresses than trees stood along the lane, calling out to travelers and latching on to the sleeves of passing prospects, as they flirted, coaxed and teased. To get to the shrine, Musashi had to literally push his way through them, scowling and avoiding their impertinent stares.

"What happened to your foot?"

"Shall I make it feel better?"

"Here, let me rub it for you!"

They pulled at his clothing, grabbed at his hands, grasped his wrists.

"A good-looking man won't get anywhere frowning like that!"

Musashi reddened and stumbled along blindly. Utterly without defense against this kind of attack, he apologized to some and made polite excuses to others, which only made the women titter. When one of them said he was as "cute as a baby panther," the assault of the whitened hands intensified. Finally, he gave up all pretense of dignity and ran, not even stopping to retrieve his hat when it flew off. The giggling voices followed him through the trees outside the town.

It was impossible for Musashi to ignore women, and the frenzy their pawing hands aroused in him took long to subside. The mere memory of the scent of pungent white powder would set his pulse racing, and no amount of mental effort could calm it. It was a greater threat than an enemy standing with sword drawn before him; he simply did not know how to cope with it. Later, his body burning with sexual fire, he would toss and turn all night. Even innocent Otsū sometimes became the object of his lustful fantasies.

Today he had his foot to take his mind off the women, but running from them when he was barely able to walk, he might as well have been crossing a bed of molten metal. At every other step, a stab of anguish shot to his head from the sole of his foot. His lips reddened, his hands grew as sticky as honey, and his hair smelled acrid from sweat. Just lifting the injured foot took all the strength he could muster; at times he felt as if his body would suddenly fall apart. Not that he had any illusions. He knew when he left the inn that this would be torture and he intended to survive it. Somehow he managed to stay in control, cursing under his breath each time he dragged the wretched foot forward.

Crossing the Isuzu River and entering the precincts of the Inner Shrine brought a welcome change of atmosphere. He sensed a sacred presence, sensed it in the plants, in the trees, even in the voices of the birds. What it was, he could not say, but it was there.

He groaned and collapsed on the roots of a great cryptomeria, whimpering softly with pain and holding his foot in both hands. For a long time he sat there, motionless as a rock, his body aflame with fever even as his skin was bitten by the cold wind.

Why had he suddenly risen from his bed and fled the inn? Any normal person would have stayed there quietly until the foot healed. Was it not childish, even imbecilic, for an adult to allow impatience to overcome him?

But it was not impatience only that had moved him. It was a spiritual need, and a very deep one. For all the pain, all the physical torment, his spirit was tense and throbbing with vitality. He lifted his head and with keen eyes regarded the nothingness around him.

Through the bleak, ceaseless moaning of the great trees in the sacred forest, Musashi's ear caught another sound. Somewhere, not far away, flutes and reeds were giving voice to the strains of ancient music, music dedicated to the gods, while ethereal children's voices sang, a holy invocation. Drawn by this peaceful sound, Musashi tried to stand. Biting his lips, he forced himself up, his unwilling body resisting every move. Reaching the dirt wall of a shrine building, he grasped it with both hands and worked his way along with an awkward crablike movement.

The heavenly music was coming from a building a little farther on, where a light shone through a latticed window. This, the House of Virgins, was occupied by young girls in the service of the deity. Here they practiced playing ancient musical instruments and learned to perform sacred dances devised centuries earlier.

Musashi made his way to the rear entrance of the building. He paused and looked in, but saw no one. Relieved at not having to explain himself, he removed his swords and the pack on his back, tied them together, and hung them on a peg on the inside wall. Thus unencumbered, he put his hands on his hips and began hobbling back toward the Isuzu River.

An hour or so later, completely naked, he broke the ice on the surface and plunged into the frigid waters. And there he stayed, splashing and bathing, dunking his head, purifying himself. Fortunately, no one was about; any passing priest would have thought him insane and driven him away.

According to Ise legend, an archer named Nikki Yoshinaga had, long ago, attacked and occupied a part of the Ise Shrine territory. Once ensconced, he fished in the sacred Isuzu River and used falcons to catch small birds in the sacred forest. In the course of these sacrilegious plunderings, the legend said, he went totally insane, and Musashi, acting as he was, could easily have been taken for the madman's ghost.

When finally he leaped onto a boulder, it was with the lightness of a small bird. While he was drying himself and putting on his clothes, the strands of hair along his forehead stiffened into slivers of ice.

To Musashi, the icy plunge into the sacred stream was necessary. If his body could not withstand the cold, how could it survive in the face of life's more threatening obstacles? And at this moment, it was not a matter of some abstract future contingency, but one of taking on the very real Yoshioka Seijūrō and his entire school. They would hurl every bit of strength they had at him. They had to, to save face. They knew they had no alternative but to kill him, and Musashi knew just saving his skin was going to be tricky.

Faced with this prospect, the typical samurai would invariably talk about "fighting with all his might" or "being prepared to face death," but to Musashi's way of thinking, this was a lot of nonsense. To fight a life-or-death struggle with all one's might was no more than animal instinct. Moreover, while not being thrown off balance by the prospect of death was a mental state of a higher order, it was not really so difficult to face death if one knew that one had to die.

Musashi was not afraid to die, but his objective was to win definitively, not just survive, and he was trying to build up the confidence to do so. Let others die heroic deaths, if that suited them. Musashi could settle for nothing less than a heroic victory.

Kyoto was not far away, no more than seventy or eighty miles. If he could keep up a good pace, he could get there in three days. But the time needed to prepare himself spiritually was beyond measuring. Was he inwardly ready? Were his mind and spirit truly one?

Musashi wasn't yet able to reply to these questions in the affirmative. He felt that somewhere deep inside himself there was a weakness, the knowledge of his immaturity. He was painfully aware that he had not attained the state of mind of the true master, that he was still far short of being a complete and perfect human. When he compared himself with Nikkan, or Sekishūsai, or Takuan, he could not avoid the simple truth: he was still green. His own analysis of his abilities and traits unveiled not only weaknesses in some areas but virtual blind spots in others.

But unless he could triumph throughout this life and leave an indelible mark on the world around him, he could not regard himself as a master of the Art of War.

His body shook as he shouted, "I will win, I will!" Limping on toward the upper reaches of the Isuzu, he cried out again for all the trees in the sacred forest to hear: "I will win!" He passed a silent, frozen waterfall and, like a primitive man, crawled over the boulders and pushed his way through thick groves in deep ravines, where few had ever gone before.

His face was as red as a demon's. Clinging to rocks and vines, he could with the utmost effort advance only one step at a time.

Beyond a point called Ichinose there was a gorge five or six hundred yards long, so full of crags and rapids that even the trout could not make their way through it. At the farther end rose an almost sheer precipice. It was said that only monkeys and goblins could climb it. Musashi merely looked at the cliff and said matter-of-factly, "This is it. This is the way to Eagle Mountain."

Elated, he saw no impassable barrier here. Seizing hold of strong vines, he started up the rock face, half climbing, half swinging, seemingly lifted by some upside-down gravity.

Having reached the cliff top, he exploded with a cry of triumph. From here he could make out the white flow of the river and the silver strand along the shore of Futamigaura. Ahead of him, through a sparse grove veiled in nocturnal mist, he saw before his eyes the foot of Eagle Mountain.

The mountain was Sekishūsai. As it had laughed while he'd lain in bed, the peak continued to mock him now. His unyielding spirit felt literally assaulted by Sekishūsai's superiority. It was oppressing him, holding him back.

Gradually his objective took form: to climb to the top and unleash his rancor, to trample roughshod on the head of Sekishūsai, to show him Musashi could and would win.

He advanced against the opposition weeds, trees, ice— all enemies trying desperately to keep him back. Every step, every breath, was a challenge. His recently chilled blood boiled, and his body steamed as the sweat from his pores met the frosty air. Musashi hugged the red surface of the peak, groping for footholds. Each time he felt for a footing he had to struggle, and small rocks would go crashing down to the grove below. One hundred feet, two hundred, three hundred—he was in the clouds. When they parted, he appeared from below to be hanging weightless in the sky. The mountain peak stared coldly down at him.

Now, nearing the top, he hung on for dear life. One false move and he would come flying down in a cascade of rocks and boulders. He puffed and grunted, gasping for air with his very pores. So intense was the strain, his heart seemed about to rise up and explode from his mouth. He could climb but a few feet, then rest, climb a few feet more, then rest again.

The whole world lay beneath him: the great forest enclosing the shrine, the white strip that must be the river, Mount Asama, Mount Mae, the fishing village at Toba, the great open sea. "Almost there," he thought. "Just a little more!"

"Just a little more." How easy to say, but how difficult to achieve! For "just a little more" is what distinguishes the victorious sword from the vanquished.

The odor of sweat in his nostrils, he felt giddily that he nestled in his mother's breast. The rough surface of the mountain began to feel like her skin, and he experienced an urge to go to sleep. But just then a piece of rock under his big toe broke off and brought him to his senses. He groped for another foothold.

"This is it! I'm almost there!" Hands and feet knotted with pain, he clawed again at the mountain. If his body or willpower weakened, he told himself, then as a swordsman he would surely one day be done in. This was where the match would be decided, and Musashi knew it.

"This is for you, Sekishūsai! You bastard!" With every pull and tug, he execrated the giants he respected, those supermen who had brought him here and whom he must and would conquer. "One for you, Nikkan! and you, Takuan!"

He was climbing over the heads of his idols, trampling over them, showing them who was best. He and the mountain were now one, but the mountain, as if astonished to have this creature clawing into it, snarled and spit out regular avalanches of gravel and sand. Musashi's breath stopped as though someone had clapped his hands over his face. As he clung to the rock, the wind gusted, threatening to blow him away, rock and all.

Then suddenly he was lying on his stomach, his eyes closed, not daring to move. But in his heart he sang a song of exultation. At the moment when he had flattened out, he had seen the sky in all directions, and the light of dawn was suddenly visible in the white sea of clouds below.

"I've done it! I've won!"

The instant he realized he had reached the top, his strained willpower snapped like a bowstring. The wind at the summit showered his back with sand and stones. Here at the border of heaven and earth, Musashi felt an indescribable joy swelling out to fill his whole being. His sweat-drenched body united with the surface of the mountain; the spirit of man and the spirit of the mountain were performing the great work of procreation in the vast expanse of nature at dawn. Wrapped in an unearthly ecstasy, he slept the sleep of peace.

When he finally lifted his head, his mind was as pure and clear as crystal. He had the impulse to jump and dart about like a minnow in a stream.

"There's nothing above me!" he cried. "I'm standing on top of the eagle's head!"

The pristine morning sun cast its reddish light on him and on the mountain as he stretched his brawny, savage arms toward the sky. He looked down at his two feet planted firmly on the summit, and as he looked, he saw what seemed like a bucketful of yellowish pus stream from his injured foot. Amid the celestial purity surrounding him, there arose the strange odor of humanity—the sweet smell of gloom dispelled.

12

The Mayfly in Winter

Every morning after finishing their shrine duties, the maidens living in the House of Virgins went, books in hand, to the schoolroom at the Arakida house, where they studied grammar and practiced writing poems. For their performances of religious dances, they dressed in white silk kimono with crimson widely flared trousers, called *hakama*, but now they had on the short-sleeved kimono and white cotton *hakama* they wore while studying or doing household chores.

A group of them was streaming out the back door when one exclaimed, "What's that?" She was pointing to the pack with the swords tied to it, hung up there by Musashi the night before.

"Whose do you think it is?"

"It must be a samurai's."

"Isn't that obvious?"

"No, it could have been left here by a thief."

They looked wide-eyed at each other and gulped, as though they had come across the robber himself—leather bandannaed and taking his noonday nap.

"Perhaps we should tell Otsū about it," one of them suggested, and by common consent they all ran back to the dormitory and called up from beneath the railing outside Otsū's room.

"*Sensei! Sensei!* There's something strange down here. Come and look!"

Otsū put her writing brush down on her desk and stuck her head out the window. "What is it?" she asked.

"A thief left his swords and a bundle behind. They're over there, hanging on the back wall."

"Really? You'd better take them over to the Arakida house."

"Oh, we can't! We're afraid to touch them."

"Aren't you making a big fuss over nothing? Run along to your lessons now, and don't waste any more time."

By the time Otsū came down from her room, the girls had gone. The only people in the dormitory were the old woman who did the cooking and one of the maidens who had taken ill. "Whose things are those hanging up here?" Otsū asked the cook.

The woman did not know, of course.

"I'll take them over to the Arakida house," Otsū said. When she took the pack and swords down, she nearly dropped them, they were so heavy. Lugging them with both hands, she wondered how men could walk about carrying so much weight.

Otsū and Jōtarō had come here two months earlier, after traveling up and down the Iga, Ōmi and Mino highroads in search of Musashi. Upon their arrival in Ise, they had decided to settle down for the winter, since it would be difficult to make their way through the mountains in the snow. At first Otsū had given flute lessons in the Toba district, but then she had come to the attention of the head of the Arakida family, who, being the official ritualist, ranked second only to the chief priest.

When Arakida asked Otsū to come to the shrine to teach the maidens, she had consented, not so much out of a desire to teach as out of her interest in learning the ancient, sacred music. Then, too, the peacefulness of the shrine's forest had appealed to her, as had the idea of living for a while with the shrine maidens, the youngest of whom was thirteen or fourteen, and the oldest around twenty.

Jōtarō had stood in the way of her taking the position, for it was forbidden to have a male, even of his age, living in the same dormitory as the maidens. The arrangement they

rived at was that Jōtarō could sweep the sacred gardens in
e daytime and spend his nights in the Arakidas' woodshed.

As Otsū passed through the shrine gardens, a forbidding
earthly breeze whistled through the leafless trees. One
in column of smoke rose from a distant grove, and Otsū
ought of Jōtarō, who was probably there cleaning the
ounds with his bamboo broom. She stopped and smiled,
eased that Jōtarō, the incorrigible, was minding very well
ese days, applying himself dutifully to his chores at just
e age when young boys think of nothing but playing and
nusing themselves.

The loud cracking noise she heard sounded like a branch
eaking off a tree. It came a second time, and clutching her
ad, she ran down the path through the grove, calling,
ōtarō! J-ō-ō-t-a-r-ō-ō!''

"Y-e-e-s?" came the lusty reply. In no time she heard
s running footsteps. But when he drew up before her, he
id merely, "Oh, it's you."

"I thought you were supposed to be working," said
tsū sternly. "What are you doing with that wooden sword?
nd dressed in your white work clothes too."

"I was practicing. Practicing on the trees."

"Nobody objects to your practicing, but not here, Jō-
rō. Have you forgotten where you are? This garden sym-
olizes peace and purity. It's a holy area, sacred to the
ddess who is the ancestress of us all. Look over there.
on't you see the sign saying it's forbidden to damage the
ees or hurt or kill the animals? It's a disgrace for a person
ho works here to be breaking off branches with a wooden
ord."

"Aw, I know all that," he grumbled, a look of resent-
ent on his face.

"If you know it, why do you do it? If Master Arakida
ught you at it, you'd really be in trouble!"

"I don't see anything wrong with breaking off dead
nbs. It's all right if they're dead, isn't it?"

"No, it is not! Not here."

"That's how much you know! Just let me ask you a
estion."

"What might that be?"

"If this garden is so important, why don't people take better care of it?"

"It's a shame they don't. To let it run down this way is like letting weeds grow in one's soul."

"It wouldn't be so bad if it were only weeds, but look at the trees. The ones split by lightning have been allowed to die, and the ones blown over by the typhoons are lying right where they fell. They're all over the place. And the birds have pecked at the roofs of the buildings until they leak. And nobody ever fixes any of the stone lanterns when they get knocked out of shape."

"How can you think this place is important? Listen, Otsū, isn't the castle at Osaka white and dazzling when you see it from the ocean at Settsu? Isn't Tokugawa Ieyasu building more magnificent castles at Fushimi and a dozen other places? Aren't the new houses of the daimyō and the rich merchants in Kyoto and Osaka glittering with gold ornaments? Don't the tea masters Rikyū and Kobori Enshū say that even a speck of dirt out of place in the teahouse garden spoils the flavor of the tea?

"But this garden's going to ruin. Why, the only people working in it are me and three or four old men! And look how big it is!"

"Jōtarō!" said Otsū, putting her hand under his chin and lifting his face. "You're doing nothing but repeating word for word what Master Arakida said in a lecture."

"Oh, did you hear it too?"

"Indeed I did," she said reproachfully.

"Uh, well, can't win all the time."

"Parroting what Master Arakida says will carry no weight with me. I don't approve of it, even when what he says is right."

"He is right, you know. When I hear him talk, I wonder whether Nobunaga and Hideyoshi and Ieyasu are really such great men. I know they're supposed to be important, but is it really so wonderful to take control of the country if you get the idea that you're the only person in it who counts?"

"Well, Nobunaga and Hideyoshi weren't as bad as some of the others. At least they repaired the imperial palace in Kyoto and tried to make the people happy. Even if they did

ese things only to justify their conduct to themselves and
thers, they still deserve a lot of credit. The Ashikaga
nōguns were much worse."

"How?"

"You've heard about the Ōnin War, haven't you?"

"Um."

"The Ashikaga shogunate was so incompetent, there
as constant civil war—warriors fighting other warriors all
ne time to gain more territory for themselves. The ordinary
eople didn't get a moment's peace, and nobody had any
al concern for the country as a whole."

"You mean those famous battles between the Yamanas
nd the Hosokawas?"

"Yes. . . . It was during those days, over a hundred
ears ago, that Arakida Ujitsune became the chief priest of
ne Ise Shrine, and there wasn't even enough money to
ontinue the ancient ceremonies and sacred rites. Ujitsune
etitioned the government twenty-seven times for help to
epair the shrine buildings, but the imperial court was too
oor, the shogunate was too weak, and the warriors so busy
ith their bloodbaths they didn't care what happened. In
pite of all this, Ujitsune went around pleading his case till
e finally succeeded in setting up a new shrine.

"It's a sad story, isn't it? But when you think about it,
eople when they grow up forget they owe their lifeblood to
neir ancestors, just as we all owe our lives to the goddess at
se."

Pleased with himself for having elicited this long, pas-
ionate speech from Otsū, Jōtarō jumped in the air, laughing
nd clapping his hands. "Now who's parroting Master Ara-
ida? You thought I hadn't heard that before, didn't you?"

"Oh, you're impossible!" exclaimed Otsū, laughing
erself. She would have cuffed him one, but her bundle was
n the way. Still smiling, she glared at the boy, who finally
ook notice of her unusual parcel.

"Whose are those?" he asked, stretching out his hand.

"Don't touch them! We don't know whose they are."

"Oh, I'm not going to break anything. I just want to
ook. I bet they're heavy. That long sword's really big, isn't
?" Jōtarō's mouth was watering.

"Sensei!" With a patter of straw sandals, one of the shrine maidens ran up. "Master Arakida is calling for you. I think there's something he wants you to do." Scarcely pausing, she turned and ran back.

Jōtarō looked around in all four directions, a startled expression on his face. The wintry sun was shining through the trees, and the twigs swayed like wavelets. His eyes looked as though they had spotted a phantom among the patches of sunlight.

"What's the matter?" asked Otsū. "What are you looking at?"

"Oh, nothing," replied the boy dejectedly, biting his forefinger. "When that girl called 'teacher,' I thought for a second she meant my teacher."

Otsū, too, suddenly felt sad and a little annoyed. Though Jōtarō's remark had been made in all innocence, why did he have to mention Musashi?

Despite Takuan's advice, she could not conceive of trying to expel from her heart the longing she cherished for Musashi. Takuan was so unfeeling; in a way she pitied him and his apparent ignorance of the meaning of love.

Love was like a toothache. When Otsū was busy, it did not bother her, but when the remembrance struck her, she was seized by the urge to go out on the highways again, to search for him, to find him, to place her head on his chest and shed tears of happiness.

Silently, she started walking. Where was he? Of all the sorrows that beset living beings, surely the most gnawing, the most wretched, the most agonizing, was not to be able to lay eyes on the person one pined for. Tears streaming down her cheeks, she walked on.

The heavy swords with their worn fittings meant nothing to her. How could she have dreamed she was carrying Musashi's own belongings?

Jōtarō, sensing he had done something wrong, followed sadly a short distance behind. Then, as Otsū turned into the gate at the Arakida house, he ran up to her and asked, "Are you angry? About what I said?"

"Oh, no, it's nothing."

"I'm sorry, Otsū. I really am."

"It's not your fault. I just feel kind of sad. But don't worry about it. I'm going to find out what Master Arakida wants. You go back to your work."

Arakida Ujitomi called his home the House of Study. He had converted part of it into a school, attended not only by the shrine maidens but also by forty or fifty other children from the three counties belonging to Ise Shrine. He was trying to impart to the young a type of learning not currently very popular: the study of ancient Japanese history, which in the more sophisticated towns and cities was considered irrelevant. The early history of the country was intimately connected with Ise Shrine and its lands, but this was an age when people tended to confuse the fate of the nation with that of the warrior class, and what had happened in the distant past counted for little. Ujitomi was fighting a lonely battle to plant the seeds of an earlier, more traditional culture among the young people from the shrine area. While others might claim provincial regions had nothing to do with the national destiny, Ujitomi took a different view. If he could teach the local children about the past, perhaps, he thought, its spirit would one day thrive like a great tree in the sacred forest.

With perseverance and devotion, he talked to the children each day about the Chinese classics and the *Record of Ancient Matters*, the earliest history of Japan, hoping that his charges would eventually come to value these books. He had been doing this for more than ten years. To his way of thinking, Hideyoshi might seize control of the country and proclaim himself regent, Tokugawa Ieyasu might become the omnipotent "barbarian-subduing" shōgun, but young children should not, like their elders, mistake the lucky star of some military hero for the beautiful sun. If he labored patiently, the young would come to understand that it was the great Sun Goddess, not an uncouth warrior-dictator, who symbolized the nation's aspirations.

Arakida emerged from his spacious classroom, his face a little sweaty. As the children flew out like a swarm of bees and darted quickly off to their homes, a shrine maiden told him Otsū was waiting. Somewhat flustered, he said, "That's right. I sent for her, didn't I? I completely forgot. Where is she?''

Otsū was just outside the house, where she had been standing for some time listening to Arakida's lecture. "Here I am," she called. "Did you want me?"

"I'm sorry to have kept you waiting. Come inside."

He led her to his private study, but before sitting down, pointed to the objects she was carrying and asked what they were. She explained how she came to have them; he squinted and stared suspiciously at the swords. "Ordinary worshipers wouldn't come here with things like that," he said. "And they weren't there last evening. Somebody must have come inside the walls in the middle of the night."

Then, with a distasteful expression on his face, he grumbled, "This may be some samurai's idea of a joke, but I don't like it."

"Oh? Can you think of anyone who would want to suggest that a man had been in the House of Virgins?"

"Yes, I can. As a matter of fact, that's what I wanted to talk to you about."

"Does it concern me in some way?"

"Well, I don't want you to feel bad about it, but it's like this. There's a samurai who has taken me to task for putting you in the same dormitory with the shrine maidens. He says he's warning me for my own sake."

"Have I done something that reflects on you?"

"There's no reason to be upset. It's just that—well, you know how people talk. Now don't be angry, but after all, you're not exactly a maiden. You've been around men, and people say it tarnishes the shrine to have a woman who's not a virgin living together with the girls in the House of Virgins."

Although Arakida's tone was casual, angry tears flooded Otsū's eyes. It was true that she had traveled around a lot, that she was used to meeting people, that she had wandered through life with this old love clinging to her heart; maybe it was only natural for people to take her for a woman of the world. It was, nevertheless, a shattering experience to be accused of not being chaste, when in fact she was.

Arakida did not seem to attach much importance to the

matter. It simply disturbed him that people were saying things, and since it was the end of the year "and all that," as he put it, he wondered if she would be so good as to discontinue the flute lessons and move out of the House of Virgins.

Otsū consented quickly, not as an admission of guilt, but because she had not planned to stay on and did not want to cause trouble, especially to Master Arakida. Notwithstanding her resentment at the falseness of the gossip, she promptly thanked him for his kindnesses during her stay and said that she would leave within the day.

"Oh, it's not all that urgent," he assured her, reaching out to his small bookcase and taking out some money, which he wrapped in paper.

Jōtarō, who had followed Otsū, chose this moment to put his head in from the veranda and whisper, "If you're going to leave, I'll go with you. I'm tired of sweeping their old garden anyway."

"Here's a little gift," said Arakida. "It's not much, but take it and use it for travel money." He held out the packet containing a few gold coins.

Otsū refused to touch it. With a shocked look on her face, she told him she deserved no pay for merely giving flute lessons to the girls; rather it was she who should be paying for her food and lodging.

"No," he replied. "I couldn't possibly take money from you, but there is something I'd like you to do for me in case you happen to be going to Kyoto. You can think of this money as payment for a favor."

"I'll be glad to do anything you ask, but your kindness is payment enough."

Arakida turned to Jōtarō and said, "Why don't I give him the money? He can buy things for you along the way."

"Thank you," said Jōtarō, promptly extending his hand and accepting the packet. As an afterthought, he looked at Otsū and said, "It's all right, isn't it?"

Confronted with a fait accompli, she gave in and thanked Arakida.

"The favor I want to ask," he said, "is that you deliver a package from me to Lord Karasumaru Mitsuhiro, who lives at Horikawa in Kyoto." While speaking, he took two scrolls down from the set of staggered shelves on the wall. "Lord Karasumaru asked me two years ago to paint these. They're finally done. He plans to write in the commentary to go with the pictures and present the scrolls to the Emperor. That's why I don't want to entrust them to an ordinary messenger or courier. Will you take them to him and make sure they don't get wet or soiled on the way?"

This was a commission of unexpected importance, and Otsū hesitated at first. But it would hardly do to refuse and after a moment she agreed. Arakida then took out a box and some oiled paper, but before wrapping and sealing the scrolls, said, "Perhaps I should show them to you first." He sat down and began unrolling the paintings on the floor before them. He was obviously proud of his work and wanted to take a last look himself before parting with it.

Otsū gasped at the beauty of the scrolls, and Jōtarō's eyes widened as he bent over to examine them more closely. Since the commentary had not yet been written in, neither of them knew what story was depicted, but as Arakida unrolled scene after scene, they saw before them a picture of life at the ancient imperial court, fastidiously executed in magnificent colors with touches of powdered gold. The paintings were in the Tosa style, which was derived from classic Japanese art.

Though Jōtarō had never been taught anything about art, he was dazzled by what he saw. "Look at the fire there," he exclaimed. "It looks like it's really burning, doesn't it?"

"Don't touch the painting," admonished Otsū. "Just look."

While they gazed in admiration, a servant entered and said something in a very low voice to Arakida, who nodded and replied, "I see. I suppose it's all right. Just in case, though, you'd better have the man make out a receipt." With that, he gave the servant the pack and the two swords Otsū had brought to him.

Upon learning that their flute teacher was leaving, the girls in the House of Virgins were disconsolate. In the two months she had been with them, they had come to regard her as an elder sister, and their faces as they gathered about her were full of gloom.

"Is it true?"

"Are you really going away?"

"Won't you ever come back?"

From beyond the dormitory, Jōtarō shouted, "I'm ready. What's taking you so long?" He had doffed his white robe and was once again dressed in his usual short kimono, his wooden sword at his side. The cloth-wrapped box containing the scrolls was suspended diagonally across his back.

From the window, Otsū called back, "My, that was fast!"

"I'm always fast!" retorted Jōtarō. "Aren't you ready yet? Why does it take women so long to dress and pack?" He was sunning himself in the yard, yawning lazily. But being impatient by nature, he quickly grew bored. "Aren't you finished yet?" he called again.

"I'll be there in a minute," Otsū replied. She'd already finished packing, but the girls wouldn't let her go. Attempting to break away, Otsū said soothingly, "Don't be sad. I'll come to visit one of these days. Till then, take good care of yourselves." She had the uncomfortable feeling that this was not true, for in view of what had happened, it seemed unlikely that she would ever return.

Perhaps the girls suspected this; several were crying. Finally, someone suggested that they all see Otsū as far as the holy bridge across the Isuzu River. They thereupon crowded around her and escorted her out of the house. They didn't see Jōtarō immediately, so they cupped their hands around their mouths and called his name, but got no reply. Otsū, too used to his ways to be disturbed, said, "He probably got tired of waiting and went on ahead."

"What a disagreeable little boy!" exclaimed one of the girls.

Another suddenly looked up at Otsū and asked, "Is he your son?"

"My son? How on earth could you think that? I won't even be twenty-one till next year. Do I look old enough to have a child that big?"

"No, but somebody said he was yours."

Recalling her conversation with Arakida, Otsū blushed, then comforted herself with the thought that it made no real difference what people said, so long as Musashi had faith in her.

Just then, Jōtarō came running up to them. "Hey, what's going on?" he said with a pout. "First you keep me waiting for ages, now you start off without me!"

"But you weren't where you were supposed to be," Otsū pointed out.

"You could have looked for me, couldn't you? I saw a man over there on the Toba highroad who looked a little like my teacher. I ran over to see whether it was really him."

"Someone who looked like Musashi?"

"Yes, but it wasn't him. I went as far as that row of trees and got a good look at the man from behind, but it couldn't have been Musashi. Whoever it was had a limp."

It was always like this when Otsū and Jōtarō were traveling. Not a day passed without their experiencing a glimmer of hope, followed by disappointment. Everywhere they went, they saw someone who reminded them of Musashi—the man passing by the window, the samurai in the boat that had just left, the rōnin on horseback, the dimly seen passenger in a palanquin. Hopes soaring, they would rush to make sure, only to find themselves looking dejectedly at each other. It had happened dozens of times.

For this reason, Otsū was not as upset now as she might have been, though Jōtarō was crestfallen. Laughing the incident off, she said, "Too bad you were wrong, but don't get mad at me for going on ahead. I thought I'd find you at the bridge. You know, everybody says that if you start out on a journey in a bad mood, you'll stay angry all the way. Come now, let's make up."

Though seemingly satisfied, Jōtarō turned and cast a rude look at the girls trailing along behind. "What are they all doing here? Are they coming with us?"

"Of course not. They're just sorry to see me leave, so they're sweet enough to escort us to the bridge."

"Why, that's so very kind of them," said Jōtarō, mimicking Otsū's speech and throwing everyone into fits of laughter. Now that he had joined the group, the anguish of parting subsided, and the girls recovered their good spirits.

"Otsū," called one of them, "you're turning the wrong way; that's not the path to the bridge."

"I know," said Otsū quietly. She had turned toward the Tamagushi Gate to pay her respects to the inner shrine. Clapping her hands together once, she bowed her head toward the sanctum and remained in an attitude of silent prayer for a few moments.

"Oh, I see," murmured Jōtarō. "She doesn't think she should leave without saying good-bye to the goddess." He was content to watch from a distance, but the girls started poking him in the back and asking him why he did not follow Otsū's example. "Me?" asked the boy incredulously. "I don't want to bow before any old shrine."

"You shouldn't say that. You'll be punished for that someday."

"I'd feel silly bowing like that."

"What's silly about showing your respect to the Sun Goddess? She's not like one of those minor deities they worship in the cities."

"I know that."

"Well, then, why don't you pay your respects?"

"Because I don't want to!"

"Contrary, aren't you!"

"Shut up, you crazy females! All of you!"

"Oh, my!" chorused the girls, dismayed at his rudeness.

"What a monster!" exclaimed one.

By this time Otsū had finished her obeisance and was coming back toward them. "What happened?" she asked. "You look upset."

One of the girls blurted, "He called us crazy females, just because we tried to get him to bow before the goddess."

"Now, Jōtarō, you know that's not nice," Otsū admonished. "You really ought to say a prayer."

"What for?"

"Didn't you say yourself that when you thought Musashi was about to be killed by the priests from the

Hōzōin, you raised your hands and prayed as loudly as you could? Why can't you pray here too?''

"But . . . well, they're all looking.''

"All right, we'll turn around so we can't see you.''

They all turned their backs to the boy, but Otsū stole a look behind her. He was running dutifully toward the Tama-gushi Gate. When he reached it, he faced the shrine and, in very boyish fashion, made a deep, lightning-quick bow.

13

The Pinwheel

Musashi sat on the narrow veranda of a little seafood shop facing the sea. The shop's specialty was sea snails, served boiling in their shells. Two women divers, baskets of freshly caught turban shells on their arms, and a boatman stood near the veranda. While the boatman urged him to take a ride around the offshore islands, the two women were trying to convince him he needed some sea snails to take with him, wherever he was headed.

Musashi was busily engaged in removing the pus-soiled bandage from his foot. Having suffered intensely from his injury, he could hardly believe that both the fever and the swelling were finally gone. The foot was again normal size, and though the skin was white and shriveled, it was only slightly painful.

Waving the boatman and divers away, he lowered his tender foot onto the sand and walked to the shore to wash it. Returning to the veranda, he waited for the shopgirl he'd sent to buy new leather socks and sandals. When she came back, he put them on and took a few cautious steps. He still had a slight limp, but nothing like before.

The old man cooking snails looked up. "The ferryman's calling you. Weren't you planning to cross over to Ōminato?"

"Yes. I think there's a regular boat from there to Tsu."

"There is, and there are also boats for Yokkaichi and Kuwana."

"How many days to the end of the year?"

The old man laughed. "I envy you," he said. "It's plain you don't have any year-end debts to pay. Today's the twenty-fourth."

"Is that all? I thought it was later."

"How nice to be young!"

As he trotted to the ferry landing, Musashi felt an urge to keep running, farther and farther, faster and faster. The change from invalid to healthy man had lifted his spirits, but what made him far happier was the spiritual experience he'd had that morning.

The ferry was already full, but he managed to make room for himself. Directly across the bay, at Ōminato, he changed to a bigger boat, bound for Owari. The sails filled and the boat glided over the glasslike surface of the Bay of Ise. Musashi stood huddled with the other passengers and gazed quietly across the water to his left—at the old market, Yamada and the Matsuzaka highroad. If he went to Matsuzaka, he might have a chance to meet the prodigious swordsman Mikogami Tenzen, but no, it was too soon for that. He disembarked at Tsu as planned.

No sooner was he off the boat than he noticed a man walking ahead of him with a short bar at his waist. Wrapped around the bar was a chain, and at the end of the chain was a ball. The man also wore a short field sword in a leather sheath. He looked to be forty-two or forty-three; his face, as dark as Musashi's, was pockmarked, and his reddish hair was pulled back in a knot.

He might have been taken for a freebooter were it not for the young boy following him. Soot blackened both cheeks, and he carried a sledgehammer; he was obviously a blacksmith's apprentice.

"Wait for me, master!"

"Get a move on!"

"I left the hammer on the boat."

"Leaving behind the tools you make your living with, huh?"

"I went back and got it."

"And I suppose that makes you proud of yourself. The

next time you forget anything, I'll crack your skull open for you!"

"Master . . ." the boy pleaded.

"Quiet!"

"Can't we spend the night at Tsu?"

"There's still plenty of daylight. We can make it home by nightfall."

"I'd like to stop somewhere anyway. As long as we're on a trip, we might as well enjoy it."

"Don't talk nonsense!"

The street into the town was lined with souvenir shops and infested with inn touts, just as in other port towns. The apprentice again lost sight of his master and searched the crowd worriedly until the man emerged from a toy shop with a small, colorful pinwheel.

"Iwa!" he called to the boy.

"Yes, sir."

"Carry this. And be careful it doesn't get broken! Stick it in your collar."

"Souvenir for the baby?"

"Mm," grunted the man. After being away on a job for a few days, he was looking forward to seeing the child's grin of delight when he handed it over.

It almost seemed that the pair were leading Musashi. Every time he planned to turn, they turned ahead of him. It occurred to Musashi that this blacksmith was probably Shishido Baiken, but he could not be sure, so he improvised a simple strategy to make certain. Feigning not to notice them, he went ahead for a time, then dropped back again, eavesdropping all the while. They went through the castle town and then toward the mountain road to Suzuka, presumably the route Baiken would take to his house. Putting this together with snatches of overheard conversation, Musashi concluded that this was indeed Baiken.

He had intended to go straight to Kyoto, but this chance meeting proved too tempting. He approached and said in a friendly manner, "Going back to Umehata?"

The man's reply was curt. "Yes, I'm going to Umehata. Why?"

"I was wondering if you might be Shishido Baiken."

"I am. And who are you?"

"My name is Miyamoto Musashi. I'm a student warrior. Not long ago I went to your house in Ujii and met your wife. It looks to me as though fate brought us together here."

"Is that so?" Baiken said. With a look of sudden comprehension on his face, he asked, "Are you the man who was staying at the inn in Yamada, the one who wanted to have a bout with me?"

"How did you hear about that?"

"You sent someone to the Arakida house to find me, didn't you?"

"Yes."

"I was doing some work for Arakida, but I didn't stay at the house. I borrowed a work place in the village. It was a job nobody could do but me."

"I see. I hear you're an expert with the chain-ball-sickle."

"Ha, ha! But you said you met my wife?"

"Yes. She demonstrated one of the Yaegaki stances for me."

"Well, that should be enough for you. There's no reason to be following along after me. Oh, of course I could show you a great deal more than she did, but the minute you saw it, you'd be on your way to a different world."

Musashi's impression of the wife had been that she was pretty overbearing, but here was real arrogance. He was fairly sure from what he had seen already that he could take the measure of this man, but he cautioned himself not to be hasty. Takuan had taught him life's first lesson, namely that there are a lot of people in the world who may very well be one's betters. The lesson had been reinforced by his experiences at the Hōzōin and at Koyagyū Castle. Before letting his pride and confidence betray him into underestimating an adversary, he wanted to size him up from every possible angle. While laying his groundwork, he would remain sociable, even if at times this might strike his opponent as being cowardly or subservient.

In reply to Baiken's contemptuous remark, he said, with an air of respect befitting his youth, "I see. I did indeed learn a good deal from your wife, but since I've had the good fortune to meet you, I'd be grateful if you'd tell me more about the weapon you use."

"If all you want to do is talk, fine. Are you planning to stay overnight at the inn by the barrier?"

"That's what I had in mind, unless you'd be kind enough to put me up for another night."

"You're welcome to stay, if you're willing to sleep in the smithy with Iwa. But I don't run an inn and we don't have extra bedding."

At sunset they reached the foot of Mount Suzuka; the little village, under red clouds, looked as placid as a lake. Iwa ran on ahead to announce their arrival, and when they got to the house, Baiken's wife was waiting under the eaves, holding the baby and the pinwheel.

"Look, look, look!" she cooed. "Daddy's been away, Daddy's come back. See, there he is."

In a twinkling, Daddy ceased to be the epitome of arrogance and broke into a fatherly smile. "Here, boy, here's Daddy," he babbled, holding up his hand and making his fingers dance.

Husband and wife disappeared inside and sat down, talking only about the baby and household matters, paying no attention to Musashi.

Finally, when dinner was ready, Baiken remembered his guest. "Oh, yes, give that fellow something to eat," he told his wife.

Musashi was sitting in the dirt-floored smithy, warming himself by the forge. He hadn't even removed his sandals.

"He was just here the other day. He spent the night," the woman replied sullenly. She put some sake to warm in the hearth in front of her husband.

"Young man," Baiken called. "Do you drink sake?"

"I don't dislike it."

"Have a cup."

"Thanks." Moving to the threshold of the hearth room, Musashi accepted a cup of the local brew and put it to his lips. It tasted sour. After downing it, he offered the cup to Baiken, saying, "Let me pour you a cup."

"Never mind, I have one." He looked at Musashi for an instant, then asked, "How old are you?"

"Twenty-two."

"Where do you come from?"

"Mimasaka."

Baiken's eyes, which had wandered off in another direction, swung back to Musashi, reexamining him from head to toe.

"Let's see, you mentioned it a while ago. Your name—what's your name?"

"Miyamoto Musashi."

"How do you write Musashi?"

"It's written the same way as Takezō."

The wife came in and put soup, pickles, chopsticks and a bowl of rice on the straw mat before Musashi. "Eat!" she said unceremoniously.

"Thanks," replied Musashi.

Baiken waited a couple of breaths, then said, as though to himself, "It's hot now—the sake." Pouring Musashi another cup, he asked in an offhand manner, "Does that mean you were called Takezō when you were younger?"

"Yes."

"Were you still called that when you were seventeen or so?"

"Yes."

"When you were about that age, you weren't by any chance at the Battle of Sekigahara with another boy about your age, were you?"

It was Musashi's turn to be surprised. "How did you know?" he said slowly. "Oh, I know a lot of things. I was at Sekigahara too."

Hearing this, Musashi felt better disposed toward the man; Baiken, too, seemed suddenly more friendly.

"I thought I'd seen you somewhere," said the blacksmith. "I guess we must have met on the battlefield."

"Were you in the Ukita camp too?"

"I was living in Yasugawa then, and I went to the war with a group of samurai from there. We were in the front lines, we were."

"Is that so? I guess we probably saw each other then."

"Whatever happened to your friend?"

"I haven't seen him since."

"Since the battle?"

"Not exactly. We stayed for a time at a house in Ibuki, waiting for my wounds to heal. We, uh, parted there. That was the last I saw of him."

Baiken let his wife know they were out of sake. She was already in bed with the baby. "There isn't any more," she answered.

"I want some more. Now!"

"Why do you have to drink so much tonight, of all nights?"

"We're having an interesting little talk here. Need some more sake."

"But there isn't any."

"Iwa!" he called through the flimsy board wall in a corner of the smithy.

"What is it, sir?" said the boy. He pushed open the door and showed his face, stooping because the lintel was so low.

"Go over to Onosaku's house and borrow a bottle of sake."

Musashi had had enough to drink. "If you don't mind, I'll go ahead and eat," he said, picking up his chopsticks.

"No, no, wait," said Baiken, quickly grabbing Musashi's wrist. "It's not time to eat. Now that I've sent for some sake, have a little more."

"If you were getting it for me, you shouldn't have. I don't think I can drink another drop."

"Aw, come now," Baiken insisted. "You said you wanted to hear more about the chain-ball-sickle. I'll tell you everything I know, but let's have a few drinks while we're talking."

When Iwa returned with the sake, Baiken poured some into a heating jar, put it on the fire, and talked at great length about the chain-ball-sickle and ways to use it to advantage in actual combat. The best thing about it, he told Musashi, was that, unlike a sword, it gave the enemy no time to defend himself. Also, before attacking the enemy directly, it was possible to snatch his weapon away from him with the chain. A skillful throw of the chain, a sharp yank, and the enemy had no more sword.

Still seated, Baiken demonstrated a stance. "You see, you hold the sickle in your left hand and the ball in your right. If the enemy comes at you, you take him on with the blade, then hurl the ball at his face. That's one way."

Changing positions, he went on, "Now, in this case, when there's some space between you and the enemy, you take his weapon away with the chain. It doesn't make any difference what kind of weapon it is—sword, lance, wooden staff, or whatever."

Baiken went on and on, telling Musashi about ways of throwing the ball, about the ten or more oral traditions concerning the weapon, about how the chain was like a snake, about how it was possible by cleverly alternating the movements of the chain and the sickle to create optical illusions and cause the enemy's defense to work to his own detriment, about all the secret ways of using the weapon.

Musashi was fascinated. When he heard talk like this, he listened with his whole body, eager to absorb every detail.

The chain. The sickle. Two hands . . .

As he listened, the seeds of other thoughts formed in his mind. "The sword can be used with one hand, but a man has two hands. . . ."

The second bottle of sake was empty. While Baiken had drunk a good deal, he pressed even more on Musashi, who had far surpassed his limit and was drunker than he ever had been before.

"Wake up!" Baiken called to his wife. "Let our guest sleep there. You and I can sleep in the back room. Go spread some bedding."

The woman did not budge.

"Get up!" Baiken said more loudly. "Our guest is tired. Let him go to bed now."

His wife's feet were nice and warm now; getting up would be uncomfortable. "You said he could sleep in the smithy with Iwa," she mumbled.

"Enough of your back talk. Do as I say!"

She got up in a huff and stalked off to the back room. Baiken took the sleeping baby in his arms and said, "The quilts are old, but the fire's right here beside you. If you get thirsty, there's hot water on it for tea. Go to bed. Make yourself comfortable." He, too, went into the back room.

When the woman came back to exchange pillows, the sullenness was gone from her face. "My husband's very drunk too," she said, "and he's probably tired from his trip. He says he plans to sleep late, so make yourself comfortable and sleep as long as you want. Tomorrow I'll give you a nice hot breakfast."

"Thanks." Musashi could think of nothing more to say. He could hardly wait to get out of his leather socks and cloak. "Thanks a lot."

He dived into the still warm quilts, but his own body was even hotter from drink.

The wife stood in the doorway watching him, then quietly blew out the candle and said, "Good night."

Musashi's head felt as if it had a tight steel band around it; his temples throbbed painfully. He wondered why he had drunk so much more than usual. He felt awful, but couldn't help thinking about Baiken. Why had the blacksmith, who had seemed hardly civil at first, suddenly grown friendly and sent out for more sake? Why had his disagreeable wife become sweet and solicitous all of a sudden? Why had they given him this warm bed?

It all seemed inexplicable, but before Musashi had solved the mystery, drowsiness overcame him. He closed his eyes, took a few deep breaths, and pulled the covers up. Only his forehead remained exposed, lit up by occasional sparks from the hearth. By and by, there was the sound of deep, steady breathing.

Baiken's wife retreated stealthily into the back room, the pit-a-pat of her feet moving stickily across the tatami.

Musashi had a dream, or rather the fragment of one, which kept repeating itself. A childhood memory flitted about his sleeping brain like an insect, trying, it seemed, to write something in luminescent letters. He heard the words of a lullaby.

> Go to sleep, go to sleep.
> Sleeping babies are sweet. . . .

He was back home in Mimasaka, hearing the lullaby the blacksmith's wife had sung in the Ise dialect. He was a baby in the arms of a light-skinned woman of about thirty . . . his mother. . . . This woman must be his mother. At his mother's breast, he looked up at her white face.

". . . naughty, and they make their mothers cry too. . . ." Cradling him in her arms, his mother sang softly. Her thin, well-bred face looked faintly bluish, like a pear blossom. There was a wall, a long stone wall, on which there was liverwort. And a dirt wall, above which branches darkened in the approaching night. Light from a lamp streamed from the house. Tears glistened on his mother's cheeks. The baby looked in wonder at the tears.

"Go away! Go back to your home!"

It was the forbidding voice of Munisai, coming from inside the house. And it was a command. Musashi's mother arose slowly. She ran along a long stone embankment. Weeping, she ran into the river and waded toward the center.

Unable to talk, the baby squirmed in his mother's arms, tried to tell her there was danger ahead. The more he fretted, the more tightly she held him. Her moistened cheek rubbed against his. "Takezō," she said, "are you your father's child, or your mother's?"

Munisai shouted from the bank. His mother sank beneath the water. The baby was cast up on the pebbly bank, where he lay wailing at the top of his lungs amid blooming primroses.

Musashi opened his eyes. When he started to doze off again, a woman—his mother? someone else?—intruded into his dream and woke him again. Musashi could not remember his mother's appearance. He thought of her often, but he couldn't have drawn her face. Whenever he saw another mother, he thought perhaps his own mother had looked the same.

"Why tonight?" he thought.

The sake had worn off. He opened his eyes and gazed at the ceiling. Amid the blackness of the soot was a reddish light, the reflection from the embers in the hearth. His gaze came to rest on the pinwheel suspended from the ceiling above him. He noticed, too, that the smell of mother and child still clung to the bedcovers. With a vague feeling of nostalgia, he lay half asleep, staring at the pinwheel.

The pinwheel started slowly to revolve. There was nothing strange about this; it was made to turn. But . . . but not unless there was a breeze! Musashi started to get up, then stopped and listened closely. There was the sound of a door being slid quietly shut. The pinwheel stopped turning.

Musashi quietly put his head back on the pillow and tried to fathom what was going on in the house. He was like an insect under a leaf, attempting to divine the weather above. His whole body was attuned to the slightest change in his surroundings, his sensitive nerves absolutely taut. Musashi knew that his life was in danger, but why?

"Is it a den of robbers?" he asked himself at first, but no. If they were professional thieves, they'd know he had nothing worth stealing.

"Has he got a grudge against me?" That did not seem to work either. Musashi was quite sure he had never even seen Baiken before.

Without being able to figure out a motive, he could feel in his skin and bones that someone or something was threatening his very life. He also knew that whatever it was was very near; he had to decide quickly whether to lie and wait for it to come, or get out of the way ahead of time.

Slipping his hand over the threshold into the smithy, he groped for his sandals. He slipped first one, then the other, under the cover and down to the foot of the bedding.

The pinwheel started to whirl again. In the light of the fire, it turned like a bewitched flower. Footsteps were faintly audible both inside and outside the house, as Musashi quietly wadded the bedding together into the rough shape of a human body.

Under the short curtain hanging in the doorway appeared two eyes, belonging to a man crawling in with his sword unsheathed. Another, carrying a lance and clinging closely to the wall, crept around to the foot of the bed. The two stared at the bedclothes, listening for the sleeper's breathing. Then, like a cloud of smoke, a third man jumped forward. It was Baiken, holding the sickle in his left hand and the ball in his right.

The men's eyes met and they synchronized their breathing. The man at the head of the bed kicked the pillow into the air, and the man at the foot, jumping down into the smithy, aimed his lance at the reclining form.

Keeping the sickle behind him, Baiken shouted, "Up, Musashi!"

Neither answer nor movement came from the bedding.

The man with the lance threw back the covers. "He's not here!" he shouted.

Baiken, casting a confused look around the room, caught sight of the rapidly whirling pinwheel. "There's a door open somewhere!" he shouted.

Soon another man cried out angrily. The door from the smithy onto a path that went around to the back of the house was open about three feet, and a biting wind was blowing in.

"He got out through here!"

"What are those fools doing?" Baiken screamed, running outside. From under the eaves and out of the shadows, black forms came forward.

"Master! Did it go all right?" asked a low voice excitedly.

Baiken glowered with rage. "What do you mean, you idiot? Why do you think I put you out here to keep watch? He's gone! He must have come this way."

"Gone? How could he get out?"

"You're asking me? You thick-headed ass!" Baiken went back inside and stamped around nervously. "There are only two ways he could have gone: he either went up to Suzuka ford or back to the Tsu highway. Whichever it was, he couldn't have gone far. Go get him!"

"Which way do you think he went?"

"Ugh! I'll go toward Suzuka. You cover the lower road!"

The men inside joined forces with the men outside, making a motley group of about ten, all armed. One of them, carrying a musket, looked like a hunter; another, with a short field sword, was probably a woodcutter.

As they parted, Baiken shouted, "If you find him, fire the gun, then everybody come together."

They set off at great speed, but after about an hour

came straggling back, looking hangdog and talking dejectedly among themselves. They expected a tongue-lashing
from their leader, but when they reached the house, they
found Baiken sitting on the ground in the smithy, eyes
downcast and expressionless.

When they tried to cheer him up, he said, "No use
crying about it now." Searching about for a way to vent his
wrath, he seized a piece of charred wood and broke it
sharply over his knee.

"Bring some sake! I want a drink." He stirred up the
fire again and threw on more kindling.

Baiken's wife, trying to quiet the baby, reminded him
there was no more sake. One of the men volunteered to
bring some from his house, which he did with dispatch. Soon
the brew was warm, and the cups were being passed around.

The conversation was sporadic and gloomy.

"It makes me mad."

"The rotten little bastard!"

"He leads a charmed life. I'll say that for him."

"Don't worry about it, master. You did everything you
could. The men outside fell down on their job."

Those referred to apologized shamefacedly.

They tried to get Baiken drunk, so he would go to sleep,
but he just sat there, frowning at the bitterness of the sake,
but taking no one to task for the failure.

Finally, he said, "I shouldn't have made such a big
thing out of it, getting so many of you to help. I could have
handled him all by myself, but I thought I'd better be careful.
After all, he did kill my brother, and Tsujikaze Temma was
no mean fighter."

"Could that rōnin really be the boy who was hiding in
Okō's house four years ago?"

"He must be. My dead brother's spirit brought him
here, I'm sure. At first the thought never crossed my mind,
but then he told me he'd been at Sekigahara, and his name
used to be Takezō. He's the right age and the right type of
person to have killed my brother. I know it was him."

"Come on, master, don't think about it anymore tonight. Lie down. Get some sleep."

They all helped him to bed; someone picked up the

pillow that had been kicked aside and put it under his head. The instant Baiken's eyes were closed, the anger that had filled him was replaced by loud snoring.

The men nodded to each other and drifted off, dispersing into the mist of early morning. They were all riffraff—underlings of freebooters like Tsujikaze Temma of Ibuki and Tsujikaze Kōhei of Yasugawa, who now called himself Shishido Baiken. Or else they were hangers-on at the bottom of the ladder in open society. Driven by the changing times, they had become farmers or artisans or hunters, but they still had teeth, which were only too ready to bite honest people when the opportunity arose.

The only sounds in the house were those made by the sleeping inhabitants and the gnawing of a field rat.

In the corner of the passageway connecting the workroom and kitchen, next to a large earthen oven, stood a stack of firewood. Above this hung an umbrella and heavy straw rain capes. In the shadows between the oven and the wall, one of the rain capes moved, slowly and quietly inching up the wall until it hung on a nail.

The smoky figure of a man suddenly seemed to come out of the wall itself. Musashi had never gone a step away from the house. After slipping out from under the covers, he had opened the outer door and then merged with the firewood, drawing the rain cape down over him.

He walked silently across the smithy and looked at Baiken. Adenoids, thought Musashi, for the snoring was thunderous. The situation struck him as humorous, and his face twisted into a grin.

He stood there for a moment, thinking. To all intents and purposes, he had won his bout with Baiken. It had been a clear-cut victory. Still, this man lying here was the brother of Tsujikaze Temma and had tried to murder him to comfort the spirit of his dead brother—an admirable sentiment for a mere freebooter.

Should Musashi kill him? If he left him alive, he would go on looking for an opportunity to take his revenge, and the safe course was doubtless to do away with him here and now. But there remained the question of whether he was worth killing.

The Pinwheel

Musashi pondered for a time, before hitting on what seemed exactly the right solution. Going to the wall by Baiken's feet, he took down one of the blacksmith's own weapons. While he eased the blade from its groove, he examined the sleeping face. Then, wrapping a piece of damp paper around the blade, he carefully laid it across Baiken's neck; he stepped back and admired his handiwork.

The pinwheel was sleeping too. If it were not for the paper wrapping, thought Musashi, the wheel might wake in the morning and turn wildly at the sight of its master's head fallen from the pillow.

When Musashi had killed Tsujikaze Temma, he had had a reason, and anyway, he had still been burning with the fever of battle. But he had nothing to gain from taking the blacksmith's life. And who could tell? If he did kill him, the infant owner of the pinwheel might spend his life seeking to avenge his father's murder.

It was a night on which Musashi had thought time and again of his own father and mother. He felt a little envious as he stood here by this sleeping family, sensing the faint sweet scent of mother's milk about him. He even felt a little reluctant to take his leave.

In his heart, he spoke to them: "I'm sorry to have troubled you. Sleep well." He quietly opened the outer door and went out.

14

The Flying Horse

Otsū and Jōtarō arrived at the barrier late at night, stopped over at an inn and resumed their journey before the morning mist cleared. From Mount Fudesute, they walked to Yonkenjaya, where they first felt the warmth of the rising sun on their backs.

"How beautiful!" exclaimed Otsū, pausing to look at the great golden orb. She seemed full of hope and cheer. It was one of those wonderful moments when all living things, even plants and animals, must feel satisfaction and pride in their existence here on earth.

Jōtarō said with obvious pleasure, "We're the very first people on the road. Not a soul ahead of us."

"You sound boastful. What difference does it make?"

"It makes a lot of difference to me."

"Do you think it'll make the road shorter?"

"Oh, it's not that. It just feels good to be first, even on the road. You have to admit it's better than following along behind palanquins or horses."

"That's true."

"When no one else is on the road I'm on, I have the feeling it belongs to me."

"In that case, why don't you pretend you're a great samurai on horseback, surveying your vast estates. I'll be your attendant." She picked up a bamboo stick, and waving it ceremoniously, called out in singsong fashion, "Bow down, all! Bow down for his lordship!"

A man looked out inquiringly from under the eaves of a teahouse. Caught playing like a child, she blushed and walked rapidly on.

"You can't do that," Jōtarō protested. "You mustn't run away from your master. If you do, I'll have to put you to death!"

"I don't want to play anymore."

"You're the one who was playing, not me."

"Yes, but you started it. Oh, my! The man at the teahouse is still staring at us. He must think we're silly."

"Let's go back there."

"What for?"

"I'm hungry."

"Already?"

"Couldn't we eat half of the rice balls we brought for lunch now?"

"Be patient. We haven't covered two miles yet. If I let you, you'd eat five meals a day."

"Maybe. But you don't see me riding in palanquins or hiring horses, the way you do."

"That was only last night, and then only because it was getting dark and we had to hurry. If you feel that way about it, I'll walk the whole way today."

"It should be my turn to ride today."

"Children don't need to ride."

"But I want to try riding a horse. Can't I? Please."

"Well, maybe, but only for today."

"I saw a horse tied up at the teahouse. We could hire it."

"No, it's still too early in the day."

"Then you didn't mean it when you said I could ride!"

"I did, but you're not even tired yet. It'd be a waste of money to rent a horse."

"You know perfectly well I never get tired. I wouldn't get tired if we walked a hundred days and a thousand miles. If I have to wait till I'm worn out, I'll never get to ride a horse. Come on, Otsū, let's rent the horse now, while there aren't any people ahead of us. It'd be a lot safer than when the road is crowded. Please!"

Seeing that if they kept this up, they would lose the

time they had gained by making an early start, Otsū gave in, and Jōtarō, sensing rather than waiting for her nod of approval, raced back to the teahouse.

Although there actually were four teahouses in the vicinity, as the name Yonkenjaya indicated, they were located at various places on the slopes of mounts Fudesute and Kutsukake. The one they had passed was the only one in sight.

Running up to the proprietor and stopping suddenly, Jōtarō shouted, "Hey, there, I want a horse! Get one out for me."

The old man was taking down the shutters, and the boy's lusty cry jarred him into wakefulness. With a sour expression, he grumbled, "What's all this! Do you have to yell so loud?"

"I need a horse. Please get one ready right away. How much is it to Minakuchi? If it's not too much, I may even take it all the way to Kusatsu."

"Whose little boy are you anyway?"

"I'm the son of my mother and my father," replied Jōtarō impudently.

"I thought you might be the unruly offspring of the storm god."

"You're the storm god, aren't you? You look mad as a thunderbolt."

"Brat!"

"Just bring me the horse."

"I daresay you think that horse is for hire. Well, it isn't. So I fear I shall not have the honor of lending it to your lordship."

Matching the man's tone of voice, Jōtarō said, "Then, sir, shall I not have the pleasure of renting it?"

"Sassy, aren't you?" cried the man, taking a piece of lighted kindling from the fire under his oven and throwing it at the boy. The flaming stick missed Jōtarō, but struck the ancient horse tied under the eaves. With an air-splitting whinny, she reared, striking her back against a beam.

"You bastard!" screamed the proprietor. He leapt out of the shop sputtering curses and ran up to the animal.

As he untied the rope and led the horse around to the side yard, Jōtarō started in again. "Please lend her to me."

"I can't."

"Why not?"

"I don't have a groom to send with her."

Now at Jōtarō's side, Otsū suggested that if there was no groom, she could pay the fee in advance and send the horse back from Minakuchi with a traveler coming this way. Her appealing manner softened the old man, and he decided he could trust her. Handing her the rope, he said, "In that case, you can take her to Minakuchi, or even to Kusatsu if you want. All I ask is that you send her back."

As they started away, Jōtarō, in high dudgeon, exclaimed, "How do you like that! He treated me like an ass, and then as soon as he saw a pretty face . . ."

"You'd better be careful what you say about the old man. His horse is listening. She may get angry and throw you."

"Do you think this feeble-jointed old nag can get the best of me?"

"You don't know how to ride, do you?"

"Of course I know how to ride."

"What are you doing, then, trying to climb up from behind?"

"Well, help me up!"

"You're a nuisance!" She put her hands under his armpits and lifted him onto the animal.

Jōtarō looked majestically around at the world beneath him. "Please walk ahead, Otsū," he said.

"You're not sitting right."

"Don't worry. I'm fine."

"All right, but you're going to be sorry." Taking the rope in one hand, Otsū waved good-bye to the proprietor with the other, and the two started off.

Before they had gone a hundred paces, they heard a loud shout coming out of the mist behind them, accompanied by the sound of running footsteps.

"Who could that be?" asked Jōtarō.

"Is he calling us?" wondered Otsū.

They stopped the horse and looked around. The shadow

f a man began to take form in the white, smoky mist. At
first they could make out only contours, then colors, but the
man was soon close enough for them to discern his general
appearance and approximate age. A diabolic aura surrounded his body, as though he were accompanied by a
raging whirlwind. He came rapidly to Otsū's side, halted and
with one swift motion snatched the rope from her hand.

"Get off!" he commanded, glaring up at Jōtarō.

The horse skittered backward. Clutching her mane,
Jōtarō shouted, "You can't do this! I rented this horse, not
you!"

The man snorted, turned to Otsū and said, "You,
woman!"

"Yes?" Otsū said in a low voice.

"My name's Shishido Baiken. I live in Ujii Village up
in the mountains beyond the barrier. For reasons I won't go
into, I'm after a man named Miyamoto Musashi. He came
along this road sometime before daybreak this morning.
Probably passed here hours ago, so I've got to move fast if
I'm going to catch him in Yasugawa, on the Ōmi border. Let
me have your horse." He talked very rapidly, his ribs
heaving in and out. In the cold air, the mist was condensing
into icy flowers on branches and twigs, but his neck glistened
like a snakeskin with sweat.

Otsū stood very still, her face deathly white, as though
the earth beneath her had drained all the blood from her
body. Her lips quivering, she wanted desperately to ask and
make sure that she had heard correctly. She couldn't utter a
word.

"You said Musashi?" Jōtarō blurted out. He was still
clutching the horse's mane, but his arms and legs were
trembling.

Baiken was in too much of a hurry to notice their
shocked reaction.

"Come on, now," he ordered. "Off the horse, and be
quick about it, or I'll give you a thrashing." He brandished
the end of the rope like a whip.

Jōtarō shook his head adamantly. "I won't."

"What do you mean, you won't?"

"It's my horse. You can't have it. I don't care how much of a hurry you're in."

"Watch it! I've been very nice and explained everything, because you're only a woman and a child traveling alone, but—"

"Isn't that right, Otsū?" Jōtarō interrupted. "We don't have to let him have the horse, do we?"

Otsū could have hugged the boy. As far as she was concerned, it was not so much a question of the horse as it was of preventing this monster from progressing any faster. "That's true," she said. "I'm sure you're in a hurry, sir, but so are we. You can hire one of the horses that travel up and down the mountain regularly. Just as the boy says, it's unfair to try to take our horse away from us."

"I won't get off," Jōtarō repeated. "I'll die before I do!"

"You've set your mind on not letting me have the horse?" Baiken asked gruffly.

"You should have known we wouldn't to begin with," replied Jōtaro gravely.

"Son of a bitch!" shouted Baiken, infuriated by the boy's tone.

Jōtarō, tightening his grip on the horse's mane, looked little bigger than a flea. Baiken reached up, took hold of his leg and started to pull him off. Now, of all times, was the moment for Jōtarō to put his wooden sword to use, but in his confusion he forgot all about the weapon. Faced with an enemy so much stronger than himself, the only defense that came to mind was to spit in Baiken's face, which he did, again and again.

Otsū was filled with grim terror. The fear of being injured, or killed, by this man brought an acid, dry taste to her mouth. But there was no question of giving in and letting him have the horse. Musashi was being pursued; the longer she could delay this fiend, the more time Musashi would have to flee. It didn't matter to her that the distance between him and herself would also be increased—just at a time when she knew at least that they were on the same road. Biting her lip, then screaming, "You can't do this!" she struck

Baiken in the chest with a force that not even she realized she possessed.

Baiken, still wiping the spit off his face, was thrown off balance, and in that instant, Otsū's hand caught the hilt of his sword.

"Bitch!" he barked, grabbing for her wrist. Then he howled with pain, for the sword was already partly out of its scabbard, and instead of Otsū's arm, he'd squeezed his hand around the blade. The tips of two fingers on his right hand dropped to the ground. Holding his bleeding hand, he sprang back, unintentionally pulling the sword from its scabbard. The brilliant glitter of steel extending from Otsū's hand scratched across the ground, coming to rest behind her.

Baiken had blundered even worse than the night before. Cursing himself for his lack of caution, he struggled to regain his footing. Otsū, now afraid of nothing, swung the blade sidewise at him. But it was a great wide-bladed weapon, nearly three feet long, which not every man would have been able to handle easily. When Baiken dodged, her hands wobbled, and she staggered forward. She felt a quick wrenching of her wrists, and reddish-black blood spurted into her face. After a moment of dizziness, she realized the sword had cut into the rump of the horse.

The wound was not deep, but the horse let out a fearsome noise, rearing and kicking wildly. Baiken, yelling unintelligibly, got hold of Otsū's wrist and tried to recover his sword, but at that moment the horse kicked them both into the air. Then, rising on her hind legs, she whinnied loudly and shot off down the road like an arrow from a bow, Jōtarō clinging grimly to her back and blood spewing out behind.

Baiken stumbled around in the dust-laden air. He knew he couldn't catch the crazed beast, so his enraged eyes turned toward the place where Otsū had been. She wasn't there.

After a moment, he spotted his sword at the foot of a larch tree and with a lunge retrieved it. As he straightened up, something clicked in his mind: there must be some connection between this woman and Musashi! And if she was Musashi's friend, she would make excellent bait; at the very least she would know where he was going.

Half running, half sliding down the embankment next to the road, he strode around a thatched farmhouse, peering under the floor and into the storehouse, while an old woman stooped like a hunchback behind a spinning wheel inside the house looked on in terror.

Then he caught sight of Otsū racing through a thick grove of cryptomeria trees toward the valley beyond, where there were patches of late snow.

Thundering down the hill with the force of a landslide, he soon closed the distance between them.

"Bitch!" he cried, stretching out his left hand and touching her hair.

Otsū dropped to the ground and caught hold of the roots of a tree, but her foot slipped and her body fell over the edge of the cliff, where it swayed like a pendulum. Dirt and pebbles fell into her face as she looked up at Baiken's large eyes and his gleaming sword.

"Fool!" he said contemptuously. "Do you think you can get away now?"

Otsū glanced downward; fifty or sixty feet below, a stream cut through the floor of the valley. Curiously, she was not afraid, for she saw the valley as her salvation. At any moment she chose, she could escape simply by letting go of the tree and throwing herself on the mercy of the open space below. She felt death was near, but rather than dwell on that, her mind focused on a single image: Musashi. She seemed to see him now, his face like a full moon in a stormy sky.

Baiken quickly seized her wrists, and hoisting her up, dragged her well clear of the edge.

Just then, one of his henchmen called to him from the road. "What are you doing down there? We'd better move fast. The old man at the teahouse back there said a samurai woke him up before dawn this morning, ordered a box lunch, then ran off toward Kaga Valley."

"Kaga Valley?"

"That's what he said. But whether he goes that way or crosses Mount Tsuchi to Minakuchi doesn't matter. The roads come together at Ishibe. If we make good time to Yasugawa, we should be able to catch him there."

Baiken's back was turned to the man, his eyes fastened on Otsū, who crouched before him, seemingly trapped by his fierce glare. "Ho!" he roared. "All three of you come down here."

"Why?"

"Get down here, fast!"

"If we waste time, Musashi'll beat us to Yasugawa."

"Never mind that!"

The three men were among those who had been engaged in the fruitless search the night before. Used to making their way through the mountains, they stormed down the incline with the speed of so many boars. As they reached the ledge where Baiken was standing, they caught sight of Otsū. Their leader rapidly explained the situation to them.

"All right now, tie her up and bring her along," said Baiken, before darting off through the woods.

They tied her up, but they couldn't help feeling sorry for her. She lay helpless on the ground, face turned to the side; they stole embarrassed looks at her pale profile.

Baiken was already in Kaga Valley. He stopped, looked back at the cliff and shouted, "We'll meet in Yasugawa. I'll take a shortcut, but you stay on the highway. And keep your eyes peeled."

"Yes, sir!" they chorused back.

Baiken, running between the rocks like a mountain goat, was soon out of sight.

Jōtarō was hurtling down the highroad. Despite her age, the horse was so maddened there was no stopping her with a mere rope, even if Jōtarō had known how to go about it. The raw wound burning like a torch, she sped blindly ahead, up hill, down dale, through villages.

It was only through sheer luck that Jōtarō avoided being thrown off. "Watch out! Watch out! *Watch out!*" he screamed repeatedly. The words had become a litany.

No longer able to stay on by clinging to the mane, he had his arms locked tightly around the horse's neck. His eyes were closed.

When the beast's rump rose in the air, so did Jōtarō's. As it became increasingly apparent that his shouts were not working, his pleas gradually gave way to a distressed wail. When he had begged Otsū to let him ride a horse just once, he had been thinking how grand it would be to go galloping about at will on a splendid steed, but after a few minutes of this hair-raising ride, he had had his fill.

Jōtarō hoped that someone—anyone—would bravely volunteer to seize the flying rope and bring the horse to a halt. In this he was overoptimistic, for neither travelers nor villagers wanted to risk being hurt in an affair that was no concern of theirs. Far from helping, everyone made for the safety of the roadside and shouted abuse at what appeared to them to be an irresponsible horseman.

In no time he'd passed the village of Mikumo and reached the inn town of Natsumi. If he had been an expert rider in perfect control of his mount, he could have shaded his eyes and calmly looked out over the beautiful mountains and valleys of Iga—the peaks of Nunobiki, the Yokota River and, in the distance, the mirrorlike waters of Lake Biwa.

"Stop! Stop! Stop!" The words of his litany had changed; his tone was more distraught. As they started down Kōji Hill, his cry abruptly changed again. "Help!" he screamed.

The horse charged on down the precipitous incline, Jōtarō bouncing like a ball on her back.

About a third of the way down, a large oak projected from a cliff on the left, one of its smaller branches extending across the road. When Jōtarō felt the leaves against his face, he grabbed with both hands, believing the gods had heard his prayer and caused the limb to stretch out before him. Perhaps he was right; he jumped like a frog, and the next instant he was hanging in the air, his hands firmly wrapped around the branch above his head. The horse went out from under him, moving a little faster now that she was riderless.

It was no more than a ten-foot drop to the ground, but Jōtarō could not bring himself to release his grip. In his badly shaken condition, he saw the short distance to the ground as a yawning abyss and hung onto the branch for dear life, crossing his legs over it, readjusting his aching hands, and wondering feverishly what to do. The problem was solved for him when with a loud crack the branch broke off. For an awful instant, Jōtarō thought he was done for; a second later he was sitting on the ground unharmed.

"Whew!" was all he could say.

For a few minutes he sat inertly, his spirit dampened, if not broken, but then he remembered why he was there and jumped up.

Heedless of the ground he had covered, he shouted, "Otsū!"

He ran back up the slope, one hand firmly around his wooden sword.

"What could have happened to her? Otsū! O-tsū-ū-ū!"

Presently he met a man in a grayish-red kimono coming down the hill. The stranger wore a leather *hakama* and carried two swords, but had on no cloak. After passing Jōtarō, he looked over his shoulder and said, "Hello, there!" Jōtarō turned, and the man asked, "Is something wrong?"

"You came from over the hill, didn't you?" Jōtarō asked.

"Yes."

"Did you see a pretty woman about twenty years old?"

"I did, as a matter of fact."

"Where?"

"In Natsumi I saw some freebooters walking along with a girl. Her arms were tied behind her, which naturally struck me as strange, but I had no reason to interfere. I daresay the men were from Tsujikaze Kōhei's gang. He moved a whole villageful of hoodlums from Yasugawa to Suzuka Valley some years ago."

"That was her, I'm sure." Jōtarō started to walk on, but the man stopped him.

"Were you traveling together?" he asked.

"Yes. Her name's Otsū."

"If you take foolish risks you'll get yourself killed before you can help anybody. Why don't you wait here? They'll come this way sooner or later. For now, tell me what this is all about. I may be able to give you some advice."

The boy immediately placed his trust in the man and

told him everything that had happened since morning. From time to time, the man nodded under his basket hat. When the story ended, he said, "I understand your predicament, but even with your courage, a woman and a boy are no match for Kōhei's men. I think I'd better rescue Otsū—is that her name?—for you."

"Would they hand her over to you?"

"Maybe not for the mere asking, but I'll think about that when the time comes. Meanwhile, you hide in a thicket and stay quiet."

While Jōtarō selected a clump of bushes and hid behind it, the man continued briskly on down the hill. For a moment, Jōtarō wondered if he had been deceived. Had the rōnin just said a few words to cheer him up, then moved on to save his own neck? Seized by anxiety, he lifted his head above the shrubs, but hearing voices, ducked down again.

A minute or two later Otsū came into view, surrounded by the three men, her hands tied firmly behind her. Blood was encrusted on a cut on her white foot.

One of the ruffians, shoving Otsū forward by the shoulder, growled, "What are you looking around for? Walk faster!"

"That's right, walk!"

"I'm looking for my traveling companion. What could have happened to him? . . . Jōtarō!"

"Quiet!"

Jōtarō was all set to yell and jump out of his hiding place when the rōnin came back, this time without his basket hat. He was twenty-six or -seven and of a darkish complexion. In his eyes was a purposeful look that strayed neither right nor left. As he trotted up the incline, he was saying, as if to himself, "It's terrifying, really terrifying!"

When he passed Otsū and her captors, he mumbled a greeting and hastened on, but the men stopped. "Hey," one of them called. "Aren't you Watanabe's nephew? What's so terrifying?"

Watanabe was the name of an old family in the district, the present head of which was Watanabe Hanzō, a highly respected practitioner of the occult martial tactics known collectively as *ninjutsu*.

"Haven't you heard?"

"Heard what?"

"Down at the bottom of this hill there's a samurai named Miyamoto Musashi, all ready for a big fight. He's standing in the middle of the road with his sword unsheathed, questioning everybody who passes by. He has the fiercest eyes I ever saw."

"Musashi's doing that?"

"That's right. He came straight up to me and asked my name, so I told him that I was Tsuge Sannojō, the nephew of Watanabe Hanzō, and that I came from Iga. He apologized and let me by. He was very polite, in fact, said as long as I wasn't connected with Tsujikaze Kōhei, it was all right."

"Oh?"

"I asked him what had happened. He said Kōhei was on the road with his henchmen, out to catch him and kill him. He decided to entrench himself where he was and meet the attack there. He seemed prepared to fight to the finish."

"Are you telling the truth, Sannojō?"

"Of course I am. Why would I lie to you?"

The faces of the three grew pale. They looked at each other nervously, uncertain as to their next move.

"You'd better be careful," said Sannojō, ostensibly resuming his trip up the hill.

"Sannojō!"

"What?"

"I don't know what we should do. Even our boss said this Musashi is unusually strong."

"Well, he does seem to have a lot of confidence in himself. When he came up to me with that sword, I certainly didn't feel like taking him on."

"What do you think we should do? We're taking this woman to Yasugawa on the boss's orders."

"I don't see that that has anything to do with me."

"Don't be like that. Lend us a hand."

"Not on your life! If I helped you and my uncle found out about it, he'd disown me. I could, of course, give you a bit of advice."

"Well, speak up! What do you think we should do?"

"Um . . . For one thing, you could tie that woman up to a tree and leave her. That way, you could move faster."

"Anything else?"

"You shouldn't take this road. It's a little farther, but you could go up the valley road to Yasugawa and let people there know about all this. Then you could surround Musashi and gradually hem him in."

"That's not a bad idea."

"But be very, very careful. Musashi will be fighting for his life, and he'll take quite a few souls with him when he goes. You'd rather avoid that, wouldn't you?"

Quickly agreeing with Sannojō's suggestion, they dragged Otsū to a grove and tied her rope to a tree. Then they left but after a few minutes returned to tie a gag in her mouth.

"That should do it," said one.

"Let's get going."

They dived into the woods. Jōtarō, squatting behind his leafy screen, waited judiciously before raising his head for a look around. He saw no one—no travelers, no freebooters, no Sannojō.

"Otsū!" he called, prancing out of the thicket. Quickly finding her, he undid her bonds and took her hand. They ran to the road. "Let's get away from here!" he urged.

"What were you doing hiding in the bushes?"

"Never mind! Let's go!"

"Just a minute," said Otsū, stopping to pat her hair, straighten her collar and rearrange her obi.

Jōtarō clicked his tongue. "This is no time for primping," he wailed. "Can't you fix your hair later?"

"But that rōnin said Musashi was at the bottom of the hill."

"Is that why you have to stop and make yourself pretty?"

"No, of course not," said Otsū, defending herself with almost comic seriousness. "But if Musashi is so near, we don't have anything to worry about. And since our troubles are as good as over, I feel calm and safe enough to think of my appearance."

"Do you believe that rōnin really saw Musashi?"

"Of course. By the way, where is he?"

"He just disappeared. He's sort of strange, isn't he?"

"Shall we go now?" said Otsū.

"Sure you're pretty enough?"

"Jōtarō!"

"Just teasing. You look so happy."

"You look happy too."

"I am, and I don't try to hide it the way you do. I'll shout it so everybody can hear: *I'm happy!*" He did a little dance, waving his arms and kicking his legs, then said, "It'll be very disappointing if Musashi isn't there, won't it? I think I'll run on ahead and see."

Otsū took her time. Her heart had already flown to the bottom of the slope faster than Jōtarō could ever have run.

"I look frightful," she thought as she surveyed her injured foot and the dirt and leaves stuck to her sleeves.

"Come on!" called Jōtarō. "Why are you poking along?" From the lilt in his voice, Otsū felt certain that he had spotted Musashi.

"At last," she thought. Until now she'd had to seek comfort within herself, and she was tired of it. She felt a measure of pride, both in herself and toward the gods, for having remained true to her purpose. Now that she was about to see Musashi again, her spirit was dancing with joy. This elation, she knew, was that of anticipation; she could not predict whether Musashi would accept her devotion. Her joy at the prospect of meeting him was only slightly tarnished by a gnawing premonition that the encounter might bring sadness.

On the shady slope of Kōji Hill, the ground was frozen, but at the tea shop near the bottom, it was so warm flies were flying around. This was an inn town, so of course the shop sold tea to travelers; it also carried a line of miscellaneous goods required by the farmers of the district, from cheap sweets to straw boots for oxen. Jōtarō stood in front of the shop, a small boy in a large and noisy crowd.

"Where's Musashi?" She looked around searchingly.

"He's not here," replied Jōtarō dispiritedly.

"Not here? He must be!"

"Well, I can't find him anywhere, and the shopkeeper

said he hasn't seen a samurai like that around. There must have been some mistake." Jōtarō, though disappointed, was not despondent.

Otsū would have readily admitted that she had had no reason on earth to expect as much as she had, but the nonchalance of Jōtarō's reply annoyed her. Shocked and a little angry at his lack of concern, she said, "Did you look for him over there?"

"Yes."

"How about behind the Kōshin milepost?"

"I looked. He's not there."

"Behind the tea shop?"

"I told you, he isn't here!" Otsū turned her face away from him. "Are you crying?" he asked.

"It's none of your business," she said sharply.

"I don't understand you. You seem to be sensible most of the time, but sometimes you act like a baby. How could we know if Sannojō's story was true or not? You decided all by yourself that it was, and now that you find it wasn't, you burst into tears. Women are crazy," Jōtarō exclaimed, bursting into laughter.

Otsū felt like sitting down right there and giving up. In an instant, the light had gone out of her life; she felt as bereft of hope as before—no, more so. The decaying milk teeth in Jōtarō's laughing mouth disgusted her. Angrily she asked herself why she had to drag a child like this around with her anyway. The urge swept over her to abandon him right there.

True, he was also searching for Musashi, but he loved him only as a teacher. To her, Musashi was life itself. Jōtarō could laugh everything off and return to his normal cheerful self in no time, but Otsū would for days be deprived of the energy to go on. Somewhere in Jōtarō's youthful mind, there was the blithe certainty that one day, sooner or later, he'd find Musashi again. Otsū had no such belief in a happy ending. Having been too optimistic about seeing Musashi today, she was now swinging toward the opposite extreme, asking herself if life would go on like this forever, without her ever again seeing or talking to the man she loved.

Those who love seek a philosophy and, because of this, are fond of solitude. In Otsū's case, orphan that she was, there was also the keen sense of isolation from others. In response to Jōtarō's indifference, she frowned and marched silently away from the tea shop.

"Otsū!" The voice was Sannojō's. He emerged from behind the Kōshin milepost and came toward her through the withered underbrush. His scabbards were damp.

"You weren't telling the truth," Jōtarō said accusingly.

"What do you mean?"

"You said Musashi was waiting at the bottom of the hill. You lied!"

"Don't be stupid!" said Sannojō reproachfully. "It was because of that lie that Otsū was able to escape, wasn't it? What are you complaining about? Shouldn't you be thanking me?"

"You just made up that story to fool those men?"

"Of course."

Turning triumphantly to Otsū, Jōtarō said, "See? Didn't I tell you?"

Otsū felt she had a perfect right to be angry with Jōtarō, but there was no reason to nurse a grudge against Sannojō. She bowed to him several times and thanked him profusely for having saved her.

"Those hoodlums from Suzuka are a lot tamer than they used to be," said Sannojō, "but if they're out to waylay somebody, he's not likely to get over this road safely. Still, from what I hear about this Musashi you're so worried about, it sounds to me like he's too smart to stumble into one of their traps."

"Are there other roads besides this one to Ōmi?" asked Otsū.

"There are," replied Sannojō, raising his eyes toward the mountain peaks sparkling dazzlingly in the midday sun. "If you go to Iga Valley, there's a road to Ueno, and from Ano Valley there's one that goes to Yokkaichi and Kuwana. There must be three or four other mountain paths and shortcuts. My guess is, Musashi left the highroad early on."

"Then you think he's still safe?"

"Most likely. At least, safer than the two of you. You've been rescued once today, but if you stay on this highway, Tsujikaze's men will catch you again at Yasugawa. If you can stand a rather steep climb, come with me, and I'll show you a path practically nobody knows."

They quickly assented. Sannojō guided them up above Kaga Village to Makado Pass, from which a path led down to Seto in Ōmi

After explaining in detail how to proceed, he said, "You're out of harm's way now. Just keep your eyes and ears open, and be sure to find a safe place to stay before dark."

Otsū thanked him for all he had done and started to leave, but Sannojō stared at her and said, "We're parting now, you know." The words seemed fraught with meaning, and there was a rather hurt look in his eyes. "All along," he continued, "I've been thinking, 'Is she going to ask now?' but you never did ask."

"Ask what?"

"My name."

"But I heard your name when we were on Kōji Hill."

"Do you remember it?"

"Of course. You're Tsuge Sannojō, and you're the nephew of Watanabe Hanzō."

"Thank you. I don't ask you to be eternally grateful to me or anything like that, but I do hope you'll always remember me."

"Why, I'm deeply indebted to you."

"That's not what I mean. What I want to say is, well, I'm still not married. If my uncle weren't so strict, I'd like to take you to my home right now. . . . But I can see you're in a hurry. Anyway, you'll find a small inn a few miles ahead where you can stay overnight. I know the innkeeper very well, so mention my name to him. Farewell!"

After he was gone, a strange feeling came over Otsū. From the outset, she had not been able to figure out what sort of person Sannojō was, and when they had parted, she felt as though she had escaped from the clutches of a dangerous animal. She had gone through the motions of thanking him; she did not really feel grateful in her heart.

Jōtarō, in spite of his tendency to take to strangers, reacted in much the same way. As they started down from the pass, he said, "I don't like that man."

Otsū did not want to speak badly of Sannojō behind his back, but she admitted she did not like him either, adding, "What do you suppose he meant by telling me that he was still single?"

"Oh, he's hinting that one day he's going to ask you to marry him."

"Why, that's absurd!"

The two made their way to Kyoto without incident, albeit disappointed at not finding Musashi at any of the places where they had hoped to—neither on the lakeside on Ōmi nor at the Kara Bridge in Seta nor at the barrier in Osaka.

From Keage, they plunged into the year-end crowds near the Sanjō Avenue entrance to the city. In the capital, the housefronts were adorned with the pine-branch decorations traditional during the New Year's season. The sight of the decorations cheered Otsū, who, instead of lamenting the lost chances of the past, resolved to look forward to the future and the opportunities it held for finding Musashi. The Great Bridge at Gojō Avenue. The first day of the New Year. If he did not show up that morning, then the second, or the third . . . He had said he would certainly be there, as she had learned from Jōtarō. Even though he wasn't coming to meet her, just to be able to see him and talk to him again would be enough.

The possibility that she might run into Matahachi was the darkest cloud shadowing her dream. According to Jōtarō, Musashi's message had been delivered only to Akemi; Matahachi might never have received it. Otsū prayed that he hadn't, that Musashi would come, but not Matahachi.

Otsū slowed her steps, thinking Musashi might be in the very crowd they were in. Then a chill ran up her spine and she started walking faster. Matahachi's dreadful mother might also materialize at any moment.

Jōtarō hadn't a care in the world. The colors and noises of the city, seen and heard after a long absence, exhilarated him no end. "Are we going straight to an inn?" he asked apprehensively.

"No, not yet."

"Good! It'd be dull being indoors while it's still light out. Let's walk around some more. It looks like there's a market over there."

"We haven't time to go to the market. We have important business to take care of."

"Business? We do?"

"Have you forgotten the box you're carrying on your back?"

"Oh, that."

"Yes, that. I won't be able to relax until we've found Lord Karasumaru Mitsuhiro's mansion and delivered the scrolls to him."

"Are we going to stay at his house tonight?"

"Of course not." Otsū laughed, glancing toward the Kamo River. "Do you think a great nobleman like that would let a dirty little boy like you sleep under his roof, lice and all?"

15

The Butterfly in Winter

Akemi slipped out of the inn at Sumiyoshi without telling anybody. She felt like a bird freed from its cage but was still not sufficiently recovered from her brush with death to fly too high. The scars left by Seijūrō's violence would not heal quickly; he had shattered her cherished dream of giving herself unblemished to the man she really loved.

On the boat up the Yodo to Kyoto, she felt that all the waters of the river would not equal the tears she wanted to shed. As other boats, loaded with ornaments and supplies for the New Year celebration, rowed busily past, she stared at them and thought: "Now, even if I do find Musashi . . ." Her troubled eyes filled and overflowed. No one could ever know how eagerly she had anticipated the New Year's morning when she would find him on the Great Bridge at Gojō Avenue.

Her longing for Musashi had grown deeper and stronger. The thread of love had lengthened, and she had wound it up into a ball inside her breast. Through all the years, she had gone on spinning the thread from distant memories and bits of hearsay and winding it around the ball to make it larger and larger. Until only a few days earlier, she had treasured her girlish sentiments and carried them with her like a fresh wild flower from the slopes of Mount Ibuki; now the blossom inside her was crushed. Though it was unlikely anyone was aware of what had occurred, she imagined everybody was looking at her with knowing eyes.

In Kyoto, in the fading light of evening, Akemi walked among the leafless willows and miniature pagodas in Teramachi, near Gojō Avenue, looking as cold and forlorn as a butterfly in winter.

"Hey, beautiful!" said a man. "Your obi cord is loose. Don't you want me to tie it for you?" He was thin, shabbily clothed and uncouth of speech, but he wore the two swords of a samauri.

Akemi had never seen him before, but habitués of the drinking places nearby could have told her that his name was Akakabe Yasoma, and that he hung around the back streets on winter nights doing nothing. His worn straw sandals flapped as he ran up behind Akemi and picked up the loose end of obi cord.

"What are you doing all by yourself in this deserted place? I don't suppose you're one of those madwomen who appear in the *kyōgen* plays, are you? You've got a pretty face. Why don't you fix your hair up a little and stroll about like the other girls?" Akemi walked on, pretending to have no ears, but Yasoma mistook this for shyness. "You look like a city girl. What did you do? Run away from home? Or do you have a husband you're trying to escape from?"

Akemi made no reply.

"You should be careful, a pretty girl like you, wandering around in a daze, looking as though you're in trouble or something. You can't tell what might happen. We don't have the kind of thieves and ruffians who used to hang out around Rashōmon, but there are plenty of freebooters, and their mouths water at the sight of a woman. And vagrants too, and people who buy and sell women."

Although Akemi said not a word, Yasoma persisted, answering her own questions when necessary.

"It's really quite dangerous. They say women from Kyoto are being sold for very high prices in Edo now. A long time ago, they used to take women from here up to Hiraizumi in the northeast, but now it's Edo. That's because the second shōgun, Hidetada, is building up the city as fast as he can. The brothels in Kyoto are all opening up branches there now."

Akemi said nothing.

"You'd stand out anywhere, so you should be careful. If you don't watch out, you might get involved with some scoundrel. It's terribly dangerous!"

Akemi had had enough. Throwing her sleeves up on her shoulders in anger, she turned and hissed loudly at him.

Yasoma just laughed. "You know," he said, "I think you really are crazy."

"Shut up and go away!"

"Well, aren't you?"

"You're the crazy one!"

"Ha, ha, ha! That as much as proves it. You're crazy. I feel sorry for you."

"If you don't get out of here, I'll throw a rock at you!"

"Aw, you don't want to do that, do you?"

"Go away, you beast!" The proud front she was putting up masked the terror she actually felt. She screamed at Yasoma and ran into a field of miscanthus, where once had stood Lord Komatsu's mansion and its garden filled with stone lanterns. She seemed to swim through the swaying plants.

"Wait!" cried Yasoma, going after her like a hunting dog.

Above Toribe Hill rose the evening moon, looking like the wild grin of a she-demon.

There was no one in the immediate vicinity. The nearest people were about three hundred yards away, in a group slowly descending a hill, but they wouldn't have come to her rescue even if they had heard her shouts, for they were returning from a funeral. Clad in formal white clothing and hats tied with white ribbons, they carried their prayer beads in their hands; a few of them were still weeping.

Suddenly Akemi, pushed sharply from behind, stumbled and fell.

"Oh, I'm sorry," said Yasoma. He fell on top of her, apologizing all the while. "Did it hurt?" he asked solicitously, hugging her to him.

Seething with anger, Akemi slapped his bearded face, but this did not faze him. Indeed, he seemed to like it. He merely squinted and grinned as she struck. Then he hugged her more closely and rubbed his cheek against hers. His beard felt like a thousand needles sticking into her skin. She could barely breathe. As she scratched desperately at him, one of her fingernails clawed the inside of his nose, bringing forth a stream of blood. Still, Yasoma did not relax the tight hold he had on her.

The bell at the Amida Hall on Toribe Hill was tolling a dirge, a lamentation on the impermanence of all things and the vanity of life. But it made no impression on the two struggling mortals. The withered miscanthus waved violently with their movements.

"Calm down, stop fighting," he pleaded. "There's nothing to be afraid of. I'll make you my bride. You'd like that, wouldn't you?"

Akemi screamed, "I just want to die!" The misery in her voice startled Yasoma.

"Why? Wh-what's the matter?" he stammered.

Akemi's crouching position, with her hands, knees and chest drawn tightly together, resembled the bud of a sasanqua flower. Yasoma began to comfort and cajole, hoping to soothe her into surrender. This did not seem to be the first time he had encountered a situation of this sort. On the contrary, it would appear that this was something he liked, for his face shone with pleasure, without losing its menacing quality. He was in no hurry; like a cat, he enjoyed playing with his victim.

"Don't cry," he said. "There's nothing to cry about, is there?" Giving her a kiss on the ear, he went on, "You must have been with a man before. At your age, you couldn't be innocent."

Seijūrō! Akemi recalled how stifled and miserable she had been before, how the framework of the shoji had blurred before her eyes.

"Wait!" she said.

"Wait? All right, I'll wait," he said, mistaking the warmth of her feverish body for passion. "But don't try to run away, or I'll get rough."

With a sharp grunt, she twisted her shoulders and shook his hand off her. Glaring into his face, she slowly rose. "What are you trying to do to me?"

"You know what I want!"

"You think you can treat women like fools, don't you? All you men do! Well, I may be a woman, but I've got spirit." Blood seeped from her lip where she had cut it on a miscanthus leaf. Biting the lip, she burst into fresh tears.

"You say the strangest things," he said. "What else can you be but crazy?"

"I'll say whatever I please!" she screamed. Pushing his chest away from her with all her might, she scrambled away through the miscanthus, which stretched as far as she could see in the moonlight.

"Murder! Help! Murder!"

Yasoma lunged after her. Before she had gone ten steps, he caught her and threw her down again. Her white legs visible beneath her kimono, her hair falling around her face, she lay with her cheek pressed against the ground. Her kimono was half open, and her white breasts felt the cold wind.

Just as Yasoma was about to leap on her, something very hard landed in the vicinity of his ear. Blood rushed to his head, and he screamed out in pain. As he turned to look, the hard object came crashing down on the crown of his head. This time there could hardly have been any pain, for he immediately fell over unconscious, his head shaking emptily like a paper tiger's. As he lay there with his mouth slack, his assailant, a mendicant priest, stood over him, holding the *shakuhachi* with which he had dealt the blows.

"The evil brute!" he said. "But he went down easier than I expected." The priest looked at Yasoma for a time, debating whether it would be kinder to kill him outright. The chances were that even if he recovered consciousness, he would never be sane again.

Akemi stared blankly at her rescuer. Apart from the *shakuhachi*, there was nothing to identify him as a priest; to judge from his dirty clothes and the sword hanging at his side, he might have been a poverty-stricken samurai or even a beggar.

"It's all right now," he said. "You don't have to worry anymore."

Recovering from her daze, Akemi thanked him and

began straightening her hair and her kimono. But she peered into the darkness around her with eyes still full of fright.

"Where do you live?" asked the priest.

"Eh? Live . . . do you mean where's my house?" she said, covering her face with her hands. Through her sobs, she tried to answer his questions, but she found herself unable to be honest with him. Part of what she told him was true—her mother was different from her, her mother was trying to exchange her body for money, she had fled here from Sumiyoshi—but the rest was made up on the spur of the moment.

"I'd rather die than go back home," she wailed. "I've had to put up with so much from my mother! I've been shamed in so many ways! Why, even when I was a little girl, I had to go out on the battlefield and steal things from the bodies of dead soldiers."

Her loathing for her mother made her bones tremble.

Aoki Tanzaemon helped her along to a little hollow, where it was quiet and the wind less chilly. Coming to a small dilapidated temple, he flashed a toothy grin and said, "This is where I live. It's not much, but I like it."

Though aware that it was a little rude, Akemi could not help saying, "Do you really live here?"

Tanzaemon pushed open a grille door and motioned for her to enter. Akemi hesitated.

"It's warmer inside than you'd think," he said. "All I have to cover the floor with is thin straw matting. Still, that's better than nothing. Are you afraid I might be like that brute back there?"

Silently Akemi shook her head. Tanzaemon did not frighten her. She felt sure he was a good man, and anyway he was getting on—over fifty, she thought. What held her back was the filthiness of the little temple and the smell of Tanzaemon's body and clothing. But there was nowhere else to go; no telling what might happen if Yasoma or someone like him were to find her. And her forehead was burning with fever.

"I won't be a bother to you?" she asked as she went up the steps.

"Not at all. No one will mind if you stay here for months."

The building was pitch black, the kind of atmosphere favored by bats.

"Wait just a minute," said Tanzaemon.

She heard the scratching of metal against flint, and then a small lamp, which he must have scavenged somewhere, cast a feeble light. She looked about and saw that this strange man had somehow accumulated the basic necessities for housekeeping—a pot or two, some dishes, a wooden pillow, some straw matting. Saying he would make a little buckwheat gruel for her, he began puttering around with a broken earthenware brazier, first putting in a little charcoal, then some sticks, and after raising a few sparks, blowing them into a flame.

"He's a nice old man," thought Akemi. As she began to feel calmer, the place no longer seemed so filthy.

"There now," he said. "You look feverish, and you said you were tired. You've probably caught a cold. Why don't you just lie down over there until the food is ready?" He pointed to a makeshift pallet of straw matting and rice sacks.

Akemi spread some paper she had with her on the wooden pillow and with murmured apologies for resting while he worked, lay down. For cover, there were the tattered remains of a mosquito net. She started to pull this over her, but as she did so, an animal with glittering eyes jumped out from under it and bounded over her head. Akemi screamed and buried her face in the pallet.

Tanzaemon was more astonished than Akemi. He dropped the sack from which he was pouring flour into the water, spilling half of it on his knees. "What was that?" he cried.

Akemi, still hiding her face, said, "I don't know. It seemed bigger than a rat."

"Probably a squirrel. They sometimes come when they smell food. But I don't see it anywhere."

Lifting her head slightly, Akemi said, "There it is!"

"Where?"

Tanzaemon straightened up and turned around. Perched

on the railing of the inner sanctum, from which the image of the Buddha was long gone, was a small monkey, shrinking with fright under Tanzaemon's hard stare.

Tanzaemon looked puzzled, but the monkey apparently decided there was nothing to fear. After a few trips up and down the faded vermilion railing, he sat down again, and turning up a face like a peach with long hair, began blinking his eyes.

"Where do you suppose he came from? . . . Ah ha! I see now. I thought a good deal of rice had been scattered around." He moved toward the monkey, but the latter, anticipating his approach, bounded behind the sanctum and hid.

"He's a cute little devil," said Tanzaemon. "If we give him something to eat, he probably won't do any mischief. Let's let him be." Brushing the flour off his knees, he sat down before the brazier again. "There's nothing to be afraid of, Akemi. Get some rest."

"Do you think he'll behave himself?"

"Yes. He's not wild. He must be somebody's pet. There's nothing to worry about. Are you warm enough?"

"Yes."

"Then get some sleep. That's the best cure for a cold."

He put more flour in the water and stirred the gruel with chopsticks. The fire was burning briskly now, and while the mixture was heating up, he began chopping some scallions. His chopping board was the top of an old table, his knife a small rusted dagger. With unwashed hands, he scooped the scallions into a wooden bowl and then wiped off the chopping block, converting it into a tray.

The bubbling of the boiling pot gradually warmed the room. Seated with his arms around his spindly knees, the former samurai gazed at the broth with hungry eyes. He looked happy and eager, as though the pot before him contained the ultimate pleasure of mankind.

The bell of Kiyomizudera pealed as it did every night. The winter austerities, which lasted thirty days, had ended, and the New Year was at hand, but as always as the year drew to a close, the burden on people's souls seemed to grow heavier. Far into the night supplicants were sounding the tinny gong above the temple entrance as they bowed to pray, and wailing chants invoking the Buddha's aid droned on monotonously.

While Tanzaemon slowly stirred the gruel to keep it from scorching, he turned reflective. "I myself am receiving my punishment and atoning for my sins, but what has happened to Jōtarō? . . . The child did nothing blameworthy. Oh, Blessed Kannon, I beg you to punish the parent for his sins, but cast the eye of generous compassion on the son—"

A scream suddenly punctuated his prayer. "You beast!" Her eyes still closed in sleep, her face pressed hard against the wooden pillow, Akemi was weeping bitterly. She ranted on until the sound of her own voice woke her.

"Was I talking in my sleep?" she asked.

"Yes; you startled me," said Tanzaemon, coming to her bedside and wiping her forehead with a cool rag. "You're sweating terribly. Must be the fever."

"What . . . what did I say?"

"Oh, a lot of things."

"What sort of things?" Akemi's feverish face grew redder from embarrassment. She pulled the cover over it.

Without answering directly, Tanzaemon said, "Akemi, there's a man you'd like to put a curse on, isn't there?"

"Did I say that?"

"Mm. What happened? Did he desert you?"

"No."

"I see," he said, jumping to his own conclusion.

Akemi, pushing herself up into a half-sitting position, said, "Oh, what should I do now? Tell me, what?" She had vowed she would reveal her secret shame to no one, but the anger and sadness, the sense of loss pent up inside her, were too much to bear alone. She sprawled on Tanzaemon's knee and blurted out the whole story, sobbing and moaning throughout.

"Oh," she wailed finally, "I want to die, die! Let me die!"

Tanzaemon's breath grew hot. It had been a long time since he had been this close to a woman; her odor burned his nostrils, his eyes. Desires of the flesh, which he thought he had overcome, began to swell as from an influx of warm blood, and his body, until now no more vibrant than a barren withered tree, took on new life. He was reminded, for a change, that there were lungs and a heart underneath his ribs.

"Mm," he muttered, "so that's the kind of man Yoshioka Seijūrō is." Bitter hatred for Seijūrō welled up in him. Nor was it only indignation; a kind of jealousy moved him to tighten his shoulders, as though it were a daughter of his own who had been violated. As Akemi writhed in tears on his knee, he experienced a feeling of intimacy, and a look of perplexity crept into his face.

"Now there, don't cry. Your heart is still chaste. It's not as if you'd permitted this man to make love to you, nor did you return his love. What's important to a woman is not her body but her heart, and chastity itself is a matter of the inner being. Even when a woman doesn't give herself to a man, if she regards him with lust, she becomes, at least as long as the feeling lasts, unchaste and unclean."

Akemi was not comforted by these abstract words. Hot tears seeped through the priest's kimono, and she went on repeating that she wanted to die.

"Now, now, stop crying," said Tanzaemon again, patting her on the back. But the trembling of her white neck did not move him to genuine sympathy. This soft skin, so sweet to the smell, had already been stolen from him by another man.

Noticing that the monkey had sneaked up to the pot and was eating something, he unceremoniously removed Akemi's head from his knee, shook his fist and cursed the animal roundly. Beyond the shadow of a doubt, food was more important than a women's suffering.

The next morning Tanzaemon announced he was going to town with his beggar's bowl. "You stay here while I'm gone," he said. "I have to get some money to buy you medicine, and then we need some rice and oil so we can have something hot to eat."

His hat was not a deep one woven of reeds, like those of most itinerant priests, but an ordinary bamboo affair, and his straw sandals, worn and split at the heels, scraped against the ground as he shuffled along. Everything about him, not just his mustache, had an air of scruffiness. Yet, walking scarecrow that he was, it was his habit to go out every day, unless it rained.

Not having slept well, he was particularly bleary-eyed this morning. Akemi, after crying and carrying on so in the evening, had later sipped her gruel, broken into a heavy sweat and slept soundly through the rest of the night. He had hardly closed his eyes until dawn. Even walking under the bright morning sun, the cause of his sleeplessness remained with him. He could not get it out of his mind.

"She's about the same age as Otsū," he thought. "But they're completely different in temperament. Otsū has grace and refinement, but there's something chilly about her. Akemi's appealing whether she's laughing, crying or pouting."

The youthful feelings aroused in Tanzaemon's desiccated cells by the strong rays of Akemi's charm had made him all too conscious of his advancing years. And during the night, as he had looked solicitously at her each time she stirred in her sleep, a different warning had sounded in his heart. "What a wretched fool I am! Haven't I learned yet? Though I wear the surplice of the priest and play the *shakuhachi* of the mendicant, I'm still a long way from achieving the clear and perfect enlightenment of P'u-hua. Will I never find the wisdom that will release me from this body?"

After castigating himself at length, he had forced his sad eyes shut and tried to sleep, but to no avail.

As dawn broke, he had again resolved, "I will—I must—put evil thoughts behind me!" But Akemi was a charming girl. She had suffered so. He must try to comfort her. He had to show her that not all the men in the world were demons of lust.

Besides the medicine, he was wondering what sort of present he could bring her when he came back in the evening. Throughout the day's alms-seeking, his spirit would be bolstered by this desire to do something to make Akemi a little happier. That would suffice; he cherished no greater desire.

At about the time he recovered his composure and the color returned to his face, he heard the flapping of wings above the cliff beside him. The shadow of a large falcon skimmed past, and Tanzaemon watched a gray feather from a small bird flutter down from an oak branch in the leafless grove above him. Holding the bird in its claws, the falcon rose straight up, exposing the undersides of its wings.

Nearby a man's voice said, "Success!" and the falconer whistled to his bird.

Seconds later, Tanzaemon saw two men in hunting outfits coming down the hill behind the Ennenji. The falcon was perched on the left fist of one of them, who carried a net bag for the catch on the side opposite his two swords. An intelligent-looking brown hunting dog trotted along behind.

Kojirō stopped and took in the surroundings. "It happened somewhere along here yesterday evening," he was saying. "My monkey was scrapping with the dog, and the dog bit his tail. He hid somewhere and never came out. I wonder if he's up in one of those trees."

Seijūrō, looking rather disgruntled, sat down on a rock. "Why would he still be here? He's got legs too. Anyway, I can't see why you bring a monkey along when you go hunting with falcons."

Kojirō made himself comfortable on the root of a tree. "I didn't bring him, but I can't keep him from tagging along. And I'm so used to him, I miss him when he's not around."

"I thought only women and people of leisure liked to have monkeys and lapdogs for pets, but I guess I was wrong. It's hard to imagine a student warrior like you being so attached to a monkey." Having seen Kojirō in action on the dike at Kema, Seijūrō had a healthy respect for his swordsmanship, but his tastes and his general way of life seemed all too boyish. Just living in the same house with him these past few days had convinced Seijūrō that maturity came only with age. While he found it difficult to respect Kojirō as a person, this, in a way, made it easier to associate with him.

Kojirō replied laughingly, "It's because I'm so young. One of these days, I'll learn to like women, and then I'll probably forget all about the monkey."

Kojirō chatted idly in a light vein, but Seijūrō's face seemed increasingly preoccupied. There was a nervous look in his eyes not unlike that of the falcon perched on his hand. All at once he said irritably, "What's that beggar priest over there doing? He's been standing there staring at us ever since we got here." Seijūrō glared suspiciously at Tanzaemon, and Kojirō turned around to have a look.

Tanzaemon turned his back and trudged off.

Seijūrō stood up abruptly. "Kojirō," he said, "I want to go home. Any way you look at it, this is no time to be out hunting. It's already the twenty-ninth of the month."

Laughing, with a touch of scorn, Kojirō said, "We came out to hunt, didn't we? We've only got one turtledove and a couple of thrushes to show for it. We should try farther up the hill."

"No; let's call it a day. I don't feel like hunting, and when I don't feel like it, the falcon doesn't fly right. Let's go back to the house and practice." He added, as though talking to himself, "That's what I need to do, practice."

"Well, if you must go back, I'll go with you." He walked along beside Seijūrō but did not seem very happy about it. "I guess I was wrong to suggest it."

"Suggest what?"

"Going hunting yesterday and today."

"Don't worry about it. I know you meant well. It's just that it's the end of the year, and the showdown with Musashi is creeping up on us fast."

"That's why I thought it'd be good for you to do some hunting. You could relax, get yourself into the proper spirit. I guess you're not the type who can do that."

"Umm. The more I hear about Musashi, the more I think it's just as well not to underrate him."

"Isn't that all the more reason to avoid getting excited or panicky? You should discipline your spirit."

"I'm not panicky. The first lesson in the Art of War is not to make light of your enemy, and I think it's only common sense to try to get in plenty of practice before the fight. If I should lose, then at least I'd know I'd done my best. If the man's better than I am, well . . ."

Though he appreciated Seijūrō's honesty, Kojirō sensed

in him a smallness of spirit that would make it very difficult
for Seijūrō to uphold the reputation of the Yoshioka School.
Because Seijūrō lacked the personal vision needed to follow
in his father's footsteps and run the huge school properly,
Kojirō felt sorry for him. In his opinion, the younger brother,
Denshichirō, had more strength of character, but Denshichirō was also an incorrigible playboy. And though he was a
more capable swordsman than Seijūrō, he had no stake in
the Yoshioka name.

Kojirō wanted Seijūrō to forget about the impending
bout with Musashi, for this, he believed, would be the best
possible preparation for him. The question he wanted to ask,
but didn't, was what could he hope to learn between now
and the time for the match? "Well," he thought with resignation, "that's the way he is, so I suppose I can't be of
much help to him."

The dog had run off and was barking ferociously in the
distance.

"That means he's found some game!" said Kojirō, his
eyes brightening.

"Let him go. He'll catch up with us later."

"I'll go have a look. You wait here."

Kojirō sprinted off in the direction of the barking and
after a minute or two spotted the dog on the veranda of an
ancient ramshackle temple. The animal leaped against the
dilapidated grille door and fell back. After a few trials, he
began scratching at the worn red-lacquered posts and walls
of the building.

Wondering what he could possibly be so excited about,
Kojirō went to another door. Peering through the grille was
like looking into a black lacquer vase.

The rattle of the door as he pulled it open brought the
dog running to his heels, wagging his tail. Kojirō kicked the
dog away, but to little effect. As he entered the building,
the dog streaked in past him.

The woman's screams were ear-splitting, the kind of
screams that shatter glass. Then the dog started howling,
and there was a battle of lung power between him and the
shrieking woman. Kojirō wondered if the beams would split.
Running forward, he discovered Akemi lying under the

mosquito net and the monkey, which had jumped in the window to escape the dog, hiding behind her.

Akemi was between the dog and the monkey, blocking the dog's way, so he attacked her. As she rolled to one side, the howl of the dog reached a crescendo.

Akemi was now screaming from pain rather than fright. The dog had set his teeth around her forearm. Kojirō, with an oath, kicked him violently again in the ribs. The dog was already dead from the first kick, but even after the second, his teeth were solidly clamped on Akemi's arm.

"Let go! Let go!" she screamed, writhing on the floor.

Kojirō knelt beside her and pulled the dog's jaws open. The sound was like that of pieces of glued wood being wrenched apart. The mouth came open, all right; a little more force on Kojirō part, and the dog's head would have split in two. He threw the corpse out the door and came back to Akemi's side.

"It's all right now," he said soothingly, but Akemi's forearm said otherwise. The blood flowing over the white skin gave the bite the appearance of a large crimson peony.

Kojirō shivered at the sight. "Isn't there any sake? I should wash it with sake. . . . No, I guess there wouldn't be any in a place like this." Warm blood flowed down the forearm to the wrist. "I have to do something," he said, "or poison from the dog's teeth might cause you to go mad. He has been acting peculiarly these past few days."

While Kojirō tried to decide what could be done in a hurry, Akemi screwed her eyebrows together, bent her lovely white neck backward and cried, "Mad? Oh, how wonderful! That's what I want to be—mad! Completely stark, raving mad!"

"Wh-wh-what's this?" stammered Kojirō. Without further ado, he bent over her forearm and sucked blood from the wound. When his mouth was full, he spat it out, put his mouth back to the white skin, and sucked until his cheeks bulged.

In the evening Tanzaemon returned from his daily round. "I'm back, Akemi," he announced as he entered the temple. "Were you lonesome while I was gone?"

He deposited her medicine in a corner, along with the food and the jar of oil he had bought, and said, "Wait a moment; I'll make some light."

When the candle was lit, he saw that she was not in the room. "Akemi!" he called. "Where could she have gone?"

His one-sided love turned suddenly to anger, which was quickly replaced by loneliness. Tanzaemon was reminded, as he had been before, that he would never be young again—that there was no more honor, no more hope. He thought of his aging body and winced.

"I rescued her and took care of her," he grumbled, "and now she's gone off without a word. Is that the way the world is always going to be? Is that the way she is? Or was she still suspicious of my intentions?"

On the bed he discovered a scrap of cloth, apparently torn from the end of her obi. The spot of blood on it rekindled his animal instincts. He kicked the straw matting into the air and threw the medicine out the window.

Hungry, but lacking the will to prepare a meal, he took up his *shakuhachi* and, with a sigh, went out onto the veranda. For an hour or more, he played without stopping, attempting to expel his desires and delusions. Yet it was evident to him that his passions remained with him and would remain with him until he died. "She'd already been taken by another man," he mused. "Why did I have to be so moral and upright? There was no need for me to lie there alone, pining all night."

Half of him regretted not having acted; the other half condemned his lecherous yearning. It was precisely this conflict of emotions, swirling incessantly in his veins, that constituted what the Buddha called delusion. He was trying now to cleanse his impure nature, but the more he strived, the muddier the tone of his *shakuhachi* became.

The beggar who slept beneath the temple poked his head from under the veranda. "Why are you sitting there playing your recorder?" he asked. "Did something good happen? If you made lots of money and bought some sake, how about giving me a drink?" He was a cripple, and from his lowly viewpoint, Tanzaemon lived like a king.

"Do you know what happened to the girl I brought home last night?"

"She was a nice-looking wench, wasn't she? If I'd been able, I wouldn't have let her get away. Not long after you left this morning, a young samurai with a long forelock and a huge sword on his back came and took her away. The monkey too. He had one of them on one shoulder, one on the other."

"Samurai . . . forelock?"

"Uh. And what a handsome fellow he was—handsomer by far than you and me!"

The humor of this sent the beggar into a paroxysm of laughter.

16

The Announcement

Seijūrō arrived back at the school in a foul mood. He thrust the falcon into a disciple's hands, curtly ordering him to put the bird back in its cage.

"Isn't Kojirō with you?" asked the disciple.

"No, but I'm sure he'll be along presently."

After changing his clothes, Seijūrō went and sat down in the room where guests were received. Across the court was the great dōjō, closed since the final practice on the twenty-fifth. Throughout the year, there was the coming and going of a thousand or so students; now the dōjō would not be open again until the first training session of the New Year. With the wooden swords silent, the house seemed coldly desolate.

Desperate to have Kojirō as a sparring partner, Seijūrō inquired of the disciple repeatedly whether he had returned. But Kojirō did not come back, neither that evening nor the following day.

Other callers came in force, however, it being the last day of the year, the day to settle up all accounts. For those in business, it was a question of collecting now or waiting until the *Bon* festival of the following summer, and by noon the front room was full of bill collectors. Normally these men wore an air of complete subservience in the presence of samurai, but now, their patience exhausted, they were making their feelings known in no uncertain terms.

"Can't you pay at least part of what you owe?"

"You've been saying the man in charge is out, or the master is away, for months now. Do you think you can keep putting us off forever?"

"How many times do we have to come here?"

"The old master was a good customer. I wouldn't say a word if it were only the last half year, but you didn't pay at midyear either. Why, I've even got unpaid bills from last year!"

A couple of them impatiently tapped on their account books and stuck them under the nose of the disciple. There were carpenters, plasterers, the rice man, the sake dealer, clothiers and sundry suppliers of everyday goods. Swelling their ranks were the proprietors of various teahouses where Seijūrō ate and drank on credit. And these were the small fry, whose bills could hardly be compared to those of the usurers from whom Denshichirō, unknown to his brother, had borrowed cash.

Half a dozen of these men sat down and refused to budge.

"We want to talk with Master Seijūrō himself. It's a waste of time to talk to disciples."

Seijūrō kept to himself in the back of the house, his only words being: "Tell them I'm out." And Denshichirō, of course, would not have come near the house on a day like this. The face most conspicuously absent was that of the man in charge of the school's books and the household accounts: Gion Tōji. Several days earlier, he had decamped with Okō and all the money he'd collected on his trip west.

Presently six or seven men swaggered in, led by Ueda Ryōhei, who even in such humiliating circumstances was swollen with pride at being one of the Ten Swordsmen of the House of Yoshioka. With a menacing look, he asked, "What's going on here?"

The disciple, while contriving to make it plain that he considered no explanation necessary, gave a brief rundown of the situation.

"Is that all?" Ryōhei said scornfully. "Just a bunch of moneygrubbers? What difference does it make as long as the bills are eventually paid? Tell the ones who don't want to wait for payment to step into the practice hall; I'll discuss it with them in my own language.''

In the face of this threat, the bill collectors grew sulky. Owing to Yoshioka Kempō's uprightness in money matters, not to mention his position as a military instructor to the Ashikago shōguns, they had bowed before the Yoshioka household, groveled, lent them goods, lent them anything, come whenever summoned, left when they were told, and said yes to anything and everything. But there was a limit to how long they could kowtow to these vain warriors. The day they allowed themselves to be intimidated by threats like Ryōhei's was the day the merchant class would go out of business. And without them, what would the samurai do? Did they imagine for a moment they could run things by themselves?

As they stood around grumbling, Ryōhei made it perfectly clear that he regarded them as so much dirt. "All right now, go on home! Hanging around here won't do you any good.''

The merchants grew silent but made no move to leave.

"Throw them out!" cried Ryōhei.

"Sir, this is an outrage!"

"What's outrageous about it?" asked Ryōhei.

"It's completely irresponsible!"

"Who says it's irresponsible?"

"But it *is* irresponsible to throw us out!"

"Then why don't you leave quietly? We're busy."

"If it wasn't the last day of the year, we wouldn't be here begging. We need the money you owe to settle our own debts before the day is out.''

"That's too bad. Too bad. Now go!"

"This is no way to treat us!"

"I think I've heard enough of your complaints!" Ryōhei's voice grew angry again.

"No one would complain—if you'd just pay up!"

"Come here!" commanded Ryōhei.

"Wh-who?"

"Anyone who's dissatisfied."

"This is crazy!"

"Who said that?"

"I wasn't referring to you, sir. I was talking about this . . . this situation."

"Shut up!" Ryōhei seized the man by his hair and threw him out the side door.

"Anybody else with complaints?" growled Ryōhei. "We're not going to have you riffraff inside the house claiming paltry sums of money. I won't permit it! Even if the Young Master wants to pay you, I won't let him do it."

At the sight of Ryōhei's fist, the bill collectors stumbled all over each other in their rush to get out of the gate. But once outside, their vilification of the House of Yoshioka intensified.

"Will I ever laugh and clap my hands when I see the 'For Sale' sign posted on this place! It shouldn't be long now."

"They say it won't be."

"How could it be?"

Ryōhei, vastly amused, held his stomach with laughter as he went to the back of the house. The other disciples went with him to the room were Seijūrō was bent, alone and silent, over the brazier.

"Young Master," said Ryōhei, "you're so quiet. Is something wrong?"

"Oh, no," replied Seijūrō, somewhat cheered by the sight of his most trusted followers. "The day's not far off now, is it?" he said.

"No," agreed Ryōhei. "That's what we came to see you about. Shouldn't we decide on the time and place and let Musashi know?"

"Why, yes, I suppose so," said Seijūrō pensively. "The place . . . Where would be a good place? How about the field at the Rendaiji, north of the city?"

"That sounds all right. What about the time?"

"Should it be before the New Year's decorations are taken down, or after?"

"The sooner the better. We don't want to give that coward time to worm his way out."

"How about the eighth?"

"Isn't the eighth the anniversary of Master Kempō's death?"

"Ah, so it is. In that case, how about the ninth? At seven o'clock in the morning? That'll do, won't it?"

"All right. We'll post a sign on the bridge this evening."

"Fine."

"Are you ready?" asked Ryōhei.

"I've been ready all along," replied Seijūrō, who was in no position to answer otherwise. He had not really considered the possibility of losing to Musashi. Having studied under his father's tutelage since childhood, and having never lost a match to anyone in the school, not even to the oldest and best-trained disciples, he couldn't imagine being beaten by this young, inexperienced country bumpkin.

His confidence, nonetheless, was not absolute. He felt a tinge of uncertainty, and characteristically, instead of attributing this to his failure to put into practice the Way of the Samurai, wrote it off as being due to recent personal difficulties. One of these, perhaps the greatest, was Akemi. He'd been ill at ease ever since the incident at Sumiyoshi, and when Gion Tōji had absconded, he had learned that the financial cancer in the Yoshioka household had already reached a critical stage.

Ryōhei and the others came back with the message to Musashi written on a freshly cut board.

"Is this what you had in mind?" asked Ryōhei.

The characters, still glistening wet, said:

Answer—In response to your request for a bout, I name the following time and place. Place: Field of the Rendaiji. Time: Seven o'clock in the morning, ninth day of the first month. I swear on my sacred oath to be present.

If, by some chance, you do not fulfill your promise, I shall consider it my right to ridicule you in public.

If I break this agreement, may the punishment of the gods be visited upon me! Seijūrō, Yoshioka Kempō II, of Kyoto. Done on the last day of [1605].

To the Rōnin of Mimasaka, Miyamoto Musashi.

251

After reading it, Seijūrō said, "It's all right." The announcement made him feel more relaxed, perhaps because for the first time it came home to him that the die was cast.

At sunset, Ryōhei put the sign under his arm and strode proudly along the street with a couple of other men to post it on the Great Bridge at Gojō Avenue.

At the foot of Yoshida Hill, the man to whom the announcement was addressed was walking through a neighborhood of samurai of noble lineage and small means. Conservatively inclined, they led ordinary lives and were unlikely to be found doing anything that would excite comment.

Musashi was going from gate to gate examining the nameplates. Eventually he came to a stop in the middle of the street, seemingly unwilling or unable to look further. He was searching for his aunt, his mother's sister and his only living relative besides Ogin.

His aunt's husband was a samurai serving, for a small stipend, the House of Konoe. Musashi thought it would be easy to find the house near Yoshida Hill but soon discovered there was very little to distinguish one house from another. Most were small, surrounded by trees, and their gates were shut tight as clams. Quite a few of the gates had no nameplates.

His uncertainty about the place he was seeking made him reluctant to ask directions. "They must have moved," he thought. "I may as well stop looking."

He turned back toward the center of town, which lay under a mist reflecting the lights of the year-end marketplace. Although it was New Year's Eve, the streets in the downtown area still hummed with activity.

Musashi turned to look at a woman who had just passed going the other way. He hadn't seen his aunt for at least seven or eight years, but he was sure this was she, for the woman resembled the image he had formed of his mother. He followed her a short distance, then called out to her.

She stared at him suspiciously for a moment or two, intense surprise reflected in eyes wrinkled by years of humdrum living on a tiny budget. "You're Musashi, Munisai's son, aren't you?" she finally asked.

He wondered why she called him Musashi rather than Takezō, but what actually disturbed him was the impression that he was not welcome. "Yes," he replied, "I'm Takezō from the House of Shimmen."

She looked him over thoroughly, without the customary "oh"s and "ah"s as to how large he had grown or how different he looked from before. "Why have you come here?" she asked coolly in a rather censorious tone.

"I had no special purpose in coming. I just happened to be in Kyoto. I thought it would be nice to see you." Looking at the eyes and hairline of his aunt, he thought of his mother. If she were still alive, surely she would be about as tall as this woman and speak with the same sort of voice.

"You came to see me?" she asked incredulously.

"Yes. I'm sorry it's so sudden."

His aunt waved her hand before her face in a gesture of dismissal. "Well, you've seen me, so there's no reason to go any farther. Please leave!"

Abashed at this chilly reception, he blurted out, "Why do you say that as soon as you see me? If you want me to leave, I'll go, but I can't see why. Have I done something you disapprove of? If so, at least tell me what it is."

His aunt seemed unwilling to be pinned down. "Oh, as long as you're here, why don't you come to our house and say hello to your uncle? But you know what kind of person he is, so don't be disappointed at anything he might say. I'm your aunt, and since you've come to see us, I don't want you to go away with hard feelings."

Taking what little comfort he could from this, Musashi walked with her to her house and waited in the front room while she broke the news to her husband. Through the shoji he could hear the asthmatic, grumbling voice of his uncle, whose name was Matsuo Kaname.

"What?" asked Kaname testily. "Munisai's son here? . . . I was afraid he'd show up sooner or later. You mean he's *here*, in this house? You let him in without asking me?"

Enough was enough, but when Musashi called to his aunt to say good-bye, Kaname said, "You're in there, are you?'' and slid the door open. His face wore not a frown but an expression of utter contempt—the look city people reserve for their unwashed country relatives. It was as though a cow had lumbered in and planted its hooves on the tatami.

"Why did you come here?" asked Kaname.

"I happened to be in town. I thought I'd just ask after your health."

"That's not true!"

"Sir?"

"You can lie all you want, but I know what you've done. You caused a lot of trouble in Mimasaka, made a lot of people hate you, disgraced your family's name and then ran away. Isn't that the truth?"

Musashi was nonplussed.

"How can you be so shameless as to come to call on relatives?"

"I'm sorry for what I did," said Musashi. "But I fully intend to make the proper amends to my ancestors and to the village."

"I suppose you can't go back home, of course. Well, we reap what we sow. Munisai must be weeping in his grave!"

"I've stayed too long," said Musashi. "I must be going now."

"Oh, no you don't!" said Kaname angrily. "You stay right here! If you go wandering around this neighborhood, you'll get yourself in trouble in no time. That cantankerous old woman from the Hon'iden family showed up here about a half year ago. Recently she's been around several times. She keeps asking us whether you've been here and trying to find out from us where you are. She's after you, all right—with a terrible vengeance."

"Oh, Osugi. Has she been here?"

"Indeed she has. I heard all about you from her. If you weren't a relative of mine, I'd tie you up and hand you over to her, but under the circumstances . . . Anyway, you stay here for now. It'll be best to leave in the middle of the night, so there won't be any trouble for your aunt and me."

That his aunt and uncle had swallowed every word of Osugi's slander was mortifying. Feeling terribly alone, Musashi sat in silence, staring at the floor. Eventually his aunt took pity on him and told him to go to another room and get some sleep.

Musashi flopped down on the floor and loosened his scabbards. Once again came the feeling that he had no one in the world to depend on but himself.

He reflected that perhaps his uncle and aunt were dealing with him frankly and sternly precisely because of the blood relationship. While he had been angry enough earlier to want to spit on the doorway and leave, he now took a more charitable view, reminding himself that it was important to give them the benefit of every doubt.

He was too naive to accurately judge the people around him. If he had already become rich and famous, his sentiments about relatives would have been appropriate, but here he was barging in out of the cold in a dirty rag of a kimono on New Year's Eve, of all times. Under the circumstances, his aunt and uncle's lack of familial affection was not surprising.

This was soon brought forcefully home to Musashi. He had lain down hungry on the guileless assumption that he would be offered something to eat. Though he smelled food cooking and heard the rattle of pots and pans in the kitchen, no one came near his room, where the flicker of the fire in the brazier was no larger than that of a firefly. He presently concluded that hunger and cold were secondary; what was most important now was to get some sleep, which he proceeded to do.

He awoke about four hours later to the sound of temple bells ringing out the old year. The sleep had done him good. Jumping to his feet, he felt that his fatigue had been washed away. His mind was fresh and clear.

In and around the city, huge bells bonged in slow and stately rhythm, marking the end of darkness and the beginning of light. One hundred and eight peals for the one hundred and eight illusions of life—each ring a call to men and women to reflect on the vanity of their ways.

Musashi wondered how many people there were who on this night could say: "I was right. I did what I should have done. I have no regrets." For him, each resounding knell evoked a tremor of remorse. He could conjure up nothing but the things he had done wrong during the last year. Nor was it only the last year—the year before, and the year before that, all the years that had gone by had brought regrets. There had not been a single year devoid of them. Indeed, there had hardly been one day.

From his limited perspective of the world, it seemed that whatever people did they soon came to regret. Men, for example, took wives with the intention of living out their lives with them but often changed their minds later. One could readily forgive women for their afterthoughts, but then women rarely voiced their complaints, whereas men frequently did so. How many times had he heard men disparage their wives as if they were old discarded sandals?

Musashi had no marital problems, to be sure, but he had been the victim of delusion, and remorse was not a feeling alien to him. At this very moment, he was very sorry he had come to his aunt's house. "Even now," he lamented, "I'm not free of my sense of dependence. I keep telling myself I must stand on my own two feet and fend for myself. Then I suddenly fall back on someone else. It's shallow! It's stupid!

"I know what I should do!" he thought. "I should make a resolution and write it down."

He undid his *shugyōsha*'s pack and took out a notebook made of pieces of paper folded in quarters and tied together with coiled paper strips. He used this to jot down thoughts that occurred to him during his wanderings, along with Zen expressions, notes on geography, admonitions to himself and, occasionally, crude sketches of interesting things he saw. Opening the notebook in front of him, he took up his brush and stared at the white sheet of paper.

Musashi wrote: "I will have no regrets about anything."

While he often wrote down resolutions, he found that merely writing them did little good. He had to repeat them to himself every morning and every evening, as one would sacred scripture. Consequently, he always tried to choose words that were easy to remember and recite, like poems.

He looked for a time at what he had written, then

changed it to read: "I will have no regrets about my actions."

He mumbled the words to himself but still found them unsatisfactory. He changed them again: "I will do nothing that I will regret."

Satisfied with this third effort, he put his brush down. Although the three sentences had been written with the same intent, the first two could conceivably mean he would have no regrets whether he acted rightly or wrongly, whereas the third emphasized his determination to act in such a way as to make self-reproach unnecessary.

Musashi repeated the resolution to himself, realizing it was an ideal he could not achieve unless he disciplined his heart and his mind to the utmost of his ability. Nevertheless, to strive for a state in which nothing he did would cause regrets was the path he must pursue. "Someday I will reach that state!" he vowed, driving the oath like a stake deep into his own heart.

The shoji behind him slid open, and his aunt looked in. With a voice shivering around the roots of her teeth, she said, "I knew it! Something told me I shouldn't let you stay here, and now what I was afraid would happen is happening. Osugi came knocking at the door, and saw your sandals in the entrance hall. She's convinced you're here and insists we bring you to her! Listen! You can hear her from here. Oh, Musashi, do something!"

"Osugi? Here?" said Musashi, reluctant to believe his ears. But there was no mistake. He could hear her hoarse voice seeping through the cracks like an icy wind, addressing Kaname in her stiffest, haughtiest manner.

Osugi had arrived just as the pealing of the midnight bells had ended and Musashi's aunt was on the point of going to draw fresh water for the New Year. Troubled by the thought of her New Year being ruined by the unclean sight of blood, she made no attempt to hide her annoyance.

"Run away as fast as you can," she implored. "Your uncle's holding her off by insisting you haven't been here. Slip out now while there's still time." She picked up his hat and pack and led him to the back door, where she had placed

257

a pair of her husband's leather socks, along with some straw sandals.

While tying the sandals, Musashi said sheepishly, "I hate to be a nuisance, but won't you give me a bowl of gruel? I haven't had a thing to eat this evening."

"This is no time for eating! But here, take these. And be off with you!" She held out five rice cakes on a piece of white paper.

Eagerly accepting them, Musashi held them up to his forehead in a gesture of thanks. "Good-bye," he said.

On his way down the icy lane, on the first day of the joyous New Year, Musashi walked sadly—a winter bird with feathers molted, flying off into a black sky. His hair and fingernails felt frozen. All he could see was his own white breath, quickly turning to frost on the fine hairs around his mouth. "It's cold!" he said out loud. Surely the Eight Freezing Hells could not be this numbing! Why, when he normally shrugged off the cold, did he feel it so bitterly this morning?

He answered his own question. "It's not just my body. I'm cold inside. Not disciplined properly. That's what it is. I still long to cling to warm flesh, like a baby, and I give in too quickly to sentimentality. Because I'm alone, I feel sorry for myself and envy people who have nice warm houses. At heart, I'm base and mean! Why can't I be thankful for independence and freedom to go where I choose? Why can't I hold on to my ideas and my pride?"

As he savored the advantages of freedom, his aching feet grew warm, down to the tips of his toes, and his breath turned to steam. "A wanderer with no ideal, no sense of gratitude for his independence, is no more than a beggar! The difference between a beggar and the great wandering priest Saigyō lies inside the heart!"

He suddenly became aware of a white sparkle under his feet. He was treading on brittle ice. Without noticing, he had walked all the way to the frozen edge of the Kamo River. Both it and the sky were still black, and there was as yet no hint of dawn in the east. His feet stopped. Somehow they had carried him without mishap through the darkness from Yoshida Hill, but now they were reluctant to go on.

In the shadow of the dike, he gathered together twigs, chips of wood and anything else that would burn, then began scratching at his flint. The raising of the first tiny flame required work and patience, but eventually some dry leaves caught. With the care of a woodworker, he began piling on sticks and small branches. After a certain point, the fire rapidly took on life, and as it drew the wind, it fanned out toward its maker, ready to scorch his face.

Musashi took the rice cakes his aunt had given him and toasted them one by one in the flames. They turned brown and swelled up like bubbles, reminding him of New Year's celebrations of his childhood. The rice cakes had no flavor but their own; they were neither salted nor sweetened. Chewing them, he thought of the taste of the real world about him. "I'm having my own New Year's celebration," he thought happily. As he warmed his face by the flames and stuffed his mouth, the whole thing began to seem rather amusing. "It's a good New Year's celebration! If even a wanderer like me has five good rice cakes, then it must be that heaven allows everybody to celebrate the New Year one way or another. I have the Kamo River to toast the New Year with, and the thirty-six peaks of Higashiyama are my pine tree decorations! I must cleanse my body and wait for the first sunrise."

At the edge of the icy river, he untied his obi and removed his kimono and underwear; then he plunged in and, splashing about like a water bird, washed himself thoroughly.

He was standing on the bank wiping his skin vigorously when the first rays of dawn broke through a cloud and fell warmly on his back. He looked toward the fire and saw someone standing on the dike above it, another traveler, different in age and appearance, brought here by fate. Osugi.

The old woman had seen him, too, and cried out in her heart, "He's here! The troublemaker is here!" Overcome by joy and fear, she nearly fell down in a swoon. She wanted to call to him, but her voice choked; her trembling body would not do as it was told. Abruptly, she sat down in the shadow of a small pine.

"At last!" she rejoiced. "I've finally found him! Uncle

Gon's spirit has led me to him." In the bag hanging from her waist she was carrying a fragment of Uncle Gon's bones and a lock of his hair.

Each day since his death she'd talked to the dead man. "Uncle Gon," she'd say, "even though you're gone, I don't feel alone. You stayed with me when I vowed not to go back to the village without punishing Musashi and Otsū. You're with me still. You may be dead, but your spirit is always beside me. We're together forever. Look up through the grass at me and watch! I'll never let Musashi go unpunished!"

To be sure, Uncle Gon had been dead only a week, but Osugi was resolved to keep faith with him until she, too, was reduced to ashes. In the past few days, she had pressed her search with the furor of the terrible Kishimojin, who, before her conversion by the Buddha, had killed other children to feed to her own—said to have numbered five hundred, or one thousand, or ten thousand.

Osugi's first real clue had been a rumor she'd heard in the street that there was soon to be a bout between Musashi and Yoshioka Seijūrō. Then early the previous evening, she had been among the onlookers who watched the sign being posted on the Great Bridge at Gojō Avenue. How that had excited her! She had read it through time and time again, thinking: "So Musashi's ambition has finally got the better of him! They'll make a clown of him. Yoshioka will kill him. Oh! If that happens, how will I be able to face the people at home? I swore I myself would kill him. I must get to him before Yoshioka does. And take that sniveling face back and hold it up by the hair for the villagers to see!" Then she had prayed to the gods, to the bodhisattvas and to her ancestors for help.

For all her fury and all her venom, she had come away from the Matsuo house disappointed. Returning along the Kamo River, she had first taken the firelight to be a beggar's bonfire. For no particular reason, she had stopped on the dike and waited. When she caught sight of the muscular naked man emerging from the river, oblivious of the cold, she knew it was Musashi.

Since he had no clothes on, it would be a perfect time

to catch him by surprise and cut him down, but even her old dried-up heart would not let her do that.

She put her palms together and offered a prayer of thanks, just as she would if she had already taken Musashi's head. "How happy I am! Thanks to the favor of the gods and bodhisattvas, I have Musashi before my eyes. It couldn't be mere chance! My constant faith has been rewarded; my enemy has been delivered into my hands!" She bowed before heaven, firm in her belief that she now had all the time in the world to complete her mission.

The rocks along the water's edge seemed to float above the ground one by one as the light struck them. Musashi put on his kimono, tied his obi tightly and girded on his two swords. He knelt on hands and knees and bowed silently to the gods of heaven and earth.

Osugi's heart leaped as she whispered, "Now!"

At that precise moment, Musashi sprang to his feet. Jumping nimbly over a pool of water, he started walking briskly along the river's edge. Osugi, taking care not to alert him to her presence, hurried along the dike.

The roofs and bridges of the city began to form gentle white outlines in the morning mist, but above, stars still hovered in the sky and the area along the foot of Higashi-yama was as black as ink. When Musashi reached the wooden bridge at Sanjō Avenue, he went under it and reappeared at the top of the dike beyond, taking long, manly strides. Several times Osugi came close to calling him but checked herself.

Musashi knew she was behind him. But he also knew that if he turned around, she would come storming at him, and he'd be forced to reward her effort with some show of defense, while at the same time not hurting her. "A frightening opponent!" he thought. If he were still Takezō, back in the village, he would have thought nothing of knocking her down and beating her until she spat blood, but of course he could no longer do that.

In reality he had more right to hate her than she him, but he wanted to make her see that her feeling toward him was based on a horrible misunderstanding. He was sure that if he could just explain things to her she would cease regarding him as her eternal enemy. But since she'd carried her festering grudge for so many years, there was no likelihood that he himself could convince her now, not if he explained a thousand times. There was only one possibility; stubborn though she was, she would certainly believe Matahachi. If her own son told her exactly what had happened before and after Sekigahara, she could no longer consider Musashi an enemy of the Hon'iden family, let alone the abductor of her son's bride.

He was drawing near the bridge, which was in an area that had flourished in the late twelfth century, when the Taira family was at the peak of its fortunes. Even after the wars of the fifteenth century, it had remained one of the most populous sections of Kyoto. The sun was just beginning to reach the housefronts and gardens, where broom marks from the previous night's thorough sweeping were still visible, but at this early hour not a door was open.

Osugi could make out his footprints in the dirt. Even these she despised.

Another hundred yards, then fifty.

"Musashi!" screamed the old woman. Balling her hands into fists, she thrust her head forward and ran toward him. "You evil devil!" she shouted. "Don't you have ears?"

Musashi did not look back.

Osugi ran on. Old as she was, her death-defying determination lent her footsteps a brave and masculine cadence. Musashi kept his back to her, casting about feverishly in his mind for a plan of action.

All at once she sprang in front of him, screaming, "Stop!" Her pointed shoulders and thin, emaciated ribs trembled. She stood there a moment, catching her breath and gathering spit in her mouth.

Not concealing a look of resignation, Musashi said as nonchalantly as he could, "Well, if it isn't the Hon'iden dowager! What are you doing here?"

"You insolent dog! Why shouldn't I be here? I'm the one who should ask you that. I let you get away from me on Sannen Hill, but today I'll have that head of yours!" Her scrawny neck suggested a game rooster, and her shrill voice, which seemed set to whisk her protruding teeth out of her mouth, was more frightening to him than a battle cry.

Musashi's dread of the old woman had its roots in reminiscences from his childhood days, the times when Osugi had caught him and Matahachi engaged in some mischief in the mulberry patch or the Hon'iden kitchen. He had been eight or nine—just the age when the two of them were always up to something—and he still remembered clearly how Osugi had shouted at them. He had fled in terror, his stomach turning somersaults, and those memories made him shiver. He had regarded her then as a hateful, ill-tempered old witch, and even now he resented her betrayal of him when he returned to the village after Sekigahara. Curiously, he had also grown accustomed to thinking of her as one person he could never get the best of. Still, with the passage of time, his feelings toward her had mellowed.

With Osugi, it was quite the opposite. She could not rid herself of the image of Takezō, the obnoxious and unruly little brat she had known since he was a baby, the boy with the runny nose and sores on his head, his arms and legs so long that he looked deformed. Not that she was unconscious of the passage of time. She was old now; she knew that. And Musashi was grown. But she could not overcome the urge to treat him as a vicious urchin. When she thought of how this little boy had shamed her—revenge! It was not only a matter of vindicating herself before the village. She had to see Musashi in his grave before she ended up in her own.

"There's no need for talk!" she screeched. "Either give me your head, or prepare to feel my blade! Get ready, Musashi!" She wiped her lips with her fingers, spat on her left hand and grabbed her scabbard.

There was a proverb about a praying mantis attacking the imperial carriage. Surely it must have been invented to describe the cadaverous Osugi with her spindly legs attacking Musashi. She looked exactly like a mantis; her eyes, her skin, her absurd stance, were all the same. And as Musashi stood on guard, watching her approach as he might a child at play, his shoulders and chest gave him the invincibility of a sturdy iron carriage.

In spite of the incongruity of the situation, he was

unable to laugh, for he was suddenly filled with pity. "Come now, Granny, wait!" he begged, grabbing her elbow lightly but firmly.

"Wh-what are you doing?" she cried. Both her powerless arm and her teeth shook with surprise. "C-c-coward!" she stammered. "You think you can talk me out of this? Well, I've seen forty more New Years than you, and you can't trick me. Take your punishment!" Osugi's skin was the color of red clay, her voice filled with desperation.

Musashi, nodding vigorously, said, "I understand; I know how you feel. You've got the fighting spirit of the Hon'iden family in you, all right. I can see you have the same blood as the first of the Hon'idens, the one who served so bravely under Shimmen Munetsura."

"Let go of me, you—! I'm not going to listen to flattery from somebody young enough to be my grandchild."

"Calm down. It doesn't become an old person like you to be rash. I have something to say to you."

"Your last statement before you meet your death?"

"No; I want to explain."

"I don't want any explanations from you!" The old woman drew herself up to her full height.

"Well, then, I'll just have to take that sword away from you. Then when Matahachi shows up, he can explain everything to you."

"Matahachi?"

"Yes. I sent him a message last spring."

"Oh, you did, did you?"

"I told him to meet me here on New Year's morning."

"That's a lie!" shrieked Osugi, vigorously shaking her head. "You should be ashamed, Musashi! Aren't you Munisai's son? Didn't he teach you that when the time comes to die, you should die like a man? This is no time for playing around with words. My whole life is behind this sword, and I have the support of the gods and bodhisattvas. If you dare face it, face it!" She wrested her arm away from him and cried, "Hail to the Buddha!" Unsheathing her sword and grasping it with both hands, she lunged at his chest.

He dodged. "Calm down, Granny, please!"

When he tapped her lightly on the back, she screamed

and whirled around to face him. As she prepared to charge, she invoked the name of Kannon. "Praise to Kannon Bosatsu! Praise to Kannon Bosatsu!" She attacked again.

As she passed him, Musashi seized her wrist. "You'll just wear yourself out, carrying on like that. Look, the bridge is just over there. Come with me that far."

Turning her head back over her shoulder, Osugi bared her teeth and pursed her lips. "Phooey!" She spat with all the breath she had left.

Musashi let go of her and moved aside, rubbing his left eye with his hand. The eye burned as if a spark had struck it. He looked at the hand he had put to his eye. There was no blood on it, but he couldn't open the eye. Osugi, seeing he was off guard, charged with renewed strength, calling again on the name of Kannon. Twice, three times she swung at him.

On the third swing, preoccupied with his eye, he merely bent his body slightly from the waist. The sword cut through his sleeve and scratched his forearm.

A piece of his sleeve fell off, giving Osugi the chance to see blood on the white lining. "I've wounded him!" she screamed in ecstasy, waving her sword wildly. She was as proud as if she had felled a great tree in one stroke, and the fact that Musashi wasn't fighting back in no way dimmed her elation. She went on shouting the name of the Kannon of Kiyomizudera, calling the deity down to earth.

In a noisy frenzy, she ran around him, attacking him from front and back. Musashi did no more than shift his body to avoid the blows.

His eye bothered him, and there was the scratch on his forearm. Although he had seen the blow coming, he had not moved quickly enough to avoid it. Never before had anyone gotten the jump on him or wounded him even slightly, and since he had not taken Osugi's attack seriously, the question of who would win, who lose, had never crossed his mind.

But was it not true that by not taking her seriously, he had let himself be wounded? According to *The Art of War*, no matter how slight the wound, he had quite clearly been beaten. The old woman's faith and the point of her sword had exposed for all to see his lack of maturity.

"I was wrong," he thought. Seeing the folly of inaction, he jumped away from the attacking sword and slapped Osugi heavily on the back, sending her sprawling and her sword flying out of her hand.

With his left hand Musashi picked up the sword, and with his right, lifted Osugi into the crook of his arm.

"Let me down!" she screamed, beating the air with her hands. "Are there no gods? No bodhisattvas? I've already wounded him once! What am I going to do? Musashi! Don't shame me like this! Cut off my head! Kill me now!"

While Musashi, tight-lipped, strode along the path with the struggling woman under his arm, she continued her hoarse protest. "It's the fortunes of war! It's destiny! If this is the will of the gods, I'll not be a coward! . . . When Matahachi hears Uncle Gon died and I was killed trying to take revenge, he'll rise up in anger and avenge us both; it'll be good medicine for him. Musashi, kill me! Kill me now! . . . Where are you going? Are you trying to add disgrace to my death? Stop! Cut off my head now!"

Musashi paid no attention, but when he arrived at the bridge, he began to wonder what he was going to do with her.

An inspiration came. Going down to the river, he found a boat tied to one of the bridge piers. Gently, he lowered her into it. "Now, you just be patient and stay here for a while. Matahachi will be here soon."

"What are you doing?" she cried, trying to push aside his hands and the reed mats in the bottom of the boat at the same time. "Why should Matahachi's coming here make any difference? What makes you think he's coming? I know what you're up to. You're not satisfied with just killing me; you want to humiliate me too!"

"Think what you like. It won't be long before you learn the truth."

"Kill me!"

"Ha, ha, ha!"

"What's so funny? You should have no trouble cutting through this old neck with one swift stroke!"

For lack of a better way of keeping her put, he tied her

to the raised keel of the boat. He then slid her sword back into its scabbard and laid it down neatly by her side.

As he started to leave, she taunted him, saying, "Musashi! I don't think you understand the Way of the Samurai! Come back here, and I'll teach you."

"Later."

He started up the dike, but she was making such a racket, he had to go back and pile several reed mats over her.

A huge red sun sprang up in flames above Higashiyama. Musashi watched fascinated as it climbed, feeling its rays pierce the inner depths of his being. He grew reflective, thinking that only once a year, when this new sun rose, did the little worm of ego that binds man to his tiny thoughts have the chance to melt and vanish under its magnificent light. Musashi was filled with the joy of being alive.

Exultant, he shouted in the radiant dawn, "I'm still young!"

17

The Great Bridge at Gojō Avenue

"Field of the Rendaiji . . . ninth day of the first month . . ."

Reading the words made Musashi's blood surge.

His attention was distracted, however, by a sharp, stabbing pain in his left eye. Lifting his hand to his eyelid, he noticed a small needle stuck into his kimono sleeve, and a closer look revealed four or five more embedded in his clothing, shining like slivers of ice in the morning light.

"So that's it!" he exclaimed, pulling one out and examining it. It was about the size of a small sewing needle but had no threading eye and was triangular instead of round. "Why, the old bitch!" he said with a shudder, glancing down toward the boat. "I've heard about blow needles, but whoever would have thought the old hag could shoot them? That was a pretty close call."

With his usual curiosity, he gathered the needles one by one, then pinned them securely into his collar with the intention of studying them later on. He'd heard that among warriors there were two opposing schools of thought regarding these small weapons. One held that they could be effectively employed as a deterrent by blowing them into an enemy's face, while the other maintained that this was nonsense.

The proponents held that a very old technique for the

needles' employment had been developed from a game played by seamstresses and weavers who migrated from China to Japan in the sixth or seventh century. Although it was not considered a method of attack per se, they explained, it was practiced, up until the time of the Ashikaga shogunate, as a preliminary means of fending off an adversary.

Those on the other side of the fence went so far as to claim that no ancient technique ever existed, although they did admit that needle-blowing had been practiced as a game at one time. While conceding that women may have amused themselves in this fashion, they adamantly denied that needle-blowing could be refined to the degree necessary to inflict injury. They also pointed out that saliva could absorb a certain amount of heat, cold or acidity, but it could do little to absorb the pain caused by needles puncturing the inside of a person's mouth. The reply to this, of course, was that with enough practice, a person could learn to hold the needles in the mouth painlessly and to manipulate them with the tongue with a great deal of precision and force. Enough to blind a man.

The nonbelievers then countered that even if the needles could be blown hard and fast, the chances of hurting anyone were minimal. After all, they said, the only parts of the face vulnerable to such attack were the eyes, and the chances of hitting them weren't very good, even under the best conditions. And unless the needle penetrated the pupil, the damage would be insignificant.

After hearing most of these arguments at one time or another, Musashi had been inclined to side with the doubters. After this experience, he realized how premature his judgment had been and how important and useful randomly acquired bits of knowledge could subsequently prove to be.

The needles had missed his pupil, but his eye was watering. As he felt around his clothing for something to dry it with, he heard the sound of cloth being torn. Turning, he saw a girl ripping a foot or so of red fabric from the sleeve of her undergarment.

Akemi came running toward him. Her hair was not done up for the New Year's celebration, and her kimono was bedraggled. She wore sandals, but no socks. Musashi squinted at her and muttered; though she looked familiar, he couldn't place the face.

"It's me, Takezō . . . I mean Musashi," she said hesitantly, offering him the red cloth. "Did you get something in your eye? You shouldn't rub it. That'll only make it worse. Here, use this."

Musashi silently accepted her kindness and covered his eye with the cloth. Then he stared at her face intently.

"Don't you remember me?" she said incredulously. "But you must!"

Musashi's face was a perfect blank.

"You must!"

His silence broke the dam holding back her long-pent-up emotions. Her spirit, so accustomed to unhappiness and cruelty, had clung to this one last hope, and now the light was dawning that it was nothing more than a fantasy of her own making. A hard lump formed in her breast, and she made a choking sound. Though she covered her mouth and nose to suppress the sobs, her shoulders quivered uncontrollably.

Something about the way she looked when crying recalled the innocent girlishness of the days in Ibuki, when she'd carried the tinkling bell in her obi. Musashi put his arms around her thin, weak shoulders.

"You're Akemi, of course. I remember. How do you happen to be here? It's such a surprise to see you! Don't you live in Ibuki anymore? What happened to your mother?" His questions were like barbs, the worst being the mention of Okō, which led naturally to his old friend. "Are you still living with Matahachi? He was supposed to come here this morning. You haven't by any chance seen him, have you?"

Every word added to Akemi's misery. Nestled in his arms, she could do no more than shake her weeping head.

"Isn't Matahachi coming?" he persisted. "What happened to him? How will I ever know if you just stand here and cry?"

"He . . . he . . . he's not coming. He never . . . he never

got your message.'' Akemi pressed her face against Musashi's chest and went into a new spasm of tears.

She thought of saying this, of saying that, but each idea died in her feverish brain. How could she tell him of the horrid fate she had suffered because of her mother? How could she put into words what had happened in Sumiyoshi or in the days since then?

The bridge was bathed in the New Year's sun, and more and more people were passing by—girls in bright new kimonos going to make their New Year's obeisance at Kiyomizudera, men in formal robes starting their rounds of New Year's calls. Almost hidden among them was Jōtarō, his gnomish thatch of hair in the same disheveled state as on any other day. He was nearly in the middle of the bridge when he caught sight of Musashi and Akemi.

''What's all this?'' he asked himself. ''I thought he'd be with Otsū. That's not Otsū!'' He stopped and made a peculiar face.

He was shocked to the core. It might have been all right if no one were watching, but there they were chest to chest, embracing each other on a busy thoroughfare. A man and a woman hugging each other in public? It was shameless. He couldn't believe any grownup could act so disgracefully, much less his own, revered *sensei*. Jōtarō's heart throbbed violently, he was both sad and a little jealous. And angry, so angry that he wanted to pick up a rock and throw it at them.

''I've seen that woman somewhere,'' he thought. ''Ah! She's the one who took Musashi's message for Matahachi. Well, she's a teahouse girl, so what could you expect? But how on earth did they get to know one another? I think I should tell Otsū about this!''

He looked up and down the street and peered over the railing, but there was no sign of her.

The previous night, confident that she would be meeting Musashi the next day, Otsū had washed her hair and stayed up till the early hours doing it up in proper fashion. Then she had put on a kimono given her by the Karasumaru family and, before dawn, set out to pay her respects at Gion Shrine and Kiyomizudera before proceeding to Gojō Avenue. Jōtarō had wanted to accompany her, but she had refused.

Normally it would be all right, she had explained, but today Jōtarō would be in the way. "You stay here," she said. "First I want to talk to Musashi alone. You can come along to the bridge after it gets light, but take your time. And don't worry; I promise I'll be waiting there with Musashi when you come."

Jōtarō had been more than a little peeved. Not only was he old enough to understand Otsū's feelings; he also had a certain appreciation of the attraction men and women felt for each other. The experience of rolling about in the straw with Kocha in Koyagyū had not faded from his mind. Even so, it remained a mystery to him why a grown woman like Otsū went around moping and weeping all the time over a man.

Search as he might, he could not find Otsū. While he fretted, Musashi and Akemi moved to the end of the bridge, presumably to avoid being so conspicuous. Musashi folded his arms and leaned on the railing. Akemi, at his side, looked down at the river. They did not notice Jōtarō when he slipped by on the opposite side of the bridge.

"Why is she taking so much time? How long can you pray to Kannon?" Grumbling to himself, Jōtarō stood on tiptoe and strained his eyes toward the hill at the end of Gojō Avenue.

About ten paces from where he was standing, there were four or five leafless willow trees. Often a flock of white herons gathered here along the river to catch fish, but today none were to be seen. A young man with a long forelock leaned against a willow branch, which stretched out toward the ground like a sleeping dragon.

On the bridge, Musashi nodded as Akemi whispered fervently to him. She had thrown pride to the winds and was telling him everything in the hope that she could persuade him to be hers alone. It was difficult to discern whether her words penetrated beyond his ears. Nod though he might, his look was not that of a lover saying sweet nothings to his beloved. On the contrary, his pupils shone with a colorless, heatless radiance and focused steadily on some particular object.

Akemi did not notice this. Completely absorbed, she seemed to choke slightly as she tried to analyze her feelings.

"Oh," she sighed. "I've told you everything there is to tell. I haven't hidden anything." Edging closer to him, she said wistfully, "It's been more than four years since Seki-gahara. I've changed both in body and in spirit." Then, with a burst of tears: "No! I haven't really changed. My feeling toward you hasn't changed a bit. I'm absolutely sure of that! Do you understand, Musashi? Do you understand how I feel?"

"Mm."

"Please try to understand! I've told you everything. I'm not the innocent wild flower I was when we met at the foot of Mount Ibuki. I'm just an ordinary woman who's been violated. . . . But is chastity a thing of the body, or of the mind? Is a virgin who has lewd thoughts really chaste? . . . I lost my virginity to—I can't say his name, but to a certain man—and yet my heart is pure."

"Mm. Mm."

"Don't you feel anything for me at all? I can't keep secrets from the person I love. I wondered what to say when I saw you: should I say anything or not? But then it became clear. I couldn't deceive you even if I wanted to. Please understand! Say something! Say you forgive me. Or do you consider me despicable?"

"Mm. Ah . . ."

"When I think of it again, it makes me so furious!" She put her face down on the railing. "You see, I'm ashamed to ask you to love me. I haven't the right to do that. But . . . but . . . I'm still a virgin at heart. I still treasure my first love like a pearl. I haven't lost that treasure, and I won't, no matter what kind of life I lead, or what men I'm thrown together with!"

Each hair of her head trembled with her sobbing. Under the bridge where her tears fell, the river, glistening in the New Year's sun, flowed on like Akemi's dreams toward an eternity of hope.

"Mm." While the poignance of her story elicited frequent nods and grunts, Musashi's eyes remained fixed on that point in the distance. His father had once remarked,

"You're not like me. My eyes are black, but yours are dark brown. They say your granduncle, Hirata Shōgen, had terrifying brown eyes, so maybe you take after him." At this moment, in the slanting rays of the sun, Musashi's eyes were a pure and flawless coral.

"That has to be him," thought Sasaki Kojirō, the man leaning against the willow. He had heard of Musashi many times, but this was the first time he had set eyes on him.

Musashi was wondering: "Who could he be?"

From the instant their eyes met, they had silently been searching, each sounding the depths of the other's spirit. In practicing the Art of War, it is said that one must discern from the point of the enemy's sword the extent of his ability. This is exactly what the two men were doing. They were like wrestlers, sizing each other up before coming to grips. And each had reasons to regard the other with suspicion.

"I don't like it," thought Kojirō, seething with displeasure. He had taken care of Akemi since rescuing her from the deserted Amida Hall, and this patently intimate conversation between her and Musashi upset him. "Maybe he's the kind who preys on innocent women. And her! She didn't say where she was going, and now she's up there weeping on a man's shoulder!" He himself was here because he'd followed her.

The enmity in Kojirō's eyes was not lost on Musashi, and he was also conscious of that peculiar instant conflict of wills that arises when one *shugyōsha* encounters another. Nor was there any doubt that Kojirō felt the spirit of defiance conveyed in Musashi's expression.

"Who could he be?" thought Musashi again. "He looks like quite a fighter. But why the malicious look in his eye? Better watch him closely."

The intensity of the two men came not from their eyes but from deep inside. Fireworks seemed about to shoot from their pupils. From appearances, Musashi might be a year or two younger than Kojirō, but then again it might be the other way around. In either case, they shared one similarity: both were at that age of maximum impudence when they were certain they knew everything there was to know about politics, society, the Art of War and all other subjects. As a vicious dog snarls when it sees another vicious dog, so both Musashi and Kojirō knew instinctively that the other was a dangerous fighter.

Kojirō was the first to disengage his eyes, which he did with a slight grunt. Musashi, despite the touch of contempt he could see in Kojirō's profile, was convinced deep down that he'd won. The opponent had given in to his eyes, to his willpower, and this made Musashi happy.

"Akemi," he said, putting his hand on her shoulder.

Still sobbing with her face to the railing, she did not reply.

"Who's that man over there? He's somebody who knows you, isn't he? I mean the young man who looks like a student warrior. Just who is he?"

Akemi was silent. She had not seen Kojirō until now, and the sight threw her tear-swollen face into confusion. "Uh . . . you mean that tall man over there?"

"Yes. Who is he?"

"Oh, he's . . . well . . . he's . . . I don't know him very well."

"But you do know him, don't you?"

"Uh, yes."

"Carrying that great long sword and dressed to attract attention—he must think he's quite a swordsman! How do you happen to know him?"

"A few days ago," Akemi said quickly, "I was bitten by a dog, and the bleeding wouldn't stop, so I went to a doctor in the place where he happened to be staying. He's been looking after me the past few days."

"In other words, you're living in the same house with him?"

"Yes, well, I'm living there, but it doesn't mean anything. There's nothing between us." She spoke with more force now.

"In that case, I suppose you don't know much about him. Do you know his name?"

"His name is Sasaki Kojirō. He's also called Ganryū."

"Ganryū?" He had heard the name before. Though not exceptionally famous, it was known among the warriors in a number of provinces. He was younger than Musashi had imagined him to be; he took another look at him.

An odd thing happened then. A pair of dimples appeared in Kojirō's cheeks.

Musashi smiled back. Yet this silent communication was not full of peaceful light and friendship, like the smile exchanged between the Buddha and his disciple Ananda as they rubbed flowers between their fingers. In Kojirō's smile were both a challenging jeer and an element of irony.

Musashi's smile not only accepted Kojirō's challenge but conveyed a fierce will to fight.

Caught between these two strong-willed men, Akemi was about to start pouring out her feelings again, but before it came to that, Musashi said, "Now, Akemi, I think it'd be best for you to go back with that man to your lodgings. I'll come to see you soon. Don't worry."

"You'll really come?"

"Why, yes, of course."

"The name of the inn, it's the Zuzuya, in front of the Rokujō Avenue monastery."

"I see."

The casual manner of his reply was not enough for Akemi. She grabbed his hand from the railing and squeezed it passionately in the shadow of her sleeve. "You'll really come, won't you? Promise?"

Musashi's reply was drowned by a burst of belly-splitting laughter.

"Ha, ha, ha, ha, ha! Oh! Ha, ha, ha, ha! Oh . . ." Kojirō turned his back and walked away as best he could in view of his uncontrollable mirth.

Looking on acidly from one end of the bridge, Jōtarō thought: "Nothing could possibly be that funny!" He himself was disgusted with the world, and particularly with his wayward teacher and with Otsū.

"Where could she have got to?" he asked again as he started tramping angrily toward town. He had taken only a few steps when he spied Otsū's white face between the wheels of an oxcart standing at the next corner over. "There she is!" he shouted, then bumped into the ox's nose in his hurry to reach her.

Today, for a change, Otsū had applied a little rouge to her lips. Her makeup was somewhat amateurish, but there was a pleasant scent about her, and her kimono was a lovely spring outfit with a white and green pattern embroidered on a deep pink background. Jōtarō hugged her from behind, not caring whether he mussed her hair or smeared the white powder on her neck.

"Why are you hiding here? I've been waiting for hours. Come with me, quick!"

She made no reply.

"Come on, right now!" he pleaded, shaking her by the shoulders. "Musashi's here too. Look, you can see him from here. I'm mad at him myself, but let's go anyway. If we don't hurry, he'll be gone!" When he took her wrist and tried to pull her to her feet, he noticed her arm was damp. "Otsū! Are you crying?"

"Jō, hide behind the wagon like me. Please!"

"Why?"

"Never mind why!"

"Well, of all—" Jōtarō made no attempt to conceal his wrath. "That's what I hate about women. They do crazy things! You keep saying you want to see Musashi and go weeping all over the place looking for him. Now that he's right in front of you, you decide to hide. You even want me to hide with you! Isn't that funny? Ha— Oh, I can't even laugh."

The words stung like a whip. Lifting her swollen red eyes, she said, "Please don't talk that way. I beg you. Don't you be mean to me too!"

"Why accuse me of being mean? What have I done?"

"Just be quiet, please. And stoop down here with me."

"I can't. There's ox manure on the ground. You know, they say if you cry on New Year's Day, even the crows will laugh at you."

"Oh, I don't care. I'm just—"

"Well, then, I'll laugh at you! Laugh like that samurai a few minutes ago. My first laugh of the New Year. Would that suit you?"

"Yes. Laugh! Laugh hard!"

"I can't," he said, wiping his nose. "I'll bet I know

what's wrong. You're jealous because Musashi was talking to that woman."

"It's . . . it's not that! It's not that at all!"

"Yes it is! I know it is. It made me mad too. But isn't that all the more reason for you to go and talk to him? You don't understand anything, do you?"

Otsū showed no signs of rising, but he tugged so hard at her wrist that she was forced to. "Stop!" she cried. "That hurts! Don't be so spiteful. You say I don't understand anything, but you don't have the slightest idea how I feel."

"I know exactly how you feel. You're jealous!"

"That's not the only thing."

"Quiet. Let's go!"

She emerged from behind the wagon, but not voluntarily. The boy pulled; her feet scraped the ground. Still tugging, Jōtarō craned his neck and looked toward the bridge.

"Look!" he said. "Akemi's not there anymore."

"Akemi? Who's Akemi?"

"The girl Musashi was talking to. . . . Oh, oh! Musashi's walking away. If you don't come right now, he'll be gone." Jōtarō let go of Otsū and started toward the bridge.

"Wait!" cried Otsū, sweeping the bridge with her eyes to make sure Akemi wasn't lurking about somewhere. Assured that her rival was really gone, she appeared immensely relieved and her eyebrows unfurrowed. But back she went, behind the oxcart, to dry her puffy eyes with her sleeve, smooth her hair and straighten her kimono.

"Hurry, Otsū!" Jōtarō called impatiently. "Musashi seems to have gone down to the riverbank. This is no time to primp!"

"Where?"

"Down to the riverbank. I don't know why, but that's where he went."

The two of them ran together to the end of the bridge, and Jōtarō, with perfunctory apologies, made a way for them through the crowd to the railing.

Musashi was standing by the boat where Osugi was still squirming around, trying to free her bonds.

"I'm sorry, Granny," he said, "but it seems Matahachi's not coming after all. I hope to see him in the near future and try to drum some courage into him. In the meantime, you yourself should try to find him and take him home to live with you, like a good son. That'd be a far better way to express your gratitude to your ancestors than by trying to cut off my head."

He put his hand under the rush mats and with a small knife cut the rope.

"You talk too much, Musashi! I don't need any advice from you. Just make up your stupid mind what you're going to do. Are you going to kill me or be killed?"

Bright blue veins stood out all over her face as she struggled out from under the mats, but by the time she stood up, Musashi was crossing the river, jumping like a wagtail across the rocks and shoals. In no time he reached the opposite side and climbed to the top of the dike.

Jōtarō caught sight of him and cried, "See, Otsū! There he is!" The boy went straight down the dike, and she did the same.

To Jōtarō's nimble legs, rivers and mountains meant nothing, but Otsū, because of her fine kimono, came to a dead halt at the river's edge. Musashi was now out of sight, but there she stood, screaming his name at the top of her lungs.

"Otsū!" came a reply from an unexpected quarter. Osugi was not a hundred feet away.

When Otsū saw who it was, she uttered a cry, covered her face with her hands for a moment and ran.

The old woman lost no time in giving chase, white hair flying in the wind. "Otsū!" she screamed, in a voice that might have parted the waters of the Kamo. "Wait! I want to talk to you."

An explanation for Otsū's presence was already taking shape in the old woman's suspicious mind. She felt sure Musashi had tied her up because he had a rendezvous with the girl today and had not wanted her to see this. Then, she reasoned, something Otsū said had annoyed him, and he had abandoned her. That, no doubt, was why she was wailing for him to come back.

"That girl is incorrigible!" she said, hating Otsū even more than she hated Musashi. In her mind, Otsū was rightfully her daughter-in-law, never mind whether the nuptials had actually taken place or not. The promise had been made, and if his fiancée had come to hate her son, she must also hate Osugi herself.

"Wait!" she shrieked again, opening her mouth almost from ear to ear.

The force of the scream startled Jōtarō, who was right beside her. He grabbed hold of her and shouted, "What are you trying to do, you old witch?"

"Get out of my way!" cried Osugi, shoving him aside.

Jōtarō did not know who she was, or why Otsū had fled at the sight of her, but he sensed that she meant danger. As the son of Aoki Tanzaemon and the sole student of Miyamoto Musashi, he refused to be pushed aside by an old hag's scrawny elbow.

"You can't do that to me!" He caught up with her and leapt squarely on her back.

She quickly shook him off, and taking his neck in the crook of her left arm, dealt him several sharp slaps. "You little devil! This'll teach you to butt in!"

While Jōtarō struggled to free himself, Otsū ran on, her mind in turmoil. She was young, and like most young people, full of hope, not in the habit of bemoaning her unhappy lot. She savored the delights of each new day as though they were flowers in a sunny garden. Sorrows and disappointments were facts of life, but they did not get her down for long. Likewise, she could not conceive of pleasure as completely divorced from pain.

But today she had been jolted out of her optimism, not once but twice. Why, she wondered, had she ever come here this morning?

Neither tears nor anger could nullify the shock. After thinking fleetingly of suicide, she had condemned all men as wicked liars. She had been by turns furious and miserable, hating the world, hating herself, too overcome to find release in tears or to think clearly about anything. Her blood boiled with jealousy, and the insecurity it caused made her scold herself for her many shortcomings, including her lack of poise at the moment. She told herself repeatedly to keep cool and gradually repressed her impulses beneath the veneer of dignity that women were supposed to maintain.

The entire time that strange girl was at Musashi's side, Otsū had not been able to move. When Akemi left, however, forbearance was no longer possible and Otsū felt irresistibly compelled to face Musashi and pour out how she felt. Although she had no idea where to begin, she resolved to open her heart and tell him everything.

But life is full of tiny accidents. One small misstep—a minute miscalculation made in the heat of the moment—can, in many instances, alter the shape of things to come for months or years. It was by letting Musashi out of her sight for a second that Otsū exposed herself to Osugi. On this glorious New Year's morning, Otsū's garden of delights was overrun by snakes.

It was a nightmare come true. In many a frenzied dream, she had encountered Osugi's leering face, and here was the stark reality bearing down on her.

Completely winded after running several hundred yards, she halted and looked back. For a moment, her breath stopped altogether. Osugi, about a hundred yards away, was hitting Jōtarō and swinging him around, this way and that.

He fought back, kicking the ground, kicking the air, landing an occasional blow on his captor.

Otsū saw that it would be only a matter of moments before he succeeded in drawing his wooden sword. And when he did, it was a dead certainty the old woman would not only unsheath her short sword but show no compunction about using it. At a time like this, Osugi was not one to show mercy. Jōtarō might well be killed.

Otsū was in a terrible predicament: Jōtarō had to be rescued, but she dared not approach Osugi.

Jōtarō did succeed in getting his wooden sword free of his obi but not in extracting his head from Osugi's viselike grip. All his kicking and flailing were working against him, because they increased the old woman's self-confidence.

"Brat!" she cried snidely. "What're you trying to do, imitate a frog?" The way her front teeth jutted out made her look harelipped, but her expression was one of hideous triumph. Step by scraping step, she pressed on toward Otsū.

As she glared at the terrified girl, her natural cunning asserted itself. In a flash it came to her that she was going about this the wrong way. If the opponent had been Musashi, trickery would not work, but the enemy before her was Otsū—tender, innocent Otsū—who could probably be made to believe anything, provided it was put to her gently and with an air of sincerity. First tie her up with words, thought Osugi, then roast her for dinner.

"Otsū!" she called in an earnestly poignant tone. "Why are you running away? What makes you flee the minute you lay eyes on me? You did the same thing at the Mikazuki Teahouse. I can't understand it. You must be imagining things. I haven't the slightest intention of doing you any harm."

An expression of doubt crept over Otsū's face, but Jōtarō, still captive, asked, "Is that true, Granny? Do you mean it?"

"Why, of course. Otsū doesn't understand how I really feel. She seems to be afraid of me."

"If you mean that, let go of me, and I'll go get her."

"Not so fast. If I let you go, how do I know you won't hit me with that sword of yours and run away?"

"Do you think I'm a coward? I'd never do anything like that. It looks to me as though we're fighting over nothing. There's been a mistake somewhere."

"All right. You go to Otsū and tell her I'm not angry at her anymore. There was a time when I was, but that's all over. Since Uncle Gon died, I've been wandering around all by myself, carrying his ashes at my side—a lonely old lady with no place to go. Explain to her that whatever my feelings about Musashi, I still look upon her as a daughter. I'm not asking her to come back and be Matahachi's bride. I only hope she'll take pity on me and listen to what I have to say."

"That's enough. Any more and I won't be able to remember it all."

"All right, just tell her what I've said so far."

While the boy ran to Otsū and repeated Osugi's message, the old woman, pretending not to watch, sat down on a rock and gazed toward a shoal where a school of minnows were making patterns in the water. Would Otsū come, or would she not? Osugi stole a glance, faster than the lightning movements of the tiny fish.

Otsū's doubts were not easily dispelled, but eventually Jōtarō convinced her there was no danger. Timidly she began walking toward Osugi, who, reveling in her victory, smiled broadly.

"Otsū, my dear girl," she said in a motherly tone.

"Granny," replied Otsū, bowing to the ground at the old woman's feet. "Forgive me. Please, forgive me. I don't know what to say."

"There's no need for you to say anything. It's all Matahachi's fault. Apparently he still resents your change of heart, and at one time I'm afraid I thought ill of you too. But that's all water under the bridge."

"Then you'll pardon me for the way I acted?"

"Well, now," said Osugi, introducing a note of uncertainty, but at the same time squatting down beside Otsū.

Otsū picked at the sand with her fingers, scratching a small hole in the cold surface. Tepid water bubbled to the surface.

"As Matahachi's mother, I suppose I can say that you've been forgiven, but then there's Matahachi to consider. Won't you see him and talk to him again? Since he ran off with another woman of his own free will, I don't think he'd ask you to come back to him. In fact, I wouldn't permit him to do anything so selfish, but . . . ."

"Yes?"

"Well, won't you at least agree to seeing him? Then, with the two of you there side by side, I'll tell him exactly what's what. That way, I'll be able to fulfill my duty as a mother. I'll feel I've done everything I could."

"I see," replied Otsū. From the sand beside her, a baby crab crawled out and scurried behind a rock. Jōtarō latched on to it, went behind Osugi and dropped it on the top of her head.

Otsū said, "But I can't help feeling that after all this time it would be better for me not to see Matahachi."

"I'll be right there with you. Wouldn't you feel better if you saw him and made a clean break of it?"

"Yes, but—"

"Then do it. I say this for the sake of your own future."

"If I agree . . . how are we to find Matahachi? Do you know where he is?"

"I can, uh, I can find him very quickly. Very quickly. You see, I saw him quite recently in Osaka. He got into one of his willful moods and went off and left me in Sumiyoshi, but when he does things like that, he always regrets them later. It won't be long before he shows up in Kyoto looking for me."

Despite Otsū's uncomfortable feeling that Osugi wasn't telling the truth, she was swayed by the old woman's faith in her worthless son. What led to her final surrender, however, was the conviction that the course proposed by Osugi was right and proper. "How would it be," she asked, "if I went and helped you look for Matahachi?"

"Oh, would you?" cried Osugi, taking the girl's hand in her own.

"Yes. Yes, I think I should."

"All right, come with me now to my inn. Ouch! What's this?" Standing up, she put her hand to the back of her collar and caught the crab. With a shiver, she exclaimed, "Now, how did that get there?" She held out her hand and shook it loose from her fingers.

Jōtarō, who was behind her, suppressed a snicker, but Osugi was not fooled. With flashing eyes, she turned and glared at him. "Some of your mischief, I suppose!"

"Not me. I didn't do it." He ran up the dike for safety and called, "Otsū, are you going with her to her inn?"

Before Otsū could answer for herself, Osugi said, "Yes, she's coming with me. I'm staying at an inn near the foot of Sannen Hill. I always stay there when I come to Kyoto. We won't be needing you. You go back to wherever you came from."

"All right, I'll be at the Karasumaru house. You come too, Otsū, when you've finished your business."

Otsū felt a twinge of anxiety. "Jō, wait!" She ran quickly up the dike, reluctant to let him go. Osugi, fearing the girl might change her mind and flee, was quick to follow, but for a few seconds Otsū and Jōtarō were alone.

"I think I ought to go with her," said Otsū. "But I'll

come to Lord Karasumaru's whenever I have a chance. Explain everything to them, and get them to let you stay until I've finished what I have to do."

"Don't worry. I'll wait as long as necessary."

"Look for Musashi while you're waiting, won't you?"

"There you go again! When you finally find him, you hide. And now you're sorry. Don't say I didn't warn you."

"It was very foolish of me."

Osugi arrived and inserted herself between the two. The trio started walking back to the bridge, Osugi's needlelike glance darting frequently toward Otsū, whom she dared not trust. Although Otsū had not the slightest inkling of the perilous fate that lay before her, she nevertheless had the feeling of being trapped.

When they arrived back at the bridge, the sun was high above the willows and the pines and the streets well filled with the New Year's throng. A sizable group had congregated before the sign posted on the bridge.

"Musashi? Who's that?"

"Do you know any great swordsman by that name?"

"Never heard of him."

"Must be quite a fighter if he's taking on the Yoshiokas. That should be something to see."

Otsū came to a halt and stared. Osugi and Jōtarō, too, stopped and looked, listening to the softly reverberating whisper. Like the ripples caused by minnows in the shoal, the name *Musashi* spread through the crowd.

18

The Withered Field

The swordsmen from the Yoshioka School assembled in a barren field overlooking the Nagasaka entrance to the Tamba highroad. Beyond the trees edging the field, the glistening of the snow in the mountains northwest of Kyoto struck the eye like lightning.

One of the men suggested making a fire, pointing out that their sheathed swords seemed to act like conduits, transmitting the cold directly to their bodies. It was the very beginning of spring, the ninth day of the new year. A frigid wind blew down from Mount Kinugasa and even the birds sounded forlorn.

"Burns nice, doesn't it?"

"Um. Better be careful. Don't want to start a brush fire."

The crackling fire warmed their hands and faces, but before long, Ueda Ryōhei, waving smoke from his eyes, grumbled, "It's too hot!" Glaring at a man who was about to throw more leaves on the fire, he said, "That's enough! Stop!"

An hour passed uneventfully.

"It must be past six o'clock already."

To a man, without giving it a thought, they lifted their eyes toward the sun.

"Closer to seven."

"The Young Master should be here by now."

"Oh, he'll show up any minute."

Faces tense, they anxiously watched the road from town; not a few were swallowing nervously.

"What could have happened to him?"

A cow lowed, breaking the silence. The field had once been used as pasture for the Emperor's cows, and there were still untended cows in the vicinity. The sun rose higher, bringing with it warmth and the odor of manure and dried grass.

"Don't you suppose Musashi's already at the field by the Rendaiji?"

"He may be."

"Somebody go and take a look. It's only about six hundred yards."

No one was eager to do this; they lapsed into silence again, their faces smoldering in the shadows cast by the smoke.

"There's no misunderstanding about the arrangements, is there?"

"No. Ueda got it directly from the Young Master last night. There couldn't be any mistake."

Ryōhei confirmed this. "That's right. I wouldn't be surprised if Musashi's there already, but maybe the Young Master's deliberately coming late to make Musashi nervous. Let's wait. If we make a false move and give people the impression we're going to the aid of the Young Master, it'll disgrace the school. We can't do anything until he arrives. What's Musashi anyway? Just a rōnin. He can't be that good."

The students who had seen Musashi in action at the Yoshioka dōjō the previous year knew otherwise, but even to them it was unthinkable that Seijūrō would lose. The consensus was that though their master was bound to win, accidents do happen. Moreover, since the fight had been publicly announced, there would be a lot of spectators, whose presence, they felt, would not only add to the prestige of the school but enhance the personal reputation of their teacher.

Despite Seijūrō's specific instructions that they were under no circumstances to assist him, forty of them had gathered here to await his arrival, give him a rousing send-off, and be on hand—just in case. Besides Ueda, five of the other Ten Swordsmen of the House of Yoshioka were present.

It was now past seven, and as the spirit of calm enjoined upon them by Ryōhei gave way to boredom, they mumbled discontentedly.

Spectators on their way to the bout were asking if there had been some mistake.

"Where's Musashi?"

"Where's the other one—Seijūrō?"

"Who are all those samurai?"

"Probably here to second one side or the other."

"Strange way to have a duel! The seconds are here, the principals aren't."

Though the crowd grew bigger and the buzz of voices louder, the onlookers were too prudent to approach the Yoshioka students, who, for their part, took no notice of the heads peering through the withered miscanthus or looking down from tree branches.

Jōtarō padded around in the midst of the mob, leaving a trail of little puffs of dust. Carrying his larger-than-life wooden sword and wearing sandals too big for him, he was going from woman to woman, checking one face after another. "Not here, not here," he murmured. "What could have happened to Otsū? She knows about the fight today." She had to be here, he thought. Musashi might be in danger. What could possibly keep her away?

But his search was fruitless, though he trudged about until he was dead tired. "It's so strange," he thought. "I haven't seen her since New Year's Day. I wonder if she's sick. . . . That old hag she went away with talked nice, but maybe it was a trick. Maybe she's done something awful to Otsū."

This worried him terribly, far more than the outcome of today's bout. He had no misgivings about that. Of the hundreds of people in the crowd, there was hardly one who did not expect Seijūrō to win. Only Jōtarō was sustained by unshakable faith in Musashi. Before his eyes was a vision of his teacher facing the lances of the Hōzōin priests at Hannya Plain.

Finally, he stopped in the middle of the field. "There's something else strange," he mused. "Why are all these people here? According to the sign, the fight is to take place in the field by the Rendaiji." He seemed to be the only person puzzled by this.

Out of the milling crowd came a surly voice. "You there, boy! Look here!"

Jōtarō recognized the man; he was the one who had been watching Musashi and Akemi whispering on the bridge on New Year's morning.

"What do you want, mister?" asked Jōtarō.

Sasaki Kojirō came up to him, but before speaking, slowly eyed him from head to toe. "Didn't I see you on Gojō Avenue recently?"

"Oh, so you remember."

"You were with a young woman."

"Yes. That was Otsū."

"Is that her name? Tell me, does she have some connection with Musashi?"

"I should say so."

"Is she his cousin?"

"Unh-unh."

"Sister?"

"Unh-unh."

"Well?"

"She likes him."

"Are they lovers?"

"I don't know. I'm only his pupil." Jōtarō nodded his head proudly.

"So that's why you're here. Look, the crowd's getting restless. You must know where Musashi is. Has he left his inn?"

"Why ask me? I haven't seen him for a long time."

Several men pushed their way through the crowd and approached Kojirō.

He turned a hawklike eye on them.

"Ah, so there you are, Sasaki!"

"Why, it's Ryōhei."

"Where've you been all this time?" Ryōhei demanded, grabbing Kojirō's hand as though taking him prisoner. "You haven't been to the dōjō for more than ten days. The Young Master wanted to get in some practice with you."

"So what if I stayed away? I'm here today."

Placing themselves discreetly around Kojirō, Ryōhei and his comrades led him off to their fire.

The whisper went around among those who had seen Kojirō's long sword and his flashy outfit. "That's Musashi, for sure!"

"Is that him?"

"It must be."

"Pretty loud clothing he's got on. He doesn't look weak, though."

"That's not Musashi!" Jōtarō cried disdainfully. "Musashi's not like that at all! You'd never catch him dressed up like a Kabuki actor!"

Presently even those who could not hear the boy's protest realized their mistake and went back to wondering what was going on.

Kojirō was standing with the Yoshioka students, regarding them with obvious contempt. They listened to him in silence, but their faces were sullen.

"It was a blessing in disguise for the House of Yoshioka that neither Seijūrō nor Musashi arrived on time," said Kojirō. "What you'd better do is split up into groups, head Seijūrō off and take him home quickly before he gets hurt."

This cowardly proposal enraged them, but he went further. "What I'm advising would do Seijūrō more good than any assistance he could possibly get from you." Then, rather grandly: "Heaven sent me here as a messenger for the sake of the House of Yoshioka. I shall give you my prediction: if they fight, Seijūrō will lose. I'm sorry to have to say this, but Musashi will certainly defeat him, maybe kill him."

Miike Jūrōzaemon thrust his chest against the younger man's and shouted, "That's an insult." His right elbow between his own face and Kojirō's, he was prepared to draw and strike.

Kojirō looked down and grinned. "I take it you don't like what I said."

"Ugh!"

"In that case, I'm sorry," said Kojirō blithely. "I won't attempt to be of further assistance."

"Nobody asked for your help in the first place."

"That's not quite right. If you had no need of my support, why did you insist that I come from Kema to your house? Why were you trying so hard to keep me happy? You, Seijūrō, all of you!"

"We were simply being polite to a guest. You think a lot of yourself, don't you?"

"Ha, ha, ha, ha! Let's stop all this, before it ends up with my having to fight all of you. But I warn you, if you don't heed my prophecy, you'll regret it! I've compared the two men with my own eyes, and I say the chances Seijūrō will lose are overwhelming. Musashi was at the Gojō Avenue bridge on New Year's morning. As soon as I laid eyes on him, I knew there was danger. To me, that sign you put up looks more like an announcement of mourning for the House of Yoshioka. It's very sad, but it seems to be the way of the world that people never realize when they're finished."

"That's enough! Why come here if your only purpose is to talk like that?"

Kojirō's tone became snide. "It also seems to be typical of people on the way down that they won't accept an act of kindness in the spirit in which it's offered. Go on! Think what you like! You won't even have to wait the day out. You'll know in an hour or less how wrong you are."

"Yech!" Jūrōzaemon spat at Kojirō. Forty men moved a step forward, their anger radiating darkly over the field.

Kojirō reacted with self-assurance. Jumping quickly to one side, he demonstrated by his stance that if they were looking for a fight, he was ready. The goodwill he had professed earlier now seemed a sham. An observer might well have asked if he wasn't using mob psychology to create an opportunity for himself to steal the show from Musashi and Seijūrō.

A stir of excitement spread through those close enough to see. This was not the fight they had come to watch, but it promised to be a good one.

Into the midst of this murder-charged atmosphere ran a young girl. Speeding along behind her like a rolling ball was a small monkey. She rushed in between Kojirō and the Yoshioka swordsmen and screamed, "Kojirō! Where's Musashi! Isn't he here?"

Kojirō turned on her angrily. "What is this?" he demanded.

"Akemi!" said one of the samurai. "What's she doing here?"

"Why did you come?" Kojirō snapped. "Didn't I tell you not to?"

"I'm not your private property! Why can't I be here?"

"Shut up! And get out of here! Go on back to the Zuzuya," shouted Kojirō, pushing her away gently.

Akemi, panting heavily, shook her head adamantly. "Don't order me around! I stayed with you, but I don't belong to you. I—" She choked and began to sob noisily. "How can you tell me what to do after what you did to me? After tying me up and leaving me on the second floor of the inn? After bullying and torturing me when I said I was worried about Musashi?"

Kojirō opened his mouth, ready to speak, but Akemi didn't give him the chance. "One of the neighbors heard me scream and came and untied me. I'm here to see Musashi!"

"Are you out of your mind? Can't you see the people around you? Shut up!"

"I won't! I don't care who hears. You said Musashi would be killed today—if Seijūrō couldn't handle him, you'd act as his second and kill Musashi yourself. Maybe I'm crazy, but Musashi's the only man in my heart! I must see him. Where is he?"

Kojirō clicked his tongue but was speechless before her vitriolic attack.

To the Yoshioka men, Akemi seemed too distraught to be believed. But maybe there was some truth in what she said. And if there was, Kojirō had used kindness as a lure, then tortured her for his own pleasure.

Embarrassed, Kojirō glared at her with unconcealed hate.

Suddenly their attention was diverted by one of Seijūrō's attendants, a youth by the name of Tamihachi. He was running like a wild man, waving his arms and shouting.

"Help! It's the Young Master! He's met Musashi. He's injured! Oh, it's awful! A-w-w-ful!"

"What're you babbling about?"

"The Young Master? Musashi?"

"Where? When?"

"Tamihachi, are you telling the truth?"

Shrill questions poured from faces suddenly drained of blood.

Tamihachi went on screaming inarticulately. Neither answering their questions nor pausing to catch his breath, he ran stumbling back to the Tamba highroad. Half believing, half doubting, not really knowing what to think, Ueda, Jūrōzaemon and the others chased after him like wild beasts charging across a burning plain.

Running north about five hundred yards, they came to a barren field stretching out beyond the trees to the right, quietly basking in the spring sunlight, on the surface serene and undisturbed. Thrushes and shrikes, chirping as though nothing had happened, hastily took to the air as Tamihachi scrambled wildly through the grass. He climbed up a knoll that looked like an ancient burial mound and fell to his knees. Clutching at the earth, he moaned and screamed, "Young Master!"

The others caught up with him, then stood nailed to the ground, gaping at the sight before their eyes. Seijūrō, clad in a kimono with a blue flowered design, a leather strap holding back his sleeves and a white cloth tied around his head, lay with his face buried in the grass.

"Young Master!"

"We're here! What happened?"

There was not a drop of blood on the white headband, nor on his sleeve or the grass around him, but his eyes and forehead were frozen in an expression of excruciating pain. His lips were the color of wild grapes.

"Is . . . is he breathing?"

"Barely."

"Quick, pick him up!"

One man knelt and took hold of Seijūrō's right arm, ready to lift him. Seijūrō screamed in agony.

"Find something to carry him on! Anything!"

Three or four men, shouting confusedly, ran down the road to a farmhouse and came back with a rain shutter. They gently rolled Seijūrō onto it, but though he seemed to revive a little, he was still writhing in pain. To keep him quiet, several men removed their obis and tied him to the shutter.

With one man at each corner, they lifted him up and began walking in funereal silence.

Seijūrō kicked violently, almost breaking the shutter. "Musashi . . . is he gone? . . . Oh, it hurts! . . . Right arm—shoulder. The bone . . . O-w-w-w! . . . Can't stand it. Cut it off! . . . Can't you hear? Cut the arm off!"

The horror of his pain caused the men carrying the improvised stretcher to avert their eyes. This was the man they respected as their teacher; it seemed indecent to look at him in this condition.

Pausing, they called back to Ueda and Jūrōzaemon. "He's in terrible pain, asking us to cut off his arm. Wouldn't it be easier on him if we did?"

"Don't talk like fools," roared Ryōhei. "Of course it's painful, but he won't die from that. If we cut his arm off and can't stop the bleeding, it'll be the end of him. What we've got to do is get him home and see how badly he's injured. If the arm has to come off, we can do it after proper steps have been taken to keep him from bleeding to death. A couple of you go on ahead and bring the doctor to the school."

There were still a lot of people about, standing silently behind the pine trees along the road. Annoyed, Ryōhei scowled blackly and turned to the men behind him. "Chase those people away," he ordered. "The Young Master's not a spectacle to be stared at."

Most of the samurai, grateful for a chance to work off their pent-up anger, took off on the run, making vicious gestures at the onlookers. The latter scattered like locusts.

"Tamihachi, come here!" called Ryōhei angrily, as if blaming the young attendant for what had happened.

The youth, who had been walking tearfully beside the stretcher, shrank in terror. "Wh-what is it?" he stammered.

"Were you with the Young Master when he left the house?"

"Y-y-yes."

295

"Where did he make his preparations?"

"Here, after we reached the field."

"He must have known where we were waiting. Why didn't he go there first?"

"I don't know."

"Was Musashi already there?"

"He was standing on the knoll where . . . where . . ."

"Was he alone?"

"Yes."

"How did it go? Did you just stand there and watch?"

"The Young Master looked straight at me and said . . . he said if by any chance he should lose, I was to pick up his body and take it to the other field. He said you and the others had been there since dawn, but I wasn't under any circumstances to let anyone know anything until the bout was over. He said there were times when a student of the Art of War had no choice but to risk defeat, and he didn't want to win by dishonorable, cowardly means. After that, he went forward to meet Musashi." Tamihachi spoke rapidly, relieved to get the story told.

"Then what?"

"I could see Musashi's face. He seemed to be smiling slightly. The two of them exchanged some sort of greeting. Then . . . then there was a scream. It carried from one end of the field to the other. I saw the Young Master's wooden sword fly into the air, and then . . . only Musashi was standing. He had on an orange headband, but his hair was on end."

The road had been cleared of the curious. The men carrying the shutter were dejected and subdued but kept scrupulously in step so as to avoid causing further pain to the injured man.

"What's that?"

They halted, and one of the men in front raised his free hand to his neck. Another looked up at the sky. Dead pine needles were fluttering down on Seijūrō. Perched on a limb above them was Kojirō's monkey, staring vacantly and making obscene gestures.

"Ouch!" cried one of the men as a pine cone struck his upturned face. Cursing, he whipped his stiletto from his scabbard and sent it flying with a flash of light at the monkey, but missed his target.

At the sound of his master's whistle, the monkey somersaulted and bounced lightly onto his shoulder. Kojirō was standing in the shadows, Akemi at his side. While the Yoshioka men directed resentful eyes at him, Kojirō stared fixedly at the body on the rain shutter. His supercilious smile had deserted his face, which now bore a look of reverence. He grimaced at Seijūrō's agonized moans. With his recent lecture still fresh in mind, the samurai could only assume that he had come to have the last laugh.

Ryōhei urged the stretcher bearers on, saying, "It's only a monkey, not even a human being. Forget it, get moving."

"Wait," Kojirō said, then went to Seijūrō's side and spoke directly to him. "What happened?" he asked, but did not wait for an answer. "Musashi got the better of you, didn't he? Where did he hit you? Right shoulder? . . . Oh, this is bad. The bone's shattered. Your arm's like a sack of gravel. You shouldn't be lying on your back, being bounced along on the shutter. The blood might go to your brain."

Turning to the others, he commanded arrogantly, "Put him down! Go ahead, put him down! . . . What are you waiting for? Do as I say!"

Seijūrō seemed on the verge of death, but Kojirō ordered him to stand up. "You can if you try. The wound isn't all that serious. It's only your right arm. If you try walking, you can do it. You've still got the use of your left arm. Forget about yourself! Think of your dead father. You owe him more respect than you're showing now, a lot more. Being carried through the streets of Kyoto—what a sight that would be. Think what it would do to your father's good name!"

Seijūrō stared at him, his eyes white and bloodless. Then with one quick motion, he lifted himself to his feet. His useless right arm looked a foot longer than his left.

"Miike!" cried Seijūrō.

"Yes, sir."

"Cut it off!"

"Huh-h-h!"

"Don't just stand there! Cut off my arm!"

"But . . ."

"You gutless idiot! Here, Ueda, cut it off! Right now!"

"Y-y-yes, sir."

But before Ueda moved, Kojirō said, "I'll do it if you want."

"Please!" said Seijūrō.

Kojirō went to his side. Grasping Seijūrō's hand firmly, he lifted the arm high, at the same time unsheathing his small sword. With a quick, startling sound, the arm fell to the ground, and blood spurted from the stump.

When Seijūrō staggered, his students rushed to his support and covered the wound with cloth to stop the blood.

"From now on I'll walk," said Seijūrō. "I'll walk home on my own two feet." His face waxen, he took ten steps. Behind him, the blood dripping from the wound oozed blackly into the ground.

"Young Master, be careful!"

His disciples clung to him like hoops to a barrel, their voices filled with solicitude, which turned rapidly to anger.

One of them cursed Kojirō, saying, "Why did that conceited ass have to butt in? You'd have been better off the way you were."

But Seijūrō, shamed by Kojirō's words, said, "I said I'll walk, and walk I will!" After a short pause, he proceeded another twenty paces, carried more by his willpower than by his legs. But he could not hold on for long; after fifty or sixty yards, he collapsed.

"Quick! We've got to get him to the doctor."

They picked him up and made quickly for Shijō Avenue. Seijūrō no longer had the strength to object.

Kojirō stood for a time under a tree, watching grimly. Then, turning to Akemi, he said with a smirk, "Did you see that? I imagine it made you feel good, didn't it?" Her face deadly white, Akemi regarded his sneer with loathing, but he went on. "You've done nothing but talk about how you'd like to get back at him. Are you satisfied now? Is this enough revenge for your lost virginity?"

Akemi was too confused to speak. Kojirō seemed at this moment more frightening, more hateful, more evil than

Seijūrō. Though Seijūrō was the cause of her troubles, he was not a wicked man. He was not blackhearted, not a real villain. Kojirō, on the other hand, was genuinely evil—not the type of sinner most people envisioned but a twisted, perverse fiend, who, far from rejoicing in the happiness of others, delighted in standing by and watching them suffer. He would never steal or cheat, yet he was more dangerous by far than the ordinary crook.

"Let's go home," he said, putting the monkey back on his shoulder. Akemi longed to flee but could not muster the courage. "It won't do you any good to go on looking for Musashi," mumbled Kojirō, talking to himself as much as to her. "There's no reason for him to linger around here."

Akemi asked herself why she did not take this opportunity to make a dash for freedom, why she seemed unable to leave this brute. But even as she cursed her own stupidity, she could not prevent herself from going with him.

The monkey turned its head and looked at her. Chattering derisively, it bared its white teeth in a broad grin.

Akemi wanted to scold it, but couldn't. She felt she and the monkey were bound together by the same fate. She recalled how pitiful Seijūrō had looked, and despite herself, her heart went out to him. She despised men like Seijūrō and Kojirō, and yet she was drawn to them like a moth to a red-hot flame.

LOOK FOR

MUSASHI
BOOK III

THE WAY OF THE SWORD

His shocking defeat of the Young Master of
the Yoshioka school has catapulted Musashi
to fame—while he himself is caught up in a
quest for harmony and beauty. But the seeds
of enmity have been sown, and now the
Young Master's fierce younger brother, Denshichirō, has challenged Musashi to a duel
to the death. Behind one swordsman stands
another—and another. Around him, friends
and lovers play out their dramas, as Musashi
is about to become one man against a hundred. . . .